"Another delightful example of Margaret Truman's keen observation of the town she used to call home."

Playboy

"Margaret Truman has settled firmly into a career of writing murder mysteries, all evoking brilliantly the Washington she knows so well.... She comes up with a totally new way of poisoning."

The Houston Post

"In this book, Miss Truman has definitely moved toward the international spy genre. She's up to the minute. And she's good."

Associated Press

"Truman's strong suit is her thorough knowledge of the Washington scene and her understanding of the perquisites of power, which she describes with enviable panache.... A good writer... in her fifth mystery novel she demonstrates an understanding of the genre which demands not simply an absorbing puzzle, but also engrossing and exotic details."

The Washington Weekly

D0054512

MARGARET TRUMAN

MURDER ON EMBASSY ROW

FAWCETT CREST • NEW YORK

A Fawcett Crest Book
Published by Ballantine Books
Copyright © 1984 by Margaret Truman

All rights reserved under International and Pan-American Copyright Conventions. Published in the United States by Ballantine Books, a division of Random House, Inc., New York, and simultaneously in Canada by Random House of Canada Limited, Toronto.

http://www.randomhouse.com

Library of Congress Catalog Card Number: 84-9209

ISBN 0-449-20621-1

This edition published by arrangement with Random House, Inc.

Printed in Canada

First Ballantine Books Edition: November 1985

29 28 27 26 25 24 23 22 21

To all those many friends and colleagues in the world of publishing who have helped produce it, this book is gratefully dedicated.

1

Geoffrey James, British ambassador to Iran, drew deeply
on a gold-banded Turkish cigarette and slowly released
the smoke toward a lethargic ceiling fan. On the other
side of a leather inlaid desk sat the Iranian foreign
minister, Falik el-Qdar. He, too, lit one of the ciga-
rettes and inhaled.

"I shall miss these, Mr. Ambassador," Qdar said.

"No need to, Mr. Foreign Minister," said James.
"Among many instructions I've left for my successor is
that Sullivan and Powell continue sending their best
Turkish in the daily pouch. I'm certain you'll be well
supplied."

"I appreciate that." Qdar leaned back in his chair
and closed his eyes. James took the opportunity to shift
his long, slender frame in his chair and to adjust a sharp
crease in his trousers. His charcoal gray pinstripe suit

was one of a dozen identical suits tailored for him by Henry Poole of London. His shirts, all white, were of Sea Island cotton and he wore only ties sanctioned by the three exclusive London clubs to which he belonged. His membership certificates were on file at Harvie and Hudson, London's famed tiemaker; such proof was demanded before any of the firm's six thousand different club ties could be sold.

Qdar opened his eyes, rubbed them, then looked across the desk at a man who'd become a friend of sorts, as possible as that could be considering Iran's recent turmoil. Qdar had succeeded Ibrahim Yazdi on November 6, 1979, forty-eight hours after the take-over of the American Embassy. A close confidant of the Ayatollah Khomeini, Qdar had been at the center of months of negotiations leading to the release of the embassy employees, negotiations that were carried out for the most part in deep secrecy and that involved diplomats from numerous countries, including Geoffrey James. Although Qdar was a loyal and vocal spokesman for the new regime and a dedicated foe of the deposed Shah of Iran, he secretly envied diplomats from Western nations, particularly the tall, well-educated, handsome, and urbane James.

"You have many pieces to put together," James said.

"Yes. There is the economy, reestablishing relations with those we've angered, and, of course, Iraq. We have lost much."

James nodded and touched his gray hair, which he combed up from a part low on his temple to cover a growing bald spot. He affirmed that the knot in his tie was where it should be, reached down and picked up a thin leather briefcase. "I must be going," he said.

Qdar held up his hand. "Before you do, you must

allow me one final gesture of friendship." He spun around in his chair, unlocked a cabinet, and withdrew a half-filled bottle of Glenmorangie single-malt Scotch whiskey. Since the Ayatollah's rise to power, it was virtually impossible to find liquor in Iran unless, of course, you knew members of the diplomatic corps who received their sacrosanct diplomatic pouches from home. "See?" Qdar said as he poured a tiny amount into each of two glasses. "I have been prudent with your last gift."

James smiled, accepted his glass, and held it up in a toast.

"Not quite yet," said Qdar. He turned again, opened the door on a small refrigerator in the cabinet, removed two tiny silver cups, and placed them on the desk. James leaned closer and examined their contents. In each was a spoonful of golden Iranian sterlet *khavyah*.

"Oh my," said James, his face an open reflection of his appreciation of what was in front of him. Of all the world's caviar, the tiny gold eggs from the sterlet variety of sturgeon was the most prized. It was seldom seen outside of Iran or Russia, so limited was its supply, and what was found invariably ended up on the tables of those nations' royalty, just as it had for the czars years ago when it was rushed to their tables wrapped in sable.

"To peace," Qdar said, raising his glass.

"Yes, quite," said James. He sipped the Scotch, licked his lips, picked up a spoon Qdar had supplied, and tasted the caviar. "Superb," he said, finishing the small amount of roe.

"It's always a pleasure providing something precious to one who has a true appreciation of it." Qdar again raised his glass. "To my friend, Geoffrey James."

"And to my friend, Falik el-Qdar. It's been an interesting experience this past year."

Qdar laughed. "British understatement at its finest. But I am glad you have found it so."

"I have."

James finished the Scotch, placed the empty glass on the desk, and stood. He was considerably taller than Qdar, something they'd joked about before. They shook hands. "I'm certain we'll meet again," James said as he walked with the easy lope of someone at home in high places. James had what his wife sometimes termed "a socialite slouch." Erect posture was for soldiers and men unsure of themselves. James's club friends also slouched and seemed to fit into their leather club chairs as though they'd been their cradles.

Qdar opened a door leading to a long corridor. Two armed soldiers who sat in straight-back chairs across from each other twenty feet from the office stood as Qdar and James passed them and proceeded down a set of stairs that led to the basement.

"My sincere best to Mrs. James," the Iranian said as they reached a secret and secure garage where James's limousine was waiting. Without Persian rugs and wall hangings to soften their voices, their words came back to them as harsh reflections off the hard gray concrete.

"I shall tell her," said James. "I spoke with her last evening. She says things are well in London—wet, of course, but acceptably so."

"I enjoyed your wet weather when I was in London. What will you do now?"

"Hard to say."

"The ambassadorship to the United States? That rumor persists."

"It would please Mrs. James. As you know, her mother was American."

"Yes, she has told me how much she would like to live there."

"I have considerable business interests to tend to in London."

"I know, but the foreign service has its advantages."

"Of which we're both aware, Mr. Foreign Minister."

An armed guard unbolted a door with considerable vigor. Qdar and James stepped into the garage. Two armed soldiers snapped to attention. A handsome young Iranian in a black suit, who'd been leaning against James's limo, opened a rear door and casually stepped back. He was six feet tall. Large soft, serene brown eyes were set in a finely etched face. His hair was thick and black and curly, like hundreds of tiny, shiny black ribbons bunched together. His name was Nuri Hafez. He'd been Geoffrey James's personal valet and driver for the past year and James had arranged for him to emigrate to London.

James and Qdar looked at each other for a moment, then extended their hands. "You fly directly home?" Qdar asked.

"No. I have business in Copenhagen."

Qdar smiled. "Miss Lindstrom is well?" he asked, his smile not fading.

James's face indicated pique, then softened and he, too, smiled. "Quite."

"My best to her."

"Of course."

"I have been privileged to know you, Mr. Ambassador," said Qdar. "You return home a hero. I have known few heroes in my life."

James glanced across the garage at Nuri Hafez. " 'No man is a hero to his valet,' " he said.

"Shakespeare?"

"Madame de Cornuel. Be well."

"Allah be with you."

James climbed into the rear of the limo and Hafez

closed the door behind him. The guards opened the overhead door. Hafez started the engine and pulled into an alley behind the Foreign Ministry. James leaned forward, slid open a Fiberglas partition, and asked, "You have everything?"

"Yes, in the trunk."

They drove to Mehrabad Airport, where they were met by representatives of the Ayatollah's internal security staff, who took the limousine, scrutinized their baggage, and escorted them to a Pan Am flight to Paris. James settled into his first-class seat. Hafez flew coach.

2

10 P.M., Saturday, November 5, 1983,
The British Embassy,
3100 Massachusetts Avenue, N.W.,
Washington, D.C.

"Even Shakespeare wrote of caviar," Geoffrey James told a small group gathered around a table in the ballroom of his resïdence at the British Embassy. On the table were silver trays of smoked Scottish salmon, pâté of pheasant, partridge, and grouse, a coulibiac of salmon with a delicate butter sauce, tiny filets of haddock in a white cream sauce, and two trays heaped with glistening black beluga caviar surrounded by bowls of chopped egg whites and yolks, onions, chives, capers, and pimiento slivers. A separate tray held piles of thin toast and lemon wedges.

"What did the bard say?" someone asked.

"He said, 'The play, I remember, pleased not the million; 'twas caviare to the general.' *Hamlet*, Act Two."

"I've never understood such reverence for fish eggs,"

the wife of the Canadian ambassador said, shaking her head and laughing.

James looked at her over half-glasses. "Fish eggs? Rather, God's gift to the educated palate."

"You must miss Iran, Mr. Ambassador," said an American under-secretary of agriculture, "having all that Iranian caviar within arm's reach."

"Yes, quite," said James. "The Iranians certainly are on a par with the Russians when it comes to"—he paused and looked at the Canadian ambassador's wife— "when it comes to fish eggs. Excuse me."

He moved gracefully through the hundreds of people attending the party to celebrate his first anniversary as British ambassador to the United States. He'd discouraged large gatherings during his first year, despite his wife's penchant for them. Marsha James, who carried herself regally and who always demonstrated an appropriate amount of British reserve, also possessed, as Geoffrey often said, "that damnable American love of frivolity she got from her mother."

The difference between them was grist for jokes among the household staff. Meg, the Irish head of housekeeping, often said that Mrs. James acted up when "the old man is too much gravel in her craw." Meg's perception of the ambassador was shared by most of the staff: a somber, calculating, mirthless stuffed shirt who held himself aloof from everyone except those to whom he was expected to display charm and wit.

James's appointment as ambassador to the United States had come as no surprise. There had been a stream of stories in the American press about his behind-the-scenes role in negotiating the release of the American hostages in Iran. He sat on the boards of numerous London banks and companies that had extensive dealings with America. And there was his wife's parentage.

Her mother was Philadelphia Main Line and had devoted considerable time and money to charitable organizations. Finally, Ronald Reagan, America's fortieth President, had eagerly accepted Prime Minister Margaret Thatcher's suggestion that James be named Britain's representative to the United States, saying to his secretary of state, "I think James will see things our way."

Marsha James stood at the east end of the ballroom beneath a Gainsborough portrait of Sir Francis Gregg. With her were President Reagan's special adviser, Dr. Werner Gibronski, and Elgin Harris, the Canadian ambassador. Gibronski had been the only member of Jimmy Carter's inner circle to have been retained by President Reagan, and his influence over foreign policy was even greater than it had been before. He was a small man, thin to the point of delicacy, with an arrowhead nose upon which sat wire spectacles. His eyes were dark and marbled, and his threadlike mouth seemed to lack lips. He spoke with a Slavic accent.

"Enjoying yourself, dear?" Marsha asked her husband.

"Yes, quite. It's all very congenial."

"One year," said the Canadian. "Do you feel American yet?"

"I daresay not," James replied, his sarcastic tone not lost on Gibronski, who wrinkled his aquiline nose and touched his temple.

"The President is well?" James asked as his eyes darted over the crowd.

"Very well, Mr. Ambassador. He sends his personal regards. Pardon me, please." Gibronski drifted away and disappeared into a knot of guests.

"Strange little man," the Canadian ambassador said conspiratorially.

"Fairly obvious, I would say," said James. He touched

his wife's arm. "I'd like a word with you, Marsha. Excuse us, please."

They found a relatively unoccupied corner of the room. "What was he saying?" James asked.

"Dr. Gibronski?"

"Harris."

"Small talk."

"Hmmmmm."

"Only that."

There had been open tension between the British and Canadian ambassadors ever since the release of the American hostages in Teheran. James had emerged the media hero, but Canada's role in preserving American lives was well documented.

The controversy had heated up when one of the released hostages, Richard Washburn, told an American underground newspaper that Geoffrey James had profited from his close association with the Ayatollah. He attributed it to unnamed sources, and the accusation died a quick death, but the shadow lingered—"The jury will ignore what the witness has said."

"What did you want to talk to me about, Geoffrey?" Marsha James asked.

"Morris and Sylvia. I'm afraid I'll have to beg off on the plans for later." Morris and Sylvia Palington were old friends from London who happened to be visiting Washington and had been invited to the party. Marsha had suggested the four of them go downtown after the party to catch a performance by British singer and actress Robyn Archer, who was touring the United States with her one-woman show, *A Star Is Torn*. James had reluctantly agreed to the plans.

"Why?" Marsha James asked angrily.

"I'm not feeling up to it."

"You're sick?"

"No, but it's been a filthy week. We'll get together another time."

"I've made reservations, Geoffrey. I was looking forward to it."

"Then go yourself."

"I resent this, Geoffrey. There are times when . . ."

"We should see to our guests." He walked away, unmoved by her cold stare following him across the large and tastefully furnished ballroom that had been the scene of countless receptions and ceremonial functions. A forty-foot-long Tabriz carpet dominated the center of the room. Three antique Austrian chandeliers cast a flattering light over the two hundred guests, some of whom sat on chairs upholstered in the same specially woven blue floral brocade that had been used in Westminister Abbey for the coronation of Queen Elizabeth II. Other chairs in rose and gold and side tables and chests in Louis XVI style from the late eighteenth century graced the room beneath carved plaster friezes of Grinling Gibbons motifs.

Some guests, particularly smokers, had spilled out of the French doors to a patio and rose garden. It was a surprisingly mild night for November and a gentle, cool breeze through the doors added freshness to the air inside. A black pianist and bass player in tuxedoes played show tunes in a corner of the room.

The embassy's head of chancery, Nigel Barnsworth, intercepted James. "What is it?" James snapped.

"You have a telephone call."

"Who is it?"

Barnsworth whispered in his ear.

"I'll call back later."

Barnsworth watched his superior negotiate the crowd with detached ease, stopping to chat with Sir Edwin Ferguson, a Scottish member of British Parliament and a business associate of James's back in Great Britain, then to a cluster of guests that included the Irish minister of commerce to the United States and a rotund, exiled Iranian journalist, Sami Abdu, who'd been a Shah loyalist and who'd escaped Iran only hours before his head was to go on the Ayatollah's chopping block.

The ambassador's personal secretary, Melanie Callender, came up to Nigel Barnsworth and said, "Good show, heh?"

Barnsworth ignored her.

They were a contrasting pair. Barnsworth, whey-faced and frail, a tick in his left eye and a perpetual sneer upon his lips, was grudgingly admitted to be the best administrator in Britain's Foreign and Commonwealth Office, but had been denied an ambassadorship throughout his career because of his foul disposition.

Callender, on the other hand, was tall and robust, a thirty-year-old from Liverpool, with cheeks the color of cherries, large, sparkling opalescent green eyes, and an irrepressible personality that could erupt into raucous laughter with minimal provocation. Because she was privy to many of James's personal contacts and phone calls, she was constantly pressed by the household staff to provide juicy gossip about the ambassador. She steadfastly refused, although there were moments when she would comment upon his dour nature. She was more vocal about Nigel Barnsworth, often referring to him as "the git" or "a nasty little snail." Never to his face, of course.

"I said, 'Good show,' " she repeated.

"Codswallop," Barnsworth said.

" 'Tis not," said Callender. "I think it's lively and lovely, just what the ambassador needs. Do him some good." When Barnsworth said nothing, Callender asked, "Why do you hate him so?"

Barnsworth cocked his head, looked up his nose, and said, "Be careful, Callender. You're not liked here." He left her and went to the main kitchen off the ball-room, where a dozen men and women were in a frenzy of activity. The head chef, who'd once created the acclaimed cuisine for London's Savoy Hotel, was busy slicing salmon so thin it was diaphanous. A young woman created flowers out of raw carrots and radishes, another peeled jumbo shrimp to replenish a dwindling supply.

The chef's wife, Eleanor, a plump woman who man-aged the kitchen while her husband concocted the em-bassy's daily bill of fare, leaned over to an assistant chef they'd brought with them from London and said, "Look who's 'ere," referring to Barnsworth. "Let's cut 'im up and plop 'im in the soup." They laughed. She turned to where a young woman was buttering thin, crustless slices of bread and said, "Get on with it, now. You know 'e hates it when the bread runs out for his caviar." The girl finished buttering, arranged the slices on a tray that also contained unbuttered toast and a fresh supply of chopped egg yolks and onions, bustled past Barnsworth, and pushed through swinging doors.

Barnsworth skirted a large butcher block cutting table and went to where Nuri Hafez leaned against a floor-to-cciling wall of stainless steel refrigerator doors, some of which were padlocked. "What are his plans tonight?" Barnsworth asked the young Iranian.

Hafez wore a white butler's jacket over a blue shirt and maroon tie. He touched the genesis of a black mustache and shrugged.

"Oh, come on, Hafez, you know. He tells you everything."

"I think they plan to be with their friends from London."

"The Palingtons?"

"I am busy, Mr. Barnsworth. Excuse me." Hafez slid along the refrigerator doors, picked up a tray heaped with orange and red vegetable flowers, and left.

"Snotty bastard," Barnsworth muttered.

"Pardon?" said Eleanor, who'd come up behind him carrying a large, gleaming kitchen knife.

"Nothing." His eyebrows went up at the sight of the knife.

"You wish something, Mr. Barnsworth?"

"No. Make certain we don't run out of anything out there."

"Yes, *sir*." She smiled and turned away.

Marsha James was standing with the Palingtons in front of a 1930s sixfold leather screen on which scenes of the Spanish Armada's attempted invasion of England during Queen Elizabeth I's reign were portrayed. "Of course we understand," Sylvia Palington was saying. "The strain," added Morris Palington. "He should have stayed in banking instead of all this diplomatic nonsense. We miss him at the club."

"We'll just leave the old stick-in-the-mud home and go ourselves," Marsha James said. "I'm not about to miss Robyn Archer."

The Argentinian ambassador to the United States, who was surprised he'd been invited, considering the Falklands tête-à-tête, fumbled with a long, thin black cigarette in a holder as James approached. The Argentinian clicked his heels, extended his hand, and said, "Congratulations, Mr. Ambassador."

"For what, for heaven's sake?"

"For one year in this country."

"How long have you been here, Mr. Ambassador?"

"Three years."

"Then congratulations are entirely more appropriate

for you." James heartily shook his hand and went to where Nuri Hafez was collecting empty glasses from a table. Although Hafez's only official duty at the embassy was to serve the ambassador, he'd offered to help during the evening's festivities. "I intend to leave soon, Nuri," James said. "I'm not feeling well. Mrs. James and the Palingtons are going off to catch a show after the party, I'm told. Please drive them."

"All right," Hafez said, continuing to put glasses on a tray.

"After you've dropped them at the theater, come back here. I'll be in my study. I might want to go out, although my plans are not firm. You needn't mention that to Mrs. James."

"Whatever you say, Mr. James."

James narrowed his eyes at the form of address used by Hafez, looked over his shoulder, then said, "I plan to retire to my study in a few minutes after I've said good-bye to those who matter. I'd like a fire, caviar from the special stock, toast, lemon, and vodka, thoroughly chilled."

"All right."

"I'll tell you when."

The musicians launched into "A Foggy Day." A young woman who'd had too much to drink shrieked with laughter, lost her balance, and fell into her date's arms. Werner Gibronski winced and moved away.

"Ah, Mr. Ambassador," said a corpulent man in a doublebreasted tan plaid suit. He had a long, thick mustache that swooped down low, flared out, and was waxed to precise points. His name was Berge Nordkild and he was Washington's most successful and famous purveyor of fancy imported foods. Most of the food for the party had been supplied by Nordkild, Ltd. He spoke with a Scandinavian accent. "Everything is to your satisfaction?"

"Yes, quite."

"A fine party befitting a fine man," said Nordkild.

"And from the looks of things, it's about to end," James said, patting him on the shoulder and moving on. He found Marsha enjoying a joke being told by a young man from the State Department's British liaison office. James waited patiently for the conclusion of the joke, which had a mildly risqué punch line. Everyone laughed except James. When the young man looked at him for a reaction, James smiled and said, "Quite good."

"Dear," James said to Marsha, indicating with his finger that he wanted her to follow him. They moved away from the group and he said, "I'm going to my study for the evening. There are cables I must go over."

"Really?" A sardonic smile crossed her lips.

"Yes, really. I'll say good night and take my leave. Nuri will drive you and the Palingtons to the show and pick you up. And please, I don't wish to be disturbed."

The smile never left her face as she said, "You really are a bastard, Geoffrey, and you become more of one every day."

"I'll see you in the morning."

"Yes, in the morning."

The ambassador went to the kitchen, where he found Nuri Hafez. "I'm going upstairs now," he told his valet. "Please bring me what I requested."

James left the kitchen. Hafez took a brass key fob from his jacket pocket, unlocked a padlock on one of the refrigerators, opened its door, and found what he was looking for, a dented tin with a lid secured by rubber bands. He removed the tin and a bottle of vodka, placed a silver bowl on a serving tray, filled the bowl with crushed ice, and carefully nestled the vodka bottle in it. Next to the bottle went a small cut-glass cup. He spooned caviar from the tin into the cup and added four lemon wedges. "I need toast," he told Eleanor as he replaced the tin of caviar in the refrigerator, secured the lock, returned the key to his pocket. "I'll be back," he said. He returned five minutes later. The toast was wrapped in a white linen napkin and was on the tray.

Hafez crossed the ballroom and almost reached the twin limestone staircases leading to the upper floors when Marsha James intercepted him. "Nuri," she said, "please bring the limousine around to the front. The Palingtons and I will be going to . . ."

"I know," he said sullenly.

She started to comment on his tone of voice, but was suddenly surrounded by a group of guests, including Werner Gibronski. "I must leave immediately," Gibronski said. He turned and bumped into Hafez, who nearly lost his grip on the serving tray. He placed it on a walnut Queen Anne table. Marsha James looked down. A lemon wedge had fallen to the floor. Hafez bent over and picked it up, looked for somewhere to put it, then walked to the kitchen, where he angrily tossed it in a trash can. Gibronski was gone by the time Hafez returned and Marsha James was saying good-bye to lingering guests. Standing next to her were the Palingtons. As Hafez picked up the tray, she said to him, "Please hurry. I don't want to be late."

Hafez went to the main hallway, a long, wide corridor with red walls and a checkerboard floor of white Vermont marble and black Pennsylvania slate. The official coronation portrait of Her Majesty Queen Elizabeth II peered down at him as he slowly climbed the stairs to the next level, where the ambassador's study was located. He paused at the door as he heard James's voice say, "Not tonight . . . I am not in the habit of being asked to apologize to anyone. Good night!" The phone was returned to its cradle with considerable force. Hafez waited a few seconds, then knocked. "Come in," James said loudly.

The ambassador had removed his shoes, suit jacket and tie, and had slipped into a red cashmere robe and slippers. "A fire," he mumbled as Hafez placed the tray on a crotchwood lyre card table decorated with brass rosettes. Hafez quickly arranged newspaper, cedar kindling, and four slender logs in the fireplace, ignited them, and stood.

"That's all," said James. "I won't be going out tonight. Drive them to the show and pick them up. Please don't disturb me."

As Hafez was about to open the door, James said, "You know, Nuri, there is an old saying about not biting the hand that feeds you." Hafez half-turned and cocked his head. "Don't give me that confused expression you're so bloody fond of adopting, Nuri. Just think about what I said. Good night."

Marsha James returned to the embassy at midnight. She was driven by two plainclothes members of the internal security staff who'd escorted her and the Palingtons to the Robyn Archer show. Mrs. James and her guests had been driven in the ambassador's limousine by Nuri Hafez, with the security men following in an unmarked sedan. When Hafez didn't show up at the end of the evening and a call to the embassy failed to locate him, Mrs. James had the guards drop the Palingtons at the Madison Hotel, then bring her home.

She was furious as she entered the front door. "Where is Nuri?" she asked the household staff, who were still cleaning up after the party.

"We don't know, ma'am."

She went to the ballroom, picked up a telephone, and dialed Hafez's room. There was no answer. She dialed the main garage. No answer there, either. She returned to the foyer and told a security guard, "Go around back and see if the limousine is there." He returned a few minutes later and reported it was missing.

"Thank you," she said. "That will be all."

Marsha James hated Nuri Hafez and the staff was aware of her feelings. No one was quite sure why she felt as she did, although they did speculate. With few exceptions, Mrs. James ran the residence, including the hiring and firing of house staff. But Hafez was out of her reach, above her control. He "belonged" to her husband.

Marsha knew her husband's sexual tastes too well to suspect any taint of "the English vice"; it was as though Hafez was a pet dog who not only preferred her husband, but who disliked, no, tolerated her.

There may have been a time when she envied the close relationship James and Hafez shared; lately she only resented it, and freely let it trigger and fuel the arguments the embassy household overheard too often.

She went upstairs and stood in the hallway. To her left was the door to his private study. Her own study was next to it, and she often took tea there before retiring, usually with her social secretary, who would brief her on the following day's activities.

She went to her study, picked up a phone, and called the kitchen. "I shan't have anything this evening," she said. She returned to the hall and paused in front of their bedroom. A maid, on her way to her own bedroom on the floor above, asked, "Can I get you something, ma'am?"

Mrs. James was startled by the maid's appearance. "Oh, no, I think not," she said.

19

"Good night, ma'am."

"Yes. Good night."

She went to her husband's study, where dim light squeezed through a narrow space at the bottom of the door. There was the smell of burnt cedar. She placed her hand on the doorknob and slowly turned it. The door slid open. She peered into a room rendered chiaroscuro by the light diffused by the green glass shade of a brass study lamp, and the waning orange glow from the embers of the fireplace.

Silhouetted against this light, she saw her husband, Geoffrey James, the soft folds of his robe draped around him. He was slumped over the card table.

She entered the room, closing the door behind her, and approached him.

His right hand held a stemmed glass that was tipped over, its contents having whitened the table's smooth finish. Toothpaste and cigarette ash; she thought automatically of one of her mother's home-repair remedies. Geoffrey's head had fallen sideways onto a silver bowl now half filled with melted ice water, a lemon wedge floating on the top.

The cut-glass caviar cup was partially submerged, and the caviar still remaining formed a black crust over his nose.

"Geoffrey," she said softly, not touching him. Then she reached, hesitated, and felt the exposed side of his face. It was cold, with the flat, gray look of modeling clay. The eye she could see was open and distended and his mouth gaped in a rictus that was half smile, half scream.

Marsha left the room, involuntarily wiping her hands on her skirt and went downstairs to the kitchen, where Eleanor was having tea with her husband. Marsha saw the plate of dainty sandwiches between them, the un-eaten remains of that evening's party.

"Something wrong, ma'am?" Eleanor asked.

Marsha heard her voice answer. "Yes, I would say there is."

3

Salvatore Morizio, a detective captain in Washington's Metropolitan Police Department, sat hunched over a chessboard in the living room of his Arlington, Virginia, condominium. "Why the hell did you make *that* move?" he mumbled as he tried to devise a strategy to counter the unexpected placement of his opponent's knight.

The phone rang. He ignored six rings before getting up and answering it. "Yeah?" he said, still thinking about his next move.

"Sal, Jake. I wake you?"

"No. What time is it?"

"One."

"Is it? It got late. What's up?"

Jacob Feinstein, chief of the State Department's 1,000-officer police force, whose mission it was to protect the lives of the vast foreign diplomatic community in the District of Columbia, said, "The British Embassy. We've got a possible death of the ambassador, but I don't have confirmation yet."

"Geoffrey James? What happened?"

"Sounds like a heart attack. Nobody's saying for sure over there."

"They had a party for him tonight."

"I know. We covered it. Want me to call when we firm it up?"

"No, no need. I think I'll . . . Sure, call me."

Morizio hung up and looked out the window. The view of the nation's capital across the Potomac River always pleased him, especially at night. It was the view that had tipped the scales in favor of his purchasing this condo instead of others he'd seen. It wasn't as spacious as he'd wanted and the sales agent had been a surly ignoramus, but there was the view, especially at night.

He returned to the couch and looked down at the chessboard. The timer had run out. He reset it, thought for a moment, then made his move. Almost instantly the computer countered with a move that would put Morizio's king in check down the road. "You bastard," Morizio said. "It was the phone. I lost my concentration." He often beat the computer, which he'd named Rasputin, in the first six levels of play, but had never been a winner at level seven.

Jake Feinstein called again. He'd confirmed that Geoffrey James, British ambassador to the United States, was dead, the apparent victim of a coronary.

"Too bad," Morizio said.

"Yeah. He wasn't the warmest guy we deal with, but he was okay. His wife's nice. Know her?"

"I've met her."

"Well, just wanted to let you know."

"No question of cause?"

"Evidently not. What are you doing up so late? You're an early-to-bed type."

"I was playing chess."

"Really? Who is she?"

"It's a he, Jake. His name is Rasputin."

Feinstein laughed. "Whatever you say, Sal. See you at the meeting."

Morizio slept soundly, was up at seven, and watched "The CBS Morning News" while eating a breakfast of melon, eggs, and an English muffin. Ambassador James's death was mentioned only in passing. He was sixty-one, Diane Sawyer said. Funeral arrangements had not been announced.

Morizio dressed in gray slacks, a gray Harris tweed jacket, white button-down shirt, and black knit tie, used a shoehorn to slip into penny loafers, and went to the living room and checked himself in a mirror. Five feet eleven inches tall, thick, close-cropped black hair with gray at the temples, dark skin and fine features. He was slender, no thanks to his life-style. He seldom exercised and ate what he wanted. Metabolism, he'd been told, insides always churning that kept him thin and gave him an ulcer at thirty, now in remission. He looked out the window. It was a sunny, clear November day and the forecast promised that the fair-weather pattern would hold for at least another two days.

He picked up the phone and dialed. "Good morning, sunshine," he said.

"Hi, Sal," Constance Lake said through a yawn.

"Up and at 'em, kid," he said. "It's a fat morning out there."

"I am up. I just finished working out."

"I'm jealous.

"Of what?"

"Of Richard Simmons. You spend every morning naked with him."

Lake laughed. "He inspires me."

"And I don't."

24

"Different inspiration. You're on your way out?"

"Yeah. Don't forget the meeting at eleven."

"I have it down. See you there."

"Right. Just remember, Richard Simmons doesn't love you. I do."

"I'll keep it in mind, Sal."

He checked his pockets to make sure he hadn't forgotten anything and went to a basement garage where he kept his car, a Chevy Cavalier he'd taken delivery on two weeks earlier. He pressed a button on the wall that opened the overhead doors and headed for the Rochambeau Memorial Bridge. Twenty minutes later he pulled into a reserved parking spot behind MPD Headquarters at Third and C streets. Having his name on a parking slot was his most prized perk since being named coordinator of intracity security, which involved liaison between MPD's 4,000 cops, the 1,200 members of the U.S. Capitol Police, and Jake Feinstein's 1,000 uniformed personnel.

"Captain Morizio," a sergeant said the minute he walked through the office door. "Urgent message." He handed Morizio a slip of paper. Written on it was the name "Paul Pringle" and a phone number. Pringle was a security officer at the British Embassy. Morizio had done him a couple of favors, including a personal one that involved Pringle's teenage daughter, Harriet, and they'd stayed in touch. Although it breached embassy rules, Pringle often filled Morizio in on embassy events that might be of interest to him.

Morizio dialed the number which, he knew, was not an embassy extension. Pringle answered on the first ring. "Hello, Sal," he said quickly. "Just arrive?"

"Yeah. Where are you?"

"A friend's. Listen to me, Sal. You've heard about the ambassador?"

"Sure. Sorry to hear it. *Was* it a heart attack?"

"That's what's being put out, but some things have occurred that make me wonder, which is why I called."

"I appreciate it. Go ahead." Morizio waved people away who started to enter his office, cradled the phone between his ear and shoulder, and poised a pen over a blank yellow legal pad.

"First, Sal, the ambassador's personal valet, a young Iranian named Nuri Hafez, has disappeared."

"When?"

"Last night. He evidently drove off in the ambassador's limo and hasn't been heard from since."

"And?"

Pringle told him about Hafez's failure to show up to drive Marsha James and her guests home after the show.

"You say he's Iranian. Did the ambassador meet him over there?"

"Yes, he arranged for him to leave Iran and to work for him as a valet and chauffeur in London. Then he brought him here."

"Any idea where he might be or why he took off?"

"None whatsoever, unless it has to do with the other thing that prompted me to call."

"Which is?"

"Kitchen scuttlebutt that the ambassador was poisoned."

"Who's saying it?"

"The chef's wife. She claims somebody told somebody else that the embassy physician, Dr. Hardin, mumbled after he'd examined the corpse that it looked like cyanide to him, not a bloody coronary. It's all seventh-hand, but I thought you'd want to know."

Morizio made a few notes, then said, "It sounds like the folks in the kitchen ought to be writing murder mysteries instead of peeling potatoes. Who did it, the butler?'' He laughed.

Pringle didn't laugh. ''The butler, Sal, or the valet.''

''The Iranian?''

''Yes. Why would he run?''

''No idea. Want me to put out an APB on him?''

''No. You're not supposed to know any of this.''

''I could do it unofficially, look for the limo.''

''All right. That might clear the water a little. Thanks. I'll get back to you later in the day.'' He gave Morizio information about the limousine and hung up.

There was a knock on his door. Before he could respond, it opened and Constance Lake poked her head in. ''Good morning,'' she said brightly.

''Hi. Come in.''

She tossed a large wine-colored leather shoulder bag on the desk and pulled up a chair. ''Kiss?'' she said, with lots of play in her voice.

Morizio picked up the yellow legal pad from the desk and frowned.

''Come on, Sal, just a peck. No one's looking.''

He peered over the pad and said, ''We go through this act every morning. Not in the office. *Never* in the office.''

Connie laughed, crossed one shapely stockinged leg over the other, and dangled a black pump from her foot. It was a morning ritual and she loved it. They'd started dating three years ago, two years after she joined MPD. Because she was a woman and because she had a master's degree in psychology, she was assigned to the rape unit, where she dealt with victims of sexual assault. At that time, Morizio was second-in-command of a tactical street-crime unit. They met on a case, liked each other, and launched the relationship with occasional dinners.

They were as different as they were similar. Morizio was a thesis away from a Ph.D. in sociology, which he'd grimly pursued at night at Catholic University. His master's degree was from Harvard in the same field, although his undergraduate work at Boston University had been in political science. He'd put in a stint with the Army, interrogating returning Korean POWs, ended up in Washington on the staff of a one-term Massachusetts congressman, spent two quiet, unsettling years with the Central Intelligence Agency, then decided to join the MPD. Sal Morizio was a cop's son. His father had been Sergeant Carlo Morizio, 12th Precinct, Boston, who'd walked a beat in the North End until his retirement and who died exactly one year after his farewell dinner.

Connie Lake was from Seattle. She, too, had come to Washington as an aide to a politician. Five feet five inches tall, fair skinned and with long hair the color of wheat, she was, as Morizio told a friend after first meeting her, "the most beautiful woman I've ever seen." It took him a year to tell her that. When he did, she replied, "Isn't it nice that you think so."

Connie's parents were Swedish. Her father, Jens Lake, had owned a succession of restaurants in the Seattle area, none of which made much money. Her mother, who was born in Malmö, Sweden, met Jens when he accompanied his parents on a vacation to visit relatives in "the old country." Connie Lake's grandmother still lived in Malmö, although Connie had never met her.

When Morizio was named coordinator of intracity security, he was allowed to pick his own staff. Connie Lake pleaded with him to join the unit. Although he was against working that closely with his lover and held out for two months, she eventually prevailed and was now his assistant.

She'd brought with her that morning a list of pending events in the city that required close coordination between MPD and the other security forces. They went over them and formulated the approach Morizio wanted to take at the weekly meeting, which was to begin in twenty minutes.

"Let me lay something on you that I picked up this morning," Morizio said. "Strictly between us."

Her eyes widened and she leaned forward.

He told her of Pringle's call without mentioning his name. When he was done relating what Pringle had reported, he asked, "What's your reaction?"

She sat back and raised her eyebrows. "Sounds like a gossipy gang in the embassy kitchen. Should be easy to corroborate."

"Why? We can't get involved unless we're invited. Section 167, the Vienna Convention, 1961. Remember?"

"I know, Sal, but if this Iranian, Hafez, is loose in the city and the limo is stolen, how could we not be invited in?"

Morizio grinned and stood, stretched his arms and twisted his neck against a pain that had suddenly developed. "Let's forget about it until after the meeting and there's more information from my contact."

"Why won't you ever share your contacts with me?" she asked.

"Because then they wouldn't be mine anymore. Come on, let's go."

As they went into the meeting, Morizio asked Jake Feinstein whether he'd heard anything about the possibility of Ambassador Geoffrey James being poisoned. Feinstein shook his head. Morizio didn't know whether he was telling the truth. The MPD was powerless to intervene in any embassy affairs without specific invitation. Each embassy was a sovereign nation within Washington, its borders and internal affairs off-limits to anyone except embassy personnel and those designated by the embassy's mother country.

The major item on the meeting's agenda was to beef up security in the Capitol Building. A recent pipe bombing in a coatroom and assaults on American personnel and property overseas had prompted an urgent review of congressional security. There was to be a special meeting that afternoon on the subject and Morizio assigned Lake to represent MPD. He had lunch in his office after the eleven o'clock meeting and spent most of the afternoon disposing of paperwork that had accumulated, including six weeks of expense accounts. It was days like this that he periodically closed his eyes and second-guessed leaving the mainstream of the MPD for what was basically a political job. He was always awash in paperwork and in attending social functions with politicians and bureaucrats. When he was with the street-crime unit, there'd been daily action that was real—cops-and-robbers, white hats and black hats. It was what a cop was supposed to be.

But those self-doubts seldom lasted long because he would remind himself of the prestige of his present job. He was known to officials in Congress, the Supreme Court, the diplomatic corps, and even the White House as *the* person on the Metropolitan Police Department to turn to when security was at stake. His father would have burst with pride—and Morizio often thought about his father. His mother was happy about his position, too, although for other reasons. She'd constantly worried about his being out on the street dealing with "scum" and she liked the fact he was finally back in a "dull job," which was the way she'd viewed his years with the CIA.

Paul Pringle called at four-thirty. "Sal, the kitchen

rumors might be true,'' he said. He sounded out of breath.

''Poisoned?''

''Perhaps. Have they contacted you about an autopsy?''

''Who?''

''The arrangements are being handled by our head of chancery, Nigel Barnsworth. He's working through the Home Office.''

''Nobody's contacted me.''

Another button on Morizio's phone lighted up. ''I've got another call, Paul.''

''I'll call you at home tonight.''

''Right.'' He pushed the other button. ''Captain Morizio.''

''Please hold for Dr. Gibronski,'' a female voice said.

''Werner Gibronski?'' Morizio asked himself.

''Captain Morizio?''

''Yes.''

''This is Dr. Werner Gibronski at the White House.'' The heavy Slavic accent left little doubt he was who he said he was.

''Yes, sir. What can I do for you?''

''I would like to discuss an urgent matter concerning the death of Ambassador James.''

''I'm afraid I don't know much about it, sir, except what I've seen on TV.''

''Perhaps you will know more after we meet. Could you be at my office within the hour?''

''Sure. Yes, sir, of course.''

''Please hold.''

A woman came back on the line and asked, ''What is your date and place of birth, Captain Morizio?''

He was momentarily taken aback, then said,

"June 22 . . ." Before he could finish, she asked where he was born. "Boston, Massachusetts."

"Thank you. Dr. Gibronski expects you within the hour. Please use the West Entrance."

All four buttons on his phone came to life. He started left to right; "Captain, Aiken in Communications. UPI is carrying a story about reports from the British Embassy that the ambassador might have been poisoned." MPD's communications center monitored both AP and UPI, as well as all four local television channels.

"Thanks," Morizio said, pushing the next button. It was the senior Washington correspondent for Reuters, the British wire service. He asked what Morizio knew about the embassy reports. "Nothing," Morizio said. The reporter pressed, but Morizio excused himself and took the next two calls, neither of which were about Geoffrey James.

He checked his watch, got up, went to the bullpen, and said to his secretary, "Ginnie, I'm on my way to the White House." She gave him her "I'm impressed" look. "Take all the calls until I get back. If Lake arrives, tell her to wait here for me. Refer all press inquiries to public affairs. I'll pop in there on my way out."

"Do I have to wait around until you get back?"

"I'd appreciate it."

"I had a dinner date and . . ."

"Do whatever you have to do."

He went to the public affairs office and pulled its chief, Rod Dexter, out of a meeting. "Look, Rod, something big is brewing at the British Embassy over the ambassador's death, a possible homicide. I'll find out more. For now, the word to the press is that my department is gathering the facts and will have a statement when those facts are organized. Until then, no comment."

4

A guard at the West Entrance of the White House confirmed that Morizio had an appointment with Dr. Gibronski, verified the date and place of his birth, and directed him to the Appointment Lobby, which had formerly housed the press room where reporters lounged in massive leather chairs, often napping in them while waiting for something newsworthy to occur. But when President Nixon took office, he floored over the White House swimming pool in a protest of sorts and moved the press corps there.

The appointment lobby had taken on a distinctly more feminine character since its media days. The walls were covered in a pale yellow silk. Ceiling, moldings, and wainscoting were painted linen white. Drapes on the tall windows were of the same yellow silk as the walls. The oak floor was polished to a high, hard glow. A large, muted antique rug of yellow and green flowers covered the center of the room. It was sparsely fur nished; two Sheraton Pembroke tables, an assortment of Queen Anne and Chippendale chairs, a small but handsome walnut bonnet-top secretary, and an eight-legged mahogany Hepplewhite sofa upholstered in a rose-colored brocatelle. Morizio sat on the couch, then stood. It was uncomfortable.

He perused a breakfront bookcase housing official gifts presented to presidents over the years, and admired a series of oil paintings of the American landscape. He was studying Winslow Homer's *Maine Coast* when a young man with a cowlick appeared and said, "Dr. Gibronski will see you now."

Gibronski's office was large and spartan. The blinds were drawn; two floor lamps and a brass desk lamp with a green shade cast pools of soft light over walls the color of talcum powder and over the burnt umber carpeting.

Gibronski was dwarfed by a massive teak desk that was completely clean—not a scrap of paper, not a pencil, not a pad or paper clip. A matching credenza behind Gibronski contained an elaborate telephone system and two individual phones—one red, one white. He was on the white phone when Morizio arrived.

A door at the side of the office opened. A man entered, came to where Morizio stood, halfheartedly offered a fleshy, cold hand, and said in a whispered British accent, "George Thorpe. Sit down."

Thorpe and Morizio took leather chairs across the desk from Gibronski, who continued a hushed conversation on the white phone. Thorpe fumbled through the pocket of a wrinkled brown tweed jacket with elbow patches and pulled out a large, fat, black cigar, carefully positioned a lighter's flame so that its heat ignited the tobacco but didn't actually touch it, snapped the lighter shut, and returned it to his pocket. He drew on the cigar, coughed, and exhaled.

Morizio observed the Englishman as he went through

34

his cigar ritual. He was big—six feet two inches, Morizio decided, and about 250 pounds. Everything about him was rumpled. He had a puffy face, heavy jowls, and the red, watery eyes and veined cheeks of a heavy drinker. The collar of his white shirt was too tight and a brown tie was ridiculously narrow against the shirt's broad expanse.

Gibronski concluded his conversation, quietly placed the phone in its cradle, and turned to face his visitors. Morizio stood and said, "Captain Morizio, Dr. Gibronski. I got here as fast as I could."

"Yes, thank you, Captain." Gibronski neither stood nor offered his hand. He stared at Morizio over half-glasses until he sat down. Gibronski was in shirtsleeves and Morizio noticed that his hands were free of rings. *As clean as his desk,* he thought.

"Mr. Thorpe represents Her Majesty's government regarding Ambassador James's death," Gibronski said in a tight, controlled voice. "He has been given authority to oversee every aspect of the disposition of the matter. He will carry out that responsibility under my supervision as it relates to this government's policies."

Morizio wanted to smile at Gibronski's flat, blunt statement. There had been no preliminary conversation, no welcome, not a cough or a pause. He simply recited it in his Slavic accent. When he was through, he sat back in a leather chair that rose above the top of his head, twined long, tapered fingers about each other, and continued peering at Morizio over his glasses.

"The point is," Thorpe said, his attention still on his cigar, "that certain unfortunate events have transpired that turn a routine death into a complicated one."

Morizio's first thought was to question the reduction of a major ambassador's life to trivia. His second thought was spoken: "What unfortunate events?"

Gibronki answered. "Under usual procedure, the death of Ambassador James would be strictly a matter for the British to resolve. However, because of indiscretions within the British Embassy, those who prosper from rumor and speculation have insisted upon"—he paused and Morizio enjoyed it—"have insisted upon . . ."

"The press?" Morizio asked.

". . . have insisted upon making it a matter of public titillation."

"What does this have to do with me?" Morizio asked.

"There will be a minor involvement of the Metropolitan Police Department. It will be in the best interests of all concerned that the appropriate channels be pursued."

"Because it looks good?" Morizio hadn't intended it to sound so cynical.

"If you wish," Gibronski said.

"Why me, Dr. Gibronski? If this is as delicate as you say, I'd think Chief Trottier would be the one to talk to."

"He agrees with us completely. He also suggests that since you coordinate Intracity Security, you should direct MPD's contribution."

"Contribution?"

"Yes. You will, of course, work under Mr. Thorpe's direct supervision. There is to be nothing undertaken without his full knowledge and approval. Above all, there is to be no public statement until I have approved it. Are there any questions, Captain Morizio?"

"Lots of them, Dr. Gibronski, but I have the feeling that they wouldn't be answered if I asked them." He smiled. "Was Ambassador James poisoned?"

Gibronski frowned.

"No offense. It's just that I don't like working in the dark."

"But you will learn to, of course," Thorpe said. "I suggest we meet each day to compare notes, as you might say. Shall we make it lunch?"

"How about the end of the day?"

Gibronski said impatiently, "Work out the details later. That's all the time I have now. Thank you." He pressed a buzzer and the young man who'd escorted Morizio to the office appeared through the side door. Morizio and Thorpe followed him to the West Entrance. "Have a nice evening," the aide said.

"Buy you a drink, Captain?" Thorpe asked.

"No, I have to get back."

"As you wish." Thorpe handed Morizio a card on which two phone numbers were printed. "My office and home," he said. "Call at any hour."

"Mr. Thorpe, there's one question you can answer better than anyone."

"Which is?"

"What's your position in this? What's your official connection with the British Government? Who are you?"

Thorpe turned up the collar of his tan trenchcoat against a stiff breeze. He smiled, patted Morizio on the back, and said, "I'm on call to Her Majesty's Government. The offer of a drink still holds."

"I'll call you," said Morizio.

Connie Lake was waiting for him at MPD. "What's going on?" she asked.

"Something I don't understand. Christ, I feel like a spook again, back in the CIA."

"Can you tell me about it?"

"Sure, but let me call the chief first."

"Want me to leave?" she asked.

He shook his head as the chief's secretary came on the line. "Captain Morizio to speak with him. Is he in?"

"One second, please."

"Sal?"

"Yes, sir."

Two things were blatantly different, Morizio realized. Donald J. Trottier, Washington, D.C.'s chief of police, had never called him by his first name before. The second thing that was different was that he'd been put through immediately.

"Sal, I'm glad you called. I understand you've spoken with Dr. Gibronski."

"Yes, sir, that's right. Just got back. There was a George Thorpe there, too."

"I haven't met him, but I understand he represents British interests in this project."

Project? Morizio thought. He remembered Gibronski's term, "contribution."

"There's lot I don't understand, sir."

Trottier laughed. "No need to, Sal. Under normal circumstances, MPD wouldn't be involved at all, but this has some high-level ramifications that take it out of the realm of the ordinary. That should be obvious with someone like Gibronski involved. We've been asked to lend certain limited support and that's exactly what we'll do. I don't know of anyone in the department better equipped to deal with something this sensitive than you. I've been reviewing your background. Really impressive. Now I remember why you were a hands-down choice to head up intracity security. One thing I don't need is a run-of-the-mill cop trying to appease heavy hitters like Gibronski." He laughed again.

Run-of-the-mill cop.

"Was Ambassador James poisoned?" Morizio asked.

"You should stop reading the newspapers."

"Was he?"

"The autopsy is going on right now."

"At MPD?"

"Under a blanket of top security, and that's the way it has to stay."

"Including me? If I'm in charge of the case, I'd like . . ."

"It's not a case, captain, it's a project."

Project, my ass, he wanted to say. Instead, he asked, "What do you want me to do?"

"Whatever this Thorpe fellow and Dr. Gibronski tell you to do. I'm counting on you to be discreet, to say nothing, and to follow their orders—and so is Commissioner Watson. It'll be over in a few days and everything'll be back to normal."

"All right."

"Nice talking to you, Sal. Keep me informed."

"If I'm allowed."

"Pardon?"

"If Thorpe and Gibronski allow me to keep you informed."

"I don't think sarcasm serves any useful purpose, Captain Morizio."

"Yes, sir, sorry. Good night."

"Good night." His voice had changed from sunny to Arctic freeze.

"Well?" Connie asked.

"What are you doing for dinner?"

"Having it with you."

"Good. Come on, let's stop by the morgue to get in the mood."

The MPD morgue was located in D.C. General Hospital. Morizio parked illegally in front of the salmon-colored stone building and he and Lake entered through the police entrance. The guard recognized Morizio and waved them through. They used the stairs to the basement instead of the elevators and pushed open a fire door. The entrance to the autopsy room was sealed by armed security guards from the British Embassy, augmented by a contingent from MPD. Morizio spotted Paul Pringle and approached him, didn't acknowledge they were friends, simply asked, "What the hell is going on?"

"Sorry, Captain. No one is to enter."

"Who's in there now?"

Pringle's superior joined them. "Captain Morizio, good to see you. How've you been?"

"Just fine. What's up?"

"Not at liberty to say."

"I'll be damned," Morizio said. "The morgue has been invaded by Great Britain."

Pringle and his superior laughed.

Morizio said to Lake in a loud enough voice to be sure Pringle heard, "Come on, let's eat. I want to be home by eleven to watch the invasion on TV."

They ate paella with black beans at Omega and washed it down with a cheap bottle of Spanish wine. Morizio told Lake of his meeting with Gibronski and Thorpe and of Chief Trottier's side of the phone conversation.

"What do you make of it?" she asked.

"I haven't the vaguest idea," he said.

"Want to know what I think?"

"Sure."

"Forget it. Go through the motions, do what they say, and let it slide. Obviously, MPD has no role in it and why should you care?"

"Because . . . Yeah, maybe you're right."

She placed her hands on his in the middle of the table and smiled. "I don't want to see you all worked up over something you can't control. I like you when you're calm, relaxed, and mellow. Come on, let's go home."

"Home" that night was his condo in Arlington. They usually decided a day in advance where they would stay the following night and the visitor packed a small bag in anticipation. They averaged four nights a week together, sometimes more, sometimes less, depending upon events at MPD. Lake had pressed months ago that they live together, but Morizio nixed the idea, saying, "I'm afraid it'll be too much like marriage."

"What's wrong with marriage?" Connie asked.

"Nothing at all, but I'm not sure I'm ready for it. I'd hate to get used to something I'm not ready for."

It was left at that, although each took turns proposing and neither was ever uncomfortable saying no. There was a tacit understanding that one day they probably would marry, but not now—and until they did legalize their relationship, he insisted that they keep their romance far removed from work. Everyone around them at MPD knew of their involvement but never mentioned it, at least to Morizio. Some of Connie's female colleagues would ask her from time to time how it was going. Her answer was always a smile and a "Hanging in there."

They slipped into matching terrycloth robes and settled in front of the TV. It was ten o'clock; the early news had just begun. "Drink?" Lake asked.

"Yeah, that'd be nice."

She returned from the kitchen with two snifters of cognac and snuggled close to him. They clinked their glasses together and said, "To us," a private little ritual.

"We'll be back in a moment with the latest on the mysterious circumstances surrounding the death of the British ambassador to the United States, Geoffrey James."

After three consecutive commercials, the anchorwoman

returned. *"An unusual autopsy was conducted today on the body of British Ambassador Geoffrey James, who was found dead at a party celebrating his one-year anniversary as ambassador to the United States. Informed sources told this station that the autopsy was performed at the Metropolitan Police Department's main morgue at D.C. General by two British physicians. Security around the morgue was extremely tight, our sources report. There has been significant speculation that Ambassador James was poisoned. Under diplomatic law, local authorities are forbidden from interfering in an embassy's internal affairs, even when it involves potential murder, unless specifically invited, which makes the use of the MPD morgue all the more interesting. The British Embassy on Massachusetts Avenue has been vehemently silent on the matter. Greg Basso with sports right after these messages."*

Morizio went to the phone.

"Who are you calling?" Lake asked.

"Ross Brown. They used his morgue. He ought to know something." Ross Brown was Washington, D.C.'s chief medical examiner.

"They told you to stay out of it, Sal."

"I know."

"Hello?"

"Ross? Sal Morizio. Sorry to bother you at home."

"That's all right, Sal. The missus and I were making love. We do it once a month and tonight's the night, but don't let it bother you."

"I almost believed you."

"Believe me, Sal. You want to know about James's autopsy."

"Yeah."

"Call the British doctors. I was told to vacate by none other than Trottier. I know nothing."

"Nothing?"

"Nothing. They used the facilities, but brought their own people. Mind if I get back to the foreplay?"

Morizio laughed. "Enjoy. Sorry to bother you."

"Don't sweat it."

Morizio returned to the couch. The folds of Connie's robe had fallen open. He was about to embrace her when the phone rang. He leaped up and went to it.

"Sal, Paul Pringle."

"I was hoping you'd call. What's going on?"

"A great deal. He was poisoned, Sal. Ricin, not cyanide."

Morizio whistled. "That's exotic," he said. Ricin, Morizio knew, was one of the world's most toxic substances, ranking right up there with botulinus. It was isolated from castor oil beans and had been considered for use as a chemical weapon during World War II. One-millionth of a gram was a lethal dose and one gram would kill almost 40,000 people. It was difficult to detect in the body—the lab boys had done a good job.

Pringle asked, "Did you have any luck with Nuri Hafez and the limousine?"

"I didn't do anything about it. Things got hectic today and I was concerned about putting out an APB and prompting somebody to wonder where I got the information about Hafez and the limo. Nothing from your end on it?"

"No. There's evidently some debate about how to handle it, but I'm not privy to those conversations. Sal, I must tell you something."

"I'm listening."

"I think I'd best sever contact with you for awhile. There's a lot at stake here and . . ." It sounded as though he'd been interrupted.

"Paul?"

43

"Yes, Sal, sorry. Someone was near. As I was saying, I'd best lay low for awhile. You understand."

"Sure I do, but before you go, who gave TV the story about the autopsy?"

"Probably someone who owes a favor, like I owe you. I'll be in touch later, but not very soon. Cheerio, Sal."

Morizio told Lake of the conversation. "I don't like it," he said. "I don't like games like this. If the British have their reasons for covering up what happened to their ambassador, that's fine, but why drag others in? Ship the body home, bury it, and forget about it."

"Sal."

"What?"

"Let's go to bed."

"You don't want to talk about it?"

"About going to bed?" She giggled.

"About James."

"No. I want to go to bed, make love, have a good night's sleep, and spend breakfast talking about murder." She took his hands, pulled him up from the couch, and turned off the living room lights. He took a detour on the way to the bedroom to pick up a discarded Kleenex she'd tossed on a table and to throw it in the kitchen wastebasket. She watched him with a bemused smile. Sal Morizio put Felix Unger to shame when it came to neatness, and tissues especially nettled him. It was a running gag between them, her cavalier attitude toward disposing of tissues and his obsession with getting rid of them. He sometimes called her "the Tissue Queen" and she would say, "And you're the Duke of Disposal."

They called each other quite different names ten minutes later, once they were in bed.

5

Willard Jones was on routine car patrol for the State Department's embassy security force. It was shortly after sunrise, but still dark enough for lights in buildings to be discernible. He'd made a pass along Massachusetts Avenue's Embassy Row and was now on his way back. He was hungry and looked forward to pancakes and sausage at his favorite diner.

Massachusetts Avenue was virtually without traffic. A stray dog crossed the wide boulevard and Jones slowed to allow him to make it safely. Jones was a dog lover and had two strays at home that he and his wife had rescued over the years.

He'd put on weight recently and his pants pressed in on his stomach. His uniform was almost identical to that worn by MPD cops, except that it had a bright yellow stripe down the side of the pants. He'd been turned down by MPD ten years ago and had settled for the embassy patrol. He liked police work. He liked uniforms.

He hugged the curb across from the South African

Embassy. The three-story white cinderblock building was dark, just as it had been during his initial run. He yawned, put the gearshift of his unmarked car into DRIVE, and proceeded at a snail's pace, stopping across from a two-story white building whose windows were covered by ornate blue metal grillwork with bronze tulips woven into the design. The number was 3005. A weathered wooden sign read: EMBASSY OF THE ISLAMIC REPUBLIC OF IRAN. It was translated below into Arabic.

The Iranian Embassy in Washington had been vacant since diplomatic relations between Iran and the United States had crumbled in 1980. It—and other buildings owned by Iran—had dramatically deteriorated, prompting constant protests from neighbors. A thick layer of leaves covered the front lawn. The flagpole was bare. Blue-and-white Persian ceramic tiles on the front of the building were stained and lifeless.

Jones was about to continue on his route when a light flickered in an upstairs window. "It's supposed to be empty," he told himself. The light continued to dance, then vanished. The window was black.

He made a careful U-turn, pulled into a driveway in front of the embassy, and shined a flashlight on large wooden front doors whose windows were covered with bronze scenes of stags, horses, and lions locked in combat.

Jones followed the driveway to the rear of the building where the garages were located. One of the overhead doors was raised a few feet. As he got out of the car, a gust of wind picked up dry leaves and swirled them into his face. He came around the front of the car, stooped, and directed the beam of his flashlight beneath the door. There was a vehicle inside. Jones pushed up on the door and it retracted with a bang.

The vehicle was a black Cadillac limousine. Its license plate designated it as belonging to the diplomatic corps. Jones entered the garage and opened the driver's door. The interior light came on. The sun visor was down. A sign attached to it read: OFFICIAL BUSINESS—BRITISH EMBASSY.

Jones stood in the garage and pondered the situation. There was no reason for a limousine from the British Embassy to be there. The Iranian Embassy had been vacant for years. All abandoned cars had been towed away. Jones looked to where he'd left his patrol car running and debated whether to call in or to give his report in person. Calling in would mean staying there—and he was already a few minutes past quitting time. Willard Jones always had trouble making decisions. This time, the decision was taken out of his hands. A man stepped into the garage through a door shrouded in shadow, came up behind Jones, and brought a tire iron down on his neck. Jones's head snapped back and his pupils disappeared behind his eyelids. A rush of air exploded from his lungs and filled the garage with an anguished, breathy scream. He pitched forward over the limousine's hood, his fingers grasping the smooth black metal as he slowly slid back toward the floor. By the time he reached it he was unconscious.

His attacker grabbed Jones's feet and dragged him into a corner of the garage, went inside the embassy, and returned moments later carrying two black leather satchels. He took keys from his pocket and climbed behind the wheel of the limo, shook his head, got out, put the keys on the seat, left the garage, pulled down the overhead door, and quickly walked to Massachusetts Avenue. The sun was higher and traffic had begun to build. He went right, passed the three-story white Embassy of South Africa and stopped in front of a park across from the British Embassy. He climbed a slight rise to where the heavily wooded park began. There was a wooden bench, and a sign that read: NORMANSTONE TRAIL—TRAIL MAINTAINED BY THE POTOMAC-APPALACHIAN TRAIL CLUB. An arrow pointed toward the British Embassy and indicated that Wisconsin Avenue was one kilometer in that direction. An arrow pointing into the park was followed by ROCK CREEK, 1K. He cast a final look at the British Embassy, then disappeared into the woods. A short time later he emerged on Rock Creek Drive, hailed a passing taxi, and told the driver, "Union Station."

6

Exterminators were at MPD when Morizio and Lake arrived that morning. Roaches had invaded the building weeks ago, but it had taken that long for money to be transferred from one fund to a new one whose file folder read: EMERGENCY FUMIGATION.

"This place stinks," Morizio said as he hung his blue suit jacket on a clothes tree in his office, slipped behind his desk, and glanced through a long memo.

"I'll give you a report on that meeting I went to on Capitol security," Lake said.

"Yeah, good," Morizio said, not looking up.

"Sal."

"What?" He looked at her.

She blew him a kiss.

"Do the report."

His phone rang and she picked it up. "Oh, hi, Jake," she said. "Hold on." She handed the phone to Morizio.

"Hello, Jake. What can I do for you?"

"We've had an incident at the Iranian Embassy on Massachusetts Avenue. One of our men, Willard Jones, was assaulted in a garage there. Somebody hit him with a tire iron. He's critical at D.C. General.''

"The Iranian Embassy? It's been closed for years.''

"There's more. In the garage where we found him is a limo belonging to the British Embassy.''

"Yeah.'' Morizio sat back and sighed.

"You don't sound surprised, Sal.''

"Sure I am, Jake, it's just that . . .'' He was guilty about not having shared with Feinstein what he'd learned earlier about the missing valet and limo. "Any idea why a British limo would be at the abandoned Iranian Embassy?''

"None whatsoever.''

"Any idea who hit your man?''

"No. You have any thoughts?''

Morizio shook his head, then realized Feinstein couldn't see him. "Not off the top of my head, Jake.''

"Well, it's your problem now, Sal.''

"Maybe.''

"He's loose in D.C. That's MPD business.''

"Let me do some checking. I'll call you later.''

He hung up and filled in Lake, whose first words were, "The valet? What's his name?''

"Hafez. Nuri Hafez.'' Morizio dialed Chief Trottier's number. "Captain Morizio here,'' he told Trottier's secretary. Trottier came right on the line. "Chief, I've got to see you right away.''

"On the British matter?''

"Right.''

"Is anything wrong?''

"Lots. Can I come up?''

"Not now. Make it an hour.''

"Yes, sir.''

Morizio told Lake, "Get over to the Iranian Embassy. Do it quietly, just be there.''

"What should I do when I get there?"

"Nothing, just don't let anything disappear. If the press is around, keep your mouth shut. You're there on routine business. Keep in touch."

An hour later Morizio sat across the desk from Donald J. Trottier, who was in dress uniform in anticipation of an awards luncheon. He was slightly shorter than Morizio and had recently put on weight, which caused his uniform to bulge. Bald, but with fringes of gray hair, he wore a thin black mustache which Morizio knew he touched up. Morizio started to tell him what had happened but was interrupted three times by telephone calls. "Can you kill that for ten minutes?" Morizio asked after the third call, pointing to the phone.

Trottier didn't like it but said, "All right, Sal." He told his secretary to hold all calls. "Now, what's so urgent?"

Morizio, conscious of the need to be quick, said in a series of staccato sentences, "One of State's security men was attacked last night at the Iranian Embassy . . . they found a British Embassy limo in a garage there . . . I know that Geoffrey James's Iranian valet—a guy named Nuri Hafez—disappeared the night of the death, along with the limo . . . I also know that . . ."

"How do you know about this valet and the limo?"

"I can't say, I just know."

"That's a hell of a thing."

"Yeah, it is."

"I'm the chief of police. I'm . . ."

"You're my boss, I know that. I held back for good reason. But now . . ."

"I find this unsettling, Captain, that one of my men would withhold such information. It could be vital."

"Of course it's vital . . . *sir*. What I want to know is why the British Embassy kept it secret."

"Evidently, it didn't. You knew."

"And now you know, but why has it been hushed up?"

"Who says it has?"

"Hasn't it? What would you call it?"

"I'd call it the prerogative of the British Embassy. The death occurred on its property and involved one of its people. That means we stay out unless we're invited in."

Morizio felt anger percolating. He'd worked for years to bring into check what was a naturally volatile temper, but there were times when he lost the battle and he was afraid this might be one of them. He took a deep breath, changed position in his chair, and said calmly and slowly, "I understand, sir, that this is British business under Vienna, 167, but we now have on the loose, in Washington, D.C., someone who has assaulted a security officer from the State Department. He's in critical condition. Not only that, I attended a meeting yesterday—with your blessing—with Dr. Gibronski and the Englishman, Thorpe, about this case. I've been told by you to keep you informed. I've been told . . ."

"You've been told, Captain Morizio, to do nothing without specific orders from Dr. Gibronski and George Thorpe. That's the way it is and that's the way it will be unless you hear differently from me. Understood?"

Morizio stood and went to the window, again to buy time against lashing out. He leaned on a sill that contained heat and air-conditioning and said, "Do I ignore this assault?"

"Yes. I would suggest you follow—to the letter—the protocol that's been established. Call George Thorpe, tell him what you've told me, and ask for his instructions. Excuse me, Captain, I have other pressing matters."

"Thank you, sir."

"Son of a bitch," Morizio muttered loudly as he went down a back stairwell to the communications center where he was told they'd just delivered carbons of wire dispatches to his office. He looked at the originals—stories of the assault on Willard Jones and of the discovery of the limousine at the Iranian Embassy.

Lake was on the line when he returned to his office. George Thorpe was there in person. "Excuse me," Morizio told Thorpe as he picked up the phone. "What's the situation, Officer Lake?" he asked.

"Officer . . .? Someone's there. Okay, Captain, it's confusing. The press are all over the place. Jake Feinstein is here. So are two units from Tactical. They want to know what the protocol is."

"Put the officer-in-charge on."

An officer with a husky voice came on the two-way. "Seal off the area," said Morizio, "and do it up at street level. Set up a normal crime-scene situation— barriers, shift guards, the usual. And put Officer Lake back on."

"Yes, sir?" she said briskly.

"When you're satisfied it's secure, report back here."

"Yes, sir." Even brisker.

Thorpe had been standing just inside the door. He'd lighted a cigar and had allowed the ash to grow to a precarious length.

"Ashtray?" Morizio asked as he hung up.

The ash fell to the green carpet. "Oh, my," Thorpe said.

"It's good for the fibers," Morizio said.

"Yes, I've heard that," Thorpe said as he dragged a shoe over the ashes and came to Morizio's desk.

"What now?" Morizio asked.

"Pardon?"

"I'm supposed to take orders from you."

"From what I've been observing, Captain, you've forgotten that."

"Do you want to run this department, Mr. Thorpe? Do you want to set up security—or a lack of it—at the scene of a crime?"

Thorpe ignored the pique in Morizio's voice. He pulled a chair close to the desk, settled his large frame into it, and leaned toward Morizio. He was wearing the same brown tweed suit he'd worn at Gibronski's office—and the same tie. His white shirt was shiny and had a white-on-white pattern in it. "Are we alone?" Thorpe asked.

Morizio blinked and looked around the room.

"*Really* alone, Captain, and I do not appreciate feeble attempts at humor."

"Get to the point, Mr. Thorpe."

"And you drop the façade of the tough, hard-boiled American *cop*, Captain Morizio. You've entered another league and are about to . . ." His voice had the tensile strength of steel. Now he smiled, sat back, puffed on his cigar, and said softly, " . . . about to strike out. Baseball."

Morizio smiled, too. "Yeah, I know. I'm a fan."

"Really? For whom do you root?"

"The Red Sox."

"Boston. I've never been able to muster enthusiasm for the game—or the city. They're both dreadfully slow."

"You like the fast lane, Mr. Thorpe?"

"At times. It's akin to sex. There are times when the slow and comfortable approach is pleasant, but then there are times when . . ."

"Why are you here?"

"To see that you don't exceed your ego boundaries."

"What does that mean?"

"A psychology major?"

"Sociology."

"Oh yes, quite. It's Officer Lake who majored in psychology."

"Are you trying to impress me that you've done your homework about me?" Before Thorpe could respond, Morizio said, "And why would you bother, about me or Officer Lake?"

Thorpe smiled and flicked his ash into a dented metal ashtray on the desk. "I admire a discreet man," he said.

"Meaning what?"

"Insisting upon calling one's lover *'Officer* Lake.' "

Morizio wanted to come across the desk at him but told himself not only would it be embarrassing, he'd be attacking his superior. "What do you want?" he asked.

Thorpe belched, excused himself, and vigorously ground out the cigar in the ashtray. "Captain Morizio," he said as he stood and walked to the door, "what should have been a simple diplomatic death has been unnecessarily complicated."

"By me?"

"In a sense, but more at the feet of your free press and those who suffer a loss of their *ego boundaries.*"

Morizio wondered whether he was referring to leaks within the British Embassy, specifically Paul Pringle. He sat with a blank expression on his face and an urge to spit, preferably in the direction of the hulk in the brown tweed suit.

Thorpe said, "There will be a press conference this afternoon in the rotunda of the British Embassy. Your Chief Trottier will be there and he requests your attendance."

"I just left him. He didn't mention it."

"He just found out about it, Captain. It's at three. I'll see you then."

"Maybe."

"No, Captain, you'll be there—at three." The hard edge was back. Then a deliberate softening once again. "By the way, I am sorry."

"For what?"

"For your Red Sox not having an especially fulfilling season."

"Rice had a good year."

"Rice. Oh yes, the Negro outfielder. I suppose he did."

It took Morizio ten minutes to calm down. When he did he called Chief Trottier's office. He was put through immediately. "I'm calling about the three o'clock press conference at the British Embassy," he said.

"Yes, Captain, I expect you to be there. There'll be a major announcement regarding Ambassador James's death. You're to say nothing. I'll handle any questions."

"Can I ask, sir, why I'm to be there with a gag on my mouth?"

"Because you are one person, Captain Morizio, and your sensitivities are irrelevant compared to affairs of state in which two major nations must resolve a difficult situation. You know, Captain, I took the time after you left to review your background. I'm beginning to wonder whether putting you in the delicate job of intracity coordinator of security was an appropriate decision. You certainly have the degrees—and your years with the Army and the CIA are impressive—but degrees and past performances don't always accurately predict a man's future performance."

"I suppose they don't, sir."

"Three o'clock. Let's go together. My car will be in front at two-forty-five."

"Yes, sir."

Morizio hung up and kicked a metal trash basket across the room. He was still limping when he arrived in front of MPD headquarters at a quarter of three.

7

George Thorpe was waiting in the foyer of the British Embassy's rotunda when Morizio and Trottier arrived. Dozens of uniformed and armed embassy security personnel, augmented by 100 members of the State Department's security force, checked IDs before allowing anyone inside the rotunda, a large, two-story circular glass building that looked from the outside like an afterthought to the embassy complex.

"Follow me," Thorpe said as he pushed into the crowd and led them to a raised platform at the Massachusetts Avenue edge of the circular room. Embassy press secretary Jack Boyington repeated into a microphone, "Ladies and gentlemen, *p-l-e-a-s-e* quiet down so that we may begin." Next to him was Head of Chancery Nigel Barnsworth. They were flanked by embassy guards.

Thorpe indicated that Trottier and Morizio should step up on the platform. Morizio grabbed Trottier by the arm and said, "What's going on?"

"I told you in the car it's all been resolved. I'll

handle any questions. What are you doing for dinner tonight?''

"Dinner?"

"At the house. The missus and I would enjoy having you."

"I've got a . . . well, I . . . that would be nice. Thank you."

They mounted the platform and Morizio looked out at 300 faces. Sunlight through floor-to-ceiling yellow drapes cast shifting patterns over the assembled. Reporters jostled for position, and still-photographers spilled out of their designated area to stake out better shooting angles.

Morizio looked up and to his right at a large heraldic embroidery of a Scottish unicorn suspended from the ceiling by gold ropes, one of four such Queens' Beastes in the room. He then shifted his attention to six embassy guards carrying automatic weapons who stood like statues on a narrow balcony above the TV cameras.

"P-l-e-a-s-e," said Boyington.

The crowd fumbled and mumbled to a tentative stillness.

"Ladies and gentlemen," said Boyington, "we appreciate having all of you here today. It was admittedly short notice, but events dictated that. At any rate, it is good of you to come. At this time I would like to introduce Head of Chancery Minister Nigel Barnsworth, who has an announcement to make to you. Minister Barnsworth."

Morizio had been watching Barnsworth during the press secretary's preliminary remarks. He was overtly nervous, and held a prepared statement in hands that trembled. He was to Morizio's right, and Morizio fixated on the tic in his left eye, which became more pronounced with each passing moment.

Barnsworth stepped to the microphone, cleared his throat three times and said in a shaky voice, "Thank you for coming."

"Was the ambassador poisoned?" a reporter shouted.

"Please, I have a statement to make," Barnsworth said.

Boyington held up his hands.

"Ladies and gentlemen, there has been a most unfortunate situation here at Her Majesty's mission to the United States," said Barnsworth. "As you know, our esteemed ambassador, Geoffrey James, has expired." A few reporters chuckled at his use of the word. Barnsworth's face colored. He cleared his throat again and continued. "At first, it was thought that coronary failure had caused the death of Ambassador James. However, further study of this tragic matter has indicated differently."

"Was he poisoned?"

"Please, allow me to continue. Those of you familiar with diplomatic law realize that events within a mission to any nation remain the sole purview of that mission. However, because of the circumstances surrounding the death of Ambassador James, this mission sought the help of its host country, the United States of America. An autopsy was performed on the ambassador by the excellent forensic division of the Washington Metropolitan Police Department. It was determined, as a result of that forensic exploration, that the cause of death was poison, to be more precise, a highly toxic and fast-acting poison called ricin."

There was a flurry of activity in the room. A series of questions came from the floor, but Barnsworth shook his head and held up a hand. "Please, ladies and gentlemen, allow me to complete my statement." When reporters continued to ask questions, Jack Boyington took the microphone and announced that if order was not restored, the press conference would be terminated. That did it, and Barnsworth continued. "Obviously, this loss has been felt deeply within this mission, and within Great Britain. It is little consolation that the identity of this great man's murderer is known."

Again, a roar of comment and question.

Barnsworth ignored the disruption this time. He cleared his throat with surprising gusto, grasped the flexible mike stand and said loudly, "Geoffrey James, Her Majesty's ambassador to the United States, was poisoned to death by one Nuri Hafez, an Iranian who had been rescued from Iran by the deceased ambassador, and who had served as his valet and chauffeur ever since. The evidence against Nuri Hafez is overwhelming and beyond debate, and an international warrant has been issued for his arrest."

The questions erupted. "Where is he?" . . . "What's his background?" . . . "Was the limousine found this morning at the Iranian Embassy connected with it?"

Barnsworth pressed on, and his words caused the reporters to cease their questioning. "A printed statement regarding the death of Ambassador James and background information on his murder has been prepared and is available for each of you at the conclusion of this conference. I would like to express Her Majesty's profound appreciation for the invaluable aid and cooperation of the United States government, and for the same spirit of friendship and help from this city's Metropolitan Police Department, Donald J. Trottier, chief of police, and Detective Captain Salvatore Morizio, coordinator of intracity security. Their contributions and professional excellence have been exemplary. That concludes my official statement."

Press secretary Boyington took the microphone and

invited questions, then immediately turned it over to Trottier, who launched into answers that sounded more, to Morizio, like a campaign speech.

Morizio hopped down from the platform. "Can I help you?" Thorpe asked. Morizio shook his head and headed for the foyer where he cornered an embassy security guard. "Is Paul Pringle here?" he asked.

"Mr. Pringle? No, I can't say I've seen him."

"Thanks."

Morizio crossed a corridor leading to the embassy's main entrance and motioned to guards at a desk behind a series of sliding bulletproof doors. He waved his ID. After some scrutiny, a button was pushed and the doors slid open. "Captain Morizio, MPD," he said. "I'd like to speak with Paul Pringle."

"Pringle." One of the guards consulted an internal directory. "Sorry, sir, Mr. Pringle is no longer with us."

"That can't be," Morizio said. "He was here a few days ago."

Another of the guards said pleasantly, "That he was, sir, but he's been dispatched to special duty back home."

"England?"

"Yes, sir, that is home."

"Can you connect me with his office?"

The guard laughed. "He doesn't have an office any longer."

"Thanks," said Morizio. "If Paul Pringle passes through on his way home, please give him this." He took a business card from his pocket, scribbled on the back—*"Paul, please call"*—and handed it to the guard.

Morizio returned to the rotunda, which had emptied out considerably. Chief Trottier was still fielding questions. George Thorpe intercepted Morizio on his way to the platform. "Anything wrong, Captain?"

"Do you know the whereabouts of Paul Pringle?"

"Pringle? Can't say that I've ever heard the name."

"He worked in security here at the embassy."

Thorpe shook his head. "That offer of a drink still holds."

"I have something else to do," Morizio said.

"Lucky man. Miss Lake?"

"I don't like you, Thorpe."

Thorpe laughed. "Pity. A drink might bring you around."

"I doubt it."

Thorpe belched, ran a large hand over his mouth, glared at Morizio and said, "Congratulations."

"For what?"

"Doing such a splendid job in this messy case. Your chief has been praising you at every turn."

Morizio looked up at Trottier, who'd answered his final question and was about to step down, then returned his attention to Thorpe, and said, "You buying?"

"Yes."

"Good. Where?"

Thorpe rubbed his hands together and furrowed his brow. "I'm partial to Timberlake's."

"I'll be there in an hour."

"I'll wait."

After confirming dinner at Trottier's house and getting directions to it, Morizio called his office and was connected with Connie Lake. "How'd it go?" she asked.

"Smashingly."

"You okay?"

"Tip-top. Look, Officer Lake, get yourself wired up and join me at Timberlake's, on Connecticut."

"Wired?"

"Yeah, but don't check anything out of Surveillance.

63

Keep it simple, grab something from my apartment and be there in an hour.''

"Who are we seeing?"

"A representative of Her Majesty's government."

"Huh?"

"George Thorpe. He belches a lot but ignore it. Got to go. See you in an hour.''

Lake immediately left the office and drove to Morizio's condominium in Arlington. She let herself in, went to the bedroom and opened the only one of three closets that was locked. Inside were shelves of electronic and photographic equipment—microphones of every description, including shotgun mikes, FM transmitting mikes, watches, tie tacs and earrings containing microphones; ultra-sensitive devices that picked up whispers through cinderblock walls, telephone taps, a microphone woven into a scarf and the newest addition to the collection, a subminiature microphone designed to be implanted in a tooth, provided a cooperative dentist could be found. There were recorders of varying sizes and shapes, blank tapes, miniature cameras and film, infrared lighting equipment and a video camera with a lens powerful enough to pick a bug off a branch at 500 yards. The collection represented one of Morizio's many hobbies. Everything in the closet was available through MPD's Surveillance Unit, but Morizio enjoyed having his own capability. Besides, anything electronic fascinated him. There was an amaranthine quality about gadgets that he felt was lacking in people, an honesty, a directness, predictability. You took care of equipment, kept it clean and serviced, and it would always be there for you, like a good dog.

Lake often kidded him about it, but over the course of their relationship she'd learned to share his appreciation of the myriad gadgets in the closet. He'd spent hours teaching her how to use and service them. Morizio was a fanatic about the care of his collection of electronic gear—batteries always removed and stored in the refrigerator, tape heads cleaned and demagnetized at prescribed intervals, tapes thoroughly erased in a bulk eraser, rewound and stored outside the machines to avoid stretching, reel-to-reel tapes stored tails-out to avoid print-through and, most important, he thoroughly checked everything before taking it on a job.

Lake chose a small Sony cassette recorder attached to a VOX switch, which meant it would record only when there was someone speaking. The recorder's internal mechanism had been modified to allow five hours of recording on a single side of the cassette. The microphone had been custom made by a small Virginia electronics firm that supplied exotic listening devices to police departments across the country. It would pick up hushed conversations across a large room even when inside a closed attaché case. She inserted batteries and a cassette, attached the microphone, and did a test. It worked perfectly. She slipped recorder and microphone into a pocket of her raincoat, reminded herself to turn it on before entering the tavern, and headed for Timberlake's, a popular D.C. neighborhood pub.

Morizio and Thorpe were in a booth when she arrived. Morizio introduced Lake to the Englishman. "Ah, yes, Miss Lake," Thorpe said, standing and extending his hand. "Or should I say *Officer* Lake?"

"Are we on duty?" she asked.

Morizio laughed, shook his head and said, "No, we're not. Call her Connie, Mr. Thorpe."

"And George will do for me," Thorpe said as he helped her off with her coat. "Check it for you?" he asked.

"No, here is fine." Thorpe hung it on the booth's

upright nearest him. "Perfect placement," Lake thought to herself as she sat next to Morizio, across from Thorpe.

Thorpe had a draft bitter in front of him, Morizio a bottle of Miller Lite. Lake ordered a white wine. The place had begun to fill up and the long bar was two deep. Thorpe raised his glass and said, "To you, Miss Lake. When Sal told me he'd invited you to join us, I was delighted."

"To all of us," she said, looking at Morizio.

They clinked glasses. Morizio said, "George and I were just getting to know each other, Connie. We've been involved, sort of, in this Geoffrey James thing and figured it was about time we knew who we were."

Thorpe laughed, burped behind his hand, sipped his beer and said, "I was telling the captain a little about myself."

"You were in Africa?" Morizio said.

"Yes, for six years, establishing trade agreements with African industrialists."

"Must have been fascinating," Lake said.

"More hot than fascinating, Connie. I've never been a fan of heat. It saps one. Don't you agree?"

"I'm from Seattle," she said. "It never gets too hot or too cold there. I like moderation."

"In everything?"

"Usually. How long have you been here in the United States?"

Morizio sat back and drank his beer as Thorpe talked about his life as a trade representative for Great Britain. Twenty minutes later Thorpe said, "I've been going on forever, it seems. Time for another round and a little about you, Sal."

They ordered. Morizio said. "There's not much to tell about me, George. I suspect you know a great deal anyway, based upon comments you made earlier."

"Earlier?"

"When we first met. I'm just a cop, a civil servant." He told a little of his Boston family, his college days and what had led to his joining MPD. Thorpe listened quietly, his only reaction an occasional raise of an eyebrow, or a smile at a humorous aside. When Morizio was through, he looked at his watch. "I have a dinner date. I really have to go."

Connie looked at him quizzically.

"Chief Trottier's house. The missus is making me dinner."

"Oh," she said.

"Have you had dinner, Miss Lake?" Thorpe asked.

"No, I thought . . ."

"I'd be delighted," said Thorpe. "That is, if your captain doesn't have objections."

"Why would he?" Lake asked.

"George is aware that we have a relationship aside from the department," said Morizio.

She was surprised that he would have admitted such a thing, but knew this wasn't the time to bring it up. She smiled at Thorpe and said, "I'd enjoy dinner and hearing more about Africa."

Now, it was Morizio's turn to be perplexed. He was certain she'd turn down Thorpe's offer.

"The food here is surprisingly good for a pub," Thorpe said, "which is why I'm partial to the establishment. I'd avoid the seafood, with the exception of oysters, and the quiches are uniformly satisfying."

"Enjoy yourselves," Morizio said, barely able to hide his annoyance that Connie decided to stay. "I'll call you later," he told her as he slipped into his coat.

"Okay, Captain."

Morizio pondered her playful use of his title, let it pass and said to Thorpe, "Maybe you'll have a chance to explain to Connie why someone who's spent his life as a trade representative ends up in charge of an ambassador's murder, George.''

"I'll do my best," Thorpe said. "Enjoy your chief's wife's cooking."

"I'm sure I will."

Morizio wanted to sit down, remove his coat, and ask the questions that were really on his mind. Instead, he shook Thorpe's hand, nodded at Connie and left Timberlake's.

He didn't leave Chief Trottier's house until eleven. Dinner was excellent, and Trottier's wife, Maureen, was as plain and straightforward as her husband was pompous. Throughout dinner Trottier claimed the reason he'd invited Morizio was to get to know his key men better. "There's a tendency for a gap to exist between a chief and his captains, Sal," he said. "I've been impressed with the way you've handled this Geoffrey James matter and wanted you to know it on a more personal level than's possible at headquarters."

"More pie?" Maureen asked.

"No, ma'am," Morizio said. "I'm stuffed. It was very good."

Morizio had hoped to find time alone with Trottier to clear up some of his confusion over the handling of the James murder. That chance never materialized. As he stood at the front door and Trottier helped him on with his coat, he asked, "Can we catch some time together, Chief? I've got questions about the James case that are bothering me."

"Nine?"

"Sure thing."

"I'd intended to hold a briefing on it anyway. There's

still protocol to be followed, even though we're out of it."

"Out of it? What about finding Hafez?"

"I'm sure he's long gone from D.C. by now. It's an international matter. We'll let them know what we know, which isn't much, and get on with things. See you at nine."

"Yes, sir. A wonderful meal, Mrs. Trottier. Thank you."

"Come again, Captain. I enjoy meeting the men my husband works with."

Morizio considered stopping by Connie's apartment on his way home but decided not to. He didn't call her either because he didn't want to wake her. She called him at midnight. He was playing chess with Rasputin. "How was dinner?" she asked.

"She's a good cook. You?"

"I've had better food, I've had worse."

"I don't care about the food. Anything come out of Thorpe?"

"It's all on tape. He's a charmer. I wish his stomach were under better control but aside from that, I enjoyed his company."

"Well, I didn't. I don't like him."

"Neither do I."

"You sound as though you do."

"Oh, Sal, that little vestige of jealousy peeks through now and then and I love you for it."

"Jealous, hell. Thorpe's not what you'd call a threat to a relationship."

"He's not *that* bad. But do you know what, Sal?"

"What?"

"One, I love you very much. Two, I'm anxious to listen to the tape with you and discuss it. And three, I sense a side of Mr. George Thorpe that would allow him to blow up his own mother if there were something in it for him.''

Morizio laughed. "He's not *that* bad."

"I think he could be. Sleep tight. See you in the office, Captain."

Morizio had just climbed into bed at two when the phone rang. An overseas operator told him to wait. A few seconds later Paul Pringle came on the line.

"Paul, I was looking for you today at the embassy. They said you'd gone home on some special assignment."

"Call it what you will, Sal. I didn't want to just leave without saying good-bye."

"I appreciate that, but what's really going on? Why the sudden departure? The James thing? Do they know you'd been in touch with me?"

"Best not discuss it on the phone, Sal, best we just drop this whole James business and get on with our lives."

"That doesn't sound like you."

"We're all different people at different times, Sal. I really must scoot. Thanks so much for all you did for me in the States, and for your continuing friendship. I've left a little token of my appreciation with the bartender at Piccadilly. Johnny, the skinny one. Just ask for the envelope with S.M. on it. Perhaps we'll meet once again. If you ever get over this way please ring up. And my best to your Connie Lake."

"Yeah, thanks. I appreciate the call, Paul. Take care."

There was the hint of a laugh. "Oh, yes, Sal, I certainly intend to do that, and I urge you to do the same."

"Count on it. Best to the family."

Morizio tossed and turned until five, then drifted into

a light sleep. He sat bolt upright when the alarm went off at seven, immediately got out of bed and showered. He called Lake. "Don't mention the meeting with Thorpe around MPD," he told her.

"I didn't plan to. Shall I bring the tape?"

"No. We'll listen to it tonight. Where are we staying?"

"Your choice."

"Here. Okay?"

"Sure. If Kissinger could get used to shuttle diplomacy, I can handle shuttle romance."

8

Morizio and Lake had a chance to talk before his nine o'clock meeting with Chief Trottier. "Did you press Thorpe on why a so-called trade rep ends up representing England in a murder case?" he asked her.

"I pursued it. Pressing's not my style."

"What did he say?"

"He said . . . well, you might as well hear it tonight. It's all on tape."

"Give me a hint."

"He said that he sometimes is called upon to perform other duties for 'Her Majesty's government.' "

"Like what?"

"Like . . . like overseeing a murder investigation that involved his country's ambassador to the United States."

"But why him? Why not somebody from Embassy Security, or Scotland Yard, or Interpol?"

"He seemed to say, Sal, that it's really not the murder that involves him. It's more a case of being on

the scene to represent a government 3,500 miles away.
I can buy that.''

''But you think he'd blow up his own mother.''

She laughed. ''An overstatement. You can hear it all
tonight. By the way, did you tape dinner at the chief's
house?''

''Of course not.''

''Just wondering. Thought we might swap tapes, like
a club.''

''I have to go.''

''Kiss?''

''Jesus.''

Trottier made it known immediately that he had only
fifteen minutes for the ''briefing'' on the James case.
Joining Morizio around a conference table were five
other officers representing public affairs, administra-
tion, tactical crime, forensics and communications.
Trottier's statement was short and direct. ''From the
standpoint of this organization, the case of British Ambassador James is closed, except to assist in the search
for the accused assassin, Nuri Hafez. All matters relating to the forensic assistance we gave the British government are sealed, unless specifically ordered open by
me. The press is to be told nothing aside from the
prepared statements they've received. Are there any
questions about this?''

Only Morizio responded. ''Chief Trottier,'' he said,
''there are areas that concern me relating to intracity
security. If the British had immediately issued a report
on Hafez and the limo, Officer Jones from State wouldn't
be in a hospital with a fractured skull and, most likely,
Hafez would be in custody right now.''

''And, Captain Morizio?''

''And . . . and, there's an assumption that Hafez is
no longer in the D.C. area. That's not been established.

I'd like to know what guidelines we're to follow in looking for him."

Trottier sighed and said, "The guidelines are exactly what I've outlined."

"But we are actively looking for the suspect in Washington. Is that right?"

"An APB has been issued."

"What about the Iranian community in the city? Are we looking for leads there?"

"We are looking for the suspect as we would any suspect, with one exception. If the averages hold, sixteen people will be murdered in the District this month. One will be a child below the age of twelve. One will be older than sixty. We now average an eighteen-percent solve-rate for all serious crimes in the District, which puts D.C. eleventh on a list of twelve area police departments. In other words, Captain Morizio, we have more pressing things to attend to than poking our noses into Great Britain's criminal business. Does that answer your question?"

"Not really, sir, but your point is well taken."

"Thank you. That will be all."

Morizio and Lake met up at six that evening. "Come on," he said, "I'll treat you to some mutton chops and a yard of beer at Piccadilly."

"I don't like mutton chops, and I don't drink beer."

"Maybe they'll make you Cockney chop suey. I have to pick something up before we go home."

They drove up Pennsylvania Avenue, past the White House, then went north on Connecticut Avenue until reaching the Chevy Chase Circle where the Piccadilly Restaurant and Pub was located. Morizio had spent evenings there with Paul Pringle, who claimed it was the only restaurant in Washington with the ambiance of a London pub, even though it was owned by Germans.

They found a legal parking space across the street from the pub's gray-and-gold awning and lighted sign, approached the entrance on Astroturf and went through heavy black double doors. A German hostess greeted them.

"Is Johnny on tonight?" Morizio asked.

"No," the hostess said. "Dinner?"

"Yeah, thanks."

They settled at a table. "I'll be right back," Morizio told Lake. He headed for the bar, which was entered from the small dining room through an archway. A pair of swords hung over it. Morizio stopped to admire a collection of old books, an antique globe and ship models in a bookcase next to the archway. Paul Pringle had donated some of the books. He was an inveterate history buff, particularly military history, and when his book collection overflowed his shelves, he gave some to friends, and to his favorite pub.

Morizio asked a barmaid whether a package had been left for him by Johnny. She rummaged through a drawer until finding an eight-and-a-half-by-eleven manila envelope with the initials S.M. written in red ink.

Morizio took it to the table and handed it to Connie.

"What's this?" she asked.

"Paul Pringle left it for me before he took off. Says it's a token of his appreciation." He mimicked a British accent.

"That was thoughtful of him."

"Yeah. Nice guy. I'd sell Rasputin to know what really sent him back to jolly ol' England."

Marizio ordered beer, and Lake had wine. Then, mutton chops for him, Dover sole for her. It wasn't until they'd finished dinner and had ordered a trifle to share that they finished reading twenty pieces of paper, some fastened together with paper clips. There was a covering note from Pringle:

Dear Sal—Sorry to vanish like this but duty calls. You've been a good friend, and I only wish I could repay what you've done for me as a stranger on your shores. But let us avoid the maudlin at all costs. What I leave you are various documents having to do with the death of the ambassador. He was a nasty sort, between you and me, and there were certainly enough people who won't wear black at his passing, including his lovely and long-suffering wife, his deputy, Barnsworth, certain of the household staff and Lord knows who else around the globe. The point is, Nuri Hafez is being pointed to as the culprit, and perhaps he is, but I wouldn't take it as Gospel. But then I know the astute detective, S. M., probably hasn't, and doesn't need an aging civil servant to tell him that.

There's a copy of the guest list in here, some of my notes about certain personalities, other bits and pieces that might entertain you. Naturally, these have appeared from the blue, the work of a demented soul terminally influenced by Dame Agatha, but one who means well.

I shall miss you, S.M. Hoist one for me from time to time at Piccadilly. God bless.

They drove to his apartment where they got into robes and poured themselves nightcaps. "What do you make of the papers Paul left?" Morizio asked.

She rubbed her eyes. "Obviously, he doesn't think Hafez killed James, although he doesn't offer anything you'd call proof. The guest list is interesting, but so what?"

"Why?" Morizio asked the middle of the room.

"Why what?"

"Why hush things up? Why George Thorpe? Why does Pringle not buy the official line? Why heavies like Werner Gibronski in the act? Why the chief treating it as though plans for nuclear destruction rode on keeping it so goddamn secret?''

She extended her hand and touched his cheek. "Sal, drop it. They've told you to drop it, and that's what you should do. There's nothing to be gained, no up-side.''

"There's still an APB out on Hafez.''

"So?''

"So, I'm still involved officially. So are you because I am.''

"What do you want me to do?''

"See what you can dig up on Rich Washburn.''

"The hostage?''

"Yeah. Maybe something he said about James from the Iranian days would shed a little light.''

"All right.''

"Did you notice the name Berge Nordkild on the guest list?''

"Sure, he's in the society pages all the time. Caters all the fancy parties.''

"That's right. Half the black tie dirges I attend are catered by Nordkild. I've met him a couple of times. Think I'll give him a call.''

"Can we go to bed now?''

"I'd like to listen to the tape you made with Thorpe.''

They finished listening at one-thirty. Morizio found it boring, heard nothing on the tape that shed any light on things. He labeled the tape, stored it in a locked cassette rack, cleaned the tape heads and turned out the lights. They snuggled together in bed, bare bodies melding like Silly Putty. She knew he would fall asleep quickly. "Sal," she whispered.

"What?''

"Do you know why I don't like chasing this James thing?''

"Why?''

"Because we have little enough time together as it is. I was hoping we could grab the long weekend over Thanksgiving and get away, maybe to the shore, Seattle to see my folks, just hole up here for four days, be alone."

"That'd be nice."

"I *know* it would be nice. The question is whether we'll do it."

"I'm all for it."

"Sal."

"I love you, Lake. Just remember that."

"I love you too, Morizio. Let's think about it."

"Absolutely. It sounds great. Uh, huh."

They awoke early, made hasty love, and were at their desks by eight.

9

"Mr. Nordkild?"

"Yes."

"Captain Salvatore Morizio, Metropolitan Police. We've met a few times."

"Yes, I recall. What can I do for you?"

"You could give me some education on fancy foods."

Nordkild laughed. "It would be my pleasure. Is this for personal or professional reasons?"

"Strictly personal. Could I visit you today?"

"Yah, that would be all right. This is the day I taste new foods. Would you like to join me?"

"I'd love it. You're sure it's not an inconvenience."

"Not when a police captain is involved. Noon? You know where my offices are?"

"Yes."

"Bring a healthy appetite."

"I'll skip the donuts this morning, Mr. Nordkild. See you at noon."

Nordkild Importers and Catering occupied a handsome four-story Georgetown brownstone on Q Street,

N.W., off Wisconsin Avenue. Morizio knew the neighborhood; his favorite bookstore, the Francis Scott Key, was a few blocks away.

He was asked to wait downstairs by a striking brunette who spoke with the same accent as Nordkild, and who was very tall. He examined what hung on the walls: testimonial letters from government figures and entertainers, covers of gourmet food magazines on which Nordkild was featured, large color photographs of Nordkild standing behind sumptuous displays of food, and a black-and-white autographed picture of Washington's top caterer presenting Jimmy Carter with an oversized peanut sculpted from chicken liver.

"Mr. Nordkild will see you now," the receptionist said. Morizio followed her to a tiny elevator. She reached inside, pushed a button for the third floor and stepped back. "Enjoy," she said.

"Right," said Morizio. *"Skoal!"*

Nordkild met him on the third floor. "Welcome, Captain. You're very prompt."

"I try to be. Nice building you have."

"Functional. Our kitchens are here on Floor Three. Floor Two has offices. My offices are on Floor Four. Come, we eat."

The tasting room was directly off a large kitchen and was decorated in muted shades of blue and pink. An elaborately set table stood in the center of the room. Gleaming Bing-and-Grøndahl handpainted porcelain china and Georg Jensen silverware rested regally on a crisp white tablecloth. Two places were set. A Grieg cello sonata played softly from speakers in the room's four corners.

"Sit, my friend," Nordkild said. "We've received samples of some interesting new foods. I hope you enjoy them."

"I'm sure I will."

They settled into comfortable Finn Juhl armchairs and two young blonde women wearing starched white uniforms arrived with trays from the kitchen. One held a variety of herring, the other four porcelain bowls filled with varieties of caviar.

Nordkild took a bottle from an ice bucket and filled two small glasses. "Akvavit," he said. "This has a dill base. Perhaps you would prefer coriander."

"I've never tasted akvavit."

"Good. I like introducing new things to new friends. Skoal!" He held his glass at eye level, nodded, smiled and tossed it down. Morizio did the same. "You like it?"

"It's strong. Yes, I like it."

"It gets better by the glass." Nordkild lifted the edge of his napkin, which he'd tucked into his collar, and wiped his drooping, waxed mustache. "We start with herring," he told Morizio. "We always start with herring. This brand is from Finland. I have not had it before. Tell me what you think."

Morizio took tiny bites. He hated herring. When asked by Nordkild what he thought, he said, "Not bad."

Nordkild laughed. "Not good, either, Captain. Hopefully, the caviar will be better."

Vodka was served in iced glasses, and one of the servers placed a white plastic spoon in each bowl of caviar. "The caviar is from America," said Nordkild. "The spoons are too, from McDonalds."

Morizio laughed.

"Caviar should never be eaten with anything metal. Doctors' tongue depressors are good. So are these little plastic spoons."

"Yeah, coke addicts like 'em, too."

"I wouldn't know about that. Begin tasting, Captain. Tell me if you think the Americans are capable of producing decent caviar."

They tasted from the four bowls, with Nordkild providing a running commentary. "At the turn of the century your Delaware River produced tons of sturgeon but you polluted yourselves out of business, and the only *real* caviar since then has come from the Caspian. Now, you have entrepreneurs from your west coast who claim to have caviar as good as the Caspian. Do you agree?"

"Don't use me as a judge, Mr. Nordkild. The only caviar I can afford is in jars at the supermarket."

Nordkild made a face. "Lumpfish or whitefish painted black. You do appreciate the difference in what you're eating now. This is quite good."

"As good as from the Caspian?"

"No."

Nordkild continued spooning from the bowls. He was obviously enjoying it. His round cheeks were flushed, and he licked his lips like a cat after lapping milk. One thing was certain, Morizio thought, Nordkild was as fat as he was for good reason. He talked between mouthfuls. "Yes, captain, there was a time when your rivers were teeming with sturgeon, so much so that barges loaded with them went up the Hudson River to be sold for a penny a pound in Albany as 'Albany beef.' "

Morizio smiled. "Times have changed," he said, reflecting on the current price of caviar.

Nordkild laughed. "Yes, indeed, captain. In those days the roe was usually discarded. People only wanted the balik."

"What's that?"

"The sturgeon's back. Smoked, it was considered a

delicacy, but not the roe. Sad. The rest of the fish ended up bait.''

"Supply and demand. What happened to the supply?"

"Pollution, neglect, stupidity.'' He guffawed and finished what was in one of the bowls. "Of course, events sometimes occur to mitigate shortages."

"Like what?"

"The vagaries of religion for one. Imagine the strain on the already limited supply of caviar if the Jews deemed it kosher."

"They don't?"

He shook his head. "Whether a sturgeon has scales or not is debatable, but Jewish leaders, after passing their piece of silk thread over a sturgeon's body and not having it snag on a scale, decided to prohibit it from their dietary laws. That's good news for the caviar-loving gentile world." A hearty laugh.

Morizio sat back and watched Nordkild consume what was left of the caviar, lean back, smack his lips, and wipe his mouth.

"Well, what's the verdict, Mr. Nordkild? Did they pass muster?"

"They're adequate, but I haven't built my reputation for settling for the adequate. No, I reject them both. Iran and Russia have little to worry about—yet."

Morizio absently picked up a spoon and slowly turned it in his fingers. He didn't look up as he said, "You were at Ambassador James's party."

"We now arrive at the obvious reason for your visit. Yes, I was there. I provided the food."

"That's what I heard. You knew him well?"

"The ambassador? As well as some, not as well as most."

"Anything strange about him that night?"

Nordkild fanned a fat hand over his face and frowned.

"Strange? No, nothing strange. I think that . . ." The waitresses appeared with two plates of goose rillettes, glazed carrots, and dauphinois potatoes. "I took the liberty of choosing the menu for us, Captain. I trust it will be acceptable."

"Looks good to me."

"Fine." A bottle of red wine was opened with care, sniffed, and tasted, then poured into their glasses. "Skoal."

"Skoal."

Morizio waited until they were well into the meal before returning to the subject of the James party. "Care to speculate on who might have poisoned the ambassador?" he asked.

Nordkild's mouth was full. He chewed, holding up a hand to bid for time, then said, "His aide, of course."

"Hafez, the Iranian?"

"Yes. Open and shut, isn't it? He flees the night of the murder, steals a limousine, hides out, assaults a police officer, and continues to run. Obviously, only a guilty man does such things."

"There could be other reasons."

"Yes?"

"I don't know what they might be at this moment, but I learned a long time ago not to jump to conclusions. All the facts might support the assumption that Hafez is guilty, but sometimes we process facts in the wrong way. It's the old cockroach theory."

Nordkild laughed. "I've not heard of such a theory."

"Yeah, a psychiatrist friend explained it to me once. He said there was this scientist who worked for years trying to teach a cockroach to respond to verbal commands. He succeeded, and the roach would jump over his finger whenever he said, 'Jump!' He cut off the roach's front legs and said, 'Jump!' It managed to get over his finger. Off came the middle set of legs. It wasn't easy, but that little roach crawled over the finger on command. The scientist finally took off the rear set of legs. The scientist said, 'Jump!' The roach just laid there. The scientist took out his notebook and observed that when a cockroach's legs were removed, deafness occurs.''

''An amusing story, Captain.''

''Yeah, I always like it. Any other ideas about who might have done the ambassador in?''

''None whatsoever.''

''How do you figure he was poisoned?''

''The method? Surely your forensic experts would know that.''

''I haven't heard. Could it have been the food?''

''That *I* provided?'' He laughed and pulled his napkin from beneath his chin. ''Caviar laced with ricin. A rich murderer's weapon. A gun would have been cheaper.''

''I guess it would have been. What do you get these days for caviar?''

''Supermarket jars are about five dollars. The real thing costs a few hundred dollars for a fourteen-ounce pound.''

''That's a lot of money for fish eggs.''

''Fortunately, there are still people with educated palates and the resources to indulge them. Would you like a doggie bag, Captain?''

''No, thanks.''

''A tin of caviar as a gift?''

''Wasted. This palate never got beyond the fourth grade.''

''You're too modest. You will have coffee.''

''Sure.''

"And dessert. I assumed from your name that you are of Italian parentage. Cappuccino pie?"

"Remember the cockroach."

"Yes, I shall never forget it."

The pie was so rich and good that Morizio wondered whether it warranted a trip to the confessional. "Excellent," he told his host. "By the way, do you happen to know someone named Inga Lindstrom?"

"Should I?"

"I made the assumption from her name that she was Scandinavian, and I assume you are, too."

Nordkild's laugh was hearty and genuine. "The cockroach, Captain."

"Swedish?"

"Originally, but I spent most of my years in Copenhagen."

"Inga Lindstrom?"

"Oh, yes. Of course I know her. She has what is undoubtedly the finest wholesale food business in Denmark. I buy a great deal from her."

"Was she involved with the ambassador?"

Nordkild's eyebrows went up and he puckered his lips. "Are you suggesting hanky-panky?"

"I'm not suggesting anything. I just wondered whether there was a connection between James and her."

"What causes you to raise her name?"

"Somebody mentioned it to me along the way, that's all." In fact, the name appeared on the materials Paul Pringle had left for Morizio at Piccadilly. According to Pringle's notes, the central switchboard had noted an incoming call from Lindstrom during the party, and that James had called the Madison Hotel later that evening and asked to be connected with her room. Pringle had concluded the note with: *The outgoing call was on the ambassador's 'private line,' but there is no such thing when it goes through a switchboard and the operator on duty is a devoted soap opera fan.''*

"Have you seen Ms. Lindstrom recently?" Morizio asked Nordkild.

"Yes. She was here only a few days ago."

"Where is she now?"

Nordkild shrugged. "She was on a selling tour of the country. I believe she said she was next going to Los Angeles."

"Well, Mr. Nordkild, this was terrific. The food was excellent."

As they waited for the elevator, Morizio said, "Ambassador James was quite a gourmet, wasn't he?"

"He appreciated fine food, including caviar without poison. He belonged to a rather exclusive diplomatic fraternity which meets twice a year to sample the best available."

"Every interest has a fraternity."

"I suppose so. Have a pleasant day, Captain."

10

"At least you got a good meal out of it," Connie Lake said to Morizio. They were in bed at her apartment. It was nine at night, and a made-for-TV movie about cops had just started. Lake had one foot out of the covers as she applied polish to her toes. Morizio leaned against the headboard and read *Esquire*'s massive 50th-Anniversary issue.

"I didn't like the food," he said.

"Sounded good to me."

"Lots of fanciness and little substance."

"Do you want to hear about Richard Washburn?"

"Yeah. Just let me finish this piece on Abraham Maslow. The guy was smart. He studied healthy people instead of sick ones."

"I did my master's thesis on Maslow."

"That's right, I forgot. Go ahead and tell me about Washburn."

"I had Bobbie Orben at the *Post* pull some clips on Washburn from the morgue." She reached over her side of the bed and took papers from a briefcase. "Here," she said.

"Who's Bobbie Orben?"

"The researcher who's always helping us over there. Speaking of morgues, I talked to Jill in forensics today."

"Strange girl."

"Why do you say that?"

Would you want your daughter to spend her life playing with the 'living impaired'?"

"I asked her about that once."

"What'd she say?"

"She said it paid the bills."

"I still wouldn't want my daughter doing it."

"She's not your daughter."

"What did she have to say about James?"

"She said they've analyzed every scrap of food from the party and haven't come up with a trace of poison."

"Maybe somebody gave it to him directly."

"Shoved it down his throat?"

"Wrapped it in a piece of bread, or chocolate."

"I suppose. What do you think of the Washburn material?"

"You haven't given me a chance to read it."

Lake worked on her toes while Morizio flipped through the clippings, which basically supported what he already knew: that Richard Washburn was the hostage most vocal and critical of diplomatic efforts to free them. He leveled charges at his own government for failing to foresee the Ayatollah's take-over and eventual siege of the embassy in Teheran. He also said that he viewed the entire diplomatic process to free them as a "pathetic sham perpetrated by people whose only motive is their own political gain." Washburn's statements were largely ignored by the press, buried deep inside long articles about the release of the hostages and their appreciation for efforts expended on their behalf. One paper, a weekly tabloid distributed free in Georgetown, devoted considerable space to Washburn's charges, including one aimed at then British ambassador to Iran, Geoffrey James. Washburn quoted Iranian friends (but never by name—he said it would endanger their lives in Iran) who claimed to have knowledge of business deals between James and the Ayatollah's government that would add to James's wealth and, according to Washburn, actually prolonged the release of the hostages. He was never more specific than that. Attempts to contact James in London had failed, according to the journalist who wrote the piece.

"What kind of business deal could James have cut with the Ayatollah?" Morizio asked Lake.

"I can't imagine. What does Iran have to offer a British business tycoon and diplomat?"

"Oil?"

"Maybe. Maybe caviar."

Lake laughed.

"Don't laugh," said Morizio. "According to Nordkild, there's only two sources of good caviar, Iran and the Soviet Union. He said it's selling for more than two hundred bucks a pound, and a fourteen-ounce pound at that. At those prices you could get rich if you had the right supply line."

"Could be drugs, Sal."

"Yeah, I was thinking that. I read that the DEA is focusing on Iran as a pipeline."

"I read that, too, but a wealthy British aristocrat like Geoffrey James doesn't become a drug pusher."

"I told Nordkild the cockroach story at lunch."

"Did he laugh?"

"He smiled."

"No sense of humor."

"He got the point, though. By the way, I mentioned Inga Lindstrom to him."

"Does he know her?"

"Yeah. They do business together, and she was here in Washington the night James died. I wonder what their relationship was, why she called him at the embassy and he called her back."

"An affair?"

"Could be. Speaking of that, you wanna fool around?"

"The polish is still wet."

"Blow on it."

She giggled. "Sal, can I ask you a serious question? Why are we even bothering with the James murder? You've been told by heavies like Werner Gibronski, MPD Chief Donald J. Trottier and that mysterious servant of Her Majesty's government, George Thorpe, to butt out, mind your own business and forget there ever was a Geoffrey James."

"Maybe that's why, Connie. Maybe if those so-called heavies didn't make such a goddamn big deal about dropping it I wouldn't have this need to know."

"It happened in the British Embassy, Sal. That's sacred ground, and you know it. If the British government wants to handle it within its own borders, that's its prerogative."

"What about Paul Pringle getting shipped off in the middle of the night, or Nuri Hafez hiding out in the abandoned Iranian embassy and assaulting one of Jake Feinstein's men? No, Connie, I just can't forget about it. I take orders and I'm good at it, always have been, but I think I'll . . ."

"Sal, you're the worst order-taker I've ever met. You're always questioning authority."

"But I never cross the line, do I? I always stop short of hanging myself."

Lake sighed deeply and leaned back against the headboard. She wanted to suggest that he might be about to cross that line in the James case but, instead, turned on her side, ran her fingertips over his bare chest, and said, "It's dry.

"Huh?"

"The polish, Sal. It's dry."

11

Morizio spent the next two days attending planning sessions about beefing up security on the Hill, and at the White House. He shuttled between federal agencies, including the Pentagon where he was secretly briefed on a plan to install surface-to-air missiles on the White House grounds in case of a surprise attack from National Airport. "Jesus, we'll end up shooting down the Eastern shuttle," he thought as he left the pentagonal-shaped building.

Connie Lake was busy, too, covering what meetings Morizio couldn't get to and holding down the office. It seemed to her that the amount of paperwork doubled each week, and there was always a journalist on one of the phones wanting to talk about Ambassador Geoffrey James's poisoning. Those calls were referred to Public Affairs, although a few did manage to get through to her. One particularly aggressive reporter from a radio station told her, "I can make it worth your while."

"Mink?" she asked. "A Rolls?" She didn't bother transferring him.

Morizio called at six. He was at a meeting of police chiefs from twelve surrounding counties and towns who'd been asked to develop lists of possible terrorists in their jurisdiction. "My wife," one had told Morizio, which summed up his view of the project.

"I don't see getting out of here until eight," Morizio told Lake.

"I'll just eat alone again," she said with exaggerated sorrow.

"I'll call you when I get back."

"Want to stay at your place?"

"Not tonight. I need a little time alone. Call you later."

She worked in the office until eight-thirty, wading through reports and analyzing a computer program that was being developed to better coordinate MPD's projects with Capitol and State Department forces. Her stomach suddenly reminded her she hadn't eaten since breakfast. She considered having something delivered, decided instead to run across the street for a fast sandwich at Jaybird's, a local hangout at Fifth and D.

Jaybird's was filled with off-duty cops. Lake was about to take the only empty stool at the bar when a female voice said, "Hey Connie." Lake turned. It was Jill Dougherty from Forensics. "Drinking on the job?" Jill asked.

"Looking for anything to fill a hole in the belly," Connie said. "You?"

"The same. I thought I'd bring something back with me. I have reports to get out."

"Join the crowd, only I think I'll eat here. Eating at my desk depresses me."

Jill laughed, her round, radiant face glowing beneath short, black, shiny hair. "That's the advantage of working in forensics," she said. "Squeaky-clean stainless steel tables, big refrigerators, and the sharpest knives and forks in town. Why don't you come back with me? The car's right outside.''

''Well, I . . . sure, why not?''

They ordered chef's salads and Tabs to go. ''I'll run you back,'' Jill said as they climbed into her car and headed for D.C. General. ''It's good to see you, Connie. Nobody beats down the door to visit me at the morgue.''

The autopsy room was empty. It was a large cold room made to feel colder by multiple fluorescent fixtures that bathed everything in a harsh, flat white light. There were four stainless steel examining tables with metal rims around them. A puddle of clear liquid (water, Connie hoped) had formed in the corner of one. Along a wall was a light box in which color photographs of recent autopsies were displayed. It reminded Lake of the giant Kodak display in New York's Grand Central Station. A TV camera was mounted high in one corner; the days of next-of-kin looking down into the face of a loved one were over. They viewed bodies upstairs, on a TV monitor.

There were white freezer doors along a wall. At the other end was a door leading to a room reserved for badly decomposed bodies. Microphones used by forensic doctors for their play-by-play of autopsies dangled from the ceiling. Lake was aware of three sounds in the room: the gentle whoosh of an oscillating fan, a hum from the fluorescent lights, and disco music from a small radio that sat on the floor in the corner. The only odor came from the salad dressing.

''It ain't much, but I call it home,'' Jill said as she pulled two stools up to the middle table, and found two small, white hand towels in a drawer. Cups for the Tab came from a water cooler at the far side of the room.

"I'm starved," said Jill.

"Me, too," Connie said. "Who was your last dinner guest?"

"On this table?" Jill grinned. "Oh, who *rested* here last? I have no idea. Probably an inept rapist or a junkie who held out on the boys."

"Pass the dressing."

They talked about many things as they ate—the Red-skins, fashions, political gossip, new TV shows. Eventually, it came around to the men in their lives. "How's the Italian stallion?" Jill asked.

"Morizio? A stallion he's not. He's busy, preoccupied, obsessed, as usual."

"Obsessed with what?"

Connie hesitated, then said, "With the James case."

"So's everybody else in D.C. It'd make a great novel, wouldn't it, British Ambassador to the United States poisoned in his own embassy by his Iranian manservant. Juicy."

"And hard to swallow, you should pardon the expression. Too pat, Jill, too many unanswered questions. For instance, you told me that none of the food you tested contained poison. How did James get it?"

Jill shrugged and filled her mouth with lettuce, saying through it, "Maybe sexually."

"Huh?"

"Like AIDS, or herpes."

"Be serious."

"I have no idea how it got into his body, Connie. Somebody must have fed it to him, maybe in a brownie. Maybe it wasn't ricin that killed him."

"Huh?"

"Maybe it was borax."

"Borax?"

"That caviar James was eating at the time of his

death contained borax. The rest of the caviar from the party didn't.''

''So?''

''So, borax was outlawed in this country by the FDA forty years ago because it left a poisonous film on baby bottles after they were cleaned with it.''

''Then why would it be in James's caviar?''

''Got me. More dressing, please.''

Lake handed it to her. ''Could borax really have killed him?'' she asked.

''Not unless he ingested a ton of it. No, it was ricin, but the borax thing interested me, that's all.''

''I'd better get back,'' Connie said.

''And I'd better get cracking on the reports. Connie, let's just forget any conversations about the James mess, okay?''

''Sure.''

''We had the riot act read to us. This thing is under a big lock and key, and I get the feeling heads will roll if anybody tries to open it.''

''I know, we're under the same restrictions. That's what worries me about Sal's interest in it.''

''Tell him to drop it.''

''I have.''

''Good. What are you doing for Thanksgiving?''

''No plans yet. I'm trying to convince Mr. Morizio to come away with me, but I'm not brimming with confidence. You?''

''Working. I swapped last Christmas for this Thanksgiving.''

''Sorry.''

''Could be worse. Ross promised to have a turkey delivered for the slaves.''

''That's nice of him.''

"Purely selfish, Connie. Gets his conscience off the hook, but we eat, so I suppose everyone wins."

"That's the way Ayn Rand would have viewed it. Drive me back. I'm bushed."

Morizio called Lake at eleven. She'd taken a warm bath and had dozed off in a large leather recliner he'd given her last Christmas. It took her a few moments to come awake and to sound intelligent. "Are you home?" she managed.

"Uh huh. What's new with you?"

She told him of her conversation with Jill Dougherty and about the borax in James's caviar.

"What does it mean?" he asked.

"I don't know, probably nothing, maybe something. I'm sleepy. I wish you were here."

"Yeah, I do . . ." His intercom buzzer sounded. "Hold on," he said. He went to the kitchen and answered the doorman's call, then returned to the living room. "George Thorpe's downstairs," he told Connie.

"Were you expecting him?"

"No."

"Why would he stop in unannounced at this hour?"

"I'll find out soon enough. Call you after he leaves."

Thorpe's large body filled the doorway. He wore a faded brown tan corduroy suit jacket, baggy tan pants and a green turtleneck whose collar had been stretched into limpness by his huge neck. "Good evening, Captain," he said. "You were about to leave?"

Morizio hadn't changed out of his suit. He looked down, then at Thorpe and said, "No, just got here. You want to come in?"

"Thank you." Thorpe stepped into the foyer and looked around. "I'm not interrupting anything, am I?"

Morizio knew he was really asking whether Connie

was there. He ignored the question and asked, "What can I do for you, Mr. Thorpe?"

Thorpe ignored his question and walked across the living room to the window. "Splendid view. I enjoy good views."

"Yeah, so do I. Like a drink?"

"That's gracious of you."

"Scotch?"

"Bourbon? I've developed a taste for it since being here."

Morizio knew Thorpe had already been drinking. There was a hitch to his speech, and unusually high color in his cheeks. Morizio went to the kitchen and filled a glass with ice and Ancient Age ten-year-old bourbon. He poured himself Cognac and returned to the living room where Thorpe had settled into a leather club chair.

"Thank you, sir," Thorpe said. He downed half of what was in his glass, nodded his approval, and said, "I'm disappointed in you, Captain."

"Really? You came here to tell me that?"

"I came here because we had agreed to meet at the end of each day. We haven't been."

"I've been busy. Besides, there's been nothing to talk about. The James . . . *project* . . . is over."

"Is it?"

"That's what I'm told."

"Being told is one thing, Captain, acting upon it is another."

"Get to the point, Mr. Thorpe. It's late."

Thorpe took a tiny sip this time and focused on his glass. He ran a finger over the rim and belched. "We had been on a first name basis," he said.

"That's right."

"But you seem hell-bent on keeping the situation official."

"How'd I do that?"

"By ignoring the simple rules, Captain. Do nothing unless instructed. Simple. So simple.

"I didn't break any rules."

"Berge Nordkild?"

"What about him?"

"Questions about Ambassador James's death."

"Idle conversation. We had a social lunch, a food-testing session actually. Of course James came up. Nordkild was at the party."

"And you had no professional interest in the questions you asked him."

"That's right." Morizio got up, took off his jacket and tossed it on the couch. He yanked his tie loose from his neck and dropped it on the jacket. He didn't want to demonstrate the anger he felt. It would accomplish nothing, be counter-productive, end up in unpleasantness. He sat down and sampled his Cognac.

"The James matter is over, Captain Morizio. It was a tragic experience that has been resolved."

"Has it? What about the valet, Hafez?"

"Under arrest."

Morizio sat up. "When?"

"Yesterday, in Iran."

"In Iran? He went back?"

"Yes. He'll be prosecuted there."

"For poisoning Ambassador James."

"Exactly."

"Why not extradite him to England?"

Thorpe laughed and extended his empty glass toward Morizio. "I'd love another. Extradite from Iran? Our Arab neighbors are not interested in the civilized manner in which we function. In some ways they have a point. Extradition would mean red tape, delays, negotiations. Have you ever lived in an Arab state, Sal?''

"Now it's Sal.''

"You prefer, 'Captain'?''

"I don't prefer anything.''

"You are, of course, now ready to accept the fact that the James case has reached its logical conclusion. There's no need to ask questions of anyone any longer. Justice has been done. If you do understand that, then first names are again appropriate.''

"And if I don't?''

Thorpe smiled. "Excellent bourbon. Please.''

Morizio, too, smiled as he went to the kitchen to refill the glass. There was something strange and inherently charming about George Thorpe. He couldn't make up his mind whether he enjoyed his company or detested him, but because there was that ambivalence, the tendency was to go along. He brought Thorpe his second drink, settled on the couch, and asked, "How do you know I talked to Berge Nordkild?''

"Irrelevant.''

"Not to me.''

"Too many things have relevancy for you.''

"What's relevant to you, Thorpe?''

"The quality of my life. I'm dedicated to direct routes, to taking highways rather than winding country roads.'' He smiled and raised his glass. "To simplicity, Captain Morizio. It's a significantly more rewarding way to live.''

Morizio drank, said, "Sometimes the simple way doesn't work.''

"It always works, Captain, if one limits the relevancies in one's life. Take me for instance. I don't own a cat or a dog, nor are there any plants in my house. There is nothing I must care for except George Thorpe.''

"Sounds dull."

"It works. Simplicity."

"Lonely?"

"Alone, not lonely." He crossed his legs and drew a deep breath before finishing his drink. Morizio hoped he wasn't about to settle in for the night.

"A nightcap, Thorpe? Then I have to turn in. It's been a long day."

"Yes, of course." He handed Morizio his glass. "Where is Miss Lake tonight?"

"Home," Morizio said over his shoulder as he headed for the kitchen. He stood in front of the sink and thought about Thorpe's claim that Nuri Hafez had returned to Iran and had been arrested. He didn't buy it. He poured the bourbon over the ice cubes and again felt anger scrape his belly. He'd been followed to Berge Nordkild's office, had probably been under surveillance all the while. He didn't like it, and by the time he handed Thorpe his glass he was ready to vent his feelings.

"Why was I followed?" he asked as he sat across from Thorpe and stared at him.

Thorpe laughed and shook his head. "Too many years as a police officer, Sal, too many years developing the paranoia common to your breed."

"My father was 'my breed.' No paranoia with him, Thorpe, just an old-fashioned virtue of liking to see justice done."

"And you, Sal? No paranoia in your generation?"

"Nordkild."

"A friend."

"He told you I had lunch with him?"

Thorpe nodded and sipped.

"Why would he bother?"

Thorpe sat up straight, consumed what was left in his

glass, and stood unsteadily. "You're a hospitable man, Sal. You pour a good drink, perhaps too good. I really stopped by to tell you about Hafez and to say how much I've enjoyed working with you. Now that it's over, there won't be a reason for us to see each other, unless you allow me to buy you lunch one day."

"That'd be nice."

"Yes, it would. Well, again, thank you." They shook hands and Thorpe walked slowly toward the door, his large feet reaching for the floor with some uncertainty. He opened the door, hesitated as though deciding whether to say something else, stepped into the hall, and disappeared in the direction of the elevators.

Morizio called Connie and woke her. "Sorry," he said. He told her briefly of his conversation with Thorpe.

"Sal," she said.

"What?"

"I'm glad it's over."

"I don't know." He started to express his doubts about Thorpe's story of Hafez but she asked him to hold them until morning. "If we were married or living together we could fall asleep while you tell me everything that's on your mind. But I'm sleepy, Sal. Tomorrow."

He tried reading Edmund Wilson's *The Thirties* but couldn't concentrate. He put on a Billie Holiday tape and settled into a level six match with Rasputin, which ended in a stalemate at three in the morning.

News of Nuri Hafez's capture in Iran was on morning television, and in the papers. What was interesting to Morizio was that most of the attributed statements were from the State Department, not the British government. The spokesman made the same point that Thorpe had, that Iran would not consider extradition but had assured the British that Hafez would be tried and, if convicted, executed under Moslem law.

Morizio tossed his newspaper on the desk and muttered, "Tried, like hell. He'll lose his head and that'll be the end of it."

The *Post* article also pointed out that Willard Jones, the diplomatic security cop who'd been attacked by Hafez, had been upgraded from critical to satisfactory. The piece ended with: *"The United States government shares the loss of the distinguished ambassador, Geoffrey James, with his native Great Britain. It is of little consolation to his family that his murderer has been apprehended and will face an appropriate punishment in his native country, and it is the wish of this government, and the government of Great Britain, that the accused be extradited to Great Britain. However, because of tensions between Iran and Western nations, this has been ruled out by Iran's leaders."*

Lake was late that morning, and Morizio didn't try to hide his pique. That was the problem with being intimate with someone who works for you, he told himself. He told her that, too, when she arrived carrying a brown bag of fresh blueberry muffins, his favorite, and hot coffee. "The super was supposed to be there at eight to fix the tub, but he didn't show until nine," she said. "You should have called," Morizio said. "I'm sorry," she said. "This is awkward," he said. "I said I'm sorry, Captain."

He smiled and handed her the morning paper. As she read it he ate two muffins and finished his coffee. "Well?" he asked.

"Like I said last night, Sal, I'm glad it's over."

"It's not."

"What do you mean?"

"You buy this garbage?"

"It doesn't matter whether I buy it or not. Somebody buys it, and that's the name of that game. Forget it, Sal. Instead of trying to complicate everything, let it go and get on with what's important to you."

"Keep it simple, huh?"

"Yes." She blew her nose and dropped the tissue in the ashtray. He put it in the waste basket and handed her a piece of paper outlining the day's schedule. She would represent him at two meetings that afternoon, while he met with the congressional budget people who funded the city of Washington, D.C.

Morizio's kid cousin was in town looking for a job, and he took her to lunch at the Market Inn. When he returned to MPD there were a dozen phone messages waiting for him. One immediately captured his attention. It was from Paul Pringle. It said: *"Urgent I see you tonight at Piccadilly. Seven? I'll wait. Paul."*

Chief Trottier called a few minutes later. He'd been going over the preliminary budget figures and saw potential problems. "Let's meet at six in my office."

"Can we make it another time?" asked Morizio. "I had plans."

"Department business?"

"Well, yes and no. It's . . ." He knew he shouldn't mention Pringle, and didn't. "No, sir," he said. "Six will be fine."

Lake got back to the office at five. "Connie," Morizio said, "Paul Pringle's in town."

"How nice."

"Maybe." He explained his conflict and asked her to get to Piccadilly by seven. "I'll join you as soon as I can. Just don't let him leave."

Morizio reached Piccadilly at eight-twenty. Lake was at a booth having a shepherd's pie. "Where is he?" Morizio asked.

"I don't know," she said. "He never showed."

Morizio had a roast beef sandwich and a glass of ale. He was visibly upset at Pringle's failing to show. Lake asked him whether the message had been taken correctly at headquarters. "Yeah, I double-checked. It's not like him, Connie. Damn it, why would he suddenly show up back in Washington unless he had something important to tell me about James."

"Sal, that's old business."

"Not for me. Where the hell is he?" He ordered another beer and kept glancing at the front door. At eleven he said, "Let's go."

"All kinds of things could have happened," Lake said.

"Yeah. Where would he stay overnight in D.C.?"

"The embassy?"

"Last place. Let's go home." He checked with Johnny, the bartender, who confirmed he hadn't heard from Pringle, paid the check, and drove to his apartment. At one, Morizio said he was going to bed. They turned off the bedside light and Connie quickly drifted into a peaceful sleep, a pleasant smile on her lips. Morizio was wide awake. He didn't want to disturb her, carefully slipped out of bed, and went to the living room where he stood at the window and watched the lights across the Potomac come and go through a ground fog. He eventually turned on a small lamp with a green shade on the desk and sat in a straight-back chair, his hand resting inches from the phone. "What the hell is going on?" he asked himself as he did drum rolls with his fingers. He placed a call to Pringle's home near London. Again, no answer. He called the Foreign and Commonwealth Office in London and was connected with the minister of security's office. A clerk informed him that no one was in yet. Morizio asked about Paul

Pringle. The clerk said he wasn't familiar with the name, took Morizio's number, and hung up. He considered calling some British law enforcement contacts he'd made over the years but wasn't sure how they could help at this point.

He turned off the light and was about to return to bed when the phone rang. The loudness of it in the black, silent room jarred him. He grabbed it before it could ring again, flipped on the lamp, and said, "Morizio."

"Captain, Schwab in Homicide. Sorry to wake you."

"You didn't."

"That's good. Captain, we wouldn't be calling you on this ordinarily except that there's an unusual circumstance with a homicide we handled tonight. It looks like a drug rubout. The victim carried ID and some papers. Your name was on one of them."

"Who's the victim?" Morizio knew the answer.

"A Paul Pringle, caucasian, male, about forty-five . . ."

"Where'd it happen?"

"Adams Morgan. A grisly one, Captain. Somebody sure didn't like him." Adams Morgan, a poor, heavily Hispanic section of inner-D.C., had one of the city's higher crime rates, particularly narcotics.

"Where's the body?"

"The morgue."

"Thanks. I'll be there right away."

He hung up and realized Connie was standing in the bedroom doorway. "Who was it?" she asked.

"Homicide. Paul was murdered tonight."

"Oh, my God."

"They said it looks drug-related."

"Paul?"

"He had my name on a piece of paper. That's why they called."

"Is he at D.C. General?"

"Yeah. I'm going down."

"I'll go with you."

"No, hang in here, Connie. I'll call you later. Get some sleep." He started into the bedroom. She touched his arm, started to cry, and wrapped her arms around him. "I'm sorry, Sal."

Paul Pringle was on one of the stainless steel tables in the morgue. An attendant led Morizio to it and pulled back the sheet that covered his body. Morizio looked down into Pringle's face. There was a bright red ring around his neck where he'd been garroted, probably with a thin metal wire. He'd been savagely beaten; his face was swollen to twice its size and was the color of blueberries.

"Autopsy?" Morizio said.

"In about an hour, captain. We did notice this." The attendant, a slight black man with sparse reddish hair, took Pringle's wrist and suspended his arm. There were needle marks in the crook of the elbow.

"He didn't use drugs," Morizio said.

"You knew him pretty good?"

"Yeah, I knew him pretty good."

"He's British, huh?" the attendant said as he replaced the sheet over Pringle's torso and face. "You want to handle next-of-kin?"

"I'll figure that out later. Thanks."

He returned to his office at MPD and called Homicide. "There's more to this than meets the eye," he told the detective. "Don't do anything with it until we have a chance to talk to Chief Trottier."

"Whatever you say, Sal, but what's going on? Why the fuss over him?"

"He was a friend."

"Sorry to hear it. A good one?"

"Yeah, and he was about to become an even better one."

12

Pringle's murder was handled by the press as just another D.C. crime until his connection with the British Embassy was revealed. Then, the story took on greater importance. His former colleagues at the embassy were scouted up and interviewed, at least those who were willing to talk. One was Melanie Callender, the ambassador's former personal secretary, who was interviewed in front of her apartment building. At first, she was composed. "Yes, I knew Paul Pringle well . . . No, I was unaware of any connection with drugs . . . He was a fine man, a good family man . . . I have nothing whatever to say about Ambassador James's death . . ." She started to cry. The TV reporter asked about Pringle's departure from the embassy shortly after the ambassador's death. "Please," Callender said, waving her hand at the camera, "no more. Two fine men are dead and I . . . I . . ." She broke down, turned, and walked quickly inside the building.

Morizio and Lake watched the interview on the six o'clock news. They were at his apartment. It had been, as Morizio put it, "a bitch of a day." He'd spent a lot of time with homicide detectives discussing Pringle's murder. Arrangements had been made with Pringle's widow to have his body returned to England for burial. Residents of Adams Morgan had been questioned by a team of investigators, as had known drug dealers. Nothing concrete had surfaced, and Homicide was still labeling it "drug-related, assailant unknown."

"It's got to be connected with James's murder," Morizio said as he turned off the TV and started an Ella Fitzgerald tape. He paced the living room. "Pringle was coming here to tell me something, and it had to do with James. What else could it have been? Somebody didn't want him talking to me and headed him off, dragged him into Adams Morgan, beat the hell out of him, held him by the throat with a wire, and pumped him full of heroin."

"You can't be sure of that, Sal."

"You got a better version?"

"No, but maybe he wasn't coming here to talk about James. Maybe he came here for another reason and just wanted to catch up for a drink with an old friend."

"Doesn't play."

She shook her head and sighed. "I don't know."

"I'm going to find out. You want a drink?"

"No. How are you going to find out?"

"By asking questions, starting with Paul's wife."

"It's not your case, Sal."

"I'm not so sure." He sat next to her on the couch. "You don't have to get involved."

"If you're involved, I want to be."

"Go talk to Callender."

"Why?"

"Woman to woman. She worked closely with the

ambassador. Maybe she'd tell you something she hasn't told anybody else. Hell, she talked to the press.''

"Do I do it officially?"

"Any way you can. You don't have to." He touched her honey hair. "They won't like it."

"Chief Trottier?"

"All of them."

"I love you, Sal, and I know how important this is to you."

"And I love you and don't want you hurt because of my craziness."

"Maybe that's *what* I love. Jake Feinstein will have Callender's address."

"Yeah, he's got addresses on everybody in D.C. who works diplomatic."

"What if somebody asks where I am?"

"In the department? Don't worry, you work for me. You're at a meeting. There's always enough meetings in this town to go around."

Connie Lake arrived at Melanie Callender's apartment house at eight the next morning. She didn't bother calling ahead, preferring to be turned away in person. Callender came on the building intercom and Lake told her who she was.

"The police? I have nothing to say to the police."

"I'm police, Ms. Callender, but from a different perspective. I don't want to talk about Ambassador James, only about Paul Pringle. My boss was a close friend of his and is heading up a special investigation. It's . . . well, it's somewhat unofficial but it's important. Paul wasn't murdered for drugs, and we all know that. What you say to me is off the record. I promise you that. I'll share it only with my boss, and that's where it stops. You talked to the press and they're only out after a story. We *care* about Paul Pringle. Please, Ms. Callender, help us.''

There was a very long pause on the other end. Finally, Callender said, ''Only for a few minutes. I'm leaving for London.''

Callender's tenth floor apartment was small and sparsely furnished, a place reflecting someone who wasn't sure how long she'd be staying. A row of suitcases stood by the door. Sun highlighted dirt on the windows. There was a tiny pullman kitchen and a faded pull-out couch. A bookcase made of boards and bricks was without books; a row of houseplants sat on the top shelf.

''Connie Lake, Ms. Callender.''

''I really am in a hurry,'' Callender said. She was visibly nervous, kept brushing away a wisp of auburn hair that tickled her forehead.

''You said you were going to London. Vacation?''

''No, for good. I've been replaced. I'll be working at the home office, I think.''

Lake wasn't sure she should sit on one of two vinyl chairs or to wait for an invitation. She sat and said, ''I would think keeping you at the embassy would be valuable for the new ambassador.''

''He hasn't been named yet.'' Callender stood over the suitcases and counted them, which she'd obviously done countless times that morning.

''I won't take much of your time, Ms. Callender. I just wanted to . . .''

''Ask what you want. Just be quick.''

Lake was aware of a tenuous resolve Callender was holding onto, a strength that could be washed away at any moment by a torrent of tears. She hoped for the tears; Morizio always said that tears brought with them revelations, something every good cop and journalist

113

understood. She also remembered she promised to talk only about Paul Pringle, not Ambassador James. "Ms. Callender, what do you think really happened to Paul?"

Callender continued to stand over the suitcases and said without turning, "Paul was a decent man. He'd never use drugs."

"We know that."

"He was different."

"How so?"

"He . . . he bloody well cared about people." The tears were ready to erupt and Lake felt like a ghoul for not getting up and hugging them away. She sat quietly and waited for Callender to continue, which she predictably did. "He cared about his family and his job," she said.

"Why do you think he came back to Washington? He left a message for my boss, Captain Morizio, that he wanted to meet him at Piccadilly. He never showed up. Now we know why."

"Piccadilly." Callender turned and brushed away that strand of hair. "He loved it there. Most of us never went because we considered it a pale imitation of home. We preferred American places, real American places. We followed baseball and ate chili. Assimilation, it's called. Paul hung on to home. He wanted a pub no matter where it was, Africa, China, Washington, D.C."

"Who killed him?"

"How would I know?" She sat heavily on one of the suitcases and pressed her hands to her mouth. "Ask Barnsworth," she said through her fingernails.

"Barnsworth? The assistant?"

"Deputy charge of mission. Nigel Barnsworth." She said it as though her mouth were filled with lemon rind.

"You're saying Nigel Barnsworth knows who killed Paul Pringle?"

114

"He knows everything, why not this? I hate him."
She stood and shook herself into a posture of dignity.
"There, I've said it. Now, please leave. I'm going
home."

"Why do you hate him?" Connie asked.

"Please, your time is up, Miss Lake."

"I'm on your side, Ms. Callender. I'm not an enemy."

"I know that."

"Why are you leaving?"

It was more a snort than a laugh. "I was told to."

"By Nigel Barnsworth?"

"Of course. He's the acting ambassador until another
is named."

"Could *he* be named?"

"No. He's a good administrator, a bloody failure as
a diplomat."

"Geoffrey James was a good diplomat, wasn't he?"

"Very good."

"Could Barnsworth have poisoned him?"

Melanie looked at Connie as though she'd uttered the
ultimate blasphemy. "That loyal, nasty little viper, that
tribute to the civil service, Nigel Barnsworth? Don't be
ridiculous."

It was Connie's turn to laugh. "From the way you
describe him, he's capable of anything."

"Yes, to further his career, but he learned long ago
that he would never be a full ambassador, not with his
snotty disposition. If he thought he'd gain an ambassadorship he'd kill his own mother, but he knows better."

Lake thought of George Thorpe and her evaluation of
him. She said to Melanie, "What about the ambassador's wife, Mrs. James? Was it a good marriage?"

Callender thought for a moment. A smile crossed her
face to indicate she'd arrived at the perfect answer to
the question. "An excellent marriage. Consistent."

"Meaning?"

"Never varying, daily hatred."

Lake hadn't expected the answer. She sat a little forward in the chair and hoped Callender would keep talking. When she didn't, she said, "The relationship between Ambassador James and his wife really isn't of concern unless it bears upon his murder and Paul Pringle. Does it?"

"No."

"Daily hatred."

"People in their position don't commit murder. They suffer and live out their lives."

"Lovers?"

"Would it surprise you?"

"Of course not."

Callender took a cigarette from her purse and lighted it. "The last vestige of Geoffrey James," she said through the smoke. "He had these flown in every day, in the pouch, his favorite fags. He knew how to live, he did."

"A little perk of the position," said Lake. "I understand diplomatic pouches are used for many . . . many personal things."

Callender's eyebrows went up and she smirked. "Oh, yes, many personal things. Fags and caviar, his excellency's passions."

"Are you that bitter?"

"Bitter? Anything but, Miss Lake. I appreciate the chance I've had to serve my government and the ambassador. I am a fortunate young woman. My future is secured, I have contributed to world understanding, and I am bursting with pride. There is no room for bitterness in that, is there?"

Callender's increasing "bitterness" made Connie uncomfortable. She considered leaving but decided to

116

ask a final question. She said, "You knew a Miss Inga Lindstrom."

"Inga? Oh, my god." Callender sat on her suitcase and lit another cigarette. "The Scandinavian goddess." She looked seriously at Lake, then said, "She looks like you. Yes, very much like you."

"Inga Lindstrom?"

"Yes. Are you Scandinavian?"

"Yes."

"I thought so. You could be sisters."

"Did she and the ambassador . . . ?"

"Have an affair. Of course they did. He had an affair with every woman who appealed to him."

It took a lot for Lake to ask it. "Does that include you?"

"According to Mrs. James."

"I don't care about Mrs. James. I'd like to hear it from you."

"You have no business asking."

"I have no business asking anything, but you allowed me here to ask questions. I'm sorry. I didn't intend to intrude on personal matters."

"Of course you did. Everything that's happened involves 'personal matters,' doesn't it? What could be more personal than murder?"

"Most murder is personal, at least according to statistics."

"Passion, jealousy, hate. I loved the movie *Casablanca*, didn't you?"

"Very much."

Callender stood and straightened her skirt. She was wearing a heather tweed suit over a dark blue blouse that bunched around her neck. She was an attractive woman, Lake realized, vital and bright and leggy. Such color in her cheeks and lips. Callender said, "Ambassa-

dor James slept with Inga Lindstrom. It doesn't matter.
Sleeping with people doesn't make one a bad person,
does it?''

"Why did the ambassador and his wife stay together?''

"His majesty and the missus? Money. Her money
carried them through for so many years. Then he found
his own money and he could divorce her.''

"Divorce?''

"It was in the works. Once his oil company succeeded in spawning millions for himself, it was time.''

"Because he didn't need her wealth.''

"It's all money, isn't it? Is there anything you can
name that doesn't rest, in its deepest roots, in money?''

"I wish I could but I've come up a blank. You.
mention Ambassador James's new wealth through his
oil company. I knew he sat on the boards of companies
but didn't know he owned an oil company.''

"Not many people did. Actually, it isn't an oil company, no drilling of wells or refineries, nothing like
that. A small bank he founded in Manchester financed
an oil brokerage firm in Scotland. It represents Scottish
oil interests to the rest of the world.''

"A middleman?''

"Yes, quite. It's been very successful.''

"Were you involved in that company?''

"Goodness, no, only peripherally, as his secretary.''

"Was Inga Lindstrom part of that company?''

"Of course not. Inga Lindstrom is very successful in
her own right with all her fancy foods.'' There was
venom in every word.

"You really hate her, don't you?''

"I hate no one, Ms. Lake. I simply dislike dishonest
people.''

"Were you in love with Ambassador James?''

Callender looked at her watch. "I must leave now. I have a taxi arriving any minute."

"You've been very generous with your time, and I appreciate it. Is there someplace in London I could contact you in the event I wanted to talk some more?"

"I gave up my flat when I came here. I'll be staying with mum and dad until I'm settled into a new job."

"Your parents live where?"

"I would not want them disturbed. Please, I'm not a rude person, but I must be off now."

"Yes, thank you again." Lake got up and they shook hands. They were the same height, and behind Callender's green eyes Lake discerned fear and confusion, and a plea for understanding, for gentleness. "Good luck, Ms. Callender."

"Thank you."

Lake went to her car and pulled a small tape recorder from her purse. She listened for a few minutes to make sure it had recorded properly, then drove back to MPD.

"I called Ethel Pringle in London," Morizio said late that night. They were at Connie's apartment. "She's handling it pretty well, but she wasn't anxious to talk about Paul. She always was a pretty cold customer, didn't like being in the U.S. She stayed pretty much by herself."

"I only met her that one time," Lake said. "She was cold, so unlike him."

"Yeah, he was loose, loved drinking at Piccadilly. We had some good times."

Lake had played the tape of her conversation with Callender for Morizio during a dinner of sausage, peppers, and spaghetti. He'd made notes, and when the final goodbyes played through the speakers, he put down his pad and pen and said, "I wonder how much they did hate each other."

"Callender and Barnsworth?"

"Mr. and Mrs. James. If he was about to divorce her, that could mean cutting her off after all those years of her supporting him, like doctors divorcing their wives after they've put them through medical school."

"Make her mad enough to poison him? I suppose so, but what about Paul Pringle? I doubt if Mrs. James is capable of the things that were done to him."

"Maybe she bought them."

"Maybe. You want me to talk to her, don't you?"

"Yeah, that'd be nice. Feel like it?"

"Callender told me she's back in Philadelphia staying with her mother. I could go up there."

"Take a shot at it tomorrow. I'll cover for you."

Lake sat back in her recliner and rubbed her eyes, stretched her long, bare legs out to their fullest extension, and said, "We're in deep, Sal. It'll kick back."

"I'll handle it, don't worry."

13

Lake took the 6 A.M. Amtrak Metroliner, which arrived in Philadelphia at 7:45. She'd only had coffee on the train and was hungry. Besides, she was too early to be calling Marsha James's family home in Bryn Mawr. She'd decided to take the same basic approach she had with Melanie Callender, but did plan to call a few minutes before arriving at the house.

She ate a large breakfast in a luncheonette on Thirtieth Street and read the morning paper. At 9:15 she went into a phone booth and dialed a number for a residence listed under Marsha James's maiden name, Girard. The family traced back, according to newspaper stories about the ambassador's wife, to Stephen Girard, who'd been the principal financier of the War of 1812.

A woman answered. Connie asked for Mrs. James.

"Not here," the woman said. Lake assumed she was a maid, asked when Mrs. James could be expected. "At noon, at lunch." Connie thanked her and hung up.

She killed the morning walking through Penn Center,

then called the Girard home at ten minutes of noon. The same woman answered. "Yes, who is calling?"

"Constance Lake of the Washington Metropolitan Police Department."

"Please wait," said the maid.

"Yes?" a different woman said.

Connie introduced herself again. "Is this Mrs. James?" she asked.

"No, this is her mother. You're a police officer?"

"Yes, ma'am."

"What a fascinating thing for a young woman to do. It would never have been allowed in my day."

Lake smiled and said, "My mother says the same thing."

"She must worry about you, my dear. You want to speak to my daughter?"

"I was hoping to. I don't want to intrude but . . ."

"She's been through a great deal, something no mother would wish upon a daughter, but that's life, is it not? We take the bitter with the sweet."

"Absolutely." Connie realized how fortunate she was to have gotten Mrs. Girard. As long as she could keep her talking, stay on her good side, there was a chance of getting to Marsha James. She listened patiently as the old woman lamented over what had happened to Philadelphia, its rising crime rate, poverty, a loss of the genteel life to which she'd become accustomed. When she was through with her monologue, she said, "I've been talking your ear off. You're a very nice young woman to indulge me."

"I enjoyed it," said Connie. She had.

"My daughter will speak with you."

"She . . ."

"Hello."

"Mrs. James?"

"Yes. You are . . ."

"Constance Lake. I'm with the Washington, D.C. MPD."

"I really have nothing to say."

"I'm not here to talk about your husband. I know that's embassy business, but the murder of Paul Pringle is another matter."

"Yes, I heard. Tragic. He seemed a decent sort."

"Yes, he was very decent, Mrs. James. I'm trying to learn more about him to help us in the investigation. It's more than official. He was a close friend of my boss and . . ."

"I'll be more than happy to speak with you. When would you like to see me?"

"I can be there in twenty minutes."

"You're in Philadelphia?"

"Yes."

"You were confident."

"I suppose I was."

"Twenty minutes will be fine. Mother insists you have lunch with us."

"I don't want to impose."

"No imposition. Good-bye."

Connie stepped out of the booth and processed what had just gone on. It was so easy, too easy. She tried to think the way Morizio would think—"No such thing as a free lunch." What are they after? She realized she'd find out soon enough, hailed a cab, and gave the driver the address.

The house had been designed by Thomas U. Walter. It was, she decided as she looked at it from the cab, French-Federal, although she wasn't sure what that meant. It was large and made of red brick. Four white columns decorated with cupids and flowers supported the roof of the front porch. A Cadillac limousine and a red Mercedes were parked in the driveway.

The maid answered her knock, took her coat, and escorted her to a cozy paneled library where a fire roared in a walk-in fireplace. Three people were in the room, Marsha James, her mother, and a distinguished looking gentleman in muted brown tweeds and a magnificent red beard streaked with white.

"Miss Lake," Mrs. Girard said as she crossed the room and extended her hand. She carried a cane but didn't seem to need it. She was a tiny woman with silver hair and blue eyes that were very much alive. A natural pink hue forced itself through wrinkled parchment cheeks. She wore a black taffeta dress gathered at the sleeves, and a white silk shawl. Strands of pearls wound around her neck, and Lake noticed immediately that four fingers on each gnarled hand held rings of varying sizes and brilliance.

"You're Mrs. Girard."

"Yes, I am. Come, meet my daughter and her guest." She took Lake by the hand and led her across the room. Marsha James sat in a white oak Wainscot chair. The gentleman stood behind her, his hand on the chair's arched, cresting back as though he were ready to pose for a family portrait.

"Miss Lake, my daughter, Marsha."

"Hello," Lake said, extending her hand. Mrs. James took it but without enthusiasm.

"And this is Sir Edwin Ferguson," said Mrs. Girard.

"Nice to meet you," Connie said.

"Yes, likewise." He seemed awkward at the introduction and did not address her directly.

"Sherry?" Mrs. Girard asked.

"Ah, yes, that would be . . ."

"Something else? My late husband used to say, 'Wine

maketh glad the heart of man,' or something like that. True for women, too. Would you prefer whiskey?''

"Scotch would be nice.''

"He drank too much but he liked it.'' She rang for the maid and gave her Connie's order. "More, Sir Edwin?'' she asked Ferguson.

"Yes, please.''

"A Scotsman through and through.''

Lake glanced at Marsha James, who seemed either bored or annoyed with what had transpired, and decided to get into a conversation with her right away. "It was good of you to see me,'' she said.

"I always wish to be cooperative.''

"I know, that's your reputation.''

Mrs. James smiled and looked down into a glass of sherry she cradled in her lap. She was dressed in a simple but expensive graphite-gray dress. A burgundy silk scarf was neatly arranged around her neck. Her shoes were black, sensible pumps, and her only jewelry was a plain gold wedding band. She glanced up at Connie and said, "You look nothing like a police-woman.''

"I take that as a compliment,'' Lake said pleasantly.

"I meant it to be. You said you wanted to talk about Paul Pringle.''

"Yes, that's right.''

"If you don't mind my putting in my two cents,'' said Sir Edwin Ferguson, "I think this is totally inappropriate. The death of that fellow has nothing to do with Mrs. James.''

"Of course not,'' said Lake, "but this murder might be linked, in some way, to your husband's death.'' She said it to Mrs. James, deliberately ignoring Ferguson.

"That's absurd,'' Mrs. James said. "They were totally unrelated. From what I read, Mr. Pringle was involved in drugs.''

''We don't believe that,'' Connie said.

''Why anyone would want to use those things is beyond me,'' Mrs. Girard said from a maple Hitchcock rocker into which she'd settled by the fireplace. ''All the criminals in Philadelphia are dope addicts. Disgusting lot.''

''Drugs and crime do go hand in hand,'' Lake said. She looked at Ferguson, who was still posturing behind Marsha James's chair. ''Are you a family friend?'' she asked him.

''Yes.''

''Sir Edwin and my husband were business associates and good friends.''

''I see.'' There was a sudden stillness in the room, broken only by the crackling of the fire. Lake said, ''This is a lovely room, so warm and inviting.''

The maid returned with the drinks, including a refill of sherry for Mrs. Girard. The old lady raised her glass and said, ''To better times, without the dopeheads.''

Connie smiled and sipped her drink.

''When's lunch?'' Mrs. Girard asked. ''I'm starved.''

''Right away, ma'am.''

They lunched at the library window, at a game table inlaid with leather. Outside was a large garden rendered gray and dormant by the pending winter. Lake was glad they were staying in the room. Besides being comfortable, it meant she could leave her purse where it was, on the mantel. The tape was rolling.

The food was simpler than she'd expected—onion soup, watery; tuna salad on a bed of lettuce; heated Pepperidge Farm rolls; and sliced tomatoes. Everyone ate quickly, and little was said. Dessert consisted of leftover apple pie and coffee.

"Delicious," said Lake.

"Very nice, mother," Marsha James said.

"With the price of food these days the farmers have all the money," said Mrs. Girard.

Marsha James sighed, got up, and returned to her chair by the fireplace. Ferguson excused himself and left the room. Connie remained at the table with Mrs. Girard, who'd sat back, her coffee cup in a very steady hand, and who was staring at Connie. "Do you really think my son-in-law's death could be related to this Pringle chap?"

"We don't know," Connie said, pleased that the topic had been reintroduced, "but we're trying to find out."

"You're wasting your time," Marsha James said, "My husband was poisoned by his valued Iranian servant, Nuri Hafez, who is in custody in Iran."

"That's debatable, isn't it?" Connie said.

Marsha James sat up straight. Her eyes opened wide and her mouth slipped into a tight sneer. "No, young lady, there is no debate about that whatsoever."

Connie was tempted to back off. Instead, she looked Mrs. James in the eye and said, "We have information that leads us to believe Nuri Hafez might have been a scapegoat."

"Good lord," Marsha James said, turning from Lake and looking into the fire. "I've never heard such drivel in my life."

"I didn't say it was a fact, Mrs. James, just that there's a possibility that Hafez did not kill your husband."

"You're not here to talk about my husband."

"Yes, I'm sorry. What can you tell me about Paul Pringle?"

"Very little. He was a quiet man, did his job, was courteous."

"Hardly a drug user's profile."

"I wouldn't know about that. There'd been rumors that he'd had personal problems."

"What kind of personal problems?"

"I have no idea. I was not involved with the security staff."

"What in God's name led you to become a police-woman?" Mrs. Girard asked.

Ferguson entered the room. "I really should be going," he announced.

"Were you involved with Ambassador James in his Scottish oil company?" Connie asked. Ferguson looked at Marsha James. Lake added, "The one financed by the Manchester bank."

"I think it's time for *you* to leave, Miss Lake," Mrs. James said, standing and smoothing her dress.

"Why is that question so out of line?" Connie asked.

"Scottish oil," Mrs. Girard said in a disparaging voice. "Next they'll be seceding from the Crown, and good riddance."

"Please, mother."

Ferguson coughed.

Lake looked at Mrs. Girard, who was smiling. It was a sweet, satisfied smile. Obviously, she reveled in the dialogue that was taking place.

"To answer your question," Ferguson said, "I am retired. It was a pleasure meeting you." He said to Marsha James, "Might I speak with you a moment?"

Mrs. James quickly got out of her chair and followed him from the room. Connie realized her time was up, and she'd get nothing more from Marsha James. She said to Mrs. Girard, who'd returned to sipping her sherry, "Did you know the young Iranian who's accused of murdering your son-in-law?"

"Never met him. Damn fool, Geoffrey was, bringing that sort with him."

Connie wasn't sure how to respond. She thought for a moment, then said, "Geoffrey was quite the ladies' man, wasn't he?"

Mrs. Girard laughed. "Yes, he did well with them, better than he did with his business and his high and mighty diplomatic nonsense. He had more bearing than brains, as my late husband would have said, but he wasn't so smart himself."

"Your . . ."

"That's right, my husband. Shock you that I'd speak this way of the dead? It shouldn't. They were all right, my husband and my son-in-law, a couple of British stuffed shirts who knew more about how to spend money than make it, spend it on the ladies."

Connie was excited over Mrs. Girard's candor. She nervously glanced at the door, then asked, "Did you know about a woman named Lindstrom, Inga Lindstrom?"

The old woman suddenly seemed to be fatigued. She closed her eyes, slowly opened them and said, "No, was she one of them?"

"I don't mean to . . ."

"Both foolish, my daughter and my son-in-law. She supported him in grand style with our money until he got enough of his own, then he decides to walk out on her for some floozy."

"Who?"

"Who cares? That secretary of his, this Inga what's-her-face, somebody. I'm past my nap time."

"Yes, of course." Connie stood, offered her hand, which Mrs. Girard took. There was less strength than in their initial handshake. "You're very kind, Mrs. Girard. I appreciate everything."

"It wasn't much of a lunch but with the prices of everything . . ." Her voice trailed off as though a tiny wind-up motor inside had wound down.

"I'll see myself out," Connie said. "Again, thank you."

Ferguson and Marsha James were in the front hall. "Thank you," Lake said.

"It was nice of you to stop by." There was an awkward silence before Mrs. James added, "I don't wish to be uncooperative, Miss Lake, but all of this has been traumatic."

"I understand." She said to Ferguson, who'd put on a tan cashmere topcoat and a snappy tweed hat, "Congratulations on your retirement. Who'll run the oil company now?"

"It's in the process of being dissolved," Mrs. James said. "It no longer exists as a business entity."

"Oh. Well, thanks again. It was gracious of you to have me to lunch."

Marsha James smiled. "I think it was mother who had you to lunch. She often invites people she doesn't know. Mother is . . . well, she's getting old and quite eccentric."

"She's nice," Connie said.

"Yes, eccentric and nice. Good-bye."

Marsha James waited until Lake had disappeared around a corner in search of a cab, and Ferguson had driven off in his red Mercedes, then went to her bedroom and dialed a number in Washington. "This is Marsha James," she said to an answering machine. "Call me at the Philadelphia number as soon as you come in."

14

Morizio had come down with a head cold the night before, which was a good excuse to leave MPD early that afternoon. He went home, made himself some soup, and started going over everything he knew about the Pringle and James murders. The papers Pringle had left at Piccadilly were spread over the dining room table. Lake's tapes of her conversations with Melanie Callender and George Thorpe played on the stereo. A lined yellow legal pad contained pages of notes Morizio made each time a thought or a potential connection came to him.

He called Ethel Pringle at 4:30. She was slightly warmer this time, not quite so standoffish although Morizio didn't categorize her attitude as friendly. He taped the conversation, and played the tape after they'd concluded their talk.

MORIZIO: "Sorry to bother you again, Ethel. This is Sal Morizio."

PRINGLE: "It's all right."

MORIZIO: "Ethel, why did Paul return to Washington?"

131

PRINGLE: "I don't know."

MORIZIO: "He didn't give you any indication, any hint?"

PRINGLE: "No."

MORIZIO: "He'd made a date to see me the night he was murdered. His message sounded urgent. Could it have been about the James murder?"

PRINGLE: "Perhaps. I really don't know anything. Thank you for calling. I know he was fond of you."

MORIZIO: "Wait, please. This accusation that he was involved in drugs. Can that be true?"

PRINGLE: (After a long pause) "Paul was troubled, was involved in things he shouldn't have been. He never shared with me, so I don't know any of the specifics. I just know the past few months have been dreadful for all of us and I would prefer to bury them. Please understand."

MORIZIO: "I think it's a damn shame."

PRINGLE: "Of course it is, it's . . ."

MORIZIO: "I'm not talking about his death, Ethel, I'm talking about his reputation. Paul Pringle never touched drugs in his life and I hate to see you and Harriet tainted by a lie."

PRINGLE: "All of it is in the past. I'm determined to start anew, and so is Harriet. Thank you."

She hung up.

Morizio played the tape again, and once more. He kept focusing on her statement—"Paul was troubled, was involved in things he shouldn't have been."

Lake walked in at five-thirty.

"How'd it go?" he asked.

"You have a cold? You sound nasal."

"Yeah. What happened in Philadelphia?"

"A lot." She pulled the tape from her coat pocket and handed it to him.

132

"You got to talk to her?"

"Sure did, and her mother, and Sir Edwin Ferguson."

"Who's he?"

"He was on the guest list. Old friend and business partner."

Morizio rewound the tape and started it. Lake made herself a drink and joined him on the couch. The words from Mrs. Girard's study were clear and complete. Morizio and Lake listened from different perspectives. For Morizio it was all new. For Connie, it enhanced memories of her day; she was back in Mrs. Girard's home.

When the tape was over, Morizio said, "There's a lot there."

"I couldn't get over Mrs. Girard's candor, but old people are like that sometimes. The tape misses the nuances, though, the looks between people, the subtle feelings."

"Tell me about 'em."

"You sound awful. Are you taking something?"

"Chicken soup, canned, and Ornade."

"Okay, here's the way it went."

They talked until two in the morning, an FM elevator-music station playing softly in the background. They went over Pringle's papers, and Morizio's notes. They had trouble creating a clear-cut scenario or establishing viable connections between the murders, but they did agree that the murders had to have been linked, in some way, although the actual acts had probably been committed by two different people—a conspiracy. Inga Lindstrom kept popping up as a missing link, and Melanie Callender took on greater importance because of Mrs. Girard's comment about her and the fact that she was involved, to some extent, in Ambassador James's Scottish oil company.

"If James was that much of a player," Morizio said, "his wife had cause to hurt him."

"But why Pringle?"

"He knew something that would incriminate the murderer, or he had something, papers, like what he left me."

Lake yawned. "I'm beat. It's been a long day."

"Tell me again about Ferguson. What was it he said, that the oil company had been 'dissolved'? That's a strange way to put it."

"He didn't say it, Marsha James did. It was almost as though she wanted the point to be made that it was gone, finished, not worth thinking about."

"Let's think about it."

"I assumed we would."

"What about James's will?"

Connie shrugged.

"Did he leave everything to his wife?"

"I don't know."

"Is she the one 'dissolving' the business?"

"Sal, I don't know."

"I don't expect you to. I'm just thinking out loud."

"You're *very* nasal."

"Yeah. I think I have a fever, too."

"Can I get you something?"

"Club soda, and let me change the music. It's putting me to sleep."

Lake went to the kitchen as Morizio changed frequencies on his FM receiver. He found a college station at around 90 playing vintage jazz—an Art Tatum solo recording of "Willow Weep For Me" was in progress. Reception wasn't good and he carefully adjusted the dial until the needle was it its maximum strength. Static continued to drift in and out, but he was willing to trade off reception for the good music.

Connie returned with a large glass of club soda and ice. She'd poured herself a glass of tomato juice.

"Let's run this through one more time," Morizio said. He drank from his glass and walked to the window. Outside, an ice storm had rolled in, turning the streets into long, wide skating rinks. It was pretty; light reflected off the glassy surfaces as though someone had randomly spilled containers of red, yellow, and green oil into water.

"Okay, Ambassador Geoffrey James is poisoned by someone within his inner circle. His wife hates him because he runs around and is about to divorce her. His secretary has a thing going with him, and maybe he's crossed her. He's got a disgruntled assistant, Barnsworth, who'd kill his sister for a real ambassadorship. His Iranian servant, Hafez, maybe isn't too happy with something that's going on. His girl friend's in town, Swedish beauty named Lindstrom, who calls him and he calls her and they don't connect. Maybe they did, who knows? He's got this partner, Ferguson, who's uncomfortable with you there, says he's retired, the business has been dissolved for some reason and . . ."

"Sal."

"What?"

"Did you hear it?"

"Hear what?"

"The radio."

Morizio cocked his head in the direction of the speakers. The Jimmy Lunceford Orchestra was playing a Sy Oliver arrangement of "Four or Five Times." "It's nice," he said.

"Not the music, what else was coming through."

"What are you talking about?"

I heard *you* before.

"On the radio?"

135

"Yes, go ahead and talk." She went to one of the speakers and pressed her ear against it. Morizio started to loudly recite the alphabet. "Change places with me, Sal."

He stood by the speaker while she went to where he'd been standing and recited "A, B, C . . ."

"I hear you," he said. "Keep going." As she continued speaking he played with the tuning dial until her voice came in stronger. "Son of a . . ."

"The room's bugged," she said.

"It sure as hell is." He went to his electronic supply closet and pulled out a tiny, thin Nuvox FM radio. He plugged in an earphone, put on his coat and shoes, and told her to keep talking while he went outside.

"Let me go, Sal. You're sick."

"No, just give me a few minutes, then start talking."

A blast of freezing rain stung his face as he left the building. He shivered as he placed the earpiece in his ear and adjusted the tuning dial to approximately 90. He continued to fine-tune until he heard Lake's voice. It was clear: "A, B, C . . ."

He walked toward the river. Her voice continued to play in his ear. It wasn't until he'd gone about eight blocks that she faded out. He stayed tuned-in as he retraced his steps, heard her say, "Sal, can you hear me? Come on back, you'll get pneumonia."

"Eight blocks," he said when he returned to the apartment. "I picked it up for eight blocks." He threw his coat on a chair, picked up the living room phone, and unscrewed the earpiece. There, nestled in cotton beneath the wired coil was a sub-miniature FM transmitter. He carefully removed it and examined it under the light. "State-of-the-art," he mumbled. He looked at Lake and said, "Remember when we looked at voice scramblers and bug sniffers last year? I wanted to buy one but it was too much money. Remember? I think what was in the back of my mind was that I'm a cop, and nobody bugs cops, do they? What a jerk."

"What about the bedroom?" Connie said.

There was a transmitter in that phone, too. "While we were in bed," he said.

"I don't really understand why it picks us up talking in a room. Why doesn't it just transmit phone calls?" she asked.

"Like I said, Connie, state-of-the-art. I've seem them demonstrated. The phone itself powers it but it's not dependent on phone transmissions. It covers a room, any room." He punched the palm of his left hand with his right fist. "Your place, too, probably. Let's get over there."

"Let's do it tomorrow. There's nobody there for them to hear anyway."

He reluctantly agreed.

They sat in the living room until almost daybreak, and each hour saw Morizio become increasingly angry. The reality was that everything they'd discussed about the James and Pringle murders had been overheard, including the tapes Lake had made with Callender, Thorpe, and Mrs. Girard, Marsha James, and James Ferguson. And, what nettled him even more, their love-making, every subtle, private, personal sound of it had been shared.

Just before Connie dozed off on his shoulder, she asked, "The department? Did they do it?"

"Who else?"

"Then they know we've been disobeying orders from the beginning."

"Yeah. I'm sorry for dragging you into it."

"Don't be. I love you."

She closed her eyes and fell asleep.

They stopped at her apartment in the morning. Both phones there had been altered, too.

Morizio went directly to the Surveillance unit at MPD and checked out a small and lightweight device that vibrated in the user's hand whenever it came close to a concealed transmitter or room bug. He went to his office, closed the door and approached his desk phone. Lake watched him as he extended his hand toward the phone. He stared at the two-by-two-inch box in his hand. It had started to vibrate. "Here, too," he said. He shut off the device and unscrewed both earpiece and mouthpiece. There was nothing except what belonged there. "It's in the line," he said, "probably downstairs in the junction boxes."

"Can they hear us now?" Lake asked.

"Not unless there's a mike somewhere in the room." He walked the office's perimeters, the device in his hand. It didn't vibrate until he came close to the phone again. "I think it's just a phone tap," he said, "but let's cool the conversations just in case."

He returned the antibugging device to Surveillance, then went to a local greasy spoon for coffee. He told her that from now on she was to stay away from anything having to do with Geoffrey James and Paul Pringle.

"I'm already in up to my throat," she said.

"But it hasn't reached the nose and mouth yet."

"What about you, Sal? You should get out, too. Maybe if we just forget it from now on nobody will care."

"Maybe, but I can't walk away, Connie. I just don't want you hurt."

"Can I make that decision?"

"Could I stop you? Sure, I can. I'm your boss. You do what I tell you to do."

"All right, then give me a direct order."

"You've got it."

She stirred the muddy bottom of her cup, laid the spoon on the Formica tabletop, and said, "I've learned a lot from you, Captain Morizio."

"Good."

"Yup, I sure have, and one of the lessons you've taught me is that sometimes people have to disobey orders for their soul."

"Don't give me a hard time, Connie."

"I wouldn't think of it. Come on, I have a meeting to go to."

"So do I," he said as they walked to the cashier's desk. "There's a semiannual luncheon of the Washington, D.C. Diplomatic Gourmet Society. Geoffrey James was a past president. They're tasting caviar, and foie gras."

"Sal," she said, holding out her upturned hands in a gesture of hopelessness. "Stay away."

"Not this gourmet. I love caviar and foie gras."

"You hate them both," she said as they stepped out to the sidewalk.

"I've developed a taste. Besides, I should keep in touch with the nation's capital's diplomatic corps. It's my job to protect them."

"Send me," she said, laughing for the first time since the previous day. "I really like caviar and foie gras."

"Get a bologna sandwich for lunch. I'll see you later."

15

The meeting of the Washington, D.C. Diplomatic Gourmet Society was held in a private room at the Watergate Hotel. Morizio took with him two uniformed members of his force; might as well make the visit look official.

He approached a woman seated outside the function room. She was tall, slender, and well dressed, about fifty he judged, one of a legion of Washington women who pass their days at social events. He introduced himself and asked who was in charge.

"Is something wrong?" she asked.

Morizio smiled. "No, ma'am, just routine."

"You'd better see Mr. Nordkild," she said. "He's inside. Would you like me to take you to him?"

"No, I know him. Thanks anyway." He told his men to take up positions in the small reception area and went in search of Nordkild.

It was early; the affair wasn't scheduled to start until noon and it was quarter of twelve. A few guests were gathered around an elaborately set horseshoe of tables. A small bar was in a corner. They were out of central-casting, Morizio thought, diplomats through and through, suits dark and immaculately tailored, shoes shined but not too glossy, drinks held as though the glasses were natural extensions of their arms. Berge Nordkild was not cut out of the same mold, however, although his clothing was obviously expensive. That was the problem with being overweight, Morizio mused. No matter how much you spent for a suit it never looked right. Nordkild might have shelled out big money for the suit he wore but it still looked like something Pinky Lee might have worn. It had very wide lapels, was double-breasted and was a greenish plaid that could have caused seasickness if you stared at it long enough.

"Mr. Nordkild, could I speak with you for a minute?" Morizio said.

Nordkild, whose back was to Morizio as he accepted a drink from a black bartender, turned, squinted, and said, "Captain Morizio, what a pleasant surprise. What brings you here?"

"That's what I wanted to talk to you about."

"Drink?"

"Sure. I have a lousy head cold."

Nordkild laughed, sending his suit into a green tidal wave. "Nothing like good whiskey for what ails you. Scotch?"

"Yeah, that'll be fine."

They walked to an unoccupied corner of the room where a folding screen shielded serving pieces and glassware from the guests. Morizio said, "I have a couple of uniformed officers outside." He tasted his drink and said, "Beats penicillin. Look, the reason I brought them is that with all the recent threats against diplomatic personnel around the world, we've decided to beef up security whenever a group of diplomats like this gets together. Better safe than sorry."

"Has there been a threat against us today, a bomb?"

"No, just preventative medicine." He grinned and sipped more Scotch.

"As you wish, Captain," said Nordkild. "Will you be staying?"

"I hadn't planned on it but I will, if it's okay with you."

"Love to have you, as I'm sure the members of the club will feel. Actually, I am not a member of this special group, but I do cater their meetings. I'm an honorary member of sorts, a diplomat without passport."

"But good caviar gets you through Customs."

"Exactly."

Nordkild twisted the ends of his mustache and said, "I assure you you'll find the quality of today's caviar superior to what we had at our lunch, and the foie gras is absolutely spectacular. Come refill your glass and I'll introduce you around."

"I know a lot of these people," Morizio said as he followed Nordkild to the bar. "My job."

"Of course, but some are undoubtedly strangers. Frankly, we end up with too many lower level embassy personnel and their female guests, usually secretaries they're trying to impress for obvious reasons."

Morizio laughed and looked around the room. More guests had arrived, some of whom were not quite so clearly cut from the diplomatic cloth, and who gave credence to what Nordkild had said. One, in particular, captured his attention, a short, stocky Arab dressed in an ill-fitting gray wool suit. He'd already heaped his plate with caviar, foie gras, and other delicacies from the table. Morizio had assumed there'd be some sort of ritual to the tasting, an order of events, but the Arab proved him wrong. Obviously, the name of the game was to eat as fast and as much as you could. He mentioned it to Nordkild, who replied, "We call these gatherings tastings, but in reality they are nothing more than an excuse to fill bellies with expensive food. Besides, labeling these gatherings 'tastings' make the members feel like gourmets. They like that."

Morizio appreciated Nordkild's candor and cynicism. He asked who the Arab was.

"Sami Abdu," Nordkild said. "He was a journalist in Iran until the Ayatollah took over. He was lucky to escape with his head, as I understand it."

Morizio recognized Abdu's name from the guest list of James's party. He told Nordkild, "I've heard of him. I'd like to meet him. He's supposed to have some good stories about Iran."

"Then allow me to introduce you," said Nordkild. "By the way, captain, anything new on your investigation of Ambassador James's death?"

"Nope, not a thing."

"I was shocked to read about the brutal murder of that fellow from the embassy, Pringle. That was his name, wasn't it?"

"That's right."

"Do you think there is any connection between the two deaths?"

"We looked into that but came up a cropper. Evidently, they were two totally unrelated incidents."

"I suppose that's good from your perspective."

"Yeah, having a conspiracy on our hands would complicate things."

Nordkild introduced Morizio to Abdu, then excused himself. Abdu suggested that Morizio get food before it disappeared, which made Morizio smile. If the food were going to disappear, it would be into the Abdu's stomach. He was already on his second overflowing plate.

Morizio went to the table and chose what he thought he could get down—tiny shrimp in a green sauce, thinly sliced Scottish salmon with capers and onion, wedges of toast intended for use with caviar, and just enough caviar and foie gras to make it look as though he was "with it." He rejoined Abdu and said, "I understand you're lucky to be standing here."

The Arab raised his eyebrows.

"The situation in Iran. My friends tell me you were lucky to get out alive."

"Oh, yes, that is true, but it is far enough in the past for me to have forgotten about it."

"Sorry I brought it up," Morizio said. He tasted his food, then said, "I'm sure you've kept up with the murder of Ambassador James."

"Yes, I read about it, and some of my press colleagues discuss it from time to time. Are you the officer in charge of that investigation?"

Morizio shook his head. "No, MPD has no official connection with the case. It happened in an embassy, which makes it strictly embassy business."

Abdu shrugged and took a large forkful of foie gras. "It depends upon how an embassy views it, does it not? When the Russian was found hanged in his embassy, they called your police force and invited you to investigate."

"That's right, but every embassy handles things differently. The British chose not to." Again, Morizio asked himself why it hadn't. He said, "I became fascinated with Ambassador James's Iranian valet, Nuri Hafez. You're Iranian, Mr. Abdu. What do you think about Hafez being arrested in Iran and facing a trial there for James's murder?"

Abdu ran his fingers over pockmarked skin while thinking of an answer. Finally, he said, "I would not want to be in that young man's shoes. The Ayatollah doesn't care about the death of a British Ambassador, but he must make a show. He will behead him."

"I don't believe he's there."

"Hafez? In Iran? Why do you question it?"

"Why don't you?"

Abdu chewed his cheek and suppressed a grin. "I suppose because I choose to believe rather than to question?"

"A journalist?"

"A survivor."

"Will Hafez have a trial?"

"Of course not. If the Ayatollah wishes to make a gesture to the Western world by executing Nuri Hafez, then that is what he will do. The Iranian way of life is different from Washington, D.C." He wiped up the last few grains of caviar from his plate, licked his lips, and said, "You must try the pressed sevruga, Captain. The berries that are damaged during processing are compressed into caviar jelly. Many gourmets consider it the finest, and I list myself among them. It is, after all, the same caviar but in a different form. It spreads so nicely on the toast."

Morizio went to the table and looked into a bowl of pressed caviar. It looked to him like blackberry jam. He smeared some on a triangle of toast while Abdu filled his plate to the edges. Morizio asked, "Do you know anything about Nuri Hafez's background?"

"I knew his family in Iran."

"You did?"

"Yes. Nuri was the black sheep of the family. He went to work for the British Embassy and had little to do with his family after that except for his older brother, Ahmad."

145

Morizio stopped eating and looked at Abdu. "You sound as though you knew the family pretty well."

"Oh, yes, although I lost touch with them toward the end. This must have been a terrible blow to them, to have their youngest son arrested for murder. We are a proud people, Captain, and this is a disgrace that the family will never overcome."

"Did you know anything about Nuri's dealings with Ambassador James?"

"No, only that he had become . . . how shall we say it . . . 'indispensable'? . . ."

"To the ambassador?"

"Yes. He was a very ambitious young man."

Morizio had the feeling that Abdu knew more about Nuri Hafez than he was willing to divulge. He put down his plate, finished his Scotch, and said to Abdu, "Another drink?"

"I am a Moslem," Abdu said.

Morizio looked at the glass Abdu held. It contained ice and an amber liquid. Abdu noticed his interest in the glass, smiled and said, "The Moslem is not only devoted to his God, he has learned over the centuries to adapt in order to survive. Were it not quite so cold in my new country, and did I not feel a flu coming on, I would never allow whiskey to pass my lips. But . . ." A bigger smile this time. "To your health, Captain." He finished his drink.

"Only for medicinal purposes," Morizio said.

"Exactly."

Nordkild, accompanied by two men, joined Abdu and Morizio. Morizio knew one of them, Boris Kaldar, the third-ranking diplomat at the Soviet Union's embassy in Washington. Kaldar recognized Morizio and shook his hand warmly. Morizio had always liked Kaldar. He was his embassy's security coordinator and had met with Morizio on a number of occasions. Kaldar's colleagues at the embassy were, in Morizio's judgment, cold and hard, stereotypes of Russian men in high position. Not Kaldar. He was in the sixties but looked younger. He was about Morizio's height and had a body of an athlete, someone who kept in good condition. His shoulders were broad, his waist narrow, and his gray pinstripe suit was carefully tailored to define the contours of his body. His face was long and narrow. He had high cheekbones, a thin nose, and blue eyes that seemed perpetually bemused. He spoke perfect English, and Morizio recalled what a good storyteller he was, enjoying long, intricate jokes that poked fun at diplomatic and governmental bureaucracy. The last time they met was when a young Russian embassy employee was found hanged inside the embassy, and Morizio had accompanied a team of detectives from MPD. The Russians, heavily shrouded in secrecy, had invited them in because of a death while the British, America's best friend, had not.

The other man with Nordkild was Elgin Harris, the Canadian ambassador to the United States. Harris was tall, angular, and reserved, a Geoffrey James type.

"Excellent caviar, Berge," Kaldar said to Nordkild.

"Could it be anything but excellent, Comrade Boris?" Nordkild said, chuckling. "It is, after all, Russian."

Sami Abdu said, "Or Iranian in Russian tins."

Kaldar laughed. "A nasty rumor created by the disgruntled Iranian caviar industry." He gently slapped Abdu on the back, and the pained expression on the Iranian's face indicated his displeasure. Kaldar said, "You couldn't sell your caviar here after you took the American hostages, and you couldn't stand the thought of only Russian caviar on American plates, to say nothing of no American money in your pockets." He winked at Morizio.

Abdu said, "Not true, Mr. Kaldar. When the Americans prohibited us from selling products here, we simply sold them to you. There was a method to our madness. We knew that if Americans could only eat the Russian product they would quickly lose their taste for caviar. What would we do when the boycott was lifted? There would be no market left."

Everyone laughed. Morizio asked of no one in particular, "Is that true, that Iranian caviar is sold to the Soviet Union and then repackaged for the U. S.?"

"It must be true," said Kaldar. "We have been told by a journalist."

Morizio asked Kaldar, "Do the Soviet Union and Iran process caviar the same way?"

"No, the methods may be the same but we Russians have a definite advantage when it comes to the art of applying the salt."

"What about the art of adding borax?" Morizio asked.

Nordkild answered that question. "It shouldn't matter to an American, Captain. You won't allow me to import caviar containing borax because of a ridiculous law enacted years ago."

"Yeah, I heard that," Morizio said. "Does it taste that much different?"

"Indeed it does," Kaldar said.

Nordkild said, "There are caviar lovers the world over who would give their right hand to have a supply of caviar with borax rather than salt . . ." He looked at Sami Abdu and added, "No offense, my Iranian friend."

"The Europeans have all they want," Kaldar said, "because there is no such law anywhere but here in America."

Morizio put his hands in his pocket and shrugged.

"It'd probably taste the same to me," he said. "I'm not what you'd call a connoisseur."

Abdu asked, "Did you enjoy it today?"

"What do you mean?" Morizio said.

"Please, Sami . . ."

Abdu cut Nordkild off. "The pressed sevruga you had has been preserved with borax, not salt."

"No kidding." Morizio looked at the table, then said to Nordkild, "If it's illegal in this country, what's it doing here?"

"Don't listen to him," Nordkild said, referring to Abdu.

Abdu laughed and said, "We're definitely breaking the law, Captain, although, as you know, the diplomatic pouch is beyond all law."

Morizio held up his hands. "Hey, I don't care. This isn't a borax bust. What do you do, bring it in a pouch?"

Elgin Harris cleared his throat and excused himself. So did Nordkild. Morizio said, "It did taste different. I liked it. Maybe I ought to get a diplomatic pouch of my own."

"Excellent idea, Captain," Kaldar said.

Morizio looked around the room and saw other familiar faces from the diplomatic corps, including personnel from the State Department. One of them, Jeb Carter, came up to Morizio, shook hands, and said, "I didn't know you were a gourmet, captain."

"I'm becoming one."

Carter, who was tall and handsome in an Ivy League way, warmly greeted Harris and Kaldar. They talked about the food at the luncheon, particularly the relative merits of beluga, sevruga, and oestra caviar. It seemed to Morizio that Carter really didn't care and only used such occasions to keep in touch with diplomats around the city. Kaldar seemed genuinely interested in caviar and knew a great deal about its history. Morizio mentioned he'd tasted American caviar at Berge Nordkild's office, and a spirited discussion developed over whether it would ever rival the Caspian Sea's product.

"The best caviar will always come from the Caspian," Abdu said.

"Not if the balance of caviar power shifts," said Carter. "Right now it's a standoff, isn't it, Mr. Kaldar?"

Morizio said, "You make it sound like the nuclear arms race."

"It is similar," said Kaldar.

Carter jumped in with, "You see, Captain, technology prevails even with something like caviar. The Russians went ahead and developed a synthetic caviar. We had no choice but to develop our own technological capability."

"You're joking," said Morizio.

"Not at all, Captain," Kaldar said. "It is true. A Soviet professor, Grigory Slonimsky, developed the technique. He uses proteins, drops them in vegetable oil and the proteins break up into little fish eggs that look and taste like caviar once dye and flavorings are added."

"Fascinating," Morizio said. He said to Carter, "You say we've developed it, too."

"That's right, over at Romanoff, but they swear they'll only use it as a second-strike against the Russians."

"A balance of power," Kaldar said.

"Maybe we should stop producing nuclear weapons and fight it out on the caviar battlefield," said Morizio.

"An excellent suggestion, Captain."

"It really looks like the real thing?" Morizio asked.

"Yes, it does," Sami Abdu said. "I have seen and tasted it. It's quite good, but its appearance bothers me.

150

It rolls out of machines like tiny ball bearings, one egg identical to the next.''

Morizio asked Jeb Carter whether he'd seen and tasted it. He shook his head.

Kaldar said, "I have tasted it. Everyone in the caviar community has had that opportunity at one time or another.''

Morizio said, "You learn something new every day. Artificial caviar. Next they'll be doing it with corn flakes.''

"Corn flakes?''

"My favorite breakfast. I should get back.''

"Me, too,'' said Boris Kaldar. "Good to see you again, Captain. Don't be such a stranger. Stop in for tea or vodka.''

"I will.''

Morizio had wanted to discuss Hafez with Sami Abdu but the Iranian begged off, claiming to be late to a meeting. "But call me,'' he told Morizio, handing him his card.

Morizio sought out Nordkild on his way out. "Thanks for having me,'' he told the fat caterer. "I enjoyed it, learned a lot.''

"My pleasure, Captain. Ignore what was said about the borax. It was only a single tin, nothing.''

"Don't worry about it,'' said Morizio. "If it were cocaine, we might have a problem, but what's a little borax between friends?''

"Exactly. Good day.''

16

The full impact of having been electronically bugged
didn't settle in on Morizio until that night. It had been a
busy day, too busy to dwell upon it, and he was ex-
hausted from so little sleep the night before. His cold
was worse; he couldn't breathe and his throat felt like
sandpaper when he swallowed. On top of everything
else, his mother called from Boston to say she'd slipped
while grocery shopping and had broken her right wrist.
She seemed unconcerned, and dismissed his offer to fly
up to see her. "It'll heal," she told him. "At least it
wasn't the whole arm."

"I just want to sleep," he told Lake. They were at
her apartment. She'd cooked bacon, put it on toast, and
poured Welsh rarebit over it. That was dinner, along
with raw stringbeans and wine. Now, they sat together
in bed. He'd brought *The Thirties* with him and was
reading Wilson's accounts of his exploits in New York
in the thirties with S. J. Perelman, Philip Wylie, and
Dashiell Hammett when his mind was suddenly filled
with visions of someone sitting in a car and smirking as

he listened to Connie and him making love. He slammed the book on the bed and swore.

"I know," Connie said, lowering a newspaper she'd been reading and looking at him. "It's come home to me, too. I was just thinking about us here, in bed, making love and . . ."

That often happened with them, thinking the same things at the same time.

"Maybe it wasn't MPD," Morizio said. "Maybe it was the State Department, or the CIA. Maybe the FBI wants something, or Thorpe, or Gibronski."

"We don't know, Sal, and maybe we never will unless what they heard is used in some way."

Morizio pulled his knees up to his chin and wrapped his arms around them. "Whoever did it knows we know, and they've lost their line to us. Does that mean they try to establish another conduit into what we're doing, or do they let it drop? Did they get what they wanted, or did we foul things up for them too soon?"

She sighed. "I feel like a character out of George Orwell, big brother and all that. I'm afraid to say anything, do anything."

"We just can't let it slide, Connie. I want to, want to forget it ever happened, but that's impossible. I dread the next time I'm with Trottier. I don't know whether I'll be able to hold back, not accuse him, blow my stack, and end up suspended."

"That wouldn't accomplish anything." She deliberately changed the subject by saying, "You said you had some interesting stories from the tasting this afternoon."

Morizio had mentioned only his conversation with Sami Abdu, and that he wanted to follow up on the Iranian journalist's knowledge of the Hafez family. Now, he told her of the exchange between Abdu, Kaldar, and Nordkild about borax being in the pressed sevruga.

"Nordkild went pale," he said, laughing, "figured he'd end up arrested for importing illegal substances. I loved it."

"But you said it was brought in in a diplomatic pouch."

"Yeah, but I have the feeling that most of it ends up with Nordkild for resale. Nice little part-time business for a diplomat, smuggle in a couple of tins of good caviar with borax, sell it to Nordkild, and let him jack up the price to people who prefer it to salt."

Lake thought for a moment, then said, "Remember a few years back when that diplomat . . . he was from some Asian country, can't remember . . . they nailed him with three or four hundred thousand dollars worth of drugs in his pouch. They found a few tins of caviar, too. Remember? It was a joke around the department."

"Vaguely. Do you think James was smuggling and got killed over it?"

"We've gone over this before. He certainly got rich after he left Iran, and that hostage's claim that he'd struck some sort of a deal with the Ayatollah might have some credence. What did we decide it could be, drugs, oil, caviar? Nobody gets murdered over a tin of caviar."

"A thousand tins? Ten thousand?" Morizio said. "A tin retails for around two hundred bucks. Smuggle in ten thousand tins, sell it at a hundred a tin and you've got a million dollars. Not bad."

"But why would anyone buy from such a source?"

"We slapped the lid on all Iranian products after the hostage take-over, remember?"

"Right, but James didn't need money. His wife's loaded."

"And his pride was empty. That's what I got from your talks with Mrs. James and her mother."

"I don't know, Sal. What about Paul?"

"He knew. What else can I assume?"

"And they'd brutally murder him to preserve a caviar business? Doesn't play for me."

"Try drugs."

"Try oil."

"Nothing illegal about selling oil."

"Depends on how you do it. There's nothing illegal about selling TV sets unless you get them off the back of a truck."

"We should find out more about James's oil company."

"Want me to?"

"You're out of it."

"Like you say, Sal, it's tough giving orders to somebody you sleep with."

He smiled, punched his pillow into the configuration he wanted, and snuggled his head into it, saying from that position, "I didn't tell you about how the tasting ended up. Did you ever hear of synthetic caviar?"

"No."

"You have now." He told her about it. "There's a synthetic everything, all plastic. What a world. Kiss me good night, I'm fading fast."

She leaned over and kissed his ear. He purred. "Synthetic, Sal? Little ball bearings popping out of a machine?"

"That's right."

"James died in a bowl of caviar."

"So?"

"No ricin found in it, just in his body. What if the poison were inside some synthetic eggs, all wrapped up nice and tight until somebody takes the fateful bite? Crunch! Dead!"

He opened his eyes and sat up. "And what's left doesn't read in lab tests because it's inside. It's possible."

"Sure it is."

"It's dumb."

"No, it's not. It is possible, Sal, really possible. At least we can check it." She got out of bed and pulled a phone from her desk to bedside.

"Who are you calling?" he asked.

"Forensics. Maybe Jill Dougherty's on late."

She was. Lake said to her, "Jill, I'm asking a big favor, and you can say no if you want, only if you do I'll never speak to you again."

"With some creeps around here that'd be a promise instead of a threat. What do you want?"

"I want to come down and run some of that caviar Ambassador James was eating when he died through another test."

"Now?"

"Right now. I can be there in a half hour Slow tonight?"

"Got a full house, but they won't disturb us."

Lake smiled and shook her head. "Can we do it? It will have to be strictly off the record, unofficial."

"Will you and your Italian friend support me for the rest of my life if I'm out on the street because of it?"

"Count on it."

"Sure, come on down, but if we suddenly get busy, keep walking."

"See ya."

Morizio asked to go with her but Connie stood firm against it, saying, "One, there's no sense in having us show up together. Two, you have a rotten cold. And three, you'll scare Jill off. I'll be back as soon as I can. Go to sleep."

Morizio slept fitfully until she returned four hours

later. She woke him up and said excitedly, "Sal, it checked out. There was artificial caviar in with the real thing."

He wiped sleep from his eyes and sat up. "You're sure?"

"Positive. We ran water over it, really turned on the pressure. The real eggs crushed but the artificial didn't. They looked exactly the same as the real thing, Sal, incredible."

"How many?"

"A dozen. There must have been more but he ate them."

"Ricin?"

"Yes. The artificial eggs are hollow and filled with it. Jill ran a preliminary patch test on it. It's ricin all right, no question about it."

Morizio got up and put on his robe. "That's how he got it, huh?"

"Evidently."

"Who did it?"

"Anyone with access to the caviar he ate."

"Comes back to Hafez, doesn't it?"

"Maybe, but why would he have a supply of artificial caviar filled with ricin?"

"Or anybody, for that matter. It's supposed to be a deep, dark secret but they agreed at lunch that anybody who spends time around caviar has seen and tasted the phoney stuff. The Iranian, Abdu, said he'd tried it."

Connie undressed and slipped into a Black Watch plaid nightshirt. She untied a bow in her hair and brushed it out as she said, "It sure rules out passion, doesn't it?"

"What do you mean?"

"It couldn't be spur-of-the-moment, that's for sure.

157

You don't just have ricin-laced artificial caviar lying around the way you do a gun or a kitchen knife."

"Are you ruling out Marsha James?"

"No, I'm just saying that whoever did it planned it for a long time, took pains to put it together."

Morizio said over his shoulder as he headed for the kitchen, "I'm hungry. Want eggs?"

"Sure."

They sat at the kitchen table and ate scrambled eggs and English muffins. Morizio had a glass of milk, Lake white wine. He asked, "How did you leave it with Dougherty?"

"I told her to do or say nothing until she heard from me. She agreed."

"She can't do that for long. Hell, she's made a major discovery, good for the career. What do *we* do with it?"

"I just work here, boss."

"In a pig's . . ."

"Why don't you just confront Chief Trottier with it, tell him what you know and insist on a further investigation."

"He'd refuse. It's still within the embassy, if that's the way they want it. It might be different if it had to do with Paul's murder but it doesn't."

She reached across the table and grabbed his wrist. "But wouldn't they want to know how the British ambassador to the United States was murdered?"

Morizio sat back and placed his bare foot on her leg beneath the table. "No, they don't want to know, and that's what really gets to me. Somebody somewhere wants this buried and forgotten, no flowers on the grave, no perpetual burning light. Why, I don't know, but it's true. Will Jill Dougherty sit on it for long enough for us to get some answers?"

"I think so."

"I'll call a friend tomorrow who might be able to help. I'd like to talk to Nordkild again, too. I need a couple of days."

"You don't have them. The rest of the week is jammed, at least according to the calendar."

"I'm sick. I've got enough sick leave stacked up to last a lifetime. Hold down the fort tomorrow, maybe the next day. We can't let this go."

"We?"

"Yeah, well . . . thanks for running over there."

"There's no way to push me away now, Captain. I'm hooked."

"So am I, and I wish I weren't."

"Don't kid a kidder, Sal. You love it."

"I want Paul Pringle's killer. That's all."

"That's enough. Let's get some sleep. The eggs were good, a little overdone but passable."

They went to the bedroom. As Morizio slipped out of his robe he said casually, "One of the eggs I used was synthetic."

"That's the way you plan to get rid of me?"

He smiled, climbed into bed next to her, and kissed her nose. "Good night," he said.

"Good night," she said.

17

Morizio left himself plenty of time to make the lunch date he'd set up with an old friend from his CIA days, Kenneth Donaldson. He made the call to Donaldson's office from a booth outside Lake's apartment. When Donaldson asked where he'd like to meet, Morizio said, "The Cafe Tatti, the McLean Mall. Noon?"

"I'll be there," said Donaldson.

Morizio took the George Washington Memorial Parkway along the Potomac, then switched to the Georgetown Pike until reaching the Virginia town of McLean. He parked in front of Tatti and waited until Donaldson drove up, parked, and was walking toward the tiny French restaurant. Morizio intercepted him on the sidewalk. "Hello, Ken, good to see you."

"Same here, Sal."

"Let's take a ride. I made a reservation someplace else."

Donaldson, who was sixty and scholarly, grinned and asked, "Who's after you?"

"I paid my taxes so I know it's not the IRS. Evans Farm okay?"

"Lunch in the country. Sounds delightful."

Morizio took a roundabout route to Chain Bridge Road in McLean, where the inn stood on forty acres of rolling land; there were fruit trees, and dozens of grazing goats, sheep and quacking ducks. He checked his rearview mirror frequently, and didn't actually approach the inn until he was certain no one was behind him. Donaldson observed quietly.

They entered the stone building, crossed a flagstone floor to the pub, and took seats at the bar. "I made a reservation inside," Morizio said, "but we're early. Besides, I could use a drink. I've got a bad cold."

"You sound it," Donaldson said. He ordered a perfect oldfashioned for himself. Morizio had Bourbon in a snifter and club soda on the side.

"Here's to seeing you again, Sal," Donaldson said. They touched glasses. "So can you tell me why all the evasiveness, or are we talking about the Redskins?"

"The Redskins for openers. Think they'll do it this year?"

They kept to football for the duration of their drinks, then went to the main dining room where Morizio chose a table for two that was in front of a fireplace, and was a decent distance from adjacent tables. They ordered another round, got salads from a salad bar, tasted the spoon bread a waitress had placed on the table, and looked at each other.

Morizio hadn't seen Ken Donaldson in awhile, almost a year he figured. They'd worked closely at the Central Intelligence Agency during Morizio's two-year stint there. It was highly classified work that involved theoretical methods of disrupting a smaller nation's cultural and economic patterns over a prolonged period of time to create a better climate for overthrow. Morizio had found the work fascinating, but there wasn't a night during those two years when he didn't question his values. That's why he resigned, not so much to join MPD but to stop questioning himself. It took up too much time.

Probably the greatest mitigating factor in his daily moral grapple was Ken Donaldson, who'd been a professor of sociology at Georgetown University for many years. He'd also been a paid, secret consultant to the CIA, commonly known as ''the Company,'' during his tenure at Georgetown. When his connection with the giant intelligence organization was revealed, along with others in similar positions at colleges around the country, the heat was on for him to resign. He did, and joined the Company full-time. Morizio and Donaldson became close, enough so for them to openly discuss Donaldson's decision to leave academia for the clandestine life. ''It was the honest thing to do,'' Donaldson often said. ''I was tired of the either-or lie that perpetrated the controversy—the University is 'pure,' the government is 'evil.' It was nonsense. There is no such thing as purity, at least not in institutions. Personal purity, perhaps, or I'd like to think so, but never when more than three people band together to create a thing, a Pentagon, a CIA, a Congress or a university. I decided to go where the evil was understood and admitted. As I said, Sal, it was the only honest thing to do.''

They used to debate it for hours, and while Morizio never completely bought Donaldson's philosophies, he admired him for being introspective enough to ponder his life, and for his willingness to talk about it, never in public, of course, but privately, with friends, like Morizio.

Morizio also enjoyed Donaldson's erudite manner,

wit, knowledge about myriad things and even his classically conservative style of dress—Brooks Brothers, from the skin out. This day he wore a herringbone jacket, blue cotton button-down shirt, and red paisley bow tie. His glasses were large and rimmed with tortoise shell. He was slender; his fingers were long and thin, like a pianist's. He was bald, and allowed the white hair at his temples to grow a little too long and to go in its own direction, a vestige of his professorial days.

Donaldson brought up boxing. He was a devoted fight fan, an unlikely passion most people thought, for so educated and sensitive a man. "It's the only true drama on television," he told Morizio as they looked at menus, "two combatants facing each other in a defined area, a third man to impose some semblance of civilization and a specified amount of time to kill each other. Each man brings all his dreams and fears into that ring hoping his body will serve him well. Do you agree, Sal?"

Morizio, who'd been listening with one ear, looked up, nodded, said his father had been a fight fan, and asked what Donaldson was having.

"The Smithfield ham, what else."

Morizio ordered a rare steak. When the waitress was gone from the table, he said to Donaldson, "I can't tell you much, Ken, about what prompted me to call you, but I am asking you to tell me something."

"Good," Donaldson said. "I hate being told things I'm not supposed to know."

"It's . . . well, it's delicate, and it's a mess."

"I assume it has to do with the death of Ambassador James."

"Why assume that?"

"I've been following it. In fact, I meant to call you but never got around to it. I also read about the death of

Paul Pringle. He was your friend. You introduced me once.''

''I did?''

''Just in passing, at a party or something. The reason I'm assuming whatever problems you're having has to do with the James murder is that Pringle's demise made it two in a row from the British Embassy. Coincidence? What do you think?''

''I think not.''

''Of course. Now, what can I do for you?''

Morizio glanced around the dining room, which had begun to fill up. He leaned close to the table and said, ''Are you still keeping up with the technology at the place?''

''Specifically?''

''What did we used to call it, 'Neutralization and Elimination.'''

''We still do.''

''Anything new?''

''Always something new, Sal. You can't spend millions in search of devices like that without having new discoveries pop up all day long, it seems. Which are you interested in?''

''Food. Methods of poison. Caviar.''

''Which took the life of Ambassador James.''

''Right. Know anything about synthetic caviar?''

He smiled.

''I've got a theory going, Ken. It goes this way. Whoever killed James used synthetic caviar eggs filled with ricin. That's why it read in his body but not in lab tests on the food itself. Is that far-fetched?''

''No.''

Morizio knew Donaldson wouldn't say more. He didn't have to. Obviously, from the way Morizio read the reply it was a confirmation that the wing of the

Company devoted to developing exotic methods of neutralization and elimination of unwanted persons had
added the phony fish eggs to its arsenal.

The waitress delivered their food and they started
eating. Morizio sat back halfway through his steak and
asked, "If my theory isn't out of the ballpark, it leads
me to another theory."

"Which is?"

"That the product in question is probably more available than we might believe." He told Donaldson of
what he knew about the Russians developing the synthetic caviar and the Romanoff Company coming up
with its own product to be used in the event the Russians put it on the market. He added that it seemed that
people involved in caviar had probably had access to it
from one source or another. He waited for a reaction.

"Sal," Donaldson said, dabbing at his mouth with a
white linen napkin, "if I were speculating what the
source might have been, I'd look to the Russians. We've
been amazingly effective in recent years receiving all
sorts of forbidden products from abroad. The balance of
payments has tipped in our favor."

Morizio translated to himself. "The U.S. espionage
network was doing its job, and synthetic caviar had
been among those state secrets delivered to the Company through agents and paid informers."

"It was good." Donaldson said, referring to his
empty plate. "Beautifully cured ham."

"It was a good steak. Ken, another question."

"Another theory?"

"No, a question. I'm under surveillance."

"By whom?"

"I thought you might know."

"Us? Nonsense. Why?"

"I don't know."

"Have you been indiscreet lately in your personal life?"

"I'm never indiscreet in my personal life."

Donaldson laughed. "Maybe the FBI. Even with Hoover dead, they continue to want files on everybody in Washington."

"No, it doesn't smell FBI." He considered telling Donaldson more about what had occurred but decided not to. They had hot deep dish apple crisp and coffee, argued over the bill (Morizio won) and left the Evans Farm Inn. They were almost to Morizio's car when Donaldson touched his arm and led him toward a clump of leafless fruit trees. He stopped, turned, and said, "Your friend, Pringle, was our man in the British Embassy."

"He was?"

"Yes. He was good, and well paid."

"I'm surprised, Ken, really surprised. Paul was very loyal to Britain. At least he always seemed to be."

"And he needed money which, as you know from your time with us, has always been the only acceptable motive for telling tales out of school. Besides, Great Britain is our best friend. He wasn't there to steal nuclear secrets, just to let us know what was what, what decisions were in the works to give us some lead time."

"I'll have to let this sink in," Morizio said.

"Of course."

"I'm surprised at something else, Ken."

"What's that?"

"That you told me."

Donaldson laughed and headed for the car. He said before opening the door, "The man's dead, he's been replaced, and you look and sound as though you need some help. Take me back to my car, Sal."

18

Morizio didn't tell Connie right away that he'd learned about Paul Pringle being on the Company payroll and working inside the British Embassy. He didn't know how to process the information, and needed a little solo time to mull it over.

He also decided that despite Donaldson's denial, it could well be that the Company had ordered the surveillance of him and Lake, and had killed Pringle. It wouldn't be the first time that someone on the CIA payroll was "eliminated" by his own people. If that were so, Morizio's probing into Pringle's death could send CIA powers-to-be in search of some fast relief.

It could also put their lives on the line. That was the problem with organizations like the CIA. They operated under a heavy blanket of secrecy, free from scrutiny and with carte blanche to take matters into their own hands for whatever reasons they deemed palatable— national security, world order, emergency situations beyond the comprehension of ordinary folk. He believed Donaldson when he said he didn't know anything about CIA surveillance of him and Connie. There was no reason for him to know. Within the CIA were highly secret pockets of operations that functioned the way an embassy did in a foreign country, no explanations to anyone else, no justifying actions, no checks and balances. "The only check and balance in this town is Jack Anderson," Morizio muttered to himself as he set up Rasputin for a match. He and Connie were staying at their respective apartments tonight. Sometimes you just had to be alone. They called each other a lot.

He lost to Rasputin, chalking it up to preoccupation with bigger challenges. He went to bed at midnight after calling Connie for the last time, took two aspirin and an Ornade and fell into a heavy sleep. When he awoke in the morning his nasal passages were clear and the scratchiness in his throat was almost gone.

He met Connie for breakfast at Booeymonger's Georgetown branch.

"You're feeling better, aren't you?" she said. He looked better than he had in days, rested, less anxious. Dark circles under his eyes had almost vanished.

"Yeah, the cold is better. I slept good."

"I'm glad."

"I feel like a weight is off my back."

She broke into a smile. "That's great," she said, "but why? What happened at lunch yesterday?"

He'd told her nothing about it. He was still afraid of talking on the phone. Besides, he didn't want to use Donaldson's name. All he'd said was that he'd had lunch with an old friend.

"Did your friend come up with anything helpful?" she asked.

"Yeah, as a matter of fact he did. He's somebody I used to work with pretty closely."

"Ken Donaldson?"

"Why do you assume it was him?"

"You mention him a lot. You used to work together at the CIA."

"Yeah, well . . . It was an interesting lunch." He picked up his spoon and looked closely at it. "I'm so goddamn paranoid I see microphones in everything."

"I know exactly how you feel. You said you were going to call 'your friend' right after we found out about the synthetic caviar. Did he know anything about it?"

"Yes. He didn't specify, but you learn over there to pick up on non-answers. Using phony roe for elimination didn't shock him."

"Elimination. N and E, neutralization and elimination. The first time you told me about that I laughed, remember, then broke into a cold sweat."

Their cheese and bacon omelets were served, along with buttered toast and raspberry jam. Morizio slowly got ready to eat, arranging things, adjusting his napkin, pouring a little pepper on the eggs. He was a devout ritualist, which always amused her, as it did now. He never started cooking unless the table was set, never left on a car trip without toll coins counted and accessible, always cut pancakes neatly into small squares before adding syrup. There were hundreds of them.

He finished arranging and said, "Connie, the fact that phony fish eggs are around Langley means enough people have had access to have killed James with them." The Central Intelligence Agency was headquartered in Langley, Virginia. "You said the other night that it ruled out a crime of passion. I agreed, but not anymore. Sure, it would take some planning, but not a hell of a lot."

"Good," she said after tasting her omelet. "They didn't overcook it."

"I'm glad." He motioned for her to lean across the table and said softly, "Paul was an informer inside the embassy. He was on the Company payroll."

"Jesus," she said.

He waved his fingers toward himself again, this time to indicate he wanted something from her. "Come on, give it to me, instant on-the-spot reaction."

"I may be a jaded female cop, Sal, but I'm still a lady."

He looked around the small restaurant, leaned over again and said, "Maybe it was the Company who killed them. It doesn't matter why because they don't need reasons that would make sense to us. It could be Langley who's keeping an eye on us, and if it is . . ."

"They could kill us, too," she said.

"You never know."

She leaned her elbows on the table and cradled her face in her hands. "Did you ask your friend about it?"

"Yes. He doesn't know anything. He would have leveled with me if he had."

"With all your smarts, Sal, you can be so damned trusting and naive."

"Believe me, I know. I trust him. I taped it. I'll play it for you.

Her eyes opened wide and she shook her head. "I don't believe you, Sal. You're furious that we've been bugged but you run around town taping everybody. Then you actually go out and record lunch with a Company spook."

"That's right," he said, not joining in the laughter that followed her initial response. "If Nixon can do it, so can I. They're just playing politics, I'm dealing with murder."

"By choice, Sal, and it's *we*, not I. *We're* dealing with murder."

"I know, I know."

She ate some of her omelet, said, "It got cold." She watched him across the table. He smeared jam on a piece of toast and idly chewed little pieces. No doubt about it, she told herself, she was terminally in love. She wondered whether the strain they'd been under lately was capable of ruining their personal relationship. She'd seen it before with friends, good, solid relationships warped by outside pressures to the extent that they could never be bent back to their original forms. She didn't want that to happen to them. Being bugged, facing MPD ire over breaking the rules, even contemplating her own murder did not frighten her. Losing Sal Morizio did.

"Sal," she said, "you said before that a weight had been lifted. Why did you say that? From what you've just told me, the weight should be heavier."

He shook his head and reached in his jacket for a cough drop. His throat was scratchy again. He sucked on the mint tablet as he said, "I want to open this thing up, Connie. That's where the weight has come from, from having to play in the dark. No more. You know what I thought about in the shower this morning?"

"No, I wasn't there." It was an unnecessary jab and she knew it.

He ignored it. "I was in the shower this morning and I said to myself, 'Sal, you're too old for this nonsense. Crusades are for kids.' That's what I told myself."

The shock at what she was certain he would say next hit her physically, caused her stomach to do a sudden flip-flop and her heart to perform a paradiddle between beats. He was going to drop it, and that was okay with her.

But then he said, "Do you know what I told myself

after I got out of the shower and was brushing my teeth?''

"No. I still wasn't there."

"I told myself that that was the whole point, that I'm not a kid and never had a crusade. I did what I was told, I grew up, got educated, made a good living, became a productive, solid citizen, made my parents proud. That's what it's all about, Connie. I never had a crusade as a kid. Now, I do, and I want to bust it wide open." He paused. "I'm going to see Trottier and Gibronski."

She felt the weight now. Her eyes teared up and she bit her lip. He placed his hands on hers and asked, "What's wrong?"

She avoided his look and said, "You're going to lose, Sal." She meant to say *we* but knew it didn't matter. If he lost, so did she.

He said, "I don't care if I lose. I just don't want to take you with me."

"And that's all I want," she said, fighting against erupting into a real, out-in-the-open cry.

He paid the check. When they were out on the street she said, "I didn't tell you that I was followed the other night when I went to test the caviar with Jill."

"Did you make the car, the driver?"

"No. I only noticed it on the way home and he kept his distance."

"You knew it was a man?"

"No, man, woman, I don't know."

"Why didn't you tell me?"

"I didn't want to compound your problems."

He jammed his hands deep into his topcoat pockets and said, "That settles it. I became a cop because I believe in white hats and black hats. I don't like bad people, want 'em off the streets, but I've been . . .

we've been treated like bad guys by our own people. I'm going to tell Gibronski and Trottier everything I know and insist upon an open investigation."

She looked at him through watery eyes and said, "Give me a kiss, Sal."

It was tentative at first—the sidewalk was crowded; two kids giggled at them. She wrapped her arms around him and squeezed hard. "I love you very much."

He held her at arms' length and said, "Trust me."

"I do, Sal, you know that, but you're up against something so big and powerful that it makes us ants. All they have to do is press down with their big toe and we're crushed."

"Nobody's going to step on anybody. I'll see you later."

He drove off thinking about what she'd said. He was glad his final words had been positive. The problem was that he didn't feel as positive as the words indicated. In fact, the weight was back bigger than ever, and he sensed that a giant calloused toe was about to cave in the roof of his car.

There was a pile of reports, publications, and memos on his desk when he arrived. He went through it quickly, tossing most of it in a wastebasket behind him. One piece of paper stopped him cold, however. It was from Communications, a UPI dispatch reporting that Nuri Hafez had been tried in Iran for the murder of Ambassador Geoffrey James, been found guilty, and had been executed by sword. There was a picture of Hafez that accompanied the dispatch. When Lake arrived a few minutes later, Morizio showed it to her. "Neat, huh?" he said.

"He looks so young."

"He was, or is."

"You don't think it happened?"

"I don't know what to believe." He gave her three assignments that would take up the afternoon and made it plain that he would like her to get on them right away. In other words, leave.

When she was gone, he called Chief Trottier's office. The chief was attending a conference in New York on organized crime and wouldn't be back until morning.

He next called the White House office of Dr. Werner Gibronski, was passed from one woman to another until he reached Gibronski's personal secretary. She was cordial, recalled who he was, and asked him to hold. She came back on the line and said, "Could you be here at two, Captain?"

"Yes, that'll be fine. Thank you." He gave her his birthdate and place of birth and hung up.

He debated taking Connie to lunch and rehearsing what he intended to say to Gibronski, but decided against it. The work he'd given her was important. More crucial was wanting to disengage her from what was about to happen. He needed her, but wanted to keep her away. Between the devil and the deep blue sea, which he found himself humming unenthusiastically on his way to a solo lunch at Clyde's, in Georgetown. He sat in the sunny atrium, had a cheeseburger, and made notes on a three-by-five card of items to bring up with Gibronski.

He noticed a car behind him as he drove to the White House, a copper-colored older Buick Regal driven by a man whose face he couldn't see through windshield glare. Morizio speeded up, then slammed on the brakes and pulled head-first into a parking spot. The Buick sped by, and Morizio got a fleeting look at the driver. He wore a tan down coat with a puffy collar bunched up around his neck and chin, and a dark cap pulled low over his forehead. Morizio read the plate, jotted it on the back of his list of items for the meeting, and continued to the White House where he was asked to wait in the reception area.

He assumed he'd be taken to Gibronski's office, where they'd last met. Instead, a perky young woman took him to a small room on Gibronski's floor but at an opposite end of the corridor. She immediately left, and Morizio took in the room. It looked like a spare office used by visiting big shots. The thick carpet was the color of dusty rose. The walls were covered in a plain silk fuchsia wallpaper. The only art was a nineteenth-century large framed lithograph of an early Washington scene—the White House standing on a snowy rise while skaters on a frozen pond waltzed in the foreground.

There was a small desk polished to burnished perfection, and two Colonnette-back armchairs upholstered in a heavy fabric only slightly darker than the carpet. Morizio sat in one of them, crossed his legs and waited. It seemed hours, was actually only ten minutes before the door opened and George Thorpe entered. He said loudly, "Captain Morizio. Good to see you again."

Morizio's response was not nearly as cordial. He said without taking the hand Thorpe offered, "I have an appointment with Dr. Gibronski."

"I know, he told me," said Thorpe. "He was called away suddenly and asked me to meet with you."

"I'm not interested in meeting with anyone except him."

"Then you might as well go home, Captain. Dr. Gibronski is gone and I'm here." He went to a single window and opened white vertical blinds. "It's a good day, Captain. The sun is shining, what birds are left are probably singing and you and I are alive and breathing." He turned, leaned against the windowsill and nodded his head to reinforce his satisfaction. "What is it about you, Sal, that keeps you from enjoying what you have instead of chasing after what you don't have?"

"I'm supposed to call you George now, right?"

"Call me what you wish. Call me Ishmael." He laughed heartily.

Morizio observed that Thorpe's eyes were heavy and bloodshot, and that there was a gravy stain on his shirt. He looked like he'd put on weight since the last time he saw him. There was a hint of stubble on his face and his hair needed combing.

Morizio got up, leaned on the back of the chair, and shook his head. "I don't get it, Thorpe, I really don't. I come here to see the President's top adviser and see you instead. You're not on the staff. You're British. This is the White House, America. Do you stand in for Dr. Gibronski for official occasions, too, or just for me?"

Thorpe slapped the top of his thighs, straightened up, and went to the other chair, sat in it and looked up at Morizio. "Why don't you sit down, Sal, and let's talk. I remember seeing a very good movie once, *Cool Hand Luke*. Did you see it? Paul Newman was in it and that actor, Kennedy. I believe he won an Academy Award. What I remember so vividly was a line Mr. Kennedy spoke to Mr. Newman after he'd tried to escape from a chain gang yet another time. Kennedy, who was the warden, said, 'What we got here is a failure to communicate.'" Thorpe said it in a southern accent. "I liked that line. I remembered it. That's what we have here, a failure to communicate, nothing more than that. Let me communicate with you, Sal."

Morizio was having trouble containing himself. He resented Thorpe being there instead of Gibronski, wanted nothing to do with the big Englishman, but wasn't sure if he should take a walk or hear what he had to say. He chose to stay. He sat, looked at Thorpe, and said, "Go ahead, communicate."

"I'll do my best. I'll try to be concise and clear so that when you leave here there is no confusion, no questioning what was meant."

"That'll be refreshing," Morizio said.

"Yes, it will, clarity is priceless. Directness."

"Highways instead of winding country roads."

Thorpe laughed again. "I'm flattered that you remembered, the way that screenwriter must feel for having written a line that at least one person remembered."

"Jesus," Morizio muttered under his breath. He said aloud, "I remember a line from a movie, too. Ever see *Network*, Thorpe?"

"Yes."

"I'm mad as hell, and I'm not going to take it any more."

"I recall that. The character Howard Beale said it, played by Peter Finch."

"You watch a lot of movies, huh?"

"Those that I know I'll like. What are you mad about, Sal?"

"Lots of things, Thorpe. Who's been following me and bugging my phones?"

He adopted an expression on his wide face of exaggerated shock. "How terrible," he said.

Morizio sensed a laugh being stifled and wanted to take a swing. He took a few breaths instead, said, "You know nothing about it?"

"God, no. I don't believe in electronic surveillance."

"Does Dr. Gibronski? Somebody does because it's been happening."

"I'm sorry, I really am. Miss Lake, too?"

"Leave her out of it."

"Certainly. You really are angry, aren't you? At whom?"

"Whoever tapped into my phone and does a lousy job tailing me in a car, whoever's been playing games and covering up."

"That sounds serious. Covering up what, Sal?"

"Goddamn it," Morizio said. He got up and went to the window, played with the wand that controlled the blinds, turned, and said, "Is this room bugged, Thorpe?"

"I rather doubt it."

"It doesn't matter. You know anything about Paul Pringle?"

Thorpe pressed his cheeks together with his fingers and grunted. "I'm not familiar with the name."

"You should read the papers instead of watching movies. He worked security at the British Embassy and was . . ."

"Oh, yes, I did hear about that. Dreadful thing that happened to him. Drugs, I heard."

"No drugs. He didn't use them."

"I only know what I read."

"I doubt that."

"Think what you will. Was he a friend of yours?"

"I knew him. He was killed because he knew something about Ambassador James's death that somebody didn't want spread around."

"You know that for certain?"

"I'd bet on it."

"Interesting theory. I'd love to know what you base it upon."

"I'm sure you would. Tell me something, Thorpe, what's the connection between James's and Pringle's murders? I figure that's a pretty safe question."

"Why?"

"Because I figure you know the answer."

It was the same change of expression Morizio had witnessed on Thorpe's face the night he visited Morizio's apartment, the wide, forced pleasant grin suddenly running into a face of granite, like one of those plastic boxes filled with colored liquid that creates shapes when you turn it upside down. His eyes were hard—Lake had said it was those eyes that caused her to think he'd do in his own mother—and they pierced Morizio. "Sit down, Captain," he said.

"Look, I . . ."

"Sit down!"

"I don't take orders from you."

"You take orders from your chief and from your president and from anyone else in a position of authority, Captain Morizio, and I am telling you to sit down."

There were many things that almost came out of Morizio. He stifled them all and sat.

"Now, you called for an appointment with Dr. Gibronski. He has asked me to represent him. What was it you wished to ask, to say?"

"It's for him, not you."

"You're being absurdly difficult. Are you always like that?"

Morizio smiled. "Difficult but adorable."

"Miss Lake."

"Don't push, Thorpe. I came here to tell Dr. Gibronski and anybody else involved in this thing that I don't like being jerked around. I don't like funny little gadgets in my telephones or goons making a right whenever I do. I know more about James's murder and Pringle's than you think."

"Perhaps you do. I'd love to hear."

"You will. I'll make another appointment with Dr. Gibronski."

"Suit yourself. Do you know what bothers me most about all of this, Sal?"

"Captain Morizio."

"Childish temper, certainly not befitting a man of your rank. I like you, Captain, yes, I really do, and that's what makes this so difficult. I like your Miss Lake, too . . ." Morizio started to respond but Thorpe held up a hand. "But you don't seem to understand where you fit in. Perhaps it's explainable. Until now you've functioned in rather restricted parameters, doing your job, keeping things moving, going by the book. But there is no book for this project. The book is written as the story unfolds. There is no index to consult for guidance when a new aspect of it arises. This is very big, Captain Morizio, very very big, which is why it is being handled in ways outside of your area of understanding. I sympathize with you. I would act and feel the same way were I in your shoes. But lacking understanding really shouldn't be an impediment to proper behavior."

"Proper behavior?" Morizio guffawed.

Thorpe's voice was the hardest it'd been since he entered the room. *"Taking orders.* Does that register with you?"

"Who do I take them from?"

"Your boss. Unless I am gravely mistaken, Chief Trottier has been explicit in his orders to you regarding the death of Ambassador James. You were told to do nothing unless instructed. You were ordered to ignore it, forget it and get on with your own area of knowledge and interest."

"What about my friend, Paul Pringle? Do I ignore that?"

Thorpe blinked and rubbed his chin. He was obviously exasperated and wanted Morizio to know it. He said, "There are times when my patience amazes me. It's so simple, but you insist on confusing it. If you keep doing that, Sal, you'll regret it."

"Now threats."

"Warnings from someone who likes you and your Miss Lake."

"Damn it, Thorpe, I told you . . ."

"Listen to me, Morizio, and listen carefully. I no longer have patience. I have a job to do, too, one I take seriously. I receive orders just as you do. The difference is that I follow them. If your own chief of police does not command enough respect from you to have his orders followed, let me invoke a higher authority."

"Like who?"

"Like me." He said it slowly and deliberately, and turned his index finger from pointing at Morizio to pointing at himself. You are dealing with matters that impact upon two major world nations. Your precious little pique at the death of a friend, your ridiculous curiosity about a death that doesn't concern you within an embassy is leading you into very deep and dangerous waters, for you and for . . ."

"Thorpe . . ."

". . . and for your Miss Connie Lake." He boomed it out, and the force of his voice caused Morizio to pull away.

"Take a vacation, Captain Morizio. Get away, relax, play golf, swim, make love—but get away. Forget an ambassador and a second-line security agent ever existed." He spoke softly. "Do it for me, Sal, for your friend. Take the highway. There are so many unexpected rewards. Winding country roads can be slippery and treacherous. Small covered bridges collapse at unexpected times, animals cross the road, drunk drivers fail to navigate the turns."

181

Morizio got up and went to the door. He stood facing it and took a series of deep, frustrated breaths.

"I'm sincerely grieved it comes to this," said Thorpe from his chair. "I truly do like you, thought we might become drinking friends at Timberlakes, or Piccadilly or wherever you felt comfortable. Chums. I thought we might become *chums*."

Morizio, now under control, slowly turned and grinned. "You're an interesting guy, Thorpe, a great case study. I also think you're a psychopath. Drinking buddies? Never drink with a psychopath. Rule One, basic street smarts. Say hello to Dr. Gibronski."

"I shall. The communication has failed, hasn't it?"

"Yup."

"I tried."

"You did."

"I regret the failure."

"You do?"

"Yes, and so will you."

"You know what you've been doing here, Thorpe? You've been threatening a police officer. I could arrest you for that."

It started as a low rumble deep inside his large belly, then slowly bubbled to the throat and out the mouth. It was the cruelest, most anger-provoking laugh Morizio had ever experienced. He was mad, frustrated and, most important, felt total impotence. He slammed the door behind him and went directly home.

It was midnight when the phone rang in Morizio's apartment. He reached over Connie Lake and fumbled for the phone in the darkness. "Hello," he said.

"Captain Morizio?"

"Yes."

"This is Chief Trottier. I want you in my office within the hour."

"I thought you were out of town until tomorrow."

"I returned on urgent business. Officer Lake. I tried her home number but no one answered. Do you know her whereabouts?"

"I, ah . . . Yes, I do."

"Please bring her with you."

"What is this about, Chief?"

"Within the hour, at my office."

Trottier's message to them was simple and direct when they arrived. "I am suspending both of you from active duty for insubordination, for failure to follow direct orders from your superior, for conduct unbecoming officers in the Metropolitan Police Department, and for gross negligence in your duties. Suspension will be *with* pay until a board of inquiry is convened and the charges can be formally investigated. You are to turn in your weapons and badges and vacate your offices by eight A. M. Further, you are to remain away from this building until the board resolves this matter, and are to have no contacts with the press. Are there any questions?"

"I'll fight this, sir," Morizio said.

Trottier relaxed the rigid posture he'd maintained during his speech. He said, "I don't like this, Captain but you force my hand. I don't understand it but evidently you do. You've been given every opportunity to avoid this but you've chosen to go in your own direction. I wish you hadn't, and I say the same thing to you, Officer Lake."

She said nothing.

Trottier slumped in a swivel chair behind his desk and rubbed his eyes with both hands. "Can I make a suggestion?"

"What's that?" Morizio asked.

"Take a vacation, a long one. Get out of Washington. Your relationship is well known around here. Go away together, far away. I promise you the suspension with pay will hold for as long as you want to stay away. You've done good jobs up until now, and I'd hate to lose you permanently, but be smart. The pressure's been on you, and maybe that's why you've gotten into this mess. Go away, on MPD. When you come back the pressure will be off and we can all get on with business as usual."

Morizio started to ask a question but Trottier stood and waved him off. "Just listen to someone else for a change," he said. "I know your father was a good police officer, and you've been, too. Don't toss it all away. I'm very tired. Good night."

Connie cried on the way home. Morizio asked why. She said, "It's embarrassing. I've never been fired from anything, never even spent two minutes in the classroom corner."

"I'm sorry."

"There's nothing for you to be sorry about," she said. "I'm sorry that it happened, not about anything you've done."

"Pigheaded Morizio," he grumbled as he parked the car and came around to open the door for her.

"I love you," she said.

"Terrific."

They sat in silence in his living room. He'd put on a tape of Samuel Barber's Adagio for Strings, and the heavy, sad music softly embraced the still, dark room.

"That's too sad," Connie said, referring to the music.

"Fitting," he said.

"Let's put on something lively, something positive."

"Why?"

"Because I don't want to be dragged down, Sal."

He laughed. "How much more dragged down can you be?"

She twisted on the couch and grabbed his face between her hands. "Let's fight it, Sal. We have nothing to lose now. We've been raped and I'll be damned if I'll just lay back and enjoy it. I'll be damned if I'll have my reputation smeared this way." She jumped up and kicked a throw pillow that had fallen to the floor. "Let's go after it."

He hadn't touched his drink. He placed the glass on the table, stood and looked toward the bedroom. "I'm tired, Connie. I just want to sleep."

"Then that's what we'll do, and tomorrow we'll turn everything upside down until we find out what it is you've been after all along."

"Ants," he said wearily.

"Ants?"

"You said we were ants. We are."

"And ants are hard working, Sal. 'Take a vacation,' Trottier said. He's gutless, Sal, they all are. We'll make it work. I promise we will."

They clung to each other in bed, then made love with an urgency that had been recently lacking. She fell asleep as he stroked her long blonde hair.

"The most beautiful girl in the world," he thought. "I'm sorry."

19

Lake slept late the next morning: "I might as well take advantage of this," she said sleepily. Morizio was out of the apartment by seven. He grabbed a bowl of corn flakes and coffee at a local diner and swung by MPD. There he pulled from his desk any papers he felt he needed, shoving them into a cardboard transfer file box, including a dispatch from Traffic Control on which was written "Federal—Official," identifying the owner of the car that had followed Morizio to the White House. "Big help," he muttered as he packed his telephone book, personal photographs and memorabilia and office Dopp kit into a large leather briefcase. He took a last look over his shoulder as he stood at the door, and went to the homicide detective's lounge. A friend, Detective Fred Scheiner, was asleep in a battered leather chair. "Hey Fred, wake up," Morizio said.

Scheiner opened one eye and growled, "What?" They didn't call him Jolly Fred around MPD for nothing.

"The Pringle murder," Morizio said. "Let me see the file."

"Why?"

"I have some leads to check against what you have."

Scheiner pulled himself out of the chair and walked into a large room where one wall was lined with scratched and stained gray file cabinets. Morizio followed. Scheiner opened a drawer and withdrew a manila folder. Typed on it was *Hom. Pringle. D.C. #2746.* He handed it to Morizio.

Scheiner left the room and Morizio sat at a long table. He pulled a pad and pen from his pocket and made notes. When he was finished, he put the file in its drawer and returned to the lounge where Scheiner and two other detectives were seated at a table and eating bagels.

"Thanks, Fred," Morizio said.

"Sure. What've you got?"

"Not much, I guess. Anything new from your end?"

"Why?"

"No leads, unless Narcotics comes up with something. What's the word from up top?"

"To let it sit," said Scheiner. "It'll stay active but there's other fish to fry."

Morizio picked up the file transfer box and started out the door.

"Moving?" asked Scheiner.

"Rearranging."

Scheiner laughed. "How's Connie?"

"Good. Quiet night?"

Another detective, Nick Vasile, yawned and stretched. "Just another pleasant evening in the nation's capital, Sal. A bustling metropolis by day but when the sun goes down, all the good, solid, decent dogooders run home and out come the night folk. A couple rapes, three homicides involving two citizens nobody'll miss, and a gay Supreme Court clerk busted for soliciting. Piece of cake. Getting paid for this job is criminal.''

Morizio remembered that he'd promised Lake to empty her desk of certain items and went to the bullpen outside his office. It had been empty when he arrived, but now there was a scattering of people starting their day at MPD. Morizio's secretary, Ginnie, was one of them. ''What are you doing in so early?'' he asked.

''You wanted that report typed by noon,'' she said. ''It's long.''

''Oh, right. Thanks, I appreciate it.''

''I'll try to get it to you before lunch.''

''Good. If I'm not here, leave it on my desk.''

''Sure. What's in the box?''

''Junk. See you later.''

He sat at Lake's desk and tried to remove what she wanted without arousing attention. The few times he glanced over his shoulder, Ginnie was watching him. Who was he kidding? In an hour the word of their suspension would be all over MPD. Some would laugh, some would be saddened, some would rejoice and chalk it up to being stupid enough to allow romance into the office, others would immediately calculate what it meant to their chances for advancement. ''The hell with them,'' Morizio mumbled as he left the bullpen and went to his car. ''You, I'll miss,'' he said to his parking space as he backed out and headed for his apartment.

Lake was up when he arrived. ''Look at this,'' he said, showing her the notes he'd taken from Pringle's Homicide file, pointing specifically to a word he'd written—''Sami.''

''So?'' she asked.

''How many guys named Sami do you know?''

''A few.''

''Sammy, maybe, with a *Y*, but not Sami with an *I*.

188

Sami Abdu, the Iranian journalist. It was written on the same piece of paper that had my name. Paul must have intended to see Abdu when he was here. Why?''

"Did you mention Paul to Abdu at the luncheon?''

"No. Paul just wrote 'Sami,' not Sami Abdu. When you just write a first name, you know the person pretty well. Am I right?''

"Sure.''

"Abdu knew the Hafez family in Iran. Hafez skipped the night of James's murder with the limo and holed up in the Iranian Embassy. Maybe Abdu knows all about that.''

"It's possible.''

"I'll find out.''

"Good. Want breakfast?''

"I had some.''

"Have some more.''

It was over a second cup of coffee that Lake announced, "Let's go to Copenhagen over Thanksgiving.''

"To visit your grandmother?''

"Sure, but that's not the only reason. I don't think we'll ever piece this thing together unless we find out about Inga Lindstrom. Do you agree?''

"Sure I do.''

"We could try and see her.''

"I want to talk to Paul's widow, Ethel, too. We could go to London.''

"We could do it all in one shot.''

"Yeah, I guess we could. You know, maybe we could get some help from that Danish cop I got friendly with when he was here. Leif Mikkelsen. Remember him?''

"Sure I do. Good idea.''

Connie took a deep, satisfied breath and bit her lower lip. Sunlight through the kitchen window sent dancing patterns of light across her face. She wore no makeup, seldom did. There was a natural healthy glow to her face that rendered the use of anything artificial overkill. Her wheat-colored hair hung loose and long over the shoulders of a teal robe that was loosely sashed about her. She always looked good to Morizio, but there were moments like this that especially captured his mental, emotional, and anatomical attention.

"It's strange being here at this hour of a weekday morning," he said. "I'm not used to it."

"It's kind of nice," she said.

"You're handling this better than I am."

"Why do you say that?"

"You look relaxed, contented. Why are you smiling?"

"I'm applying the glass half-full theory to what's happened instead of half empty. I wanted time for us over Thanksgiving and now we'll have it. I know it's not the ideal way to have it come about, but as long as it did, we might as well take advantage of it. It could be a nice trip, Sal, productive and relaxed. We could use it."

He sat back and frowned. "I promised my mother I'd see her over the holiday. Maybe I should go up now, spend a day or two with her in lieu of Thanksgiving."

"Will she be terribly disappointed?"

"No, she's a glass half full person, too. Besides, there's plenty of family for her to cook for, at least a dozen."

Lake smiled, leaned forward, and took his hands. "I'll go with you. We could go up tonight. I haven't seen your mother in awhile."

"Good. Let's do it. She loves surprises. In the meantime."

She raised her eyebrows and tilted her head.

"I'm suddenly in need of a nap and some serious cuddling."

She let loose with a throaty, wicked laugh and said, "Beneath that conservative, businesslike façade is an inveterate lecher."

"Just trying to get with the half full philosophy," he said, taking her hand and leading her from the kitchen.

"Well?" his mother said after she'd registered shock at finding them at the front door, and after they'd settled down in the living room of her house on K Street, "You have news, don't you?"

Morizio looked at Lake, laughed and said, "Lots of it, Mom, but nothing you'd be interested in." He told her that they were working closely together on a case that he couldn't discuss, and were taking a vacation over Thanksgiving to London and Copenhagen. "That's why we came up now," he said, "because I won't be here."

His mother, who had gracefully aged into a stunning older woman with coal-black hair pulled back into a tight chignon, appeared to be saddened by the news. "I hope you understand, Mom. I'd love to be here . . . we both would . . . but . . . ."

"I thought you were here to say you were getting married."

Morizio coughed, Connie laughed. "It's okay by me," she said.

"We'll surprise you one day," Morizio said.

"You're not a kid anymore, Sal," said Mrs. Morizio.

"I'd love a drink," Morizio said. He went to the kitchen where he made drinks for himself and Connie, poured a glass of red wine for his mother. He could hear his mother talking about how she worried about his growing older without a good wife.

"Here's to good health to everyone," he said as he returned from the kitchen. They toasted. "And don't you worry about your son, Mrs. Morizio, he's doing just fine."

"Is he?" she asked Connie.

She nodded.

"Good," said his mother. "I'll whip up some spaghetti with shrimp sauce. It's his favorite, Connie. Did he tell you that?"

"Yes, he did." Lake got up, put her arm around the older woman's shoulder, and said, "I'll help. I'm a good second woman in the kitchen. I know how to stay out of the way. Besides, you're working with one arm." They disappeared into the kitchen, leaving Morizio alone with his drink. He wished he had some good news to bring his mother, a promotion, plans for marriage, a pending grandchild. In fact, he realized, he had nothing to report but trouble, and he was glad he'd decided to mention nothing of what had happened. Hand-in-hand with that was a strengthened resolve to clear his and Lake's name. If it meant a lot to them, it would mean the world to his mother.

The return flight to Washington a day and a half later was uneventful, except for an Associated Press item Lake discovered in the Boston *Globe* she'd been handed by the flight attendant. It was a small story buried deep inside the paper. The headline read: D.C. CATERER IN DRUG BUST.

One of Washington, D.C.'s most successful and respected caterers was arrested late last night at his Georgetown offices and has been charged with possession of, and conspiracy to sell cocaine. Officials confiscated an estimated $2 million worth of the controlled substance from his office.

The accused, Berge Nordkild, is a fixture in Washington's social scene, catering some of its poshest events for political and industrial leaders and organizations. In addition, he is a leading wholesaler of imported gourmet foods to retail outlets throughout the northeast.

A spokesman for the Drug Enforcement Agency, Fred Mayer, whose agency worked closely with Washington Metropolitan Police Department in the investigation leading to the arrest, said, "Mr. Nordkild has been under investigation for some time. We consider his illegal operation to be a major one in the eastern United States, and are confident that a significant pipeline of illegal drugs has been disrupted."

There was, of course, a larger story in the *Washington Post,* and Nordkild's arrest was reported on local television. Nordkild's attorney, Joseph Turner, one of Washington's best, issued a flat denial of the charges against his client and had asked the court to reduce the original bail of $750,000 to $50,000.

They unpacked, made coffee, and discussed the news about Nordkild. Morizio wanted to call the caterer's office but Lake dissuaded him. "He won't talk to you or anyone, Sal," she said, "not with something like this pending. Maybe in a couple of days. Besides, we've got other things to do today. I want to call Georgia Watson at the American Petroleum Institute." Connie and Georgia had been classmates at Washington State University, and although they saw little of each other in Washington, D.C., Connie was hopeful that Georgia, who worked in the institute's research department, could dig up something on Geoffrey James's Scottish oil interests.

"I also want to book our trip," Connie said.

Morizio called the Piccadilly Pub, asked when Johnny would be tending bar and was told Johnny was on days that week. Morizio decided to have lunch there. Johnny wouldn't know about the suspension, which would allow Morizio to mix a personal approach with an official one.

They agreed to meet at Lake's apartment at six.

Piccadilly was filling up fast when Morizio arrived at 12:30, mostly businessmen and government workers from the area. He perched on a corner barstool, greeted Johnny, ordered a Beefeater martini on the rocks. He watched Johnny work, a consummate pro, juggling a barrage of orders from waitresses at the service bar, taking care of customers at the bar, and keeping up with housekeeping, ringing sales on an ancient cash register, a captain of a small efficient ship in which every inch of space counted, every item in its proper place if it were to navigate the heavy seas of a brisk lunch trade.

There was a lull; customers served, waitresses satisfied for the moment, glasses washed and stacked. Johnny, who was very tall and thin, and who wore tight black pants, a white shirt, and a clip-on black bow tie, came to Morizio's end of the bar. "Well, Captain, how's things?"

"Not bad, Johnny. You?"

"Never changes. Fill 'em up, wash 'em out." He laughed, causing a prominent Adam's apple to go into action. "Anything new about our friend?"

"No, but I thought you might help."

"Not much for me to offer, Captain, except condolences. You two were good buddies, I know."

"Johnny, let me ask you something. They've accused Paul of using drugs. Did you ever see anything that would support that?"

He rubbed his chin and looked toward the ceiling. "No, can't say that I have. Not the type, if you know what I mean. Paul was . . . well, he enjoyed his ale and

. . . Ooops, excuse me.'' Three waitresses had suddenly apppeared at the service bar and verbalized their orders simultaneously. It wouldn't be easy talking to Johnny, never was with a busy bartender, and Morizio wondered whether he'd do better later that night. He was about to take a table when Johnny returned. "Drugs," he said. "Nasty business, but not for him. I'd bet my tips on it."

"That's the way I feel," Morizio said.

"I told the other guy the same thing yesterday."

"Who's that?"

"The British investigator who was in asking about Paul. Big, burly fellow, pleasant. Put 'em away, too, he does, four bourbons while he sat here." He laughed.

"Thorpe," Morizio thought. He asked.

"Never got his last name, called himself George. Works for the British Embassy."

"Does he?"

"Another, Captain?"

"Yeah, sure."

Johnny refilled Morizio's glass and took care of other customers. When he returned Morizio said, "This investigator from the Embassy, George, you said, what was he asking?"

Johnny again assumed a thoughtful expression. "He just wanted to know about Paul when he was here, who he saw, hung around with. I mentioned you, as a matter of fact."

"Who else?"

"His buddies. He had a lot of 'em as you know, and the Arab."

"What Arab?"

"Big heavy guy, as big as the investigator. They used to meet up here, not a lot but sometimes. The Arab left a package for Paul with me now and then."

"You told the British Embassy investigator that?"

"Sure. I do something wrong?"

Morizio laughed. "Of course not. You don't know the Arab's name, do you?"

Johnny shook his head and looked around to see if anyone needed another drink. He said to Morizio, "Paul just said he was a friend." He chuckled. "The Arab drank pretty good, too. I thought Moslems didn't drink."

"They don't, unless there's a reason."

"He must have had plenty of reasons, all right."

"Thanks," Morizio said, tossing a ten dollar bill on the bar.

"On me," said Johnny.

"The hell it is," Morizio said. "You'll get me suspended."

Morizio didn't stay for lunch. He went to Fio's on Northwest Sixteenth where he had homemade pasta in tomato sauce, a side order of oiled, garlicky vegetables, and a glass of wine. He wanted to talk to Connie but didn't know where to reach her. He tried Shevlin Travel but they hadn't seen her. He called the American Petroleum Institute and was told Miss Watson was out to lunch, probably with Connie, he thought. He fished out Sami Abdu's card and called the number on it. No answer.

The true fascination of his suspension started to set in. He wanted to go to his office at MPD but couldn't. He'd lost his base, was hanging around trying to kill time. He considered going to a movie but knew he wouldn't enjoy it. He ended up walking through the Smithsonian's Air and Space Museum for an hour, then drove to Connie's apartment where he let himself in, turned on TV, and watched an old movie, calling Abdu's number at every commercial break.

Connie walked in promptly at six. "How'd it go?" she asked.

"Paul used to meet Sami Abdu at Piccadilly," he said, "and Abdu gave him packages. Thorpe was in there yesterday asking about Paul. The bartender told him about Abdu."

Lake sat on the couch and kicked off her shoes. "What do you make of it?" she asked.

"I haven't figured it out yet. I've been watching TV."

She smiled, came to him, and kissed his forehead. "Well," she said, "I accomplished a lot. I had lunch with Georgia Watson. She's on the case, promises to call me tomorrow with what she can find. And, my good friend, we are booked to London and Copenhagen." She pulled two packets from her purse and handed them to him. He opened the one with his name on it and went through it. They were leaving the day after tomorrow, on Pan Am's evening flight to London, and would connect three days later on SAS to Copenhagen. Their hotels in both cities were confirmed—the May Fair in London and the d'Angleterre in Copenhagen. He put everything on a table next to his chair, looked at Lake, frowned, picked up the airline ticket again, and examined it closely. "First class?" he said.

"Yup. We are going first class, Captain."

"What are you, crazy? It's a fortune."

"What better way to spend a fortune than on ourselves. Have you ever flown first class before?"

"No, have you?"

"No, and I'm very excited about it."

He sighed and sat back. "I don't know, Connie," he said.

"About what?"

"About . . . well, I feel as though I'm losing control

over everything." He told her about his anxiety that afternoon, not having an office to go to. "I almost went to a movie, in the afternoon of all things."

She laughed, sat on the chair's arm and rubbed his neck. "I know, Sal, I know. That's why we have to clear this up once and for all. I just think we might as well live well in the bargain. It's the best revenge, isn't it, living well?"

"That's what they say, but this might all be premature," he said. "The reason for going to Copenhagen is to see Lindstrom. Maybe she's not there. She travels a lot."

Lake smiled like a contented cat. "She's there. I called, said I represented a catering house in suburban Washington and was considering making a trip to talk business with her. Her secretary—I suppose that's who I talked to—she said 'Ms. Lindstrom expects to be here for the rest of the month.' See? Even that works out."

He grinned. "You're all right, Lake."

"Even better than that, Morizio. I'm terrific. Now, what about Thorpe asking about Paul at Piccadilly?"

"I'm assuming it was Thorpe. Johnny never got a name but said he called himself George, was British and big, drank a lot. Who else? I've been trying to call Abdu all afternoon but he's been out."

"Try him again."

"Let's just stop over there. I have his address."

"But if he's not there . . ."

"If he is, I'd just as soon see him face-to-face. I don't want to be put off on the phone. I'll go. You make dinner."

"Sure, and I'll eat it alone. I'll come with you, then you can buy me dinner someplace fancy to inaugurate our vacation."

"You call this a vacation?"

"I call it taking what I can get. Give me a minute to freshen up."

Sami Abdu lived in an older two-story house off Connecticut Avenue, close to the National Zoological Park. Morizio and Lake parked across the street. It was dark outside; light from every window in the house projected a yellow patchwork quilt on the sloping front lawn.

"He's home," Morizio said.

"Somebody's home," Lake said.

They rang the bell. It was answered almost immediately by Abdu. He had the bug-eyed, sweaty look of someone who'd been interrupted in the midst of a nefarious act, or who'd just stumbled on a dead body. Either way, he was happy, even relieved at seeing Morizio. "Captain, come in, please come in."

Morizio started to introduce Connie but Abdu was too preoccupied to listen. He quickly led them along a hallway carpeted with layers of Oriental rugs to a small living room crowded with heavy furniture. It was in total disarray, papers and clothing strewn everywhere, tables upside down, drapes ripped from their rods. "Look," Abdu said, spreading his arms wide to indicate the room. "They have been here."

"Who?" Lake asked.

Abdu shrugged, picked up what was left of a red-and-white ceramic vase that had fallen to the floor and threw it against the couch. "Look what they've done to me."

"Somebody wants something you have pretty bad," Morizio said. "What about the other rooms?"

"The same."

Morizio thought Abdu was about to cry. He slapped him on the shoulder and said, "Let's take a look." Abdu was right. Every room in the house had been turned upside down, including the bathroom and kitchen. They returned to the living room. Lake and Morizio sat on a couch while Abdu paced the room, which wasn't easy. He had to thread his way through furniture and debris.

"All right, Mr. Abdu, what do you think they were after?"

"How would I know?" he said, wringing his hands.

"Is anything missing that you know of?" asked Lake.

"No. There was money in the bedroom but it is still there. I have works of art they broke. Pigs."

"What about information, Mr. Abdu? Letters, research, stories you were working on?"

Abdu thought for a moment. He sat heavily in a large upholstered armchair and shook his head. "There is nothing to interest anyone except me."

Morizio glanced at Connie before saying, "You fed a lot of information to Paul Pringle. What was it?"

Abdu straightened and ran his hand over the front of his white silk shirt, his fingers fluffing a mass of black chest hair exposed through its unbuttoned top. He appeared to be offended at what Morizio had said, and confused. He adopted a haughty expression and said, "I don't know what you're talking about."

"I think you do, Mr. Abdu. You used to meet Pringle at a pub called Piccadilly, near Chevy Chase Circle on Connecticut Avenue."

Morizio and Lake waited for a response. The confusion increased on his face. "How do you know?" he asked weakly.

"A lot of people told me. What did you and Paul Pringle meet for, Mr. Abdu? What did you give him when you met?"

"Nothing." His voice raised in pitch. "We were friends, that's all. Friends."

"Let's stop playing games," Morizio said. "Look around you. You're a marked man. Whoever broke in here knows what I know, that you were feeding information to Paul Pringle. Pringle's dead, had his throat narrowed, his face bloodied, and enough heroin pumped into him to shut him down. You're next."

It was chilly in the room. Two windows were partially open, and cold air poured through them. Abdu started to sweat, which spurred Morizio to continue. "Pringle was involved in some pretty heavy things, Abdu. The people he was involved with don't play by the same rules you and I do. There are no rules, no niceties." He thought of Thorpe. "It's called the straight road philosophy. You get on it and reach your destination as fast and simply as possible. Something . . . someone gets in your way, you run them over, leave them spots on the road. Understand?"

Abdu visibly was trying to collect his thoughts and to pull himself together. He ran his fingertips over his forehead, looked at the moisture on them, then forced a smile. "I am not being an hospitable host. A drink?" he asked.

"Keep your drink," Morizio snapped. "You're a dead man, Abdu, and all the booze in the world won't change that. There's only one thing will, and that's me. I can make you sure you live, or I can leave you out on the highway. Your choice."

Abdu looked at Morizio, then at Connie. He raised his hands in a gesture of helplessness. "What did I do?" he asked.

"You tell us," Connie said.

"I did nothing. Pringle wanted to know certain things and I told him. Is that a crime?"

"Depends," Morizio said, "but it doesn't matter. The important thing is to tell me what you told him and let me figure out a way to keep everybody's skin in one piece. What did Pringle want to know?''

"About Hafez.''

"Nuri Hafez?''

"Yes, and his family. I knew them in Iran.''

"Yeah, you told me that.''

"That's all, Captain, nothing else. When Hafez came here to work with Ambassador James I became his friend. Does that make sense? We are Iranians in a foreign country. I helped him.''

"How. What'd you do for him?''

"Nothing specific. He had questions, problems, and he came to me.''

"What kind of problems?''

"Adjustment problems.''

Morizio shook his head. "I don't think you value your life very highly, Mr. Abdu.''

"Why do you say that?''

"You're lying. You don't believe me when I say that this mess you're sitting in is only a warning. It doesn't matter whether they found anything or not. What does matter, my friend, is what you know, what you told Pringle. He's dead because of what *he* knew, and you're next.''

Morizio's words moved Abdu physically, as though he'd poked him in the neck. Morizio narrowed his eyes and said in the concerned tones of a close friend, "Let me help you, Sami. I'm the only one who can. We're narrowing in on who killed Ambassador James and Paul Pringle. We can make it right. Officer Lake here will back me up.''

"Officer?'' Abdu said. "You are a policeman?''

"Woman,'' Connie said, smiling.

"Of course,'' He stood and extended his hand. "My pleasure. Please excuse me.'' He left the room.

"Go with him," Morizio told Lake. She did, and Morizio quickly moved through the living room, picking up papers from a desk, rummaging through a wastebasket. He had to assume that the information Pringle got from Abdu had to do with Pringle's CIA role within the British Embassy. It could also have been for his own personal use, but Morizio doubted it. Somehow Abdu's claim of simply being a friend to Hafez, one Iranian helping another, didn't play for Morizio. There had to be more.

When Connie and Abdu returned, Abdu was carrying a large water glass filled with whiskey. He extended it toward Morizio and said, "You are sure you want nothing?"

"All I want is the truth, Mr. Abdu, so that no one else, starting with you, gets killed. How much did Pringle pay you for the information you gave him about Nuri Hafez?"

"Not much."

Confirming that he'd been paid anything told Morizio that Pringle wanted the information for the CIA, not for his personal use. "A thousand a month?" Morizio said.

Abdu laughed. "If it had been that much I would have given him more."

"How much?"

"It depended. He paid me for each thing I told him, five hundred dollars here, a little more or less there."

"Did he tell you what he intended to do with it?"

"No." Abdu took a healthy swig from his glass and winced as the warm, brown alcohol hit his throat and stomach. Connie did, too, as she watched him.

"What *did* you tell him about Nuri Hafez?" Morizio asked.

Abdu shrugged. "His family, what he does in the embassy."

"How would you know what he did in the embassy?" Lake asked.

"He would tell me. We were friends."

"What'd he tell you?" asked Morizio.

"That he . . . what does it matter?"

"You're a whore, Abdu," Morizio said.

"I resent that," Abdu said.

"You want me to pay you? You want five hundred dollars to tell me about Nuri Hafez like Pringle paid you? Jesus, I'm here to save your miserable life and you're shaking me down."

"I said nothing."

"Good," said Morizio. He turned to Lake, "Come on, let him sit in this mess and wait for the big guy with the steel wire."

"Wait."

Abdu sat in a chair, defeat on his face. "If I tell you," he said, "can you promise me that you will protect me?"

Morizio and Lake were both thinking of the same thing, of their suspensions. Connie said, "We'll do everything we can."

"That is not a promise."

"It's the closest thing you have to a promise, Abdu."

Abdu finished what was in his glass, looked around his living room and grimaced. "Nuri had business with the ambassador." He said it so softly that Lake and Morizio had to ask him to repeat it, which he did.

"What sort of business?" Morizio asked.

"Caviar," Abdu said.

"Smuggling?" Connie asked.

"Yes. Nuri and his brother made a deal with a fishing combine in Iran. Instead of caviar being supplied to the Ayatollah's fishing minister, it was sent directly out of Iran. The fishermen were paid ten times what the government would pay them. Everyone took a risk. To be caught doing such a thing would mean death, but the rewards were large enough."

"Wait a minute," Morizio said. "Are you saying that the British ambassador to the United States, Geoffrey James, was in on this?"

Abdu looked at the floor. "Yes," he said.

"They split the profits?" asked Lake.

"I don't know the financial arrangement."

"Except yours," Morizio said. "Your friend, Nuri Hafez, told you this and you sold it to Paul Pringle."

Yes.

"Some friend."

"I must live, just as you must live. This is an expensive city."

Morizio waited a few moments before responding. He knew he had the Iranian on the ropes. He was telling tales out of school, was admitting to selling out a friend and a countryman. He was also exhibiting basic instincts—survival, fear. The break-in had shaken him; he believed that his life was in jeopardy. Honor was one thing. Waking up in the morning, taking a deep breath, and discovering that the lungs worked was another.

"Did Nuri Hafez kill Ambassador James?" Morizio asked.

Abdu's head snapped back. He looked at Morizio as though he'd uttered a blasphemy, had defiled an Arab woman, or feasted on pork at noon during Ramadan.

"I didn't say he did," Morizio said, "but everybody else does. I'm asking."

"It does not matter," Abdu said.

"It did to Ambassador James," Lake said.

Abdu stood and pressed his hands to his corpulent belly, as if there was something inside struggling to come out. "When the ambassador died," he said slowly and softly, "Nuri knew that he would be blamed. It did not matter if it was a heart attack, as it was first thought. The ambassador, Nuri's protector, was dead. He came to me and asked for my help."

"You gave it to him," Connie said.

"Of course. He was my friend. I had a key to the Iranian Embassy. I took him there."

"You?"

"Yes. I did not see him again after that."

Lake stepped close to Abdu. "Did he kill the ambassador?" she asked.

"I told you it did not matter. Once he was dead, Nuri had lost all protection, as though his house had blown away, leaving him to the winds."

"Very poetic," Morizio said.

"We are a poetic people," said Abdu.

"And practical," Lake said.

"That, too," said Abdu.

"Sal, please," said Lake. Morizio stifled a smile. She knew what was going on and was playing the game. She continued. "He didn't do anything wrong, Sal. He's a victim. He's been broken into, robbed, violated."

He sneered and punched the back of a chair. "Sure, take it easy, she says. See what happens, Abdu, when you put a female in a cop's uniform? You get sentiment instead of action. You know what that's worth to you? Zero! *Bubkes!* That's a Jewish word. How do you say it in Arabic? How do you say *dead* in your language?"

"Please," Abdu said.

"What about Berge Nordkild?" Morizio asked. "You involved in that, running drugs from Iran?"

"That is a lie."

"Everything with you's a lie, Abdu."

He was close to breaking down. He extended his hands palm-up and said, "I have told you the truth. I do not know why Pringle paid me for what I knew about Hafez. I do not know anything about drugs and Berge Nordkild. I escaped Iran to save my life, and now it is in as much danger as if I had stayed there. This is America. You are American. Help me."

Morizio glanced at Connie, then asked, "Where's Hafez?"

"Dead," said Abdu.

"He's not dead, Abdu, and you know it."

"Let's go," Morizio said to Lake.

"What about me?" Abdu asked.

"What about you?" Morizio parroted. "You haven't leveled with us. You tell us bits and pieces, whatever you figure will keep us happy. Not enough, Abdu. The next time they come through the window they'll be looking for you, not what you have."

"I have been honest with you," Abdu said.

"Depends on how you define it," said Morizio. He knew that Connie was sympathetic to his predicament and would have preferred to drop it. He didn't share her feelings. Their timing had been perfect. They had a live one on the string and Morizio wasn't about to let him off the hook. Abdu was scared, and fear was a powerful asset when in the right hands. He decided to take advantage of it. He stepped close to Abdu and said in a harsh, threatening voice, "You're pathetic, Abdu. You're sitting here in the middle of your own mess wondering who's going to do you in, the Ayatollah, the mailman, the woman you're sleeping next to, your best friend. You're dead, Abdu, a former journalist who made a few bucks selling out his friends and . . ."

"I read it."

"Yeah, so did I. Answer me this. If he's not dead, where would he be?"

"Copenhagen."

"Why do you say that?" Lake asked.

"That is where he went when he left Washington. The caviar comes through there. It is a free port."

"He's there?" Morizio asked.

"He's dead," Abdu said, "but you ask hypothetical questions."

"What about Inga Lindstrom?" Lake asked.

"I don't know her."

"Come on, Abdu, of course you do," Morizio said scornfully.

"I've never met her," Abdu said in a sing-song voice. "I've heard of her. What does she matter?"

"Maybe a lot," Morizio said. "I want to know more about Hafez and this caviar scam."

Abdu threw up his hands. "What can I tell you?"

"More than you know," Morizio shouted. He turned to Lake and said, "Come on, let's go."

"What about me?" Abdu asked.

"What about you?" Morizio said.

"You promised."

Morizio laughed. It was deliberately cruel but he didn't care. That was the problem, you sometimes got carried away in the role of tough cop. "Close the windows," he said.

"Sal," said Lake, "be reasonable. They might come back."

"Exactly," Abdu said.

"Take a vacation," Morizio said.

"Vacation? Where do I take a vacation?"

"Your choice, just get out of Washington for awhile, someplace sunny with pretty girls in skimpy little bathing suits and tall jelly bean drinks. It's that time of year.''

Abdu stared at him.

"Stay at my place," Morizio said, "at least for the night.''

"You're serious?"

"Yeah, I'm serious, but I have lots of questions. That's the deal, a safe bed for answers.''

"I understand a deal," Abdu said. He smiled, exposing gold in two teeth. "You're a good man, Captain.''

"I'm a survivor like you, Abdu, that's all. Close the windows and let's get the hell out of here.''

20

"Well, what do you think?" Lake asked in the first-class cabin of a Pan Am 747, 38,000 feet over the Atlantic.

Morizio stretched and yawned. "Yeah, it's okay," he said.

He didn't want to admit how much he was enjoying the opulence of first class, the footrest that turned the massive seat into a bed, the little slippers on his feet, linen and China and white-and-red carnations on his tray. He'd had Beefeater gin in a chilled snifter and canapés of pâté with grapes, eggs with anchovies and sea-food. Now, the flight attendant served caviar and smoked salmon.

"Does this caviar contain borax?" Morizio asked the young woman.

"I don't know," she said, "but I'll find out."

"Nah, don't bother," he said. "Just curious."

She served them and moved on. Morizio tasted his caviar, turned to Lake and said, "you can have it."

"I'll take it. It's excellent."

"I'll never develop a taste for it, not after everything that's gone down." He spooned his portion onto her plate. "Do you think it's really possible that this whole thing, two murders, us being suspended is because of salty fish eggs?"

She shrugged and put some of the caviar on a small wedge of toast. "Let's hope we find out in the next few days, Sal."

After rare roast beef carved at their seats, and champagne, they fell asleep, ignoring the in-flight movie. They were awakened hours later by the sound of the captain's voice over the intercom. London was getting close, and breakfast was being served.

"How do you feel?" Lake asked.

"Pretty good." In truth, he felt even better than that. He was glad they were making the trip. It felt good to get away from the city that had been the scene of so much grief in past weeks, and it occurred to him, although he didn't express it to her, that if things didn't work out in London and Copenhagen, if they failed to shed any light on their dilemma, maybe they'd just stay in Europe, bum around, tell the world, especially MPD, to go to hell. Could he do it, he wondered, throw away a life that had been carefully charted and executed? He decided not to answer the question because it probably would have been a "No," and he preferred "Yes."

Although the young Cockney taxi driver talked nonstop from the moment they entered his cab at Heathrow Airport, Morizio thoroughly enjoyed the ride to the May Fair Hotel on Stratton Street, in the heart of London's fashionable Mayfair section. He couldn't get over the taxi itself, spotlessly clean and wonderfully spacious, a far cry from the dirty, cramped vehicles of Washington and Boston.

Their room was large and tastefully furnished and

appointed. Morizio flipped on the color television and watched a documentary on Australian wildlife over the BBC as he and Lake emptied their suitcases. When everything was put away, they ordered up club sandwiches, two bottles of Ben Truman lager, and a pot of tea. Morizio stripped down to his shorts, put on his robe and opened a leather shoulder bag. In it was an array of electronic equipment. He inserted fresh batteries and cassettes in each of two identical recorders, advanced the tapes past the white leader, plugged in microphones the size of hearing aid batteries, and tested them. He substituted a black ring for one of the mikes, slipped it over the phone's earpiece, and called the desk. "I'd like to leave a wake-up call for six," he said. "Yes, sir," the operator said. He hung up and played back their brief conversation. Perfect. He rewound the tape and pulled out a small address book. "I'm going to call Ethel Pringle, see if I can see her tonight."

The phone rang a dozen times at Ethel Pringle's home. When she answered she sounded out of breath. Morizio checked to see that his tape was rolling and that the recording needle moved, then said, "Hello, Ethel, it's Sal Morizio."

There was a long pause. "Hello," she said. "I'm sorry, I'm . . ."

"I won't hold you up, Ethel. I'm here, in London, and want very much to see you."

"Oh, I really don't think I can."

"Just for a brief chat, Ethel. I think . . . I think that under the circumstances it might be *nice* if you saw me. I need your help, just the way you and Paul needed mine a few years ago." He hoped he'd be successful in pricking her conscience.

"When?" she asked in a voice dripping with resignation.

"Tonight? Tomorrow? Whatever is convenient for you."

Another pause, even longer this time. "Perhaps tomorrow," she said, "in the morning, at Harriet's shop."

"Sure, that'd be fine. I'd like to see her, too. What time, and where?"

"Ten. It's the Little Soldier Shop, on Curzon, near Park Lane."

"I'll be there. Will you have had breakfast?"

"Yes."

"Okay, thanks, Ethel. I'm looking forward to it."

He played the tape back for Lake, who was in a lacy, short pink nightgown and who wore her blue Pan Am slippers from the flight. When the recorded conversation was finished, Lake said, "Harriet, the daughter. What happened there, Sal? I asked you once and you said it was too private. The rules have changed, haven't they?"

"I guess they have," he said. He joined her on the bed. "I promised Paul I'd never talk about what happened, and I wanted to keep my word."

"I understand, but now there's a . . ."

"I know, I know. It wasn't anything terrible, but it was to Paul. His daughter, Harriet, got pregnant. Hell, she was only sixteen or seventeen when it happened. Paul was beside himself. Ethel tried to convince her to have an abortion but she refused. She wanted the kid, and there wasn't much he could do about it. He asked me for help and I arranged for her to have the child in a home for unwed mothers outside of Boston. I knew the people who ran it pretty well, knew they'd keep it confidential. She had a baby boy and never came back to Washington. Ethel took her directly from the home to London. As far as I knew she was living with friends or some distant relatives. I asked Paul about it once but he wouldn't discuss it. He told me she was doing fine, had opened some sort of shop in London, and was very happy."

"What about the boy?" Lake asked. "He's still with her?"

"I assume so. She wanted him so bad that I can't imagine her ever giving him up."

"Who was the father?" Lake asked.

"No idea," said Morizio. "I figured Paul knew, but he never told me. He wanted it buried and that was that."

"Thanks for telling me, Sal. I like to feel I'm a full partner."

"No doubt about that," he said. "How about a nap?"

"You're on," she said.

"What about dinner?" he asked.

She'd been reading travel guides on the plane. "The Red Lion Pub in Mayfair sounds good," she said. "It's not far. And then, I thought, what we need is a good murder mystery. The Mayfair Theater's right downstairs, and Georgia Watson, who just came back from London, says the play is terrific. It's called *The Business of Murder*. It's been running for years. Game?"

"Sure, why not?"

They called in a reservation, curled up together and didn't awaken until the operator called at six.

They enjoyed the evening, an early dinner, a good play, and sleepy love-making at the end. Morizio was up early. Lake lingered in bed. He showered, skimmed the newspaper that had been left at their door, and carefully arranged the recording equipment in his raincoat. He looked outside. It was gray and misty. "London weather," he said.

"I'll trade it off against the tourist crush anytime," Lake said from bed. She'd declined his offer of breakfast in the room. "I just want to sleep a little longer," she said. "Good luck with the Pringle ladies."

He had porridge and toast in the hotel's coffee shop, asked the doorman how to get to Curzon Street, and walked in that direction. He was early; the doorman said it would take him ten minutes and it was 9:15. He strolled up Stratton to Curzon and took a left, as he'd been instructed. It occurred to him as he strolled along, stopping now and then to look in a shop window, that he was actually in London. It hadn't made any difference the night before, but now it did. He'd always wanted to visit London but never seemed to find the opportunity, or the time. He was like his father in that respect, reluctant to travel far from home unless pushed into it. His mother had managed to get his father to spend an occasional weekend on Cape Cod, and once they even took a week's vacation to Nova Scotia. Morizio tried to encourage his father to get away, especially after he'd retired. He'd even yelled at him once. His mother had been complaining that they never went anywhere and Morizio took her side. The result was his mother telling him to speak respectfully to his father and to mind his own business.

He took deep breaths as he approached the wide boulevard of Park Lane. Across it was Hyde Park, gray and lifeless in the moist, cold mist of London in November.

He didn't notice the shop until he was almost past it. It was on the second floor of a small, older building. A tiny sign—red lettering on a faded blue background, said: *Little Soldier Shop: Military Miniatures: H. Worth—Prop.*

Morizio smiled. It was fitting that Paul Pringle's daughter ended up with such a shop, if owning a shop was her ambition. Her father had been a history buff, particularly military history, and miniature figures held a special fascination for him. He'd talked to Morizio about the hours he spent creating authentic figures of soldiers of history and of the world, painstakingly painting and arranging them in appropriate groupings. He had thousands, he said, most of them in London. The back bar at Piccadilly held a dozen or so tiny military figures, gifts from Pringle to Johnny and the management. He also had what he termed, "as good a collection of books on military dress as anyone in the world."

He'd given Morizio two hand-crafted miniatures of South Wales Borderers as a Christmas gift, as well as a book about that regiment. Pringle often asked Morizio, "How are they?" as though they were prize dogs, or fragile family mementos. "Tip-top," Morizio always answered, "all spit and polish." And they'd laugh.

What was particularly interesting to Morizio was Pringle's focus on the Mexican-American War that spanned 1846 to 1848. He knew it in intimate detail, every battle, the underlying political forces that shaped it and, most of all, the military organization of the opposing armies, every battalion, regiment and rag-tag volunteer militia. The United States' Third Regiment was his favorite: "The best disciplined regiment the U.S. had to throw against the Mexicans," he said. From a uniform perspective, however, he preferred the Mexicans who, even though there was little money and few facilities to produce the uniforms, always added brilliant splashes of color. Mexico's Fourth Light Infantry Regiment especially pleased him. It had been issued uniforms that differed dramatically from other light regiments—dark blue coats with green collars, piping, and arabesques; crimson lapels, cuffs, and turnbacks with eagle decorations on the turnbacks; and medium blue trousers with crimson piping down the legs.

Pringle bragged that he had a complete collection of miniatures from the Fourth Regiment, two battalions of eight companies, grenadiers and fusiliers, drummers, buglers, and fifers, right down to surgeons and chaplains, every detail of their uniforms perfect, British Brown Bess muskets and Baker rifles, iron bayonets and sabres meticulously crafted and placed in the tiny soldiers' hands.

Pringle had photographed most of his collection in color, and he'd showed Morizio the photographs of the Mexican and American armies. "Evidence of a misspent youth." Morizio had said, "Why weren't you out bashing grannies?" and Pringle had laughingly agreed. "One day," he said, "when I retire from Her Majesty's service, I'd like to open a shop back home and sell to collectors. They're quite mad, you know, will pay shocking prices to round out their collections."

Morizio remembered those words as he stared at the small sign, and was sad. Pringle's dream had become a reality, but he wasn't around to enjoy it. He opened the downstairs door and peered up the shabby staircase, drew a breath and went up.

The door leading to the shop itself had a window insert. Morizio looked inside and saw a young woman behind a counter. He knew it was Harriet, although the few years since he'd seen her had changed her. She looked a lot older than she was; a young-old matron with a round, sad, pale face and short mousey-brown hair. She wore a bulky brown turtleneck sweater and a shapeless black wool skirt that was too long. He heard a child squeal, then the sound of running small feet.

He knocked. Harriet looked at the door. Her face was fearful, a bird frozen by the imminent attack of a cat. Morizio opened the door and a bell clanged. He stepped inside, closed the door behind him, and said, "Harriet?"

The sound of her name seemed to startle her. She started to say something, hesitated, then said, "Yes."

"Captain Morizio, your father's friend."

"Yes, hello."

"Did your mother tell you I was coming?"

"Yes, she did. I was surprised."

"That I was coming?"

"Yes. I don't know why. Mother didn't say."

He approached the counter, looked around and said, "What a beautiful shop."

"Thank you."

There were miniature figures everywhere. Many were military miniatures, but there were an equal amount of period pieces, women in sweeping gowns, men in high hats in carriages behind the reins of handsome horses, children skating on mirror ponds, statesmen, beggars, rogues, and mythical heros: a Tom Thumb world in a tiny London shop.

"Your father would have loved this," Morizio said.

She didn't answer. A small boy entered from a back room and eyed Morizio. "Hello," Morizio said.

The boy stood silent and still. "Go on now," Harriet said, "I've got business here."

Morizio stepped closer to the boy, crouched down and smiled. "Hi," he said. "I'm Sal." He extended his hand.

The boy giggled and turned his head.

"Get away with you now," Harriet said.

"Your son?" Morizio asked.

She glared at him. "You know it is."

Morizio nodded, felt foolish at having asked the question. He stood and said, "He's a handsome boy."

"Thank you." She made a menacing gesture at her son and he disappeared into the back room.

"Is your mother here?" Morizio asked.

"Not yet. Excuse me." She followed the boy into the back and closed the door. Morizio walked about the shop. Many of the collections were beneath glass, and had labels identifying them. He looked up at squadrons of tiny aircraft suspended by white thread from the ceiling. "Incredible," he told himself as he returned to the counter and listened for sounds from the back room. His eyes scanned the counter. There were dozens of catalogues piled on one end, two large general ledgers in green bindings, a sales receipt book, pens and pencils, and a few pieces of unopened mail. He picked up the envelopes and quickly perused them. The second one stopped him cold. It was addressed to Harriet Worth, and bore the return address of Melanie Callender. The front door opened and he dropped the envelopes to the counter, turned and faced Ethel Pringle.

"Hello, Ethel," he said, smiling and taking a step to her. She looked good, a striking difference from her daughter. Her blonde hair was stylishly fashioned into youthful soft curls. Her makeup was heavy without being garish, and she wore a smart navy blue suit, a white blouse open enough to expose the beginning of her breasts, and expensive gold jewelry. He felt sorry for Harriet. Men would turn to look at the mother, not at the daughter.

"Good morning," she said. "I'm sorry I'm late. It couldn't be helped."

"Doesn't matter. I've been examining the shop. It's marvelous. Paul would have . . ."

"Paul is dead, Captain. Where is Harriet?"

"In the back, with her son."

"Bryan's here?"

"Yeah, I met him. Handsome little kid."

Ethel Pringle ignored his compliment, went to the counter, picked up the envelope from Melanie Callender, and put it in her purse. She stepped to the back door, opened it and said, "Come out, Harriet."

"In a moment, mother."

There was a long period of silence between Ethel and Morizio. He was determined to play it right, to defer or attack depending upon what his instincts dictated. He was aware of the pressure of time and the ramifications of squandering it. He had them here together, Paul's widow and daughter, probably the only chance he'd have. He needed answers.

"Harriet's married?" he asked, trying to sound casual.

Ethel frowned.

"I saw the name downstairs, H. Worth. I assumed she'd married someone named Worth."

"She chose it for business purposes, and to keep people from prying into her life." Her tone was carbon steel.

"I'm not here to pry, Ethel," Morizio said gently. "I'm in trouble because of Paul's murder and I need help."

A trace of a smile crossed her lips. "Tit-for-tat," she said.

Anger came and went. Morizio said, "I didn't help you and Harriet because I wanted a favor later," he said. "I don't work that way. Paul was a friend."

"And you helped disgrace a family."

Morizio didn't understand. He said, "I thought I did the right thing. Paul said Harriet was determined to have the child and he told me that you agreed."

"Goddamn it!"

"Ethel, if Paul misrepresented things, I'm sorry, but . . ."

"It is none of your business," she said.

"It was then."

"But it is not now."

A series of thoughts slipped in and out of Morizio's mind. He was angry at being slapped in the face after having helped. He also wondered why Melanie Callender would be writing to Harriet Pringle, or Worth, whoever she was. To ask would admit to snooping. He decied to wrap that question into a package of other questions and started asking—"Did you know Paul was on the CIA payroll?"—"Did you ever meet his Arab friend, Sami Abdu?"—"What did you mean when you told me on the phone that he was involved in things he shouldn't have been?"—"What caused him to be murdered, Ethel?"—"You and Harriet have been getting checks from Melanie Callender for a long time now. Why?"

He was shooting in the dark but felt it was worth it. If the envelope didn't contain a check, she'd deny it which, by itself, could open a discussion of why Callender had been in touch with them. He waited for a reply. There wasn't any, at least from Ethel. But Harriet, who'd appeared from the back room, asked, "How do you know that?"

"Be quiet," her mother said.

"Why?" Morizio asked, ignoring Ethel and staring hard at her daughter. "I helped you once, remember, when you needed it. You were grateful then, or so your father told me. I need your help now, really need it. I have to find out who killed your father so that I can reclaim my own life. Please, tell me what I need to know and I'll disappear. You'll never hear from me again.''

Now, he wished the mother weren't there. He was confident he could break Harriet down, appeal to her sense of fair play, even threaten her if necessary and take advantage of youth's natural inclination to fear the worst.

"You have no right," Harriet said. "What you did for us was good, but it would have worked out even if you hadn't. My father . . ."

"Harriet!"

"My father was in trouble. That's why he died."

Her mother took a threatening step toward her. The girl stiffened and stuck out her chin. "I don't want him here, mother, any more than you do. But he is. You told him he could come. This will never end unless he gets what he wants."

Ethel leaned against the counter and glared at Morizio. "God, how I hate the policeman's mentality," she said.

As much as he disliked seeing either of them distraught over his presence and questions, Morizio was pleased with the way the conversation was going. If they believed that this 'policeman's mentality' would result in not letting go, so much the better. "You're right, Harriet," he said, "I won't let go of this until I get what I want. I'd like it to be pleasant and friendly, but that's your choice. I have an appointment with Scotland Yard this afternoon, and they'll turn on the screws if I tell them to. This is murder, Harriet, not a purse snatch."

"Paul was a private man," Ethel said. "He never discussed his business with us."

"But this shop was paid for by money he made from

sources outside his embassy job, the Central Intelligence Agency, maybe drugs.''

"That's not true," Harriet said, her voice rising with indignation. "My father would never do anything like that."

"I got the feeling from you, Ethel, that he was in pretty deep with something bad." He emphasized the last word.

"He . . ." She turned her back to him and pressed her hands on the counter. "He was a good man, Captain, foolish but good. He provided for his family.

"I know that," Morizio said, coming up behind her, "but he knew something that got him killed. What was it?"

Neither woman said anything.

"Did he know who killed Ambassador James?"

Ethel turned. "Of course not."

"Why are you so sure?"

"He would have told."

"You? You said he never discussed business with you."

"Someone. He would have told someone."

"Sami Abdu?" He remembered the envelope from Callender. "Melanie Callender? Were they close? Is she sending you money to keep you quiet?"

"She sends us money to compensate for my father's death," Harriet said.

"Why? Was she responsible?"

"We British are different than you are, Captain," Ethel said. "We take care of our own." She smiled. "Socialized medicine."

Morizio shrugged and shook his head. "I could understand that if you were receiving a widow's pension from the British government, but why Melanie Callender, a secretary?"

"Procedure, that's all," Ethel Pringle said.

"Strange one," said Morizio.

"As you wish."

He hadn't realized until that moment that he disliked her, and if he weren't after something he would have told her what was on his mind. He held it in check and said, "I don't want to take any more of your time than necessary. Is there anything you can tell me that would shed light on Paul's murder?"

Harriet looked to him as though she had something important to say. She turned to her mother, who ignored her and continued to stare at Morizio. "Harriet?" he asked. "Please. Don't make me turn this into a messy official investigation."

"Mummy, I think . . ."

"Do what you want. You're a fool, always have been. God knows how much we've tried to shelter you from your own ignorance but you haven't a twit of a brain to protect yourself."

"Harriet," Morizio said softly.

"Daddy came here the day he was leaving for America. He said that he was . . ." She started to cry.

"Oh, stop it," her mother said, "and say what you will."

Morizio wanted to slap her. He looked at Harriet, who'd mustered some control. "Daddy came here and told me that if anything ever happened to him the answers would be in a book."

"What book?" Morizio asked.

"About Mexico."

"Is it here?"

She shook her head, pulled a lace hanky from her purse, and wiped her eyes.

"Where is this book?" Morizio asked.

"Daddy said you would know."

224

"Me? Is it in the United States, in Washington?"

"I think so."

"Had enough, Mr. Chief Inspector? Satisfied?" Ethel Pringle asked as she grabbed her purse from the counter and moved toward the door.

"No."

She snorted and drew back her upper lip.

"Why?" Morizio asked, slapping the side of his raincoat.

"Why what?" Ethel Pringle said.

"If he told you where the answers were, why didn't you call me, call somebody, do something, for Christ sake?"

"Why should we have?" Ethel said. "It doesn't matter why it happened. He chose to throw in his lot with the bad ones and got what usually comes from that. Go to bed with dogs, you get up with fleas." She slowly turned toward her daughter as she said it, which caused Harriet to gaze at the floor.

"And you didn't care." Morizio couldn't keep the disgust from his voice.

"I care about me, Captain, and about Harriet. Whatever he left in his precious book—he had so many of them—could only hurt us. The boy . . . you know the story."

"Of course."

"The boy was born in disgrace. He . . ."

"Mother, please," Harriet said, glancing at the closed door to the back room. She looked at Morizio through red, wet eyes as though to invoke some power within him to make it all disappear.

"You'd best be quiet, Harriet. This is all because of you."

"You know, Ethel, this is unnecessary," Morizio said.

"And you shut up. You're as responsible as they are."

"They?"

"Paul and her. The three of you wouldn't listen. There was no need to give birth to a bastard. I screamed at both of them to listen to reason, to be smart for once in their lives, but they'd have none of it."

Morizio pressed his hand against the tape recorder in his pocket and said to Harriet, "If your father told you anything else that might help me find this book, please try to remember."

She shook her head.

"Nothing?" he said.

"No. He said you'd know."

The door to the back room opened and Bryan Worth came into the shop. "Hi, champ," Morizio said.

"Mummy," the boy said, pushing against Harriet's legs and casting a frightened glance at his grandmother.

"He's a fine looking boy, Harriet," Morizio said. "Take good care of him. He deserves it."

Ethel Pringle had already left the shop and was on her way down the stairs. Morizio followed her to the street. "I'm sorry, Ethel, to upset you," he said, meaning it.

"All the upset in my life has already been done to me, Captain. Paul and her, now you. I won't let it happen again, and I warn you that whatever you find in Paul's precious book, it had better not pertain to Harriet and Bryan. Do you hear me?"

"Yeah, I hear you, Ethel, but is that why you didn't follow up on what Paul had told Harriet? It isn't the worst thing in the world, you know, to have a child out of wedlock."

She looked right and left before saying, "Have you a daughter, Captain?"

"No."

"Then be quiet," she said in a harsh whisper, her face thrust close to his, her lips quivering. An empty taxi came around the corner and she hailed it, climbed into the back, slammed the door behind her, and disappeared from Morizio's view.

21

Connie and Morizio enjoyed an elegant dinner in the Savoy Hotel's River Room—turtle soup with sherry and potted shrimps as appetizers, haddock in cream sauce as their entree, which had been touted in *The Best of London*, and vanilla ice cream for dessert. They were utterly relaxed, and they lingered over cups of rich, dark coffee. They tried to avoid the James and Pringle murders but failed.

Morizio had played the tape of his confrontation with Ethel and Harriet Pringle in their hotel room that afternoon. As usual, it raised more questions than it answered. What book, and where was it? Why was Melanie Callender sending money to the Pringles? Those were the two "biggies"; many smaller questions spun off of them.

"Let's dance," Lake said as the Savoy's jazz-influenced orchestra launched into another set. Morizio hated to dance because he didn't know how, which made him feel naked and vulnerable on a dance floor.

He reluctantly joined her and she told him he danced better than he thought he did.

"Thanks," he said, not believing a word. He stopped dancing, stepped back and said, "It must be Piccadilly."

"In Washington?"

"Yeah, where else would Paul assume I'd know where he put the book?"

"It's possible," Connie said, stepping close and attempting to get him to move again.

"Let's sit," he said.

They had more coffee, and the maître d' bought them an after-dinner drink.

"I ought to go back to Washington," Morizio said.

"Why don't you call?" Lake suggested.

"Call Johnny? Yeah, I could do that, but I'm sure he wouldn't know what I'm talking about. You don't leave something that valuable in a bartender's hands."

"But why worry about it now?" she said. "You said you wanted to try and contact Callender. I think you should, and I'll go to Copenhagen and see if I can catch up with Inga Lindstrom. We might as well do everything possible while we're here, Sal. It's only a few more days before we head back anyway."

They stayed up late in their room at the May Fair and reviewed what they knew up to that point. Melanie Callender was now a more important figure, and they decided Morizio should be the one to approach her. He could capitalize on his meeting with the Pringles, which would make him more convincing.

Before turning out the light they reviewed what Georgia Watson had dug up on Geoffrey James's Scottish oil company. Not much, it turned out. It was an oil brokerage operation, buying oil from Scotland and reselling it to other countries. It had functioned, according to Watson, in a legal manner, possessed all the appropriate

licenses and legal documents. Watson was surprised
that the company had been folded upon James's death.
It had been impressively profitable and had every ex-
pectation of continuing to be, which would have benefitted Marsha James. There had been no effort to sell
the firm. It was simply being dissolved by Mrs. James,
who'd become chief operating officer and major stock-
holder under the terms of her husband's will.

"We already knew all that," Morizio had said when
Lake first told him.

"Yes, but the big question is *why*? If you're sitting
on a rich company you don't just close the doors. You
sell it for a profit."

"Maybe Marsha James doesn't have a nose for business. Maybe she hates it."

"But there are others involved, the Scotsman, Edwin
Ferguson, for one. He's a businessman."

"She held the big hunk of stock," Morizio said.
"Maybe he didn't have any choice but to go along."

They left it at that. Georgia Watson said she'd continue to look into it, and Lake promised to call when
they returned from Europe.

The next morning Morizio went through all the
Callenders in phone directories for London and envi-
rons until reaching Melanie Callender's parents. Her
father answered, a pleasant man who informed Morizio
that his daughter was away "on holiday" but would
return in two days. Morizio left his name and the
number of the May Fair, thanked him, and hung up.

"If we wait around for her we'll blow the flight to
Copenhagen," he said.

Connie thought about it. "Why don't I just go as
scheduled and you catch up after you've talked to her?
I've got to spend time with my Aunt Eva anyway, and

if you're really delayed I'll pop over to Malmö to see my grandmother.''

He went with her to the airport, promised he'd join her as soon as he'd made contact with Callender, kissed her good-bye, and watched her vanish through a doorway leading to her flight.

He killed the day by shopping: a Mackay tartan kilt from the Scotch House and a silk umbrella from James Smith and Sons for Connie; a walking stick that concealed a sword for himself, also from Smith's; a beautiful cut-glass compote from W.G.T. Burne for his mother; and an assortment of small gifts from Marks and Spencer for nieces and nephews. He returned to the May Fair late in the afternoon and took a nap, had a drink in the hotel bar and Talaparu duckling for dinner in the Beachcomber Restaurant. He felt very alone, and wished Lake were there. He was told at the desk when he retrieved his room key that Miss Lake had called, and would call again. He went to his room and called the d'Angleterre Hotel in Copenhagen. Miss Lake was "out for the evening." He left a message, turned on TV, got into bed, and promptly fell asleep to a BBC commentary on the state of the British economy which, judging from the announcer's voice, wasn't doing very well.

Constance Lake sat with her Aunt Eva Nygaard in the d'Angleterre's Restaurant Reine Pedauque. Aunt Eva, who was in her early sixties and who was a vegetarian, had had a steamed vegetable plate. Lake had feasted on *Kalvefilet Niçoise med friske krydderurter fransk sennep, piskeflode og pommes croquettes.* Veal Niçoise with herbs, mustard, cream, and potato puffs.

"It was wonderful," Connie said.

Her aunt, a wrinkled, tanned flower child, smiled and sat back. She wore a beige roughhewn sack dress, a necklace of handhammered copper dangles, and a copper bracelet. Her hair, brown streaked with gray, was pulled back tight. She wore no makeup and her nail polish was cracked and peeling. Stories in the family about Aunt Eva were legend. She'd been at the forefront of the movement in the early seventies to turn an area of picturesque Christianshavn into the *fristaden*, or free town of Christiania, where hundreds of young bohemians dealt openly in drugs, lived a communal lifestyle, raised large families without benefit of marriage in abandoned army barracks that could only be described as hovels, and who were immune from Danish law. "We finally convinced the Supreme Court that it was better to have them there than roaming around Copenhagen," Eva explained to Connie during dinner. "That wasn't really why we wanted Christiania established but it worked."

Connie enjoyed listening to Eva. Although the older woman espoused avant-garde philosophies and eschewed anything smacking of commercialism and wealth, she lived a rich existence, thanks to the estate of one of her late husbands who'd made a lot of money in real estate. Currently, she was living with a young artist whom she billed as a student, but who Lake was certain was her lover.

"Tell me more about this young man of yours," Eva said. "He's not the only one, is he?" She sounded as though an admission of it would be a potent shock.

"Yes, he is," Connie said, laughing. "One at a time, Aunt Eva. That's me."

Eva sighed and sipped her tea. "I suppose you *have* time," she said into her cup.

The table next to them was occupied by two men, one American, the other Danish. Both were middle-aged and well dressed. Connie had eavesdropped on their conversation and surmised that they were in the food business. She wanted to talk to them. Eva, noticing that Connie had cocked her head in their direction, leaned across the table and said, "We'll have them join us."

It dawned on Connie that Eva assumed she was interested in the men personally. She started to correct her, then realized it didn't matter how they got to talk. She nodded, and Eva said loudly, "We should join tables. It's the custom."

Connie and the Danish gentleman were taken aback at Eva's loudness, but the American laughed. Connie had been aware throughout the evening that he'd been looking at her. She smiled at him and said, "Your table or ours?"

"Yours, by all means," he answered. He introduced himself as Mark Rosner, president of Rosner Foods of New York. His Danish dinner companion was Erl Rekstad, a food exporter.

They ordered three brandies; Eva never touched alcohol because it "bloated one." There was lots of preliminary chitchat, with Rosner asking Connie questions like: "First time in Copenhagen?" "Business or pleasure?" (A hint of a leer). "Husband couldn't make it?" "Danish? You look Danish."

Connie answered pleasantly and bided her time until she could ask her own questions. She kept an eye on Eva, who seemed to be enjoying it.

"She's beautiful, isn't she?" Eva said to Rekstad, referring to Connie.

"Very," he said. "And you are, too."

Eva smiled coyly and patted his hand.

"Your wife couldn't make it?" Lake asked Rosner.

"No, no wife," he said.

"Oh. Rosner Foods. What sort of foods?"

"Fancy foods, outrageously expensive and sinfully good. Do you like fancy foods?"

"I prefer expensive ones," said Lake.

"Caviar tastes?"

"Especially caviar. Do you import it?"

"Of course. Do you have a favorite?"

"You mean Iranian or Russian?"

Rosner laughed. "Yes, that too, but I was thinking of beluga, servruga, oestra, pressed, or whole . . ."

"I love all of it."

"That's what I like to hear," Rosner said. He said to Rekstad, "A devoted fan."

"That's good," said the Dane. Eva had now rested her hand on top of his and left it there.

"You must know Berge Nordkild," Connie said, hoping it wouldn't prove to be a sore subject.

"Berge? Of course I know him. He just got himself in a lot of trouble."

"Yes, he did," Connie said. "I was shocked."

"You know him well?"

"Quite well." Let him find out differently later, she thought.

Rosner asked what she did in the United States.

"I'm a . . . a consultant."

Rosner raised his eyebrows and finished his brandy. "What do you consult on?" he asked.

"Design. Interior design."

Connie noticed the puzzled expression on Eva's face. She smiled at her and raised her eyebrows. Let her think she was reserving some vestige of her anonymity in case the evening progressed.

"I've been thinking of having my offices redone," Rosner said. "Maybe you'd be interested in the commission."

"Maybe I would," Lake said. She snapped her fingers as though a sudden thought had hit her. "Someone else you may know, Inga Lindstrom."

"Inga?" Rekstad said, sliding his hand from beneath Eva's. "You are Inga's friend?"

This was a different ballgame, Lake knew. Copenhagen was his home field. A simple local phone call to Lindstrom would reveal any lie. She said, "No, I've never met her, but mutual friends back home suggested I look her up when I was here."

"You look like her," Rekstad said.

"Yes, I've been told that," Connie said. "I thought I'd call her tomorrow."

"I am sure she is here," said Rekstad.

"Oh, good."

Rosner laughed. "Yes," he said, "nobody in the caviar business is away this week."

Lake didn't want to pounce on his comment too quickly. She sipped from her snifter, glanced at him and said, "This *is* the week, isn't it," hoping she sounded like she knew what she was talking about.

"Once every three months," Rosner said to Rekstad. "Like the old joke goes, tonight's the night." They both laughed.

"I'd love another drink," Connie said.

"You've got it," Rosner said. *"Tjener,"* he called to a waiter.

Eva complimented Rosner on his pronunciation and suggested that after the next drink they all go to her home where she would entertain them. "I have no liquor in the house," she said, "but I have excellent marijuana and cocaine."

"Jesus," Connie thought, thinking of Morizio.

"I prefer akvavit," Rekstad said.

"Plebeian," Eva said, squeezing his hand. He withdrew it.

"I'm fascinated with the whole mystique of caviar and this special week in Copenhagen," Lake said.

"There is a certain circus quality to it," Rosner said. "Never used to be this way, but that's what's exciting about the international food business. A flood here, an overthrow there and the game changes."

Connie laughed, trying to convey that she understood.

"You know, Erl," Rosner said, "as chaotic as it's gotten, there are advantages. Prices have gone down, the quality hasn't suffered, and it's a hell of a lot more fun than placing phone calls. Besides, it gives me an excuse four times a year to get out of the house and come to Copenhagen."

Lake looked at him, and he knew what she was thinking. "I mean the office," he said. "It's boring as hell just sitting behind a desk."

"Of course," she said. "No wife, my foot," she thought. She looked at Rekstad, who seemed to be feeling his drinks. His eyes were protruding and watery, and his mouth had drooped. Aunt Eva had pushed close against him, her fingers tightly entwined with his.

"I'm dying to see what goes on this week," Lake said. "I've heard so much about it from Berge and other friends in the food business. I'd hate to leave without experiencing it."

Rosner screwed up his face and looked at her. Had she blown it, she wondered. Had she overplayed it?

"What's the big deal about buying smuggled-in caviar off the docks?" he asked.

She took a page from Eva's book, pressed against him and said, "It's exciting, dealing in smuggled goods. I suppose it's tasting the bitter, unattainable fruit."

"God, it's working," she thought as he put his arm around her and said into her ear, "I know what you mean. Want to come with me?"

"Sure," she said. "What happens?"

"We buy caviar."

"Where?"

"On the docks. They run it in in small boats."

Rekstad frowned at Rosner. Evidently he didn't like him talking about what was supposed to be a well-kept secret.

"I'd love it," Connie said.

"Tomorrow?" Rosner asked.

"Sure."

"What about tonight?"

"What about it?"

"We should get together and plan our strategy."

"It's that complicated?"

"It's that simple. I'm staying here at the d'Angleterre. Where are you staying?"

"With Eva."

"Stay with me."

"I'd rather not."

"Why?"

"I don't know you."

"You will."

"Over a period of time."

He pulled away from her as though someone had slipped another disc into his computer, another piece of seduction software. He said, "Let's forget about caviar and stick to more important things."

"Like?"

"Like the rest of the evening." He grinned and whispered in her ear, "What's with your friend? She's a little old for this, isn't she?"

"She's young at heart, younger than I am."

"Sorry to hear that," Rosner said. "You ought to get with it. This is Copenhagen. Everybody's 'young at heart,' as you put it."

Connie smiled pleasantly. "What about going to the docks? What dock? Where does it happen?"

"In Christianshavn."

"Oh."

"Been there?"

"No."

"Interesting part of town."

"That's where the commune is."

"Right. You can't believe what pigs they are, all the misfits."

"Any particular dock in Christianshavn?"

"Along the main canal, on Overgaden."

"You're going tomorrow night?"

"Uh, huh. Still coming with me?"

"I'm not sure I'm free. Can I call you?"

"Sure. How about dinner tomorrow night?"

"I'll call you."

"I have the distinct feeling I'm being dismissed."

Connie shook her head and looked at Eva, who had Erl Rekstad roaring with laughter at something she'd said. "Ready to go home, Eva?" Connie asked.

"We're all going home," Eva said.

Connie shook her head. "My headache's worse," she said. "Let's go."

Rekstad stood unsteadily and kissed Eva's hand. Rosner took a final shot at Connie. "Come on," he said, "I'll buy you a nightcap in my room."

"Thank you, no," Connie said. She shook his hand. "I enjoyed meeting you. If things work out for tomorrow I'll call you."

"Sure you will."

"Don't count it out. Good night." She took Eva's arm and propelled her out of the restaurant and into the lobby. "I told him I was staying with you," she said. "Let's make it look that way."

Eva giggled. "Why all the fuss? You should go with him. He's nice. I like his nose."

"His nose?"

"He has a kind nose."

"Aunt Eva."

"American girls are strange," Eva said as they left the hotel and stood on Kongens Nytorv, in the middle of the King's New Square. They crossed the busy intersection to a park. Lake looked back and saw Rosner and Rekstad saying good-bye in the lobby. Rekstad came outside and climbed into a cab, and Rosner went into a richly paneled bar off the lobby.

"I think it's safe to go back," Connie said to Eva.

"To see him? He looks lonely."

"It was good to see you again, Aunt Eva. It's been what, five years since you visited in America?"

"Yes. It was good to see you, too. My love to your mother and father."

They kissed. "Where's your car?" Connie asked.

Eva pointed down the street to a black Saab. "I'll call you tomorrow," Connie said. They kissed again and Eva walked away.

Lake checked the lobby, quickly got her key from the desk and took the small leather-lined elevator to the second floor, which was considered the first floor. Her room number was 102. The phone was ringing as she entered. She quickly picked it up and sat on the bed.

"Connie?" Morizio asked.

"Hi, Sal. How are you?"

"Lonely. I miss you. How are you doing?"

"Good, but I miss you, too. Let me tell you what happened tonight." She replayed the evening with Aunt Eva and the two men. There was silence on Morizio's end when she was done. "Sal?" she said.

"Yeah, I'm here. This Rosner, he's staying at the hotel?"

"Yes. I managed to avoid him when I left Aunt Eva."

"That's good." His voice was muffled and flat.

"Sal, are you jealous?"

"Don't be ridiculous."

"You are." She laughed. "I think it was great what happened. I know where the caviar comes in, and that's worth something. What luck being here the one week every three months when it happens."

"I agree, Connie, I really do. What are you doing now?"

"Now? I'm going to bed. I'm beat."

"I wish I were there."

"So do I. Callender should be back tomorrow. Then you can get here."

"Right. I can't wait. Look, if I can see her early enough I'll be there tomorrow night. I'll grab the last flight."

"Great. I'll be waiting."

"Okay. Take care of yourself."

"You, too. I love you."

"That goes double for me."

Connie was up early. She opened French doors that led to an asphalt roof over the d'Angleterre's front entrance and took deep breaths. It was a stunning morning, bright sunshine, a cloudless deep blue sky and springlike air. "Unusually mild," Erl Rekstad had commented the night before about Copenhagen's recent weather.

She left the doors open as she turned on the radio, found an open space on the floor and went through a half hour of calisthenics. She missed Richard Simmons, thought of Morizio's comments about him, and smiled.

She stood under pulsating hot water from the shower for twenty minutes, vigorously soaping herself and washing her hair. She'd brought her own small hair dryer but didn't have to use it; there was one built into the wall. The towels were warm from having been on a heated rack, and Lake had draped the white terrycloth robe that came with the room over the rack. It, too, was toasty warm.

There was a small bar and refrigerator in the room, stocked with wines, whiskeys, juices, and mixes. She had a glass of Solita orange juice, sat at a desk, and organized things for the day. She looked at Inga Lindstrom's address:

Lindstrom Import-Export: 7–12k Overgaden neden Vandet, Christianshavn, Denmark. She wondered if it were close to Overgaden, the street Rosner had mentioned. She studied a street map she'd purchased at the airport. The streets were across a canal from each other in Christianshavn.

She rigged her raincoat with tape recorder and microphone, dressed in a tan camel-hair blazer, cranberry tweed skirt, and white blouse and went downstairs for breakfast in the terrace, a room surrounded by glass and decorated with hundreds of plants. She'd decided not to call Lindstrom ahead of time. Just showing up had worked with Callender in Washington, and she hoped it would in this instance, too. She had a continental breakfast and read the European *Herald Tribune*. The waitress was a pleasant middle-aged woman who refilled Lake's coffee cup every time she took a sip.

"I'm going to Christianshavn," Lake said. "Can I walk there?" It looked on the map that she could, but map mileages could be deceiving.

"*Ja*," the waitress said, "or you could take the boat from Nyhaven. It's only a few blocks."

The idea of a boat ride appealed. Lake had assumed that the famed Copenhagen passenger boats that traveled the canals would have stopped running once the tourist season ended. She received directions to the Nyhaven dock, said, "*Tak*," which meant "Thank you," the only Danish word she knew, and started walking. The streets were filled with robust people on bicycles and on foot, and Lake reminded herself that she, too, was of Scandinavian stock. It was hard for her to focus on approaching Inga Lindstrom. How nice it would be to simply be on vacation, to soak up Copenhagen without the pressures of clearing their names. That hit her hard, the fact that she and Sal had ended up in a state of dishonor, suspended from jobs they liked and worked hard at. It wasn't fair. They'd tried to do the right thing and had ended up being punished. For what? For caring? What was wrong with people? Were they all so frightened that doing what was right became wrong? She was angry, could have cried, except that she wouldn't. "Damn it," she mumbled as she approached the Nyhaven dock where a broad, flat boat called the *Kobenhaven* was loading passengers. Lake paid her 160 krona and took a seat. The captain looked like a boat captain was supposed to look, face rendered leather by a lifetime in the sun, a white capped hat at a jaunty angle, a confident expression that promised he wouldn't run them into a piling or a shifting sand bar.

A teenage boy flipped the rope free of a spike and they backed into the canal. Lake sat back and watched Copenhagen slide by, bridges with impossible names; the Stock Exchange with a serpent's tail on top; the current Christiansborg Palace: the previous five castles, dating back to 1167, having been destroyed by fire and pillage; red brick buildings covered with ivy, churches and government institutions in which bureaucracy flourished as it did in Washington—"Could this mess have happened here?" Connie asked herself. "Probably," she answered.

They passed fishing boats and luxurious passenger liners, tattoo parlors and seedy bars; the Hydrofoil dock that ran people across to Malmö, Sweden, where her grandmother lived, lovers kissing as they sat in the sun, old men drinking beer and smoking pipes. They stopped at designated areas to discharge and pick up new passengers, mostly tourists reveling in the mild weather while natives bundled up against it and chose enclosed, heated transportation.

They entered Christianshavn's main canal and Connie took in the sights on both sides. Overgaden, where Mark Rosner had said the caviar transactions took place, was lined with well-kept apartment buildings and quaint little restaurants. There were trees and brightly painted window frames on the red and gray buildings, and every apartment had flower boxes beneath its windows.

The other side of the canal, Overgaden neden Vandet, contained a series of warehouses, yellow and red and gray brick with hoists in between. Lake squinted to read the numbers; 7–12 was on a three-story modern structure with numerous windows that was attached to one of the warehouses.

The *Kobenhaven* docked and Lake disembarked into the midst of a bustling Christianshavn. Salty commercial fishermen repaired flaking boats alongside counterculture men and women preparing for another leisurely day with earnest determination. Lake was reminded of Seattle where hundreds of miles of waterfront were peacefully shared by residences and industry.

She crossed a pedestrian bridge over the canal and

walked along Overgaden naden Vandet until reaching
7–12. There was a vertical row of signs in front, gold
lettering on a black background. At the top was *Lindstrom
Import-Export*. Lake went inside and read a building
directory. Lindstrom's offices were on the next floor.
She climbed a staircase, paused in front of a wooden
door with the company name etched in gold leaf, decided not to knock and entered. The reception area was
panelled in light oak. A display case to her left held a
variety of canned foods illuminated by recessed fluorescent fixtures. The carpeting was a black, hard-finished
industrial grade. Chairs for visitors were covered in
orange vinyl. A young blond man wearing a white shirt
and red tie sat behind a desk. He glanced up from his
newspaper. "*God morgen,*" he said.

"Good morning," Lake said. "I'd like to see Ms.
Lindstrom."

"American?"

"Yes."

He smiled. "My brother lives in America."

"Oh? Where?"

"Minnesota."

"I've never been. Does he like it?"

"*Ja*. You have an appointment with Ms. Lindstrom?"

"No. I won't take much of her time. I'm a friend of
Berge Nordkild . . ." She hesitated, then added, "And
Erl Rekstad."

The young man's blond eyebrows went up; Lake
wasn't sure at which name. "You are here on business?"

"Yes, I am. I can probably explain it better to Ms.
Lindstrom. It's complicated, business and pleasure. I'm
sure she'll want to talk to me."

"*Undskyld,*" he said, getting up and going to a door
that led from the room. "*Vaer sa venlig at vente.*" He

244

smiled. "I am sorry. I forget. I should speak English. Please wait."

He returned a few minutes later and said, "She has someone with her now. It won't be long."

Connie passed the next twenty minutes browsing through a copy of *Copenhagen This Week* she'd brought with her from the hotel. The Glyptotek Museum was on the cover, and inside was a day-to-day listing of events around the city: chamber concerts at every hour of the day, jazz festivals, readings, theater, tours and guided walks, organ recitals, trotting races and craft demonstrations; and always music, bluegrass and jazz and opera. She hoped she and Morizio would have time to enjoy a little of it. It dawned on her that the next day was Thanksgiving. It was easy to forget it, not being home.

The door opened and a tall, slender blonde appeared. They *did* look alike, Connie thought, could have been sisters. Lindstrom wore a tailored suit the color of blanched straw. Her blouse, full of ruffles and with large pearl buttons, was deep purple. She wore black, high-heeled pumps. She was deeply tanned; her eyes were large and very blue. "Miss Lake," she said, crossing the room to Lake and extending her hand. "Sorry to keep you waiting."

Connie stood. "I'm sorry to barge in without an appointment," she said.

Lindstrom's smile was big and bright, perfect teeth rendered whiter by her bronze skin. "No problem. This is a light day. You say you're a friend of Erl Rekstad."

"Yes, not close friends but . . ."

"I called him. He speaks highly of you."

"Does he?"

"Yes. He said you were together last night, with Mark Rosner. Interesting men."

"Yes, they were very . . . very pleasant."

"And Berge Nordkild? You know him?"

"Yes, in Washington."

"You know, of course, of his recent trouble."

"Yes. I was so sorry to hear it."

"He deserved it, I fear. Come, we'll talk in my office."

"The lady's sharp," Lake thought as she followed her through the door. "I'd better be on my toes."

Lindstrom's suite of offices was spacious and flooded with light from floor-to-ceiling windows. Connie sat in a brown Hans Wegner armchair, one of a pair in front of a large Danish modern desk. Lindstrom asked, "Coffee, tea? Akvavit?"

Connie had had akvavit with Aunt Eva and hadn't liked it. "Tea," she said.

Lindstrom ordered it over the phone, sat behind her desk, dangled one long leg over the other, and said, "So you're here from Washington. My receptionist said it was business and pleasure. Pleasure is easy in Copenhagen. What business are you on?"

Connie had anticipated this moment and had decided to be honest and direct. She thought for a moment, framed her words, and said, "I'm a police officer, Ms. Lindstrom. I'm with the Metropolitan Police Department in Washington. I'm not here officially, but I do have a vested interest in the Geoffrey James and Paul Pringle murders."

Lake waited for a response. Lindstrom sat passively, her eyes on Connie. Finally, she said, "And?"

"There are questions that concern you, Ms. Lindstrom, that might help us fit some pieces into the puzzle."

"What questions?"

"All right, to begin with . . ."

Lindstrom held up a hand. "Before you begin, Miss

Lake, let me say that one of the murders you mention means nothing to me. His name was Pinger?"

"Pringle, Paul Pringle, a security officer at the British Embassy in Washington."

"Never heard of him."

"You didn't read about his murder?"

"No."

"All right, then we'll stick to Ambassador James. You knew him."

"Yes, I did. You do realize I have no obligation to answer any questions about his death. I'm happy to help, but please understand that it's out of a desire to cooperate, nothing more."

"Of course, and I appreciate it. I'm sure you've been interviewed before about Ambassador James's murder."

Lindstrom nodded. The young man from the reception desk arrived carrying a tray. He placed it on the desk. "Anything else?" he asked Lindstrom.

"Nej. Tak. Ah, ja. Vil De Bestille en samtale for mig til London? En time."

"Ja." He left the room.

Lake wished she understood Danish. The only thing she knew was that it had to do with London.

"Your tea," Lindstrom said. They poured and sat back. "Now, your questions."

Lindstrom's composure impressed Lake. She didn't seem the least bit concerned at having an American police officer visit her and ask questions about an ambassador's murder. She was in complete control of herself, beautiful and charming and friendly without becoming patronizing.

"Ambassador James called you at the Madison Hotel the night he was killed."

"Yes."

"Why?"

"He wanted to see me. No, to be more precise, I wanted to see him."

"About what?"

"About what?" She raised champagne eyebrows and grinned. "About love."

"You were in love with Ambassador James?"

"Yes, very much."

"You were having an affair?"

"I suppose when you're in love with a married man and share his bed, it must be called an affair. How unfortunate."

It was going to be too fast and neat for Lake. She'd expected some cat-and-mouse exchanges, some attempt on Lindstrom's part to couch her answers, but there was none of that. The lady was more impressive by the minute. "How long had you and the ambassador been seeing each other?"

Lindstrom shifted position in her high-back leather chair and adopted an expression of honest reflection. "A long time, years, ever since Iran."

"You were there?"

"In and out. I did business there."

"And you met him and . . ."

"Yes, and fell in love."

Lake had to fight against a growing feeling that she was intruding into Lindstrom's personal life. She wouldn't have liked it herself. She continued. "Did you see him the night he died?"

"No. He wouldn't come to the hotel."

"Why not?"

"He said he was tired. We argued."

"I see."

"Anything else?"

"Should there be? I'm sorry, I don't mean to be flippant, Miss Lake. Geoffrey's death was a great shock to me. I've lost not only a good friend but the only man I've ever really loved.''

''I'm sorry,'' Lake said.

''Thank you.''

''You said you'd met the ambassador in Iran. There was a rumor that he'd benefitted from the American hostages being taken captive, that he had business dealings in Iran. Do you know anything about that?''

Lindstrom shook her head. ''I'm sorry, I don't. More tea?''

''No, thank you. Miss Lindstrom, what about the smuggling of caviar from Iran through Copenhagen. You knew Nuri Hafez, didn't you?''

Lindstrom's eyes opened and she formed a bridge over her lap with her fingers, rapidly tapping them together. ''He's dead.''

''Yes, so I've read. Was he involved with the ambassador in any . . . well, any caviar trade that might have been illegal?''

Lindstrom laughed and poured more tea into her cup. ''Miss Lake, Geoffrey James was many things, some good, some bad, but one thing he was not was a smuggler . . . of anything.''

''What about Nuri Hafez? Did you know him?''

Lindstrom returned to a relaxed pose in her chair, her teacup in her hands, steam rising gently into her face. ''Yes, I knew him.''

''Because of Ambassador James.''

''Yes, and here in Copenhagen.''

Lake's heart tripped at Lindstrom's easy admission. She asked, ''What was he doing here in Copenhagen?''

''Smuggling caviar.''

''I thought you said . . .''

''I said that Geoffrey James would not be involved in anything like that. He wasn't, but Nuri was. He and his brother in Iran took advantage of the political turmoil there and undercut the state caviar commission by paying fishermen much more than they were receiving from the government. They devised an elaborate means of spiriting the caviar out of Iran and to Copenhagen. They made a lot of money, Miss Lake, particularly from America where Iranian goods were banned.''

Lake blew an imagined strand of her hair from her forehead and poked at a note pad with the tip of her felt pen. ''I understand it's still going on.''

''Smuggling? Yes, it is.'' She smiled warmly and took a cigarette from a tile box on her desk. ''Smoke?'' Lake declined. Lindstrom lighted the cigarette, recrossed her legs and slowly exhaled.

''Are you involved in caviar smuggling?'' Lake asked.

''If I were, do you think I'd admit it? Look, Miss Lake, Copenhagen is a free port. That doesn't mean that illegal products are accepted here more readily than other cities, but things are a little easier. That's all, just a little easier.''

''Is the caviar coming through here connected with Nuri Hafez and his brother?''

''I wouldn't know. My assumption is that once Nuri was executed, their operation stopped. You must understand, Miss Lake, that my only knowledge of Nuri Hafez's trade in caviar stems from what Geoffrey told me. He was furious when he learned that a trusted servant had abused his position for profit. Had Geoffrey ever suspected that Nuri would do such a thing, I can assure you he'd never have fought to bring the boy out of Iran.''

''Yes, I believe that,'' Lake said. ''Did he confront Hafez about it?''

''Of course.''

''How did Hafez react?''

"With sullen anger."

"Enough to murder Ambassador James?"

Lindstrom looked surprised that Lake would even ask such a question. She said, "That's exactly why he *did* murder Geoffrey."

Now it was Lake's turn to register surprise. "You say it, Ms. Lindstrom, as though you haven't a doubt in the world."

"I don't. Do you?"

"Yes."

"Based upon what?"

"Instinct, pieces that don't quite fit. There's a great deal that you naturally wouldn't be aware of."

"Such as?"

"I'm really not at liberty to say."

Lindstrom stubbed out her cigarette in a tile ashtray that matched the cigarette case. "But you expect me to be open and candid with you."

"Yes. It happens to be the position I'm in."

Lindstrom's face had hardened. Now, it was soft again as she said, "I understand. The difference is that I have nothing to hide, no reason to withhold everything I know. That's why I'm talking to you at all about it. There's tremendous comfort in not having things to hide, isn't there?"

"I was brought up that way, Ms. Lindstrom."

"So was I. Have you been told that we look alike?"

Lake laughed. "Yes."

"Who told you, Berge?"

"No. Melanie Callender, for one."

Lindstrom lighted another cigarette. "The ever-faithful secretary. She was madly in love with Geoffrey, you know."

"I surmised that."

"He had an interesting effect upon women, magnetic. It was part charm, part power. Your Dr. Werner Gibronski once said in an interview that the reason women found *him* attractive was because women love power.''

"I remember reading that," Connie said. "What about Mrs. James? Did she know?"

"About me? Of course. I was never on her A-List for parties."

Lake wasn't sure where to lead the conversation. She mentioned Sami Abdu's name, which caused Lindstrom to chortle. "A fat fool," she said of him. "Harmless."

"What about Nuri Hafez?" Lake asked. "When did you last see him?"

"Shortly before he returned to Iran. He hid here in Copenhagen for a week after leaving the States. He came to see me, wanted to borrow money. I refused."

"Why didn't you contact the police? He was a fugitive."

"Because I felt it was not in my best interest."

Once again, Lake was taken aback by Lindstrom's candor. There was never a moment of doubt of what answers to give, never a hitch in her voice, nothing to indicate calculation. She was "a piece of work," as Morizio would say.

"You're sure Hafez is dead?" Lake asked.

"I read the same newspapers as anyone else, Miss Lake. I hope you're not offended but I really must go now. I have someone else to see."

"Offended? Hardly. I barged in here, asked you personal questions, received honest answers, and had tea to boot. Thank you very much."

"I enjoyed meeting you. Please give my best to Erl and Mark, and Berge, if you ever see him again."

Lake stood. She asked, "Do you think it's true about Berge?"

"Probably. People like him become rich but remain greedy. I'm sorry that it happened. He was a friend and a very good customer." She walked Lake to the door. "Any last minute questions?"

"Just one. Mark Rosner seemed to indicate that the smuggled caviar was . . . well, not unfamiliar to you."

Lindstrom smiled. "Whatever I sell can be openly and proudly displayed. The smuggled variety of caviar tends to have a distinct fishy odor, no matter how fresh it is. Thank you for stopping by."

22

Approximately an hour after Lake left Inga Lindstrom's office, Sal Morizio parked a rented Austin in front of Melanie Callender's house in Blackheath, a suburb southeast of London. It hadn't been an easy trip. Driving on the "wrong" side of the road for the first time had left him shaken, especially at the numerous "roundabouts" he encountered.

The street contained neat, narrow rowhouses. He thought of the opening segment of "All in the Family." It could have been Queens, New York, except for the orange tile roofs.

A little dog behind the Callender's chain-link fence barked at him as he approached the gate. "Just a little dog," he thought. "Little dogs bite the most," he reminded himself. He tentatively wiggled his fingers at the animal. It continued to bark, but at least it wasn't growling. He flipped up the latch, talked baby talk to the dog, and stepped into the yard. The dog wagged its tail and sat up. "Yeah, nice doggie," Morizio said as he climbed six brick steps to the front door. He rang the bell and heard it sound inside. A squat, ruddy-cheeked man wearing an old gray cardigan sweater over another sweater and baggy pants opened the inside door.

"Mr. Callender?" Morizio shouted through the glass storm door.

"Yes, sir," the man said. He had trouble with the lock on the outer door. "Good morning," he said once he'd opened it.

"Good morning," Morizio said. "Mr. Callender?"

"Yes, sir."

"I'm Salvatore Morizio. I called a few days ago for your daughter, Melanie."

"Right you are. I remember. She's home now. Been on quite a holiday, she has, but these young people do better than mum and me ever did. Been everywhere."

"Yeah, they do get around, don't they?"

"That they do. Come in, come in. A Yank, are you? Nothing but good feelings about Yanks in this house. Come on, don't be shy. This missus has the teapot goin', like she always has, plenty for the whole bloody neighborhood. Makes the best tea in England, she does. Better than all those fancy places where they charge a bloody fortune. In, come in, don't mind him." He pointed to the dog. "Name's Blitz, harmless little devil but he thinks he's a German Shepherd. That's why the name."

Morizio was ushered into a narrow, dark hallway. Ahead was a kitchen where a stout woman worked at a double sink. "Ada, we've got a visitor," Mr. Callender said cheerfully. "That nice young Yank who called for Melanie a few days back."

Ada Callender stopped what she was doing, wiped her hands on her apron, and approached Morizio. "Hello," she said, a sudden wide smile splitting her round, red face like someone had taken a knife to a watermelon. "I'm a mess, I know," she said. "Wasn't expecting a visitor."

"Yeah, I'm sorry just to stop by like this but . . ."

"You'll make him a cup of your best tea," Mr. Callender said. He vigorously shook Morizio's hand. "Name's Basil Callender, Mr. Morizio. What did you say your first name was?"

"Sal. Is your daughter home?"

"Yes, she is. Sound asleep. She got in late last night. These young people, they do things we never did."

"Yes, sir, that's for sure."

Basil Callender and Morizio sat in a cozy living room heated by a coal stove, although Morizio noticed central heating vents. Family photographs stood on a mock fireplace mantel, layers of rugs, knitted caftans piled on a red tweed couch, dark wood tables topped with glass and a manikin in one corner on which an RAF uniform was fitted, leather helmet, goggles, and all. Morizio asked about it.

"My uniform," Basil Callender said. "Didn't get much time in because I took some Kraut lead early in the going, but I did my best."

Ada Callender brought their tea. "I heard her stir," she said. "She'll be up and around soon. I'll tell her you're here."

"Don't disturb her," Morizio said.

"Time a body was up and around anyway," Mrs. Callender said.

The next twenty minutes passed slowly. Not that Basil Callender didn't do his best to make it interesting. He showed Morizio his scrapbook from World War II, photographs of his buddies, his aircraft, and of him in the hospital. There were family pictures, too, many taken when Melanie was a child. Morizio feigned interest but his mind wasn't on it. Mrs. Callender returned, and said, "She'll be with us shortly. Excuse me, I've got to get back to my kitchen."

Mr. Callender kept talking as he produced more scrapbooks, recounting flying exploits and boasting about his family. Melanie, he told Morizio, was quite the celebrity, winging off to America and then becoming personal secretary to the British ambassador. They'd been proud enough when she'd passed her exams for the civil service and was immediately assigned to the diplomatic service, but working directly for a major ambassador abroad was a crowning moment. "He chose her personally," Melanie's father said. "Yes, indeed, Mr. James personally pointed to our little girl and said, 'I want you.' "

"It must have been quite a shock when he died," Morizio said.

"Oh, yes, a sad day for the Crown and for us. Murder! Dreadful thing. Of course, we don't discuss it. Melanie's not supposed to talk about it and she doesn't. She has obligations, she does, and she takes them seriously. She does her job and keeps her mouth shut, God bless her."

They were halfway through the fourth scrapbook when Morizio heard footsteps. He looked toward the hall and saw Melanie standing in the doorway. She was wearing a pink and blue plaid button-down shirt beneath a gray jumper. Her auburn hair was pulled back into a loose bun and tied with a pink ribbon. Morizio's initial reaction was to her beauty. Maybe handsome was a better word. Tall and strong and healthy. It had occurred to him while waiting that he'd never told her father or mother why he wanted to see her, and they'd never asked. Would she recognize his name from his having been in charge of diplomatic security for Washington, D.C.? Had Lake mentioned him when she visited her?

He got up and said, "Hello, Miss Callender, I'm Sal Morizio."

"Hello," she said. "My mother said you were here. Is there something you want?"

"I'd called when you were away on vacation . . . holiday, I guess you call it . . . and left a number. When you didn't call I thought I'd find the house and drop in. I hope you don't mind."

Callender looked at her father. "Yes," she said, "daddy gave me your message. I didn't know who you were. I don't call back people who don't specify why they're calling."

Morizio glanced at Basil Callender, who was overtly uncomfortable with his daughter's lack of courtesy. He cleared his throat and said, "Mr. Morizio's from the States. I told him Yanks are always welcome in this house."

Melanie smiled and nodded that she understood, said to Morizio, "That's right, we have a fondness for Americans. Now, please tell me why you've visited us. It was nice of you but . . ."

"We have a mutual friend, Constance Lake. She spoke with you just before you left Washington."

Melanie was silent while she shuffled her thoughts. She pressed her lips together and said, "Oh, yes, Miss Lake. What a lovely person. She told me you might visit when you were in London. How is she?"

"Fine. She's in Copenhagen."

"A wonderful city."

There was a long, pointed silence. Morizio had the feeling that Melanie didn't want to discuss anything in front of her father, and was trying to figure out how to gracefully get rid of him. She was bailed out by her mother, who called from the kitchen, "Basil, could you come here for a minute?"

The moment he was gone, Callender stepped close to Morizio and said, "How dare you barge into this home? I told Miss Lake that I did not want my parents bothered about what happened in Washington. I resent this deeply."

Morizio didn't flinch from the anger that her brilliant green eyes exuded. He looked into them and said quietly, but firmly, "And my life is on the line because of what happened to the ambassador and Paul Pringle. I deeply resent *that*. Paul Pringle was a friend. I just left his widow and daughter and they raised a hell of a lot of questions, most of them involving one Melanie Callender." He decided to invoke Scotland Yard as he'd done with Ethel Pringle. "I'm working through colleagues at the Yard, Miss Callender, and I'm not leaving London until I get to ask my questions, and until everyone comes up with the right answers."

Basil Callender poked his head around the corner. "More tea?" he asked.

Morizio kept looking at Melanie as he said, "I'd love some."

"It won't be a moment."

"We'll go somewhere else," Melanie said. "I don't want to talk in the house."

"Whatever you say."

She went to the kitchen, returned a few minutes later saying, "I told him I'd promised our friend, Miss Lake, to show you the Blackheath Coin Shop. Since you have such limited time, we'd better do it now."

He got the message and said to Basil Callender, "I'm a coin collector, Mr. Callender. I understand the Blackheath is one of the best shops in London."

"It is, it is," he said. "I've got some beauties from the war. Only take a jiffy."

"Why don't you get them spread out, daddy, and we'll look when we come back. Mr. Morizio only has a few hours."

"Good idea. You'll stay for lunch? The missus usually comes up with a good hot lunch."

Morizio looked at Melanie but said to her father, "We'll see, Mr. Callender, how things go." Melanie got the point, judging from the angry flash in her eyes.

They took Morizio's rented car. Melanie drove. She slammed it into low gear and peeled away from the curb, taking the closest corner as though she were on a racetrack. It was especially frightening for Morizio because, as far as he was concerned, they were on the wrong side of the road. They sped along Lee Road, then veered left onto Duke Humphrey Road which led into a large park. It split just after crossing Charlton Way, and Callender stayed left, on Black Heath Avenue. A reservoir slipped by quickly as she roared toward a large building, passing a sign that read: *Flamsteed Ho Museum.* Callender went around the back of the building and parked beneath a tall, bare tree. She turned off the ignition and faced him. "Now," she said, "ask your bloody questions, then leave me alone."

"Sure you don't want to do this over a beer?"

"Not on your nelly!"

"What's that mean?"

"It means get on with it. A beer. What nerve."

"Okay, no beers. Just fast questions. Why are you sending checks to Ethel Pringle?"

She smiled. "I'm not."

"Like hell you're not. Oh, we're going to play games. All right, checks to Harriet Pringle, or Harriet Worth."

Callender looked straight ahead and sighed. Morizio

could feel the tension in her body. Her right foot tapped on the accelerator and she tightened and loosened her grip on the steering wheel. She didn't look at him as she said, "It should be fairly obvious to you."

"Explain."

"The child. I know who you are, for God's sake. Paul told me about how you helped when that pathetic girl got herself preggers."

"Preggers?"

"Pregnant. With child. You arranged for her to have it in that home."

"That's right. So why the act back at your house?"

"Because I keep business out of that house, and I intend to continue doing it. The check is for the support of Bryan Worth. It will continue until he reaches the age of eighteen."

"Why are *you* paying?"

"*I* don't pay, I administer. I administer many things because I am a good administrator."

"Who do you administer for? Who's Bryan Worth's father?"

She said nothing.

"I think I know."

"Really?"

"Yeah. I think your boss, Ambassador Geoffrey James, got Harriet Worth pregnant. It keeps coming back to that."

"You're wrong."

"Convince me."

"I don't have to do that."

"Maybe you do, Miss Callender. I don't think you understand what's going on here. Everything was nice and neat. Your boss is murdered inside the embassy, which makes it Great Britain's business. It probably could have stayed that way except somebody got careless and leaked out the fact that it wasn't a heart attack. That meant showtime.''

"Pardon?''

"Time to shuck and jive. Fake cooperation with the police, a half-hearted autopsy, pressure from some big people in both governments to seal it up and forget about it. But that's hard to pull off, Miss Callender, damned hard. Along comes Paul Pringle who knows too much. He ends up dead. That's where I come in. I try to do my job and all of a sudden I'm in deep, and so's Connie Lake. Don't you see? This whole mess isn't as nice and neat as you'd like it to be. Sorry, but that's reality. And I promise you one thing, Miss Callender. I'll take you down with me if I have to. I'll put out the word that Melanie Callender has a big mouth, spilled everything to me. I know a lot, and nobody could argue if I pointed to you as the source.''

"You're vile, as bad as any of them.''

"I started off good. Yeah, now I'm vile. You know what Al Capone said?''

"Who?''

"Al Capone, a famous Chicago gangster. He said, 'Kindness and a gun gets you further than kindness alone.' I don't like guns but I'm against a wall. There's a lot of guns pointing at me and Connie and I'm ready to fire back. I don't give a damn who I hit, including a nice, bright, dutiful daughter named Melanie Callender.''

She abruptly turned away.

"Look at me,'' he said.

She resisted at first, then slowly turned to face him. Her eyes were moist and he was tempted to put his arms around her. He didn't want to hurt her, disrupt her life, but that's exactly what had happened to him and to Lake. They came first. He decided to soften up. "Look, Miss Callender, I really am a nice guy, and so's Connie

Lake. We may get married once this mess is over, but if I don't get to the bottom of it we don't have much of a future. I know you haven't done anything wrong, that you're probably just one of many loyal and hard-working people who've gotten sucked into this for one reason or another. It doesn't matter to me whether James fathered Harriet Pringle's child unless it bears on getting to the truth about two murders. I need to know some things, and there aren't many people who might have the answers. Please, I'm not out to hurt anyone, especially you. I just want to keep us from being hurt for the rest of our lives.''

He looked into her eyes for a sign that he was getting through. She slowly closed them, shutting him out of her thoughts. There was a barely discernible tremble in her lower lip and she swallowed hard. When she opened her eyes they were calmer. She said, ''I'm afraid. I shouldn't be talking to you, to anyone about what happened.''

''Yeah, I understand. I'm afraid, too, but sometimes the things that scare us go away when we stand up to them. Just answer some simple questions and I'll get lost. But understand one thing, Miss Callender. I'm not leaving until I have my answers. I'll stay here for the next ten years, I swear. My career is at stake, too.''

''Nigel Barnsworth is Bryan's father.''

''The assistant ambassador?''

''Head of chancery,'' she corrected.

''Whatever,'' he said, drawing a breath and leaning back against the seat. ''Okay,'' he said, ''tell me this. Did it have any bearing on either the murder of Ambassador James or Paul Pringle?''

''I don't know. I don't see how. I was simply told to manage certain bank accounts and to disperse funds from them. One was a monthly check to Harriet Worth.''

"You did that from the embassy in Washington?"

"Yes."

"And you still do it here?"

"Yes."

"What bank?"

"A small bank here in London. We worked through Barclay's in the States."

"Did the ambassador have something to do with this London bank?"

"He was on its board."

"Did he know about Barnsworth and Harriet?"

"Yes."

"And he approved the process."

"Process?"

"The situation you just described."

"Evidently."

Morizio chewed his cheek. He was hungry, and his stomach growled. "You said you managed certain bank accounts. More than one. What were the others?"

"I can't answer that."

"Why not?"

"Because I have responsibilities. Do you have responsibilities? Do you have things you mustn't divulge to outsiders?"

"Of course, but things happen to change the rules. Murder's one of them."

"For you, perhaps, not necessarily for me."

"Because you were involved?"

"Involved? In murder? You're daft."

"And getting daftier every minute." He wanted her to smile. She didn't.

A museum guard walked past the car and glanced inside. Morizio nodded at him. He kept walking. Morizio said to Callender, "Tell me about Ambassador James's oil company."

Callender furrowed her brow and shrugged. "I told Miss Lake what I knew, which was practically nothing."

"You didn't get involved in its operation?"

"No."

"Why has it been shut down instead of sold?"

She seemed surprised that he knew, asked where he'd heard it.

"From good sources within the oil industry, and from Marsha James."

"Really?"

"Yeah, and it bothers me. Supposedly it was a going business, making millions. He dies and leaves it in his will to his wife. What does she do? Instead of running with it she walks away, doesn't even sell it."

"There was nothing to sell," Callender said so softly that Morizio asked her to repeat it. "There was nothing to sell. The company was built on certain contacts Ambassador James had made. When he was gone, those contacts were lost. There was nothing tangible to sell, no tankers, no refineries, not even a desk or chair."

"Why couldn't Mrs. James keep up the contacts? What about his partners, the Scotsman, Ferguson?"

"If you believe anything, Mr. Morizio, believe me when I say I knew nothing about the company."

"Let me throw out a couple of other names. Nuri Hafez, George Thorpe."

"What about Nuri Hafez? He's dead. He killed the ambassador and paid for it. As far as Mr. Thorpe is concerned, best to let that lie. He's a very important person in the employ of the Crown."

"He tells me he represents trade and business interests."

"That is my understanding."

"What else?"

"About him? Believe me again when I say I know nothing more than what I've just said. I know he's held in high regard at the Home Office, and whenever he visited the embassy he was treated like a V.I.P."

"He was close to the ambassador?"

"Yes, although they were not close friends. It was all official business, as I understand it."

Morizio sensed he was letting her get away. She'd slipped into an 'I don't know anything' routine. He added a rough edge to his voice as he asked, "What about the ambassador's will? What did he leave his wife besides the oil company?"

"Very little. He didn't have much aside from the oil venture. Oh, he wasn't a pauper. He had his business interests here in Britain and he was highly respected within the business community, but the major money had always been hers."

"Marsha James's?"

"Yes. Unfortunately, she . . ." She turned away from him and started tapping her foot again.

"Unfortunately what?"

"It's none of my business, or yours."

"Don't pull back now, Miss Callender. Trust me, help me understand."

"It isn't anything terribly revelatory. Mrs. James's family money had run low. He . . . the ambassador had invested a good deal of it in ventures that were not successful, aside from the oil company."

Morizio thought for a moment, then said, "He didn't do very well by his wife, did he? He loses her money, finally starts a business that succeeds but is of no value to her when he dies. What's she going to do?"

Callender let out a sarcastic laugh. "She's been taken care of. No need to worry about Mrs. James."

"How?"

"The British civil service takes very good care of its own. I should know. I see that she receives her check every month."

"You? Why you? Why isn't her pension paid by the government?"

"It is, but I administer that account."

"Like the Barnsworth account for Harriet Worth."

"Yes, I suppose. Because of everything that occurred at the embassy in Washington, a separate set of accounts was established. It's my new job, one I'd like not to lose because of you, Mr. Morizio."

"You won't lose anything because of me."

"If anyone knew I'd talked to you . . ."

"They won't, as long as you keep talking to me. How much does Mrs. James get?"

"A large sum."

"Every month."

"Yes."

"For the rest of her life."

"Until I'm told not to send it."

"As long as she keeps getting money, you have a job."

"Perhaps. I hope it works out that way."

"They pay you good?"

"Quite."

"More than you were making before?"

"That's personal."

"Sure. How much to Mrs. James?"

"I won't answer that. I'm certain her pension is public knowledge. The sum is not."

"I'll check through my contacts at Scotland Yard and your home office."

"You said you wouldn't do anything to . . ."

"Save me the time and trouble. How much? Skip the pounds, give it to me in dollars."

"A quarter of a million dollars a year."

He whistled.

"I should get back."

"Sure." She started the engine. "By the way," he said, "you have a nice family. I like them."

"I love them. They're very proud of me."

"So I gathered."

"I'd like them to remain so."

"Why shouldn't they?"

"You tell me."

"You have nothing to worry about. Anything else you can tell me?"

She shook her head. "Actually, I feel better about this."

"About talking to me?"

"Yes. Nothing I've told you is a deep, dark secret. I was afraid I'd say something wrong, share a secret I shouldn't, but the fact is I don't know any secrets."

"I'm glad you feel that way."

"Should I come in?" he asked when they reached her house. "I was invited to lunch."

"I prefer that you not. Please understand."

"Sure. Thank your parents for me."

"Yes. I'll say you had to catch a plane."

She got out of the car and started toward the front door, stopped, turned, and said, "Don't ever come here again." She ran the rest of the way to the house.

He had a banger and a beer at a pub on the way back to London, returned the rented car with profound relief after narrowly avoiding two potential accidents, and took a taxi to the May Fair. He tried Lake at the d'Angleterre; no answer in her room. He left a message that he'd called and would call again, packed his things in anticipation of checking out and took a taxi to the

London Times' offices where, with some friendly help from a librarian, he read back issues that dealt with Geoffrey James and his days as ambassador to Iran. He was totally engrossed in it and was surprised when he looked at his watch and saw it was a few minutes past five. He'd booked SAS's last flight to Copenhagen, which left Heathrow Airport at nine. He put away the notes he'd made, thanked the librarian and used his telephone credit card to call Lake from a booth on New Bond Street. She still wasn't there. He had two drinks at the May Fair bar, a quiet dinner in the restaurant, checked out, and was on his way to the airport at eight.

"Enjoy your visit?" the driver asked.

"Yeah, very much," Morizio answered. He was sad that he was leaving. "I intend to come back soon," he told the driver.

"That's good," said the driver.

"This was business," Morizio said. "Next time it'll be for pleasure."

23

A harried waiter in a tuxedo at Els Restaurant served Connie Lake her dessert, three kinds of sherbet garnished with slices of fruit. Els was a favorite spot with Copenhagen natives, small, inexpensive, and good. Lake wouldn't have known about it except for her dinner companion, Mark Rosner.

She'd decided to make contact with him again after talking to Inga Lindstrom. Knowing where the caviar was delivered was one thing, having easy access to it was another. She wanted to be with someone who could point the way and clear any barriers. She would have preferred Erl Rekstad (and knew Morizio would, too), but was reluctant to call him. Maybe his wife would answer. Besides, he was too close to Lindstrom if only by virtue of physical proximity.

Rosner was easy. She called his room, reminded him of his dinner invitation, and . . . well, there they were at Els.

"Satisfied?" Rosner asked.

"Very. The food was excellent."

"And no tourists. Ready for the lowlife?"

Lake laughed. "Is it that bad?" she asked.

He shook his head and laughed, too. "No, but there is a certain forbidden quality to it. Funny, right after the hostages were taken and Iranian caviar dried up in the States, I received a call from a friend in Paris. He told me that 'good stuff' would be arriving in Copenhagen and that I should be on hand. I laughed at him, but I couldn't resist seeing what it was all about. I flew here and met this skinny Iranian wearing a U of Penn tee-shirt, sneakers, and jeans. I didn't trust him and made him open every can he was selling. It was all excellent quality caviar, the best. I had two hundred thousand in cash with me and I gave it to him. The next time I came back, about three months later, he was in a three-piece suit and had a blonde Danish bimbo on his arm. We've been doing business ever since."

"What a marvelous story," Lake said, thinking of Nuri Hafez. "I can't wait to see it in person."

He laughed. "It's not like a movie, Connie, where sinister characters stand in alleys while a drop is made. It used to be like that but not anymore. It's all in the open, like a flea market. The boats come in, we check our shipments, hand over the cash, and enjoy the rest of the evening. It's pretty boring, but it's still a good excuse to come to Copenhagen every three months."

"Let's go," she said.

He helped her on with her coat and they stepped out onto Skrandboulevarden. The mild November weather had continued; it was like an early spring night. Rosner hailed a cab and told the driver, "Overgaden, Christianshavn."

The temperate night had lured hundreds of people out of their homes and into the streets of Christianshavn. An accordion player entertained a cluster of people on

one corner, a wizened old man manipulated hand pup-
pets on another. Men and women grouped together in
cafes, their laughter spilling out into the long narrow
street and across the canal. Boats tied to either side
were filled with bodies and beer, and the heavy sweet
odor of marijuana hung over certain ones.

"What now?" Connie asked after Rosner had paid
the driver.

"We have a drink and wait. We have to end up over
there, but there's no sense in standing around." He
pointed directly across the canal where a few people
had gathered.

He led her to a small restaurant and they took stools
at the bar, near the front window. He ordered a Tuborg,
she a glass of Aqvavit. Rosner waved to a table of men
at the rear of the restaurant.

"Buyers?" Lake asked.

"Uh huh. The handsome guy in the vested blue suit
is a competitor from New York. The little one with the
funny mustache is from Los Angeles. I don't recognize
the third one."

"And they've come all the way to Denmark for
caviar," Lake said.

"All the way for *money*," Rosner said, sipping his
beer. "These Iranians are delivering the best. How
they get it out of Iran is beyond me, but they do, and
we turn a big profit back home."

A limousine pulled up in front, an elderly man got
out, entered the restaurant, spotted Rosner, and said,
"*Bon soir*, Rosner."

"*Bon soir*, Henri," Rosner said. The man gave Connie an admiring look before going to the table and
joining the others. Rosner said to her, "He's from
Paris. Funny old guy. He damn near came to blows
once with a German over a batch of caviar, right here

on the docks.'' He chuckled. ''It's not gold but it comes close, black gold.''

Lake called the d'Angleterre from a booth near the bar. ''Have I any messages?'' she asked. The operator told her of Morizio's call. ''Mr. Morizio will be arriving tonight,'' Connie said. ''Please see that he has a key to my room, 102, and ask him to wait for me. I should be there by eleven.''

The men from the table left together and climbed into the Frenchman's limo. Rosner finished his beer and said to Connie, ''Let's go. Time to do business. By the way, don't be offended if I don't introduce anyone to you. They can be a little paranoid. Just stick close to me and take it in.''

They walked down Overgaden to where Torvegade spanned the canal, crossed, and doubled back along the strip of warehouses on the Overgaden neden Vandet side. By the time they arrived there were a dozen well-dressed men waiting for caviar. Three young Arab men wearing jeans, sneakers, and windbreakers sat with their feet dangling from the dock. Two gray vans approached, stopped and their young Arab drivers turned off the headlights and joined their friends. One lighted a joint and passed it around.

Lake took note of their location. It was about two hundred yards from Inga Lindstrom's office building. ''What now?'' she asked Rosner.

''What do you mean?''

''Is it like an auction, highest bidder and all?''

He shook his head. ''It used to be. I was lucky because, thanks to my friend from Paris, I was here early in the game. He had the European market sewed up and I had the U.S., but the word got around and the vultures descended. It got pretty cutthroat until Inga set up the system.''

"Inga?"

He looked at her strangely. "Yeah, you knew that, didn't you?"

"She told me a little about it," said Lake. She'd have to be careful, she realized. She'd led Rosner to believe that she was closer to Lindstrom than was the case which, undoubtedly, contributed to his decision to bring her. That, and the prospect of an affair. She'd better be careful on both counts, she told herself.

Rosner evidently wasn't about to dwell on her slip. He said, "It costs us more now to go through her but it's worth it. We used to have to make the buy here on the docks, catch a chartered plane to Stockholm and connect there with an Icelandic 707 that made a three A.M. stop before continuing to New York. That's one of the problems with caviar, it's so damn perishable. Thank God those days are over."

Lake took a chance. "Because of the setup with Inga."

"That's right. Now we can enjoy another night in Copenhagen and fly home in the morning, like civilized human beings." He looked up the canal to one of two inlets from the Inderhavnen Canal, which separated the city from Christianshavn, "I think they're here."

Lake looked in the same direction and saw the bouncing beams of a searchlight mounted on a small power boat. A second boat followed. There was an instant electricity in the group. She smiled as she thought of a dozen well-to-do businessmen from around the globe, their pockets bulging with cash, waiting for a shipment of illicit goods. She looked up and down the dock for signs of police, or Customs officials. Nothing. Evidently, everything was tied up in a neat package, with Inga Lindstrom's finger on the bow. Copenhagen, the "free port," she thought. Famous for "free love," too. Free everything? Evidently.

The boats, eighteen-foot cabin cruisers, slid up to the dock. Their lean young pilots tossed lines to the Iranians on the dock, who secured them to pilings. They conversed in their native tongue, and there was a lot of laughter. Lake could see other people in the boats' cabins but they were in shadow, and didn't join the others on the dock.

She walked with Rosner to the first boat where the Iranians had formed a chain, a bucket brigade of caviar. Tins of the precious sturgeon roe had been packed in styrofoam freezer chests, which were being stacked on the dock. One thing was certain: the sturgeon were running in the Caspian; gourmands would not lack the the top-quality Iranian caviar around the globe for the next three months.

Connie moved closer and saw that each chest had a label. The handwriting was crude and difficult to read. Most labels contained initials: M.R.—P.Y.—B.N.—L—J.K. About a third of the cases had the word *Meen* written on them. She tugged on Rosner's coat sleeve and asked what it meant.

"Uncommitted," he said hastily. "First to come, first to get. I think it's an Arab word."

"Who decides?"

He scowled at her. "Come on, who else? Inga."

"I know *that*, but how does *she* decide?"

"Bucks. This is a light trip for me. I've got overstock back home. If I didn't, I'd pick up some of the uncommitted at whatever price I can negotiate with her."

Lake watched the rest of the unloading process. When all the chests were on the dock, the buyers inspected their shipments. Rosner removed a can from one of his chests, opened it, and scooped caviar from it with his finger. He offered it to Connie, who declined. He tasted, grunted, nodded his approval, and replaced the can in the chest. One of the boat drivers, whom Lake had noticed was not as happy-go-lucky as the others, approached Rosner and stood passively in front of him. *"Kwiyis,"* Rosner said. "Here." He pulled an envelope from his inside jacket pocket and handed it to the Iranian, who went to the next buyer, and the next. The older gentleman from Paris had taken a small spoon from his pocket and used it to taste from several cans. He, too, paid the Iranian collector, who hopped down onto one of the boats and disappeared inside the cabin.

"That's it," Rosner said. "It goes to the warehouse overnight, and we meet up with it again at the airport in the morning. "Well, what do you think? As exciting as you thought it would be?"

Connie laughed. "No," she said. "I'd love to see the next step, though, the warehouse."

"Why?" he asked.

"Just curious."

"Call Inga. She'll give you a tour."

"I know she will but . . . I'm curious, Mark. Why bother even coming here at all? You could pay Inga for the shipment and have it sent to you."

He laughed. "And miss another excuse to come to Copenhagen? Not on your life. Besides, it's not that simple. The money has to be paid directly to the Iranians."

"Why?"

"Beats me, but that's the way it's set up. Inga bills us her fees through normal channels and gets paid like · every other purveyor. There'd be a problem with shipping documents, too. The papers that accompany the shipment identify us by name, and we're the only ones

who can accompany it through Customs. That's the
way it is, and who's to argue?''

"I understand."

"Good. Let's go back to the hotel and make sense.''

"Make sense?"

"Carry things to their logical and human conclusion.''

"Logical and . . . Look, Mark, I have a big problem.''

"What is it?"

"A very jealous fiancé.''

He grinned. "You should meet my wife.''

"I'd rather not, but you'll meet my fiancé. He's at
the d'Angleterre. We've been traveling together, but he
had business in London.''

"He's there now?"

"Yes.'

He chewed on his lip and looked around. Everyone
from the buyer group was gone. The last van had
started its engine and was pulling away for its short run
to Lindstrom's warehouse. The soft sound of the street
corner accordionist melded with laughter from a bar
across the canal. "You know what you are?'' Rosner
said.

"What?"

"A very beautiful woman who's also a . . .''

She put her index finger to her lips. "Don't be
crude.''

He put his hands on his hips and shook his head.
"You've never been in Copenhagen before, have you?''

"I told you at dinner I hadn't.''

"Beautiful women are a dime a dozen here.''

"So?"

"So, they all have the same equipment. Understand?''

"I'm well aware of that. I'm glad. It gets me off the
hook.'' She smiled and touched his arm. "Thanks for
the tour, and for dinner. I loved both.''

"That's wonderful." His sarcasm was not to be missed.

"Look, you go on back and enjoy the evening. I have to stop in and see a friend before I meet up with . . . *him*."

"What's his name?"

"Sal. What's your wife's name?"

"Linda."

"Thanks again."

"Sure you won't come back with me?"

"Positive."

"Don't wander around Christianshavn too long. It's quaint, but can be rough."

"I'll be careful."

She walked with him to Torvegade where he hailed a cab, shook her hand, and winked as the taxi pulled away.

She looked back up the dock to where they'd been, and beyond. The vans had stopped in front of the warehouse attached to Lindstrom's office building. Their lights were on, their motors running. A large metal overhead door lifted and the vans drove inside, the door slamming shut behind them.

Lake started walking toward the warehouse, then stopped. She looked across the canal, which although only fifty yards wide seemed, at least at that moment, to divide two different worlds that were miles apart. The world on the other side was lively and carefree. There was life there. On her side, there was only stillness, and menace. The warehouse seemed to have grown into massive, threatening black shapes against a light sky.

She resumed walking, her footsteps kicking back at her from the pavement. She glanced into the shadows on her left and imagined there were eyes trained upon her. She looked over the edge of the dock into oil-slicked water and shuddered at the thought of falling.

There was a scraping noise to her left. She turned and saw the blazing copper eyes of a greasy gray cat. It was gone in an instant.

This was the point of no return, she told herself as she continued walking, not daring to stop. Up until then she'd considered returning to the hotel, meeting up with Morizio and coming back together. But, the caviar would be gone by morning. She thought of Berge Nordkild and his recent drug arrest, and of Inga Lindstrom. Could there be a connection between her caviar and his narcotics? She wondered, too, whether the Lindstrom caviar setup was linked, in even a tangential way, with the murders of Geoffrey James and Paul Pringle. Pringle had been accused of dealing with drugs. And, there was Nuri Hafez. Was he really dead? Had his involvement with the Iranian pipeline contributed to the events that had caused her and Morizio so much personal grief? She kept walking because what she wanted more than anything was to arrive back at the d'Angleterre with answers to all their questions. It would be good to see Morizio's face if she could make that happen.

She'd turned off the tape recorder once Rosner got into the cab. Now, she turned it on again and talked as she walked, recounting her thoughts and observations. She stopped talking when she reached the warehouse. She listened, heard nothing. The large overhead door was closed, its seal tight; no light showed around or beneath it.

A narrow alleyway between the warehouse and the three-story glass office building was shielded from the street by a tall red board gate. It looked to be open a crack and Lake went to it. A slide latch hadn't been secured. She pushed on the gate and it swung open with a rusty moan. She tensed and waited for a reaction to the noise. Nothing. She looked into the alley and noticed a shaft of light coming from beneath a steel door at the far end. She went to it and turned the knob. It was locked. A few feet farther into the alley was another door half the height of the one she'd tried. It was more like an internal submarine hatch; a person of normal height would have to double over to get through it. Its handle was of the latch variety. She slowly turned it and pushed. The door swung open easily. She bent over and looked inside. It was difficult for her to know what was there because it was dark, except for moonlight that filtered through dirt-crusted windows high on a back wall. "What the hell," she said in a whisper. She also said for the tape recorder, "In an alley next to a warehouse adjacent to Lindstrom's office building. Time about nine-thirty. About to enter small door at rear of alley."

Once inside, she was thankful for the moon. Without it the hallway would have been coal black. She moved slowly, her hand in front of her, eyes straining to see as much as moonlight would allow. She heard voices from a room to the right and looked for a door. There wasn't one. She continued to the end of the hall where a steel ladder attached to the wall led to an open trap door in the ceiling. The voices were louder now as she climbed the first three rungs of the ladder and poked her head through the opening. It was a large empty attic. There were no windows, but light glowed from an opening in the floor a hundred feet to her right. She completed her climb and tested the floor. It seemed solid. She took a step toward the light and stopped. The boards didn't creak. She took another step, then another until she was in a position to view the downstairs on an angle. Men below were talking and laughing. She was about to move into a better position to observe when there was the dull thud of a heavy door being shut, then the harsh rattle of chains lifting the overhead door. A rush of cool air came up through the opening in the floor and it felt good. The attic was hot. There was more laughter, then vehicle doors closing and engines starting. She went to the edge and looked down. The vans that had transported the caviar from the dock drove from the warehouse and into the street. One of the young Iranians hopped out and activated a switch that caused the heavy metal door to descend.

Connie waited a few minutes, then tentatively tested a rickety wooden ladder. She reached the bottom and surveyed the area. The only illumination was from a work light in a far corner, just enough for her to see that she was in the middle of a large storage room. Steel cargo containers were piled at one end, hundreds of cardboard boxes at another. A hill of empty pallets and two forklifts were in the middle of the room.

The back wall, which butted up against the hallway through which she'd entered the building, contained a corner-to-corner and floor-to-ceiling bank of walk-in refrigerators. Above each set of doors was a tiny glowing red light. She opened one of the doors. Chilled darkness. She scanned the outside wall and noticed sets of rocker switches. She pushed the first one, which produced nothing, then pushed the second and a dim light came to life inside the refrigerator.

She entered and saw that the labeled freezer chests had been stacked on slatted wooden shelves. She opened the first case to her left and removed some of the caviar tins. The labels read: *Caviar—Product of the Soviet Union—Sevruga, Oestra, Beluga,* depending on the tin's contents. Those processed with little salt said *Malosol.*

The chests were grouped according to whose shipment they comprised, and each group had a packet of papers with it. She opened one that was addressed to a food broker in Dallas, Texas. In it were bills-of-lading, Customs releases, port-of-origin forms, and tax declarations, all executed with fancy seals and scrawled signatures. She replaced those papers and went to Mark Rosner's shipment. His envelope also contained the necessary official papers.

The next order was addressed to *Nordkild Importers and Catering, Washington, D.C.* Lake read it aloud for the tape, and included the question, "Why another shipment to Nordkild now that he's been arrested?" She provided a possible answer as she removed the lid of one of the chests and took out a can—"The order was in before his arrest." Then she asked, "Will it still be shipped to him, or will Lindstrom hang on to it?"

She slipped off the rubber bands that secured the lid and looked inside. Black, oily sevruga caviar glistened in the light of the tiny bulb. She pushed her little finger into the roe and held up the can to judge how far her finger had invaded, relative to the tin's depth. It seemed to her that she hadn't reached bottom. She placed the can on a shelf, took a Kleenex from her purse, wiped her finger on it, then spread it out, and dumped the contents of the caviar onto it. She found a nail file in her purse and used it to pry around the tin's metal bottom. It came loose and fell to the floor. Lake held the can close to her face. "Sure," she said as she visually examined a plastic pouch of white powder. She slit it open with the file, smelled it, removed some, and tasted it. Cocaine, just the way it tasted during her MPD narcotics training sessions.

She replaced the false bottom, managed to get most of the caviar back into the can, wadded up the tissue and jammed it in her coat pocket. She carefully adjusted the rubber band over the top, talking for the tape all the while, put that can in her purse, and repeated the test on a can from a chest labeled simply—*Lindstrom*. The result was the same, cocaine beneath a false bottom. That can, too, went into her purse.

Should she check other shipments for signs of drug smuggling? She decided not to take the time. Her visit had paid off, and what seemed monumentally important now was to get back to the safety of the hotel, where Morizio would be waiting. Her heart beat faster; fear and excitement joined forces.

She hadn't been aware of the musty cold of the refrigerator because she'd been busy. Now, she shivered, and her nostrils tightened against the smell. One final look around. Everything was in place.

"What?" she said. There had been a noise outside. She slowly turned and looked into the warehouse but saw nothing—until a shadow ten feet tall fell across the floor.

Then, the light in the refrigerator went out.

"Oh," she said.

And the heavy steel door slammed shut.

24

Midnight.

Morizio prowled Room 102 at the d'Angleterre, checking his watch and going in and out the French doors to the roof. He went downstairs at 12:30 and told the desk he'd be in the bar in case there was a call for him. He thought a drink would relax him, but it didn't. He gulped it down and returned to the room where he went through Connie's belongings. Her tape recorder was gone, but there were tapes, each carefully labeled. He inserted one in his recorder and listened to her conversation with Inga Lindstrom. He found it interesting but it shed little light on Connie's whereabouts.

Once the Lindstrom interview ended, there were a series of comments from Connie, notes and observations, and she recounted, in detail, her dinner with Mark Rosner, Erl Rekstad, and Aunt Eva. Although Lake didn't specifically say it, it was clear to Morizio that she intended to go to the docks when the caviar shipment arrived. "Damn it, why didn't you wait for me?" he said aloud. The answer was obvious. She wasn't sure when he'd arrive and didn't want to miss the opportunity.

"Is that where you are?" he wondered as he got up, swiped a used Kleenex from a night table and tossed it in a basket. He looked at his watch. 1:15. He took a Copenhagen phone directory from beneath a Danish *Bibelen* in a night table drawer, found the listing for hospitals and called them all. No American woman had been admitted that night was the unanimous response.

He found a listing for Eva Nygaard and called the number. Eva answered. There was music and laughter in the background. Morizio introduced himself. "Ah, yes, Constance's young man. How are you?"

"Worried," said Morizio. "I can't find Connie."

"Really. Perhaps she's out."

"Of course she's out, but where? We were supposed to meet here at eleven."

"You're at the hotel?"

"Yes."

There was a pause. Eva then said, "Is there anything I can do?"

"Probably not. I was hoping she was with you."

"I wish she were. I'm having a party. Why don't you join us and we can wait for her together. Leave a message at the desk and . . ."

"No thanks. I'd rather stay here."

"All right. I'm sure everything's fine, just a mix-up. She'll be there. She seems to be a responsible young woman."

"Yeah."

"She's very fond of you, very loyal."

"Yeah, I . . . thanks. Maybe we'll get to meet."

"Please call and let me know when she arrives. I stay up very late."

"I will."

At three, he called the desk and asked what room Mark Rosner was in. "Ring him," he told the operator.

"Sir, it's . . ."

"Just call him. He's expecting the call."

The phone in Rosner's room rang ten times before he picked it up and mumbled, "Hello?"

"Mr. Rosner?"

"Yes."

"My name's Salvatore Morizio. My fiancée, Constance Lake, told me about you."

"Oh." There was a long silence. Finally, Rosner said, "Yes, she told me about you, too. I don't really know her. We had a drink . . . a whole group . . . just a . . . I mean, I was with some friends and so was she and . . ."

"Jesus, calm down, I'm not calling about *that*. Look, Rosner, she was supposed to be here at the hotel at eleven. It's three. She's not here. Do you know where she is?"

"She's not here. Three? Three in the morning? God, I . . ."

"Yeah, sorry to wake you and I wouldn't have unless I was worried. I *am* worried."

"Three. She's not there. I don't know what to tell you, I . . ."

"You haven't seen her tonight?"

"No, I . . . well, yeah, I did, as a matter of fact. We had a fast dinner and then we . . ."

"Where'd you have dinner?"

"Where? A place called Els. It was quick, just a fast dinner before we went to the docks."

"What docks? Where the caviar comes in?"

"You . . . yes, as a matter of fact. She told you?"

"That she was going? Yes. You did go?"

"Sure. I left her there."

"On the docks? Alone?"

"Hold on, it was her decision. I asked her to come back here with me but . . . I mean, I just asked her out of courtesy, didn't want to see her wandering around down there. I warned her. It's pretty, Christianshavn, but there's . . ."

"When did you leave her?"

"I don't know, around ten-thirty, I guess. Can't be sure."

"Where *exactly* did you leave her?"

"Well, let's see. It was on the corner of . . . of the street that crosses the canal . . . Torvegade, it's called . . . at Torvegade and Overgaden neden Vandet. Sorry, my pronunciation's not too good."

"Spell them for me."

Rosner did his best.

"How would you like to take a ride?"

"A ride? Now?

"Yeah, right now."

"I can't, I . . ."

"Mr. Rosner, I'm a cop, so's Connie. We're here on a murder case."

"She said she was . . ."

"An interior designer." Lake had mentioned that in her taped notes.

"That's what she said. You're both cops?"

"Right, and I have to find her, *now*. I'll meet you in the lobby in ten minutes."

Morizio stood by the desk until a sleepy Rosner arrived. He extended his hand and said, "I'm Mark Rosner."

"Sal Morizio. Let's go."

They took one of two cabs from in front of the d'Angleterre and went to where Rosner had left her. "Wait," Morizio told the driver. He and Rosner stood on the street and looked in the direction of where the caviar drop had been made. Rosner explained what had happened. "Let's go," Morizio said.

Rosner led him to where they'd taken delivery of the caviar. "What next?" Morizio asked.

Rosner shrugged, pulled up the collar of his Chesterfield coat against the cold, wet fog and said, "It goes to the warehouse."

"Which warehouse?"

"Down there, at Lindstrom Foods."

"Inga Lindstrom."

"You know her, too."

"Sure. Show me."

Morizio checked the roll-up main door and the gate to the alleyway. Both were secured, although he was able to unlatch the gate. He looked into the alley, saw nothing. "What time does Inga get in in the morning?" he asked.

"Tomorrow . . . I mean this morning it'll be early. We pick up."

"Your caviar."

"Yes. Listen, Mr. Morizio, none of this has to do with the caviar, does it?"

"Why should it? Is it illegal?"

Rosner laughed. "No, of course not, we cut a few corners but . . ."

"I don't like caviar, and I don't care who does or how they get it. I want my partner back."

"Sure, I understand. *Partner*. Connie said you were engaged."

"Right. Can you think of a better partnership?"

Another laugh from Rosner. "No, I guess not."

Morizio pondered what to do next. He looked back at the waiting taxi and said to Rosner, "I appreciate you coming with me like this. I really do. Why don't you go back to the hotel and get some sleep.''

''I'm wide awake now. I have to be back here at eight.''

''Whatever. By the way, what was Connie wearing when you last saw her?''

Rosner had trouble recalling. ''I think she had on a blue blazer, dark blue, and a turtleneck. Yeah, that's right, a powder blue turtleneck. And a raincoat.''

''Skirt?''

''Yes.''

Morizio gave him a ''you dummy'' look.

''A skirt. Black, gray, something dark. And shoes, low shoes, I think.''

''Good. Did she tell you why she was going to hang around here after you left?''

''A friend, she said. She wanted to see a friend.''

''No names.''

''No.''

''She mentioned Inga Lindstrom?''

''Sure.''

Morizio nodded. ''Anything else you can tell me?''

''No. I'm sorry. I hope you find her. She's very nice and, if you don't mind my saying so, very loyal to you.''

''You put her to the test?''

Rosner grinned, sheepishly. ''I wouldn't put it that way,'' he said. ''Can I ask you a question?''

''Sure.''

''Was that why she had dinner with me, to get closer to this case you're on?''

''Could be. Then again, maybe she was just testing herself. You're a nice looking guy.''

''Thanks.''

''One favor.''

"Sure."

"Keep your mouth shut about this, at the hotel, back home, anywhere."

"All right, I will."

"Good. Go ahead and take the cab. I'm going to hang around."

"Why don't you come back with me and wait until it gets light. Maybe she'll call."

It dawned on Morizio that he had no other choice, although the idea of waiting impotently infuriated him.

He left Rosner at the d'Angleterre elevator, bounded up the stairs to his floor and went to the room. There hadn't been any messages.

Fifteen minutes later, his recorder in his pocket, he took another cab back to Christianshavn. This time he had it stop on the other side of the canal, directly across from Inga Lindstrom's warehouse and offices. He stood alone on the street. The only sounds were from metal spars and fittings clanking against boat masts in a moderate breeze, creating a dissonant metallic symphony. The temperature was dropping fast; Morizio shivered against it and stood in a doorway, his eyes trained across the canal. He decided to take a walk to keep warm, glancing every few minutes back at the warehouse.

A fisherman greeted him from his boat. "Any place I can get a cup of coffee?" Morizio asked.

The fisherman screwed up his face, said, "*Jeg taler ikke Engelsk.*"

"Oh," Morizio said. "Coffee. Cafe."

"*Kaffe.*"

"Yeah."

"*Kaffe.*" The fisherman waved him on to his creaky, peeling boat and poured two cups from a large thermos. Morizio smiled, held up his cup, and said, "*Skal!*"

The fisherman laughed and returned the toast, then

went about his chores. Morizio sat on the gunwale and enjoyed the warmth the coffee provided. He wished he could have talked to the fisherman, asked about the area and the warehouse and the comings and goings of its employees. Morizio spoke, and could understand, a modicum of French and Spanish, but Danish was out of the question. He'd never heard anything like it. German might have helped but his knowledge of that was to count from one to ten.

He knew there couldn't be a refill when he saw headlights turn down Overgaden neden Vandet and head for Lindstrom's warehouse. Another vehicle quickly followed. They stopped, the overhead door was raised and they vanished inside.

"Thanks," Morizio told the fisherman as he handed him his cup. The fisherman nodded and resumed splicing line. Morizio walked to Torvegade, crossed the canal and approached the warehouse. He heard a car behind him. He didn't want to be noticed so he quickly turned and walked toward another building, as though he belonged there. The car sped by. Morizio looked over his shoulder, saw that the driver was a blonde who looked like Connie Lake. He moved into a position to see her park where the vans had been, get out, and quickly walk to the three-story glass building attached to the warehouse. "She gets an early start," he muttered.

He waited until she'd disappeared inside, then quickened his step until reaching the building. Lights were on upstairs; the windows were pungent yellow squares against the surrounding darkness. He noticed that a faint orange streak was now on the eastern horizon. Daybreak in Copenhagen. "Thanksgiving," he realized. Would he have something to give thanks for? "We'll see," he said as he reached into his coat pocket, activated the recorder, and went to the front door. It was open. He stepped inside, read the lobby board, went up the stairs, and paused outside Lindstrom's offices. Knock or walk in? Walk in, was the decision.

His sudden appearance startled Lindstrom, who stood in the reception area, the telephone in her hand. She placed her other hand over the mouthpiece and asked, "Yes, what do you want?"

"Inga Lindstrom?"

"Yes . . . wait . . ." Into the phone she said, "There is no argument. That is the way it will be done." She put the phone down hard. "Who are you?" she asked. She was annoyed, and a little concerned.

"Salvatore Morizio, Miss Lindstrom, Washington, D.C. Police. I work with Constance Lake."

She muttered something in Danish under her breath, probably an expletive, Morizio decided. "You're here early," Morizio said.

She extended her hands. "Is there something wrong with that?"

"Early birds catch worms, I'm told. Connie Lake. Where is she?"

"Where is she? Is this some sort of a joke?"

"It sure as hell better not be. She was here last night."

"Was she? Excuse me, I have work to do."

She walked into her office, Morizio at her heels. "Get out!" she said.

"Not until I get answers. I'll get 'em by myself, or with the Danish police, one way or the other."

"Then get the police. Why should that be of concern to me?"

"I'll figure out something. Look, Miss Lindstrom, I'm here for only one reason, and all the tough talk doesn't help. I want to find Connie Lake. She was supposed to meet me at the d'Angleterre last night but never showed. I found out she was down here on the docks when the caviar arrived, and stayed around after everyone else went home. I need your help. I'd like it pleasantly.''

If she was surprised that he knew about the caviar delivery, she didn't show it. She said, ''You and your friend have a strange way of soliciting help.''

''My friend and I are engaged to be married.''

''Congratulations.''

''Thanks. Now, can you help me? *Will* you help me?''

''How?'' She sounded sincerely confused.

''You talked to her yesterday afternoon.''

''Yes. I was kind enough to allow her to barge in here and to give her my time.''

Morizio, ignoring the cutting edge of the comment, asked, ''Did she say anything that might indicate what her plans were for the evening?''

''No. Christianshavn can be dangerous at night.''

Morizio walked to the window. A few commercial fishing boats slid slowly through the water on their way to the open sea, and lights had erupted in windows across the canal. The horizon was now magenta. The tiny black silhouette of a jet aircraft moved across it like a marker in an arcade video game. Morizio felt tired and grubby. He ran his hand over stubble on his chin and cheeks and rotated his head against an ache in his neck. He said without turning, ''I'd like to look around.''

''Be my guest,'' Lindstrom said.

Morizio faced her. ''I'd like to see everything, everywhere.'' Her smile nettled him. He said, ''Where do I start?''

''Wherever you wish to start.''

He opened a door leading to other offices, checked

each one, then returned to where she sat behind her desk, legs crossed, a cigarette held too casually between her fingers, as far as he was concerned. "What else is there?" he asked.

She extended her arms.

"You have the whole floor?"

"I have what you've seen."

"What about your warehouse?"

"It's next door."

Morizio realized someone else was there. He turned. It was Lindstrom's male secretary. Lindstrom said, "Kai, this is Mr. . . ."

"Morizio."

"Mr. Morizio. He would like a tour of our facilities. Would you please accompany him."

Kai started to protest. "*Undskyld, jeg Forstar Dem ikke* . . ." The expression on Lindstrom's face left little doubt that she meant it. "All right," he said. "What do you want to see?"

"The warehouse," said Morizio.

"They're loading," Kai said to Lindstrom.

"Mr. Morizio will find that interesting, too," she said. "Go. I have work to do."

"I'll be back," Morizio said.

"I look forward to it," Lindstrom said. She'd placed half-glasses on her nose and was reading through an invoice.

Morizio followed the secretary downstairs to the street. "Is there anything particular you wish to see?" Kai asked.

"No. Just take me inside."

They entered through the first door in the alley, which led directly into the warehouse. The two vans were there; young Iranians were loading caviar into them from the refrigerators. "What are they doing?"

Morizio asked. "Loading shipments to go to the airport," Kai said.

"Shipments of what?"

"Many things, herring, caviar, salmon . . ."

"Can I see?"

"See what?"

"What's in the shipments."

"No, sir. These are private shipments. Froken Lindstrom would . . ."

Morizio walked away from him and stepped in front of one of the loaders. He read the label on the chest he carried—it was a food importer in Chicago. He stepped aside and headed for the wooden ladder that led to the attic, Kai at his heels. "What's up there?" Morizio asked.

"Nothing."

He climbed the ladder and looked through the opening. It was empty. He came down and prowled behind the pallets and containers. "Where the hell are you, Lake?" he muttered.

"Sir, I . . ."

"What else is here?" Morizio asked. "What other rooms?"

"None," said Kai. "The refrigerators . . ."

Morizio went to the first set of refrigerator doors and opened them. Everything was black inside. "How do you put on the lights?" he asked as he reached for the first set of rocker switches.

Kai moved quickly to intercept him. "Not that switch," he said. "That controls the cooling. If it's turned off an alarm rings in the offices. This one." He pushed the second switch.

Morizio entered the refrigerator and quickly surveyed it. Its shelves were empty. He looked in every corner, then came out and went to the second set of doors, opened them and pushed the second switch on the panel. The light on, he peered inside. It, too, was empty.

"Sir, I must ask you what is going on," Kai said from the doorway. "Froken Lindstrom said you wished a tour, but this is . . ."

The next set of refrigerator doors were already open. Morizio pushed past Kai and followed one of the Iranians inside. The shelves were almost bare.

"Excuse me," Kai said, "I must call her." He walked across the warehouse to a wall phone near the front door. An Iranian picked up a chest from the shelves, circumvented Morizio, and disappeared outside.

Morizio stepped close to the few freezer chests that remained on the shelves. They were labeled *Lindstrom*. "Damn it," he said aloud, not at anything specific but at the situation in general. He was about to open one of the chests when something on the floor caught his attention, a wadded-up piece of white Kleenex stained with black. He bent over, picked it up, and held it to the light. "You were here, Tissue Queen," he said. He sniffed it. Fishy. Caviar. One of the Iranians stared at him. "A minute, no *mas,* go on, leave me alone." He could see Kai across the main floor, still on the phone, his hand punctuating an animated conversation.

Morizio desperately scanned the refrigerator, the floor, ceiling, every shelf. He might have missed it because it was black, and light from the small bulb didn't penetrate the furthest recesses of the shelves. What kept that from happening was a pinpoint of metallic reflection from the digital counter on Connie's tape recorder. A cut-out in the black leather case allowed the counter to be read even with the case on. Morizio's heart tripped. He looked over his shoulder, saw that he was alone, and grabbed the recorder, held it in his hand, squeezed it, whispered a string of obscenities. He jammed it in his coat pocket and stepped outside. Kai was on his way across the room. "Froken Lindstrom has told me that . . ."

"Forget it," Morizio said. "Thanks for the tour. I'll be back."

"She told me that . . ." Kai yelled as Morizio almost ran from the warehouse, into the alley, to the street. "Jesus," he said as he walked toward Torvegade. He was sweating. He yanked his tie loose from his neck and opened the top button of his shirt. He reached the crossing, paused, looked back, then went over the canal and sat heavily in a metal chair outside a cafe that had just opened. The owner, an old man wearing a red shirt and blue apron, called from inside, *"Hvad onsker De?"*

Morizio figured he was asking for an order, said, "Coffee. Just coffee."

"Kaffe?"

"Yeah, kaffe." He removed Lake's recorder from his pocket and examined the tape. It had run to the end. He checked the batteries. Dead. He took his recorder from his coat, transferred the tape and rewound it. It seemed to take forever—His coffee was served. He tasted it. Good, hot, and thick. The tape was at its beginning. He pushed *Play* and held the small speaker to his ear.

An hour later, and after two more cups of Danish coffee, sound ceased from the recorder. The final words came from Lake's lips—"It's dark and cold. I don't know who closed the door . . . I'm putting this on a shelf, in a corner . . . I just dropped a tissue on the floor . . . Tissue Queen to Duke of Disposal . . . Christ, I'm scared . . . I don't know . . ." There was a great deal of rustling noise as she evidently pushed the recorder into a corner. Now, her voice wasn't as immediate, but it was still loud and clear . . . "They're opening the door . . . Sal, I'm sorry . . . I love . . ."

The sound of magnetic metal latch disengaging. "Hi," Lake said. Morizio wanted to cry. Something in Arabic. "No, goddamn it, get your hands off . . ." There was an ear-piercing scream, scuffling, more foreign words by a male voice, the door slamming shut . . . and silence, tape hiss . . .

"Mejerigtig?" a waitress who'd reported for duty asked Morizio. He still held the recorder to his ear, the "hissssss" a lingering connection to Lake.

"What?"

"American? You want breakfast? Eggs, bacon . . ."

"No, nothing, nothing. Here." He pulled out whatever kroner he had in his pocket and slapped it on the table.

"Tak," the waitress said.

"Definitely," Morizio said as he got up and walked away. He saw an empty taxi, got it and told the driver to take him to the d'Angleterre. "Fast," he said. "You understand English? Drive fast."

The driver laughed and drove the way all Danish cab drivers drive at all times, suicidally fast.

He checked the desk for calls, as though Connie would be in a position to make one. Nothing. Room 102 was cold; he'd left the French doors open. He slammed them shut, sat on the edge of the bed, and forced himself into a calmer frame of mind. He called Mark Rosner's room. No answer. The desk said Mr. Rosner had checked out.

Morizio summoned from memory the name of the one Danish police officer he'd once met, Leif Mikkelsen, deputy chief inspector in charge of Copenhagen's *politi*'s famed "flying squad." Mikkelsen had participated in an exchange program in which three Washington, D.C.

police officers went to Copenhagen for a month, and three Danes came to Washington. Morizio had become friendly with the rumpled, red-cheeked Mikkelsen, a Jutlander who spoke with a deep, throaty accent and who had, according to his biography, graduated from the Danish police college at Aalborg with the most perfect grades in the school's history. Mikkelsen didn't look especially brilliant, Morizio had decided during that month in D.C., but looks were deceiving. The Dane had a mind like a computer.

He called the number listed for the Copenhagen *politi*. Someone answered in Danish, then easily shifted to flawless English. He put Morizio on hold. Seconds later a throaty voice said, "Captain Morizio. What a surprise."

"Hello, Leif," Morizio said. "Yeah, it is a surprise, and an urgent one. Glad you're in so early."

"I never left, caught a nap on a couch. Not an easy night."

"Sorry to hear it. Look, can I come over and see you right away?"

"You're in Copenhagen?"

"Yeah."

"By all means. I was about to go out for breakfast. Perhaps you could join me."

"We'll see."

"Is Miss Lake with you?"

It hit Morizio in the gut like a fist. "No, she's not, and that's the problem. She was with me but . . . I'll be there as fast as possible."

"I'll be waiting. I'll clear you downstairs."

The taxi driver pulled up in front of police headquarters on Hambrosgade, near the river. It was an imposing building, if only because of its dour, somber architecture, its original gray stone almost black now, concrete steps worn away by millions of shoes. Morizio went to an office immediately to his right that had a sign—*Information*. He introduced himself to the uniformed officer, who immediately escorted him to another officer manning a booth at the main entrance. Morizio looked through an arch into a circular courtyard that looked like an ancient Roman arena. Its walls went up three stories, the mortar as dirty as outside. At its far end was a huge tarnished metal statue of a man holding a rifle above his head.

The guard made a phone call, and a young officer appeared from behind the statue, crossed the courtyard, and said to Morizio, "Right this way, sir." They retraced his steps over pavement of uneven squares and rectangles, went around the statue, and entered an interior hallway. Morizio realized the building was in the shape of a trapezoid as they climbed stairs leading to a section identified by the sign—*Kriminalpoliti*. The young officer stepped back and allowed Morizio to precede him into the area. "In there," he said, pointing to an office. "Thanks," Morizio said. He stopped at the open doorway and saw Mikkelsen behind his desk stuffing papers into a briefcase.

"Leif."

Mikkelsen looked up, smiled and said, "*Godmorgen*, Sal." He came around the desk and they shook hands. "What a pleasant way to conclude a thoroughly unpleasant night. Come, sit down. Oh, I mentioned breakfast. Hungry?"

"Yeah."

"Then we go eat." He put on a black topcoat and gray hat and led Morizio back the way he'd come, stopping only to tell a female officer, "I will be back soon."

Five minutes later they were seated at a table in a small, attractive restaurant a block away, on the corner of Rysensteensgade and AankerHeegarde. It was called Politigaarden. They sat in the front section; a raised area to the rear contained the bar. The small tables were covered with crisp green tablecloths. A flowered lampshade with fringe hung over the table. On the walls were large black-and-white vintage photographs of Danish policemen.

"It is handy," Mikkelsen said.

"Yeah, like Jaybird's. Remember?"

"Of course I do." He rubbed his hands together, squinted across the table at Morizio, and said, "You look as anxious as you sound. What's wrong?"

Morizio started to tell the story but the waitress interrupted him. "Bacon and eggs," he said to Mikkelsen. "*To bacon og aeg,*" Mikkelsen told the woman.

She brought coffee. Now, Morizio told Mikkelsen in detail of everything that had happened, going right back to the beginning, to Washington and Ambassador James's murder. Mikkelsen listened impassively. When Morizio was finished, and the breakfast plates had been cleared and fresh coffee poured, the Dane sat back, took out a pipe, tamped tobacco in it, lighted it, puffed, and said, "How terrible. I'm sorry. I have followed the James murder but only through gossip and an occasional report. Interpol informed us when you put out your APB on the young Iranian, Hafez, but when we learned he'd been executed in Iran, we cancelled it, of course."

"Of course."

"What can I do, Sal?"

"Help me find Connie."

"All right. Let's go back to the office and get the missing person people on it."

Morizio hesitated.

"What's the matter?"

"That'll take too much time," Morizio said. "I think

we've got to move faster. Look, Leif, obviously Inga Lindstrom is involved. The tape is clear that Connie was there and was abducted from that warehouse.''

"It doesn't mean Lindstrom had anything to do with it. I'm afraid, Sal, that I'd need more than the tape to go on to put the pressure on her. She's a leading citizen, a solid businesswoman. Besides, you say you looked the place over this morning, found nothing.''

"But if we press her, Leif, maybe she'd . . .''

Mikkelsen shook his head. "I know how you feel, but it's wrong, at least from our position. You say the male voice on the tape spoke Arabic. We could fan out through the Arab community here and . . .''

This time it was Morizio's head that shook. "Same problem, Leif, too much time. What Connie found last night is worth killing for. It always has been.'' He answered the Dane's puzzled expression. "I know damn well that all of this is bound up in the murder of Ambassador James and Paul Pringle.''

"You're suggesting that Inga Lindstrom is part-and-parcel of that?''

"Yeah, I am. I think it has to do with illegal caviar and drugs and Iran and Copenhagen. Connie talked into the tape, Leif, about finding cocaine in the bottom of those caviar cans, some addressed to Lindstrom herself, some to Berge Nordkild in the States who's just been busted on narcotics.''

Mikkelsen drew on his pipe and looked at the ceiling. He seemed to be going through a weighty internal debate about whether to say what he was thinking. He put his elbows on the table, the pipe still in his mouth and held by both hands, glanced left and right, looked Morizio in the eye and said slowly, quietly, "We've been working with your DEA people, Sal. We know about Lindstrom and the drugs from the Middle East.''

"You have?"

"It's top secret, and we're close to a resolution. The tape could be valuable to us in building our case."

"Yeah, I'm sure it could, but right now I don't care about cases. I care about Connie. I want her back."

"Yes, I understand. I was less than truthful before about Lindstrom. The truth is I don't want to jeopardize *our* case."

Morizio's initial reaction was anger, but then he reminded himself that he probably would have taken the same position, had the roles been reversed. Mikkelsen was in a tough spot, between a rock and a hard place. He had his official responsibilities, yet wanted to aid a friend. He tried to help the Dane out of his dilemma by saying, "Let's forget Lindstrom for now. What I want to know, Leif, is where Connie might be. If she'd been abducted—and the tape doesn't leave any doubt about that—where might she be? Where would they take her, hide her . . . kill her?"

"Christiania."

"What's that?" He then remembered Lake talking about the free city within Copenhagen, and that her Aunt Eva had been instrumental in bringing it about. "Yeah, I know something about it, Leif. That's your best guess?"

"Yes, of course. It's filled with criminals, people running, hiding."

"Okay," said Morizio, "let's assume she's there. That narrows it down. Can we go in, really hit the place, conduct a sweep-and-search?"

"No."

"Why?"

"It's off limits to us, unless we obtain a court order. Christiania is sacred ground legally."

The irony of it hit Morizio hard. It was like an

embassy, a little country unto itself, free from whatever rules applied outside. "How long for a court order?" he asked.

"Days."

"Days?"

"Our courts are very sensitive about Christiania, Sal."

Morizio's anger permeated every word. "Are they so goddamn sensitive about innocent people being murdered?"

"Yes, that, too, Sal. Please, I understand your feelings, but these are the rules."

"Rules."

"Rules. Yes, rules, Sal. They can be changed—should be changed—but until they are, we live by them, you and I. From what you told me you broke the rules back home and have ended up suspended. Sometimes it is worth it to break rules and take the consequences, but take them we must. No, I cannot order a search of Christiania, at least not quick enough to satisfy you."

"All right, what *can* you do?"

"Talk to key people. We have a few officers of Middle Eastern ancestry who have good contacts within that community. They can ask around. I'll put them to it immediately. There are others whom I can call and ask questions of. I will do that, too."

"And what do I do?"

Mikkelsen shrugged, tapped ashes from his pipe into an ashtray, and put the pipe in his pocket. "Go to the hotel. I'll call you in a few hours."

"I can't just go back and sit around the room."

"Have a drink. Nap."

"Come on, Leif."

He smiled. "Here I am suggesting to you what I could not do under similar circumstances. I'm sorry. Come back with me."

"No, I will go to the hotel. I've got some other things I want to do. You'll call me if you hear anything."

"Of course."

They walked back to the entrance to police headquarters. Morizio handed Mikkelsen a wrinkled photo of Lake. A freezing rain had started to fall. It stung their faces. "Sal, I will do everything possible," Mikkelsen said, shaking Morizio's hand.

"I know you will. Thanks."

"I'll call you in a few hours."

Morizio walked to Puggaardsgade and searched for a taxi. They were scarce, as in every city when the weather turned nasty. He walked in the direction of the d'Angleterre until he came across a cab discharging a passenger, slumped in the back seat of the brand new Opel Rekord, and gave in to his fatigue. The driver literally had to yell at him after they'd pulled up in front of the hotel.

He called Lake's Aunt Eva. The phone rang a dozen times before she answered. "Sorry to wake you," he said, "but it's important."

"Did she arrive?"

"No."

"Where is she?"

"That's what I'm trying to find out. Look, Aunt Eva, we don't know each other but we have something in common, and that's loving Connie. I want your help."

"I will do anything."

"Come to the hotel."

She groaned. "I just went to bed an hour ago."

"Yeah, I'm tired, too. Look, if we don't act fast Constance Lake will be dead."

Eva gasped.

"So come on, Eva, get over here."

"Within the hour."

They sat in his room and he told her what he wanted, access to Christiania. "You're a big shot there," he said. "They trust you, know you're not out to hurt them. Take me there . . . ask around . . . see if anyone's willing to talk about an American woman being held there against her will."

"Yes, I will do this," Eva said. She stood, went to a mirror, dabbed at hastily-applied makeup with a Kleenex, and dropped it on the dresser.

"Runs in the family," Morizio said as he deposited it in a basket.

"What?"

"Not important. Come on."

They drove in Eva's Saab down Borsgade, across Knippels Bro and to Torvegade, then past the baroque 1682 Our Saviour's Church and to the entrance to the free city, Christiania. Morizio observed it from the car. The former military barracks looked as though they'd collapse in a gentle breeze. The entrance was strewn with debris. Dozens of people congregated in front, Hell's Angels types with spikes protruding from black wrist bands and belts, young women, some with babies in sacks on their backs, a couple of men asleep against the wall even though the freezing rain continued to fall, and dogs—dogs everywhere, skinny and yellow-eyed, listless and without obvious attachment to anyone.

"This is it, huh?" Morizio said.

They approached the gate, and Morizio suddenly felt very out of place and vulnerable, the way he did on a dance floor. Their progress was scrutinized, he in his Burberry raincoat and shined shoes, Eva in a shocking pink slicker with rhinestones at the collar and alligator boots. No one challenged them, however, which Morizio had expected, and they were soon inside, following rutted dirt roads between the dilapidated buildings, stepping over puddles, eyes glancing left and right at clusters of people whose dress, manner, and attitude established them as belonging there.

"Eva."

They turned to face a young woman with brunette hair and wearing a flowing flowered skirt and bulky tan knit sweater. Morizio was glad that someone had recognized Eva.

"Bettina," Eva said warmly, grabbing the girl by the shoulders. "I was hoping to find you."

Morizio looked up at one of the barracks and wondered whether Connie was in one of its rooms, bound and gagged, raped, mutilated, dead.

"Sal, this is Bettina," Eva said. Morizio nodded at the girl, who was very pretty and whose smile was wide and open. "Bettina sits on the Christiania Council," Eva said. "She's part of the political structure here."

"I wish you wouldn't put it that way," Bettina said. "I don't like politics."

Eva laughed. "Even here there is a need for rules, huh, Bettina? I want to ask you something."

"Hvad?"

Eva took her arm and they walked to where they could speak privately. Morizio glanced at them from time to time but didn't want to appear to be eavesdropping. He watched the comings and goings of the counterculture village. There were makeshift stands from which drugs were sold openly. Others offered food, and one featured weapons—knives in assorted sizes and styles, handguns, rifles, whips, bamboo blow-guns, and metal discs with razor-sharp blades meant to be tossed like a Frisbee.

Eva returned. "Come," she said. Morizio nodded at Bettina and followed Eva.

"What's up?" he asked.

"She's here."

"You know that?"

"Yes. Come, let's walk a bit."

She led him to a torn, faded yellow and blue awning supported by four tent poles. Beneath it sat four couples. A girl nursed a baby while her mate drew on a water pipe. The other couples seemed dazed, their eyes lifeless, staring into the light, cold rain as though it might provide a vision. Eva said in a hoarse whisper, whisper, "She is here with a young Arab. They arrived last night."

"Where?"

"In a building used by transients. There are many of those."

"I don't doubt it. Take me."

"Maybe we should think a bit before going."

"Think about what?"

"About what to do when we get there. It is not like knocking at someone's door to borrow a bottle of akvavit."

Morizio had to smile. She was right. He couldn't call Leif Mikkelsen and arrange for a S.W.A.T. team to circle the building. It occurred to him that he couldn't do that in Washington, either. MPD didn't have S.W.A.T. teams. He was weaponless. He turned and looked back at the weapons stand. "Excuse me," he said.

"How much?" he asked the bearded young man at the stand, pointing to a crude sawed-off shotgun with a scarred buttstock.

"Fem hundrede."

"English."

"Fifty U.S."

"Here." Morizio tossed two twenties and a ten on the counter. "Shells?"

"Ti."

"Come on, English."

"One dollar each." .

"Give me six." He laid another six dollars down. The vendor handed Morizio the shotgun. He examined it. It was a pump-action breechload. He pumped it, injected shells, jerked it shut. He looked at the young man and said, "It had better work."

"It works," he said, smiling. "But not here. No shooting here."

"Yeah, right." He slipped the shotgun under his coat and rejoined Eva.

"I don't like that," she said, having observed the transaction.

"I'll worry about that."

"There is no violence here in Christiania."

His expression was one of incredulousness. "Connie is kidnapped and held against her will and you tell me violence is against the rules?"

"I simply tell you of the rules here. It was part of the agreement with the city government. If there is violence, it is reason for the city police to enter. No one wants that."

"I'd love it. Let's go."

"All right."

"Before we do, though, how come you found out so easily that Connie was here?"

Eva smiled. "Christiania is no different than any other community. They need believers like me to stand tall for them when there is trouble. What is it you say in English, 'Scratch each others' back'?"

"Something like that."

They left the protection of the awning and followed the winding, muddy road to the far end of the commune. Eva stopped, pointed. "See? That red building is where the visitors stay. Bettina tells me that Connie and the Arab are there.''

It occurred to Morizio that if they were observed by the Arab from a window, it might panic him into doing something foolish with Connie. He also decided he didn't need Eva any more, but didn't want her too far away in case some negotiation in Danish was necessary. He pointed to a low board shack to the left of the red building. "Go there and wait," he said.

"For what?''

"For me to call you, in case I need you.''

"I will go with you.''

"No, please, listen to me. I appreciate everything you've done . . .'' He wanted to say "Get lost," but was more tactful. "Just do as I say. Did your friend tell you what room Connie was in?''

"She said the top floor, southeast.'' She pointed to a corner of the red building.

"See you later,'' Morizio said as he quickly walked toward a row of tents, hoping the Arab hadn't seen the American with the raincoat and shiny shoes. If not, Morizio had surprise on his side. If he had . . .

He passed the tents until reaching a point where the entrance to the red building was only twenty feet away, pressed the shotgun against his body, and crossed the open area. He paused in the doorway, looked back, saw that Eva had done what he'd said, and turned his attention to the lobby of the red building. It was dismal and in disrepair, and there was the strong odor of cabbage, garlic, and urine. A stairway was ahead of him. He crossed the lobby and started up, pausing at the second-floor landing to remove the shotgun from beneath his coat. "You'd better work, goddamn it,'' he mumbled as he continued his climb, hoping he wouldn't meet anyone coming down.

When he reached the top floor his needs shifted. Now, he wanted someone who could pinpoint the room in which Lake was being held. He got his wish. A door leading to a communal bathroom opened and a short, chubby girl stepped into the hall. Morizio grabbed her by the neck and shoved her against the wall, the shotgun pressed to her temple. He wished he knew Danish, said in English, "Not a word or you're dead. Understand?"

Wide, frightened brown eyes testified that she did.

"American woman, blonde, with an Arab. They came here last night. Which room?"

She said nothing. "You don't understanding English?" he said in the stage-whisper he'd been using.

She nodded, gulped, shook her head against the shotgun's barrel. "Please, I'm American."

"You are? Jesus. Good. Tell me, and tell me fast. Where are they?"

"Why?"

"Tell you later. Which room?"

Her eyes looked to her right.

"Which one?"

Her head slowly came up and a finger pointed to a door on the left side of the hall, at the end.

He leaned his face close to hers and said, "I'm going to let you go, but you stay here, right here, in the hall. Understand? No sound, no movement. Just stay here or . . ."

"I understand."

He was tempted to ask where in the States she was from, why she was there, all of it. The sociologist in him. Time for that later.

He approached the door she'd indicated, looking back to make sure she hadn't moved. She hadn't, not a muscle, still pressed against the wall as though he were

311

holding her. He put his ear to the door, heard muffled voices, male and female.

He didn't have any doubts about his next move. He took a step back, raised his foot and rammed it against the flimsy door. It flew open, coming off its top hinge. Morizio leaped into the room and assumed a combat stance, the shotgun at the ready.

Lake was sitting on the floor, a pea-green army blanket wrapped around her. Her abductor stood at the window. "One move, you bastard," Morizio snarled, "and you're with Allah."

Lake scrambled to her feet and came to Morizio, who although he held the shotgun on the young Arab was concentrating on her. He put a free arm around her and pulled her close.

"Sal, it's all right. He's not armed. He didn't hurt me. God, it's good to see you."

"You're okay?"

"Yes."

Morizio now faced the swarthy man, and it hit him just a shade slower than Lake said it. "It's Nuri Hafez, Sal, and everything's going to be all right."

25

It was the first direct flight they could get to the States. It left at two that afternoon, and they had to scramble to make it. Morizio called Leif Mikkelsen, told him Lake was safe and that they were leaving immediately for Washington. He concluded the conversation with, "Thanks for everything, Leif. I promise that as soon as I square things away back home I'll be in touch about the tape. Whatever I can do to help nail Inga Lindstrom will be my pleasure."

Lake called her grandmother in Malmö, Sweden. The old woman didn't speak English but her housekeeper did. Lake promised to return one day for a visit. She felt terrible to have gotten this close and not seen her grandmother, but she knew time was of the essence. She shed a few tears after she hung up.

After her call to Malmö, Lake went to the local travel agent and arranged to trade in their first-class return tickets for three coach seats. There wasn't any problem booking the two o'clock flight to New York. It was light, always was that time of year, she was told.

Aunt Eva had gone home. Lake called her, thanked her profusely for everything she'd done and promised her, too, that she'd be back as soon as possible, "To *enjoy* Copenhagen this time."

They checked out of the hotel at noon and took a cab to Kastrup Airport, checked their luggage and found a dark corner of the airport bar. Lake and Morizio had beers. Nuri Hafez ordered a Coke.

"They didn't question it," Morizio said, referring to the false passport Hafez used. "Must be a good one."

Hafez nodded. He'd said little since they left Christiania. Morizio had expected him to be edgy but that wasn't the case. The handsome young Iranian was calm to the point of placidity. There was profound sadness in his face, though, his large brown eyes looking through and beyond Morizio to something only he could see and comprehend. He wore a glove-soft brown leather jacket over a chambray work shirt. His jeans were tight and faded, his engineer's boots highly polished. He'd brought nothing with him except the bogus passport. "I don't need anything," he said when Morizio offered to stop at his house to pack a bag.

They remained in the bar until only a few minutes before flight time, walked quickly to the gate, boarded, and settled in their seats, Lake and Morizio together in a two-seat section, Hafez directly in front of them next to the window. They'd made sure during seat selection that no one would sit next to him.

"You have a lot of explaining to do," Morizio said to Lake as the giant aircraft rolled down the runway, groaned against gravity, and lumbered into the air. Almost immediately it was wrapped in fog, wings undulating in unsteady air, wing-tip lights creating a strobe effect through dense, gray clouds.

"Let's wait," she said, nodding at the back of Hafez's seat. "By the way, Sal, happy Thanksgiving."

It was a disgruntled laugh. "Yeah, you, too."

Turkey was served in honor of the American holiday. Morizio finished his, got up and went to the lavatory. He looked down at Hafez when he returned to his seat. Hafez was sleeping soundly, his head against a pillow on the window, a blue blanket pulled up to his neck.

"Okay, let's talk," Morizio said to Lake. "He's asleep."

"I wish I were," she said. "It was a tough night."

"I'm sure it was."

Lake had told Morizio enough to keep them in motion between Christiania and their flight. She'd evidently tripped an alarm in Lindstrom's office when she pushed the wrong rocker switch. Hafez, who was with Lindstrom at the time, was dispatched to check on what had happened. He slammed the door on Lake and called Lindstrom from the warehouse. She instructed him to get rid of Lake. He took her to Christiania.

"Why didn't he kill you?" Morizio had asked.

"He's not a killer," Lake had answered. "He's never killed anyone in his life."

Hafez told Lake during their night together that he'd initially stayed in Christiania after fleeing Washington. He'd hated it there and soon moved to a house owned by a friend in the Iranian section of the city. Lindstrom considered that unsafe and arranged for him to live in the tiny, idyllic coastal town of Falsterbo, Sweden, about twenty miles from Malmö, where Lindstrom owned a summer cottage. Hafez was provided a false set of papers and a car, and when it was necessary for him to come to Copenhagen, he used the frequent hydrofoil service from Malmö.

Lake hadn't told Morizio much more than that, except that as her night of captivity progressed, she found herself engaging in long, probing conversations with Hafez. She realized that he was a victim of many forces, and had become severely disillusioned with everything that had happened to him, and with his current state of affairs. It had taken awhile, Lake told Morizio that morning, to gain Hafez's full confidence, but once she did, the entire tenor of the situation changed. She asked him direct questions, and he answered them. No, he had not killed Ambassador James but knew he would be blamed. He didn't know the murderer, but assumed it was Nigel Barnsworth.

"What else did you ask him?" Morizio had asked her that morning.

"Lots of things, Sal, but later," she'd said. "The important thing is that I've convinced him to return to Washington with us to clear his name, and to help us clear ours. He knows his days are numbered here in Copenhagen, that Lindstrom will probably get rid of him."

"Kill him?"

"Yes."

Morizio had asked other questions, but was always met with, "All of it later, Sal, I promise. Let's just get out of here before he changes his mind."

"If he does, we'll call in the Danish police. I made contact with that guy I knew, Leif Mikkelsen."

"And we'll lose Hafez to them," Lake had said. "We need him back in Washington."

Morizio knew she was right and didn't press further. But now, on the plane, it was time.

"Okay, Connie," he said, "lay it all on me, every step, nice and slow."

"All right. He was . . ."

"Hafez?"

"Yes, Hafez was as close to the ambassador as he was because of what he knew from James's days in Iran. Listen to this, Sal. James knew at least a month in advance that the Ayatollah planned to take over the American Embassy. He knew every detail of the plan, the timetable, the works from his friend, Falik el-Qdar. He could have contacted American authorities, or his own people, but he didn't. Instead, he cut a deal with the new regime allowing him to buy Iranian oil at reduced prices, run it through a brokerage operation, and sell it to the Western world, including the United States. It was like what you told me about caviar, the Iranians selling it to the Russians who slapped their own labels on it to get around the American embargo."

"A swine. A traitor."

"Grade-A."

"Okay. Hafez knows about it, uses it as a wedge to get James to bring him to England, then to Washington?"

"Exactly. But our young friend isn't all sweet and innocent. He saw a chance to get rich himself in caviar. That's where Lindstrom came in, James's mistress, one of them at least. Nuri's brother in Teheran set up the network, paying fishermen a lot more than the state fisheries would. This, by the way, was done *without* any sanctions by the Ayatollah. James went along, more for the kick of it, I guess, and the chance to have a constant supply of caviar for his own dinner table. He let Lindstrom and Hafez work it out, which they did, and it functioned smoothly for awhile . . ."

"Until James wanted out."

"Wrong, at least not yet. Our Ms. Lindstrom got greedy and saw bigger dollars than fish eggs. She went around Nuri, contacted his brother, and started using the caviar pipeline for drugs. Her primary middleman in the States was Berge Nordkild. Nuri didn't like it.

Running caviar was one thing but heroin, cocaine . . . That was *big* trouble, and he knew it. He balked, told the ambassador, who blew his stack. But James couldn't do anything about it. He was swimming in illegal Iranian oil. He couldn't blow the whistle because they'd return the favor.''

"Makes sense." A flight attendant served them brandies they'd ordered. "To progress," Morizio said, clinking with her glass.

"I'm afraid to. We've made some but . . ."

"But, what do we do with it? I've been thinking about that, too."

They sipped their drinks in silence. Lake, who was at the window, looked out. The skies had broken and the rippling blue Atlantic Ocean was visible through puffy white clouds that looked dense enough to sit on. She was filled with conflicting emotions, her elation at finding Hafez butting heads with the reality of arriving with him in a few hours in New York, then to Washington, then . . . what then? Visions of her night with Hafez flooded her, then disappeared as she willed them away and focused on the here-and-now, and the tomorrow of their situation. She could see the back of Hafez's head around the corner of his backrest, thick black curls resting on his neck, the edge of his blue shirt collar lost in them. Were they being smart in taking things into their own hands? Maybe it would have been better to turn him over to Danish authorities and work through them to fill the gaps that still existed. Maybe this, maybe that. It had to work, one way or the other. It had to.

"Connie."

"Yes?"

"Everything you found out from Hafez is good, but how does it relate to the murders, especially to Paul

Pringle. From what you've said, I think there's more probability now that Hafez did kill James, no matter what he says. But Paul, did he know about the oil and the drugs? Did you ask Hafez that?''

"Yes. He assumes that Paul knew everything and was killed to keep him from revealing it, but he doesn't know for certain.''

"Neither do we.''

"Maybe we will soon, Sal. What do we do once we arrive? Do we waltz him into MPD? I promised him we'd be on his side and do whatever we could to protect him. He's still a fugitive because he's alive. We're harboring a fugitive. You realize that.''

"Of course I do. Damn, I knew from the minute I read about his so-called trial and execution in Iran that it was a phony.''

She squeezed his arm. "That's what I forgot to tell you. Nuri's *brother* was executed, but not for Geoffrey James's murder. He got caught in the caviar mess and lost his head for stealing from the state. For some reason, the Ayatollah put it out that it had been Nuri. He either did it on his own, or in concert with somebody else who wanted that story public.''

"Okay,'' Morizio said, sitting up and finishing the little bit of brandy that remained in his snifter. "We arrive in New York, grab the shuttle to D.C. There we are, two suspended cops and an international fugitive. What's next?''

"We call someone, I suppose.''

"Who?''

"Chief Trottier?''

"No.''

"Werner Gibronski?''

"The last one I'd call. All that'll result in is George Thorpe arriving on the scene. Maybe it has to be Trottier.

Maybe we can strike a deal with him in return for Hafez.''

"I don't want to betray him, Sal. We can't do that.''

"I don't either, Connie, but we can't hide him forever. All I want is time to chase down the book Paul is supposed to have left for me.''

"Piccadilly?''

"I'll start there. I thought of Abdu, but he's a journalist. Paul never would have trusted him. If it isn't Piccadilly, I'm lost. It's the only link with Paul I can think of that he might have used. Jesus, I wish he hadn't read so many spy novels. All he had to do was tell me.''

"He was afraid.''

"For good reason, I guess, judging from how he ended up.''

"So, who do we call when we get back?''

He said it through clenched teeth. "It has to be Trottier. I don't see an alternative, unless what I come up with from Paul dictates something else. Let's not call anybody until we get to that point.''

Hafez woke up and went to the lavatory. "How are you?'' Connie asked as he returned to his seat.

"Fine," he said softly. "Excuse me.'' He disappeared behind the backrest.

Morizio looked at Lake. He leaned close and said, "Do you have any doubts about his coming back with us?''

"What do you mean?''

"It's so easy.''

"Not if you spent a night in a cold room like I did.''

"Ah, come on, Connie, I'm not minimizing that, and you know it. It's just that . . . I was thinking of the cockroach theory.''

She screwed up her face.

"He's coming with us because we *assume* he wants to clear his name and help us clear ours. What if there's another motive?"

"Like what?"

"I don't know."

"We have to go with what we have."

"Yeah. I just wish I was sure what that was."

Late that afternoon they arrived on time at New York's Kennedy Airport and took a limousine to LaGuardia in time to catch the six o'clock shuttle to Washington. There'd been a tense moment at Kennedy Customs. The official took his time processing Hafez through Passport Control, checking the photograph against his face, slowly going through his passport's pages, asking questions that Hafez answered calmly and to the official's satisfaction. He waved him through. Then, the suitcase Morizio had given Hafez for appearance's sake was thoroughly searched, every item of Morizio's clothing removed and scrutinized, the bag's lining carefully patted down. Morizio expected Hafez to be taken to a separate room for a personal search but it didn't happen.

Morizio continued to be impressed with the young Arab's demeanor. Nothing seemed to rattle him, the same tranquil expression stayed on his face whether he was sleeping or being interrogated. It wasn't until they approached Washington in the Eastern 727 that Morizio discerned a hint of anxiety.

"What will we do?" Hafez asked Connie.

"In Washington?" She looked across Hafez at Morizio.

"Any ideas?" Morizio asked Hafez.

He shook his head, his eyelids coming down slowly over his big brown eyes, then raising. Nuri Hafez blinked slower than anyone Morizio had ever met.

"Your apartment?" Lake said. "Mine?"

"I don't think so, not until it's resolved. They might have slapped another bug in them and . . ."

"I know where the key to the Iranian Embassy is," said Hafez.

"The Iranian Embassy? Might make sense, Sal," Connie said.

"Yeah, not a bad idea," Morizio said. "We won't be there long, just until I can dig up what Paul left. All right, the Iranian Embassy it is. That's okay with you?" he asked Hafez.

"I suggested it."

"Yeah, you did." Hafez's manner irked Morizio but he didn't say anything.

They walked through Washington's National Airport, grabbed a cab, and Morizio gave the driver his address in Arlington. They went immediately to his basement garage and took his Chevy Cavalier to 3005 Massachusetts Avenue, the abandoned Iranian Embassy. Morizio waited for a lull in traffic, then drove down the driveway to the rear garages and parked behind them, out of sight from the road. The key to one of the back doors was beneath a large, heavy concrete planter. Hafez moved it aside, found the key, opened the door, reached to his left until coming up with a large flashlight, switched it on, and led Morizio and Lake through the dark interior until reaching a room in the middle of the building. "This is where I stayed," he said. "There are no windows."

"No windows?"

Hafez explained. "Security. It is where the most important meetings took place."

Three of the walls were red and blue ceramic tiles depicting Islamic scenes. The fourth wall, a short one, held a large fireplace. There were ashes in it. Split logs, kindling, and a pile of newspapers were on the hearth.

Morizio flipped a wall switch. "There is no electricity," Hafez said. "I used the flashlight and the fire."

"What about smoke?"

"No one seemed to notice it," Hafez said.

"I'd love a fire," Lake said. "It's freezing in here."

It was cold and damp. The building had been vacant for a long time. "No one will see a fire," Hafez repeated.

"We'd have light, too," Lake said.

Morizio thought about it for a minute, then said, "Okay. We won't be here long anyway."

Hafez made the fire, and the eruption of crackling orange flames provided instant warmth and light.

"I'm hungry," Hafez said.

"So am I," Morizio said, "but we're not ordering in a pizza." He motioned for Lake to leave the room with him, taking the flashlight and leading the way. When they were far enough away to not be heard, he said, "I've got to get over to Piccadilly. What do you think? Can we both go, or do you think he'll bolt?"

"I don't think he'd do that, Sal, but why take the chance?"

"Because I don't like the idea of leaving you alone with him."

She touched his cheek. "Sal, I'd feel the same way except that I've already been in a worse situation alone with him. I really believe he's harmless, just wants this mess over with as much as we do. I'll be all right, believe me."

"I wish we had a weapon. I meant to get one from the apartment but completely forgot."

"It doesn't matter. I'll be fine. Just be quick. Do you think Johnny's on duty?"

"If he's not, I'll find out where he lives."

"We could wait until morning, go back to one of the apartments and get some sleep."

"You could sleep?"

She smiled. "No."

"I'll hurry. Just watch out for yourself."

"I will, don't worry." She closed the gap between them and embraced him, her lips finding his. They remained linked for a long time. When she pulled away she said, "I love you."

"And I love you. Maybe it'll all work out, huh?"

"Maybe. Let's hope. Go on, get going."

She accompanied him to the door and he handed her the flashlight. "See you," he said.

"Yeah, see you."

He drove as fast as he thought he could get away with to the Piccadilly Pub. It was a disturbing period of time alone in the car. He worried about Lake being with Hafez, worried about whether he'd be able to find what Pringle had left for him and, even, whether it would provide enough answers to resolve everything. He was also acutely aware of the reversal in his life. He'd always enjoyed being a cop, riding tall on the side of law and order, nothing to hide, nothing to fear. But now, as he backparked into an empty space near Chevy Chase Circle, he felt *guilty*. He was a suspended cop working outside the same system in which he'd been so comfortable all those years. He'd prowled around London and Copenhagen like a private detective, sneaked back into his own country hoping no one would recognize him and the international fugitive he was harboring, entered through back doors of an abandoned foreign embassy like a sneak thief. He drove slowly so as not to arouse suspicion of . . . *the police*.

Maybe even worse was the realization that there

didn't seem to be anyone he could trust. They'd decided on Chief Trottier, but he represented only the best of a bad bunch. He felt very much alone, except for Lake. Thank God for her, he thought. He really did love her, need her, more than ever.

Morizio had expected Piccadilly to be relatively quiet. It was, after all, Thanksgiving, families at home eating turkey and watching football, which was what he wished he was doing.

He was wrong. Piccadilly was full, mostly young people. A game was on color TV. The hostess greeted him by name as he came through the big black double doors. He grunted in reply and looked through the arch to the bar. Johnny was there, chatting with customers. "Beautiful," he said as he headed in that direction. He stopped, turned and went to the bookcase containing the old books. There wasn't much light; he squatted and squinted as he tried to read the titles. Some were Paul Pringle's. Which ones? He straightened up and went to the bar.

"Hello there," Johnny said. "Long time, no see."

"Yeah," Morizio said, sliding onto a stool.

"Martini, lager?"

"Gin, on the rocks. And Johnny, I've got to talk to you."

"My pleasure." He poured Morizio's drink, placed it in front of him, leaned his tall, angular frame over elbows on the polished bar and said, "What's up?"

Morizio glanced right and left—the couples on either side were engrossed in their own conversations—and said, "I just learned that Paul Pringle left me something very important. Do you have it?"

"Have what?" Johnny laughed.

"I don't know. No, strike that. Look, he put some important papers in a book. I don't know which book it was, or where he left it, but I'm betting on you, or the pub."

Johnny turned serious and rubbed his chin. A customer called for a refill but was waved away. "He gave me so many books, Captain."

"He did?"

"Well, maybe not that many, but enough. He knows . . . *knew* I sort of like my history, and when he had too many for his shelves he gave them away."

"I know that, Johnny. He gave me some, too, but this one is special. Let's narrow it down. You remember when Ambassador James was murdered?"

"Sure. They still talk about it here. The date? I don't . . ."

"November Fifth. Okay, did he give you any books after that?"

"He might have. Let me see . . . hmmmmm . . . hard to recall, Captain." His face lighted up. "Oh, sure, of course he did. In fact, he said one of them was his particular favorite. That's right. He told me that it's one you'd especially like, too. He kidded about it, said you'd be mad he didn't give it to you."

Morizio drew a deep, relieved breath and tasted his drink. Johnny took care of other customers, then returned.

"What book was that?" Morizio asked.

"The Mexican War. You know how he loved that. I never could muster up much enthusiasm but . . ." He laughed. "Funny fellow, Paul, always saying this book was his favorite or that one. I didn't take it too seriously."

"What did you do with it?"

"The book?"

"All the ones he gave you after James died. How many were there?"

"A dozen, I suppose, maybe ten. I sold them."

Somebody snapped a big, fat rubber band inside Morizio. He picked up his glass and drained it.

"It was after he died, Captain. The missus was on my back about having all those dusty relics around the house, like Paul's wife did with him. I figured it didn't matter anymore, so I boxed 'em all up and sold them."

"Jesus."

"The man was dead, Captain. Besides, better to have them where they were appreciated. That's what Paul would have wanted."

Morizio didn't want to push Johnny into a defensive corner. He smiled, said. "Give me another drink, Johnny, but don't go away."

Five minutes later Morizio continued the conversation. "You say you sold them. Where, at a garage sale?" He hoped not.

"No. Can't stand them damn things. I sold them to Goldberg, the book fellow. You've met him here."

"Yeah, sure, the big guy. What's his name, Ben?"

"Right. I told him I had all these books and he said he'd love to have them. He didn't pay much, but you know how those people are. I brought them in one day, put them in the trunk of his car and he paid me."

"How long ago?"

"A week, maybe, maybe less, maybe a few days more. Can't be sure."

"Goldberg's shop's in Georgetown, right?"

"I think so."

"You don't have a card, an address?"

"Sorry, Captain, I don't."

"All right. Thanks, Johnny."

"That last one's on me."

"Good. See you later." He laid a five dollar bill on the bar and headed for the public phone in the foyer. He went through the Yellow Pages until finding *Goldberg,*

Benjamin—Rare Books. He dialed the number and let it ring thirty times. Nothing. He wasn't surprised. It was Thanksgiving, but you never knew about those book collectors. They kept strange hours, did strange things.

He checked the residential listing for Benjamin Goldberg. There were a bunch, but he found one with the same address as the bookstore, probably a brownstone with the shop down, the apartment up. He called the number. This time it was picked up on the sixth ring.

"Ben Goldberg?"

"At times. Who's this?"

"Captain Salvatore Morizio, Washington Metropolitan Police Department. We've met at the Piccadilly Pub."

"Sure. So formal. How are you, Sal?"

Goldberg had obviously remembered him a lot better than the other way around. "I'm fine, but I've got a big problem that you can help with."

"You want Thanksgiving dinner? We're just finishing but you're welcome to come over."

"No, I don't want a meal Mr. . . . Ben. What I want are the books you bought about a week ago from Johnny, the bartender at the Piccadilly."

"The shop's closed."

"Open it for me. It's official, Ben, police business involving murder."

"Who?"

"Yours if you don't cooperate."

"I get the feeling this is not as official as you say it is."

"Feel what you will, I'm telling you this is important. Nothing to worry about from your end, but I need those books. They belonged to a friend of mine who was killed, Paul Pringle, and . . ."

"I know. Johnny told me how he came to own them.

Come on over. The shop's right downstairs, but I can't promise that I have them all. Some were sold."

Morizio's heart sank. "How many?"

"No idea."

"Do you still have the one on the Mexican-American War?"

Goldberg laughed. "The only way I'd know that is to look. We'll do it together."

Morizio parked at a hydrant in front of Goldberg's shop and rang the upstairs bell. A light came on in the foyer and a large black shape behind white curtains descended the stairs. Goldberg opened the door. "Happy Thanksgiving, he said.

"Happy Thanksgiving."

"A drink? I have guests upstairs."

"Thanks but . . ."

"Come on, let's take a look."

They entered the shop through another door from the foyer. There were books everywhere, piled on the floor, on shelves that sagged beneath their weight, on desks and windowsills, chairs and a couch. It was a discouraging sight to Morizio. It'd take a month to go through them all.

But then Goldberg navigated his bulky body through the stacks with the skill of a downhill racer skirting gates and said, "Johnny's books are over here." He picked up a stack from the couch, maneuvered other stacks on the desk to make room and plopped them there. The third book in the pile attracted Morizio's hand like a magnet *Armed Conflict: The Mexican-American War, 1846–1848*. "Please, let it be you," Morizio said as he opened the hardcover book and thumbed through it. There was nothing there that shouldn't have been, just printed pages and illustrations.

"Is that the one?" Goldberg asked.

"No," Morizio said.

"Perhaps the others. Look through. I'll check on what's going on upstairs. Be back in a minute."

Morizio examined the other books in the stack. The same. Goldberg returned with his wife, Betty, whom he introduced to Morizio. "Are you sure you won't join us?" she asked. "We have enough turkey to . . ."

"No, thanks, I . . . Maybe a leg or something to chew on. I haven't eaten in awhile and . . ."

"Of course," she said. "Sure you won't have a drink?" her husband asked.

"A Coke? Seven-Up. Whatever."

"Tell me," Goldberg said to Morizio after his wife was gone, "what precisely are you looking for?"

"That's the problem, I don't know. I learned in London that Paul Pringle, the guy who used to own these, left me some important information about a murder case, two as matter of fact, including his own."

"Yes, I remember him from Piccadilly. Nice fellow. He appreciated history."

Morizio was too dejected for historical banter. "It was a shot in the dark," he said. "A book. What book? I had this dumb faith that I'd come back, pick up that Mexican-American War book, find a neatly typed set of notes that solves everything and off I'd go."

Betty Goldberg arrived with a plate of turkey and a large glass of soda. "Thanks," Morizio said as he picked up a leg and took a bite. He thought of Lake back at the embassy, cold and discouraged and hungry. Maybe I could bring a doggy bag, he thought.

Ben Goldberg picked up one of Pringle's books, a history of the Crimean War, and ran stubby fingers over the inside of the front and back covers, saying as he did it: "I bought a book once from an estate . . . it sat here for a year. One day I picked it up and admired the

330

binding, felt a bulge inside the front cover . . ." He laughed. "There it was, beneath the glued-on paper, a will that had never been probated."

"Yeah?"

"I found important papers another time, too, wedged into a book's spine." He picked up another of Pringle's books and checked it.

Morizio held the Mexican-American War volume in his hands. He opened the front cover and ran his fingertips over it. It was bulky, felt like padding underneath. He looked at Goldberg. "Check this," he said. He handed it to Goldberg, who used his fingers. "Right you are," he said. He searched the desktop, came up with a double-edged razor blade, and carefully slit the inside front cover. Beneath its pasted-on decorative page was a single sheet of white bond paper, folded in half. He handed it to Morizio, who unfolded it. Its neat type ran margin to margin, top to bottom. He moved beneath a lamp and read it.

Sal—As I write this I anticipate seeing you soon. I'd do it now, tell you in person what's in this letter, but there are still loose ends to tidy up. Once I've done that, I'll sit with you over a drink and explain everything. But, and I have come to learn the necessity of facing reality, there is always the possibility that I shall never see you again. What has happened in recent days renders each of us irrelevant. Greater forces have determined the course of events with Ambassador James. Still, I am unable to simply allow it to slide into obscure history. There must be someone else who knows, and I've chosen you. Sorry. It certainly isn't an act of friendship to make you a party to it but I happen to believe in Sal Morizio.

I couldn't mail this to you, nor could I telephone and tell you what is in this letter. They seem to know everything, Sal, because they have the where-

withal to listen to our conversations and to read our most personal correspondence. Don't debate it, friend. They do, and they take advantage of it.

Enough preface. I must keep this to one page. I learned too much, know too much about James's demise to allow me the luxury of guaranteed old age. James was poisoned by the Crown. That's right, Sal, the British government. He was too embarrassing to us to be allowed to live. He sold out your embassy personnel in Iran for profit. They—your government and mine—found out about it and worked together to resolve it. Real hands-across-the-sea. Our people didn't want it to become public, and we promised to take care of it in our own way, with our own people. And we did. To be honest with you, Sal, I do not know precisely who placed the poison in the ambassador's caviar. Barnsworth received the order, which I intercepted, but I doubt if he did the actual deed. It could have been anyone, a housekeeper, a maid, the secretary, another security person, whomever. Perhaps Barnsworth did lace the caviar. He is loyal to higher authority to a fault, and James was no longer his higher authority.

Don't let me lead you astray. It wasn't all national pride and international cooperation. There was a practical side to it, too. Imagine the lawsuits your hostages could bring against the Crown. Imagine it, Sal. And the bad press. Untenable, beyond imagination. We took care of James in a time-honored manner. He was eliminated. It was to have been a heart attack, body wrapped quickly and shipped home, sterling servant of the Crown buried with high honors. But the best-laid plans went haywire. The press. And me, calling you. The show was on, press conferences, your Chief Trottier playing the game because of larger stakes than simply law enforcement. Don't judge him harshly. He took orders, as we all did. Well, I say modestly, excluding you, and me.

I'm running out of room on this single page. What else? James was a bastard, weak and ineffectual but with some sense of business. Pity his wife, and beware a large Englishman named Thorpe. Her

Majesty's hitman guised in the respectable role of trade representative, but with the blood on his hands of Africans and Indians, Orientals and even his own. British citizens who strayed, slipped, were indiscreet. He was in charge of James's unfortunate demise, and the cover-up. He didn't do very well, and his head is on the line, too. He has the sensitivity of a mole, Sal, the conscience of a Hitler. There is always the "greater good" with Thorpe, which reduces smaller, true values to the expendable.

I wish I hadn't come into possession of these facts. It bloody well gets in the way of the retirement dream, tiny soldier shop, pipe in mouth, and leisurely days whiled away reading history, painting my miniature heroes in bright colors and enjoying my grandson, thanks to you. Harriet is a good girl, slow-witted but decent, a classic female victim of the male Barnsworth. He told her he loved her. Damn him. He pays. I mustn't fault that. The Crown pays. Mrs. James will be taken care of for the rest of her life to keep her mouth shut, to allow her husband's Scottish oil company to die a simple death so that its "business" never becomes public knowledge. What a crew, Sal. But not so unusual, huh? Human nature. Greed. I've known it, and assume you have, too.

End of page, Sal. I hope you never have to find this because it would mean I am still alive. But I don't expect that to be the case, and I trust in your ingenuity. Say hello to Johnny if I miss that opportunity. It's gone so fast, this life of mine. I'm smiling. Until now it's been rather dull. Hello to Connie Lake. Hello to you. Of all the Americans I've met, you're the best, Sal. You care. What a precious commodity. Paul.

"Well?" Goldberg said as Morizio put the paper in his jacket pocket and swallowed against a large lump in his throat.

"That's it. Thanks."

"I'm glad you found it. Of course, my book is now damaged."

"Gee, I . . ."

"Just kidding. Sure you won't join us upstairs? Nice group, all family."

"I can't, but thanks for letting me barge in on Thanksgiving."

"Glad I could help."

Morizio looked at the plate of turkey. "Maybe I could take this with me. I have a friend who . . ." He realized there was no way he could explain.

"Of course. One minute."

Goldberg returned from upstairs with a large plastic bag filled with turkey. Two smaller bags contained stuffing and mashed potatoes. Morizio emptied the platter Betty had brought into the larger bag. "I appreciate it," he said, feeling foolish, like a bag lady at a city welfare agency.

"See you again at Piccadilly," Goldberg said as Morizio left.

"I hope so. Thank your wife for me, and happy Thanksgiving."

His car had a ticket, which he tossed into the gutter. He drove slowly, trying to remember everything he'd read in Pringle's letter. He couldn't deal with it, the broad ramifications, the issues it raised. "Jesus," he muttered as he pulled up to a corner, got out, and pushed a dime into a public phone. He dialed a number, waited for it to be answered. "Hello?" a female voice said.

"Mrs. Trottier, this is Salvatore Morizio, Captain Morizio. I'm sorry to bother you at home on a holiday but . . ."

"Happy Thanksgiving, Captain," she said. He could

334

hear music and laughter in the background. "I'll get Don for you."

"Hello."

"Chief, this is Sal Morizio."

"Yes."

"Sorry to bother you but . . ."

"You're back."

"Yeah, I . . . you knew I was away?"

"Yes. What can I do for you?"

"I . . . I have to see you right now."

"Now? It's Thanksgiving. I have family here and . . ."

"It's . . ." He couldn't find a word that would convey what he felt. "It's goddamn important, Chief. I have Nuri Hafez with me, and a letter that explains the murder of Ambassador James, Paul Pringle, everything. I have it all. I . . ."

"You have Hafez with you?"

"Well, not exactly. He's with Officer Lake and he's willing to straighten everything out. I have the proof."

"Of what?"

"You son of a bitch."

"What did you say to me?"

"Jesus, look, I don't give a flying . . . I'm sorry, I've gone through a lot."

"Excuse me," Trottier said. He returned to the phone a minute later and said, "I understand, Sal. You took me by surprise, that's all. Of course I'll meet with you. Where are you?"

Morizio hesitated. Was he doing the right thing? It had occurred to him earlier in the evening that a better approach might be to go to the press, to Jack Anderson, Woodward and Bernstein, maybe even one of his casual acquaintances at local radio and TV stations. But that frightened him, too. Their needs didn't match up. They'd view it as a story. He needed resolution within MPD, for himself and for Lake.

"Where are you now, Sal?"

"In a booth in Georgetown. I'm heading back to meet Lake and Hafez. They're at . . . okay, they're at the Iranian Embassy, 3005 Mass. Ave."

"Why there?"

"Hafez had a key. Are you coming now?"

"Yes."

"Alone?"

A pause. "Yes, if that's what you want."

"Good. Come down the driveway to the rear of the building. The door is the first one you come to after the garages. I'll leave it open. I don't know if there's a buzzer. There's no electricity. Knock when you get there. Knock loud, yell. I'll come down and get you."

"All right. Give me some time to explain to my guests. We eat late. We were just sitting down."

"Yeah, well . . ."

"I'll be there inside an hour."

"Okay."

This time he didn't worry about driving too fast. He took Lake aside the minute he arrived and showed her Pringle's letter. "That's it, isn't it?" she said when she was finished reading it. "We've got it all."

"I think so. It's scary as hell. I can't even begin to deal with a friendly government like Great Britain getting together with our top people to plan a murder."

"Assassination, Sal. There's a difference to them."

"Greater good. It's still murder, and Paul's death sure as hell doesn't rank as an assassination."

"To them it does. It's awful, I agree, but that's what Gibronski and Thorpe and Trottier were telling you all along."

"And I couldn't buy it."

"I'm glad you couldn't. There's got to be room for personal honor in the midst of national goals. There has to be."

"We'll find out soon enough."

They returned to the tiled conference room where Nuri Hafez was adding a log to the fire. He looked at them as though he wanted to know what had occurred, but he didn't ask. Morizio said, "Everything's going to work out, Hafez. I found what I was looking for, and it makes it plain you didn't kill anyone. This will be over soon. You did the right thing coming back with us. We're all going to be cleared very soon."

Morizio remembered the food he'd brought from Goldberg. "It isn't much, especially for Thanksgiving, but maybe it's the best holiday dinner we'll ever have." He tossed Pringle's letter on the table and held up the plastic food bags. They tore them open at the seams and used them as plates, ate with their fingers, savoring every bite, Morizio and Lake looking at each other and smiling.

"How did Trottier sound?" Lake asked.

"Annoyed at first, but he came around. Paul was right. We shouldn't judge him too harshly. He was just doing his job, too, like . . ." They heard what sounded like an automobile in the driveway.

"He's here," Morizio said.

"I think it was on the street," Lake said. She looked at her watch. It's only been forty minutes. He said an hour."

"I told him to open the door and yell." He looked at Hafez, said, "The person who's coming here is the chief of police for Washington, our boss, Chief Trottier. We'll tell him the story, show him what I found when I was out and go from there. You've trusted us all along, Hafez, and I want you to keep doing it. We have as

337

much to gain as you do, and going through the proper channels is the only way. We all stand together. In some ways this has worked out better than we ever hoped for. We'll take it a step at a time and . . ."

"Sal."

Morizio looked at Lake, who was looking through the door into the hall. A bouncing flashlight beam came closer, and there were heavy footsteps. Then, the large, dark figure of a man filled the doorway.

"Thorpe," Morizio said, sheltering his eyes from the light the Englishman trained on him.

"Sal," Thorpe said. "Happy Thanksgiving. It looks as though you've feasted."

"Goddamn it," Morizio said, taking a step toward him. "What the hell are . . ." He stopped when he saw the .357 Magnum in Thorpe's other hand.

"The three of you move closer to the fireplace and raise your hands. Do it now!"

"You're crazy, Thorpe," Morizio said as he started to comply with the order. "I've already talked to Chief Trottier and . . ." Wasted, empty words, he knew, and the awareness of it brought a stinging bile to his throat. So did the sudden, sinking realization that in all the excitement and confusion of the past few hours he'd never thought about having a tape recorder rolling. Lake? Had she thought of it? He knew she hadn't. He wanted to call time out, to correct the lapse in professionalism. "Jesus," he muttered.

"Why this?" Hafez asked Morizio as he stood with his back to the fire, his hands above his head. Morizio didn't have any answers. He was trying to think, to calm down, to analyze the situation they were in and to make a sound judgment how to handle it. His attempt at reason was short-lived, however. He'd been looking at Thorpe, and at the weapon in his hand, but his eyes shifted to the conference table where he'd laid Paul Pringle's letter after showing it to Lake. Thorpe saw it too, and quickly scooped it up.

"That's my property," Morizio said.

Thorpe laughed as he scanned the letter in the light of a flashlight on the table.

"That's mine," Morizio shouted. He moved toward Thorpe. The sound of the magnum's discharge reverberated off the tile walls in a deafening explosion. The shell hit above the fireplace, sending wood raining down on Lake and Hafez.

"The next one finds the heart," Thorpe said casually. He waved the gun. "Move," he said, "that way."

Morizio stepped back into line with Hafez and Lake, and they stepped sideways, away from the hearth and to the nearest long wall. Thorpe crumpled up Pringle's letter, stepped near the fireplace and tossed it into the flames. They shot up as they licked away at the new fuel, and in seconds the charred remains of the letter were part of the other ashes.

"You bastard," Morizio said to Thorpe, reaching for Connie's hand.

"Don't do anything foolish," Thorpe said.

"What do you think, Thorpe, that you destroyed the only copy?" Morizio said, forcing a laugh into his voice. "Copies have gone to the appropriate people. You're not as smart as you think you are.

"I'll have to take that chance, won't I?"

"We know everything, Thorpe," Morizio said, "about you and your murders—Ambassador James, Paul Pringle, others. You're scum, the game's over."

"I quite agree," Thorpe said. "So here we have the infamous Nuri Hafez. I've been looking forward to meeting you, young man. Obviously, reports of your demise were exaggerated." He laughed. "Come forward. Let me see you. Come, come, toward the fireplace. Let the light shine on your face.''

Hafez looked at Morizio, and Morizio could feel emotion from the young man, fear, confusion, as though he were asking Morizio for guidance. Morizio didn't have any, for Hafez or for himself.

Hafez did as instructed by Thorpe, and flames from the fireplace played across his young, handsome face, catching his eyes for split seconds, dancing away, black curls glistening, then falling into momentary shadow as the eyes caught the light again.

''You've done a fine job, Sal,'' Thorpe said.

''Meaning?''

''You've broken all the rules, defied all authority, and yet have come up with a fugitive of international repute, a brutal murderer of an esteemed world diplomat and of a loyal security agent named Pringle. Obviously, your brief holiday from duty is over. In fact, I can guarantee it.''

''Wrong, Thorpe,'' Connie said. ''Hafez didn't kill anyone and you know it. You're the one, perhaps for some vague nationalistic aim, but the killer nonetheless.''

''You're very sweet,'' Thorpe said, smiling. ''What a shame that you couldn't have dissuaded your lover here to take another tack, to honor tradition and higher authority, to . . .'' He said it to Morizio, his smile broadening '' . . . to take the highway instead of those treacherous winding country roads he seems so fond of. Pity. We could have forged a wonderful friendship, the three of us, lunches together, good conversation, sparkling moments of laughter and companionship between chums. I would have liked that. I don't have much of it, unfortunately, because it seems the world is full of people like you, knights on their white horses, veins filled with what they consider honor and integrity, all that bloody nonsense that gets in the way.''

"Of what?'' Morizio asked.

"Of life. Those misguided souls do not usually live long, Sal. Their purified blood runs before its time.''

"You're big on threats, Thorpe.''

"And quite good at carrying them out. It's my profession.''

"My brother," Hafez said softly.

Thorpe raised his eyebrows. "What about your . . . deceased brother?''

"You killed him.''

"No, of course not. There are others in this world who are able to separate ideals from practical actions. Your brother lost his head, as it were, because our friends in Iran understood the necessity of not only punishing him for his crimes against the state, but for telling the world it was you. We needed that to give us time to find you and to make sure *you* were punished.''

"The punishment's over," Lake said. "I don't know about large, international matters, but I do know that even governments must stand accountable for their actions.''

A smile from Thorpe, then a belch which he covered with his hand. "Part of your sweet nature, Miss Lake, is your wonderful naiveté. I like that in a woman.''

"If I had a gun," Morizio said, "I'd . . .''

"But you don't," said Thorpe. "I do, and . . .''

Lake and Morizio looked at each other. Morizio said, "And what, Thorpe?''

"And it is time for the guilty to pay.''

The flashlight on the table was aimed at Nuri Hafez's chest and face. Thorpe raised the gun, held it with both hands, and squeezed the trigger. Again, the room exploded with sound as the bullet left the barrel and struck

Hafez squarely between the eyes. His face disappeared; bright red blood burst over the room like a huge firework in a black sky on the Fourth of July, pellets of crimson splattering Morizio and Lake's faces, tiny pieces of bone stinging them like red ants.

Another discharge before Hafez's faceless body fell, this one opening a gaping hole in his chest and driving him back into the fire.

Lake's scream was as loud as the revolver's discharge. She fell toward Morizio, who grabbed her and held her up. He slumped back against the wall, his head hitting the red and blue tiles.

Everything was still, except for the lingering vibrations of explosion and scream, and a sickening change in the sound from the fireplace as Hafez's hair and skin ignited, accompanied by a pungent odor.

"I'll call the police," Thorpe said. "I thought Mr. Hafez was about to draw a weapon. Pity. Much might have been learned from questioning him. Good job, Sal. You, too, Miss Lake. You'll undoubtedly be commended by your chief." He went to the fireplace and dragged Hafez out by his legs. "It's over," he said, "finally over." He looked to where Morizio and Lake leaned against each other. "You've been splendid throughout this," he said. "Bloody splendid." He belched and left them alone.

26

THE SEATTLE TIMES, SUNDAY, JUNE 24.

*Constance Birgit Lake, daughter of Mr. and Mrs.
Jens Lake of Seattle, was married yesterday to Salvatore Morizio, son of Mrs. Lucille Morizio and the
late Carlo Morizio, Sr. of Boston. Justice Glenn
Beers, a friend of the bride's family, performed the
ceremony, which took place in the Cabinet Room at
the Four Seasons Olympic Hotel.*

*The bride, who was attended by her sister Karin,
wore a simple white silk suit. Miniature white roses
and Dendrobium orchids were woven into her up-
swept hair. The groom was attired in a navy vested
suit. Carlo Morizio served as best man for his brother.*

*The new Mrs. Morizio was recently appointed
assistant director of the privately funded Seattle Wom-
en's Crisis Center. A former policewoman with the
Metropolitan Police Department in Washington, D.C.,
she holds a master's degree in psychology from
Washington State University. Her father is a retired
Seattle restaurateur.*

*Dr. Morizio, the son of a policeman, was also a
member of the Metropolitan Police Force before
taking a post at the University of Washington where*

he is associate professor of sociology. He earned his undergraduate degree in political science from Boston University, received his master's in sociology at Harvard and recently was awarded his Ph.D. in sociology from Catholic University.

Following a honeymoon in London and Copenhagen, the couple will reside in Seattle.

Margaret Truman has won faithful readers with her works of biography and fiction, particularly her ongoing series of Capitol Crimes mysteries. Her novels let us into the corridors of power and privilege, poverty and pageantry in the nation's capital.

She lives in Manhattan with her husband, Clifton Daniel, distinguished journalist, author, and editor. They have four sons and two grandchildren.

MARGARET TRUMAN

Published by Fawcett Books.

Call toll free 1-800-793-BOOK (2665) to order by phone and use your major credit card. Or use this coupon to order by mail.

__MURDER IN THE SUPREME COURT	449-20969-5	$5.99
__MURDER IN THE SMITHSONIAN	449-20959-8	$5.99
__MURDER ON EMBASSY ROW	449-20621-1	$5.99
__MURDER AT THE FBI	449-20618-1	$5.99
__MURDER IN GEORGETOWN	449-21332-3	$5.99
__MURDER IN THE CIA	449-21275-0	$5.99
__MURDER AT THE KENNEDY CENTER	449-21208-4	$5.99
__MURDER AT THE NATIONAL CATHEDRAL		
	449-21939-9	$5.99
__MURDER AT THE PENTAGON	449-21940-2	$5.99
__MURDER ON THE POTOMAC	449-21937-2	$6.99
__MURDER AT THE NATIONAL GALLERY	449-21938-0	$6.99

Name_____

Address_____

City_____State_____Zip_____

Please send me the FAWCETT BOOKS I have checked above.
I am enclosing $_____
   plus
Postage & handling* $_____
Sales tax (where applicable) $_____
Total amount enclosed $_____

*Add $4 for the first book and $1 for each additional book.

Send check or money order (no cash or CODs) to:
Fawcett Mail Sales, 400 Hahn Road, Westminster, MD 21157.

Prices and numbers subject to change without notice.
Valid in the U.S. only.
All orders subject to availability.   TRUMAN